TO DO OR DIE

Max Adams served as an officer in the British military for over twenty years. A keen historian, his personal and professional experience of weapons and tactics brings an unusually high degree of authenticity to these novels.

Max Adams is a pseudonym.

First published in 2010 by Pan Books
an imprint of Pan Macmillan, a division of Macmillan Publishers Limited
Pan Macmillan, 20 New Wharf Road, London N1 9RR
Basingstoke and Oxford
Associated companies throughout the world
www.panmacmillan.com

ISBN 978-0-330-51033-2

3 5 7 9 8 6 4 2

A CIP catalogue record for this book is available from
the British Library.

Typeset by Ellipsis Books Limited, Glasgow
Printed by CPI Mackays, Chatham ME5 8TD

Visit **www.panmacmillan.com** to read more about all our books
and to buy them. You will also find features, author interviews and
news of any author events, and you can sign up for e-newsletters
so that you're always first to hear about our new releases.

TO DO
OR DIE

MAX ADAMS

PAN BOOKS

CHAPTER 1

3 SEPTEMBER 1939

'Fuck this for a game of soldiers,' Eddie Dawson muttered.

He relaxed his grip on the sling, lowered the Lee-Enfield .303 rifle from his shoulder, closed his eyes briefly and again took stock of his surroundings. To his front, the ground sloped away gently, the uncultivated field an unattractive patchwork of tussocks and wind-blown shrubs and bushes. Behind him lay a wood – in fact little more than a large copse – that echoed with the raucous cries of rooks. It was late afternoon, grey and cold, and his view down the field was blurred by the curtains of steadily falling rain. Dawson was chilled to the bone, soaking wet, really uncomfortable and thoroughly pissed off.

He was lying in a shallow ditch that ran in a more or less straight line across the top of the field. His feet and heavy boots were actually submerged in the few inches of brown stagnant water – the all-pervasive farmyard smell clearly indicated the reason for its colour – at the bottom of the trench.

Even outside the ditch, the ground was sopping wet,

caused by the driving rain that had been lashing the area since first thing the previous morning, and, despite the allegedly waterproof groundsheet Dawson was lying on, and the gas cape – a garment of dubious utility, made of thin rubberized material, printed with a camouflage pattern and normally intended to be worn like a poncho – draped around his shoulders, his army battledress had managed to absorb the water with considerable efficiency, and he was soaked right through to his army underwear. After almost four hours in more or less the same position, he was now lying in what amounted to a cold, sopping wet, heavy and all-enveloping cocoon of khaki brown serge.

The only thing he possessed that wasn't wet was the breech of his Lee-Enfield, which was fitted with a canvas cover against the pounding rain.

'Shut up, Dawson. Keep your eyes front.'

The order came from the man lying directly to his right, who was in every way in precisely the same physical state as Dawson, but who sported corporal's stripes on his arm. Baker was the NCO – non-commissioned officer – in charge of the six-man section. Dawson was the second-in-command, the 2 I/C, a lance-corporal.

'This is a complete waste of bloody time, Corp, and you know that as well as I do.'

'Just fucking shut up and do what you're told.'

Corporal Baker's irritation was tempered by the fact that Dawson's opinion fairly closely matched his own, but there was nothing he could do about it. The orders he'd been given were simple and explicit. The six members of his section were to guard the field – the obvious approach to the wood – against a possible enemy

advance, and the shallow ditch was the best cover they'd been able to find when they'd arrived there just after midday. The only good thing was they hadn't needed to actually dig themselves in – the ditch was already deep enough to conceal them.

'You said that three hours ago,' Dawson said, 'and I've seen bugger-all so far. Even the sodding rabbits have gone home.'

Dawson's ill-temper wasn't surprising. Watching and waiting for something to happen is incredibly boring, in this case compounded by the conditions and the fact that all they'd had to eat since breakfast were the dry 'compo' rations from that morning. They hadn't even been able to light a stove to have a brew-up, as it might compromise their position. A supply of hot tea is as essential for morale as bullets are for rifles, so, while it was Eddie Dawson who complained, all six men felt pretty much the same.

'We've got our orders,' Baker snapped.

Dawson looked at him. 'And they made sense to you, did they? I wouldn't put it past that bastard MacKenzie to send us out here when he knows that the action's somewhere else. He's had it in for me ever since we got here.'

'He's had it in for you, Dawson, because you're an insubordinate bastard. Now just shut up and keep watching.'

At that moment the soldier lying on Baker's right-hand side spoke, his voice low and urgent.

'Bottom of the field, two hundred yards, ten o'clock, by the hedge. I just saw movement down there.'

Immediately, every one of the six men snapped to high

3

alert as they stared down the slope through the grey curtains of falling rain.

'I don't see anything,' Baker murmured. 'Are you sure?'

'Yes. Look, there it is again.'

And this time they all saw it. A shadowy figure, a rifle clutched in his hands, crept around the end of the hedge close to the bottom of the grassy hillside, perhaps 200 yards away. The man crouched down in the undergrowth and appeared to scan the field in front of him. Other soldiers, perhaps half a dozen in all, materialized from the gloom behind him and fanned out across the field, forming a line.

'Right, here they come,' Baker said, somewhat unnecessarily. 'Check your weapons, men. Make every shot count, but wait for my order before you fire. Set your sights to one hundred yards.'

Each of the six men was armed with a .303 rifle, a Number 4 Mark 1 Lee-Enfield, or SMLE, the standard weapon of the British army since the turn of the century and one of the best bolt-action rifles ever made.

Each of the soldiers obediently adjusted the flip-up adjustable aperture micrometer rear sight as the corporal had ordered. Obviously Baker wanted there to be no mistakes – at 100 yards even a very average shot would expect to be able to hit a man-sized target with that rifle, and none of the six soldiers lying in the ditch was average. The weeks they'd spent on the rifle range at Catterick had honed their skills in that department.

Below the patrol, the slowly approaching figures separated and formed a line that extended almost all the

way across the field. Then they started walking slowly up towards the wood at the top of the hill.

But as Dawson picked out a target and watched the line of advancing men, a sudden thought struck him.

'Corp,' he said urgently, his voice barely above a whisper, 'where are the rest of them? There should be more than that, surely?'

Baker glanced at him and looked back down the hill at the approaching soldiers.

'I count only five,' he said, his voice equally low.

'So do I,' Dawson replied. 'The rest of them could be holding back in reserve, but I don't think so. This looks like a diversion. They're trying to out-flank us.'

Baker considered this for a couple of seconds, then nodded.

'You could be right,' he conceded and raised his voice slightly, so that the other members of the patrol could hear him. 'Take Richards and Watson. Get behind us and cover our backs.'

Dawson nodded and slid backwards, deeper into the shit-filled ditch, then climbed out the other side, crawling through the scrubby bushes that flanked the uphill slope. He checked all around him, scanning the perimeter and looking towards the wood, and to his left and right. Moments later the other two soldiers joined him.

'I'll watch the wood,' Dawson said, gesturing towards the top of the hill. 'You two take one side each.'

They spread out, making use of what little cover they could find, each ducking down behind one of the clumps of stunted bushes that dotted the hillside between the ditch and the wood.

They'd barely got into position before Dawson

spotted three men just leaving the tree-line, probably only 100 yards away, their weapons and battledress clearly visible.

'Corp – they're behind us as well,' Dawson called, keeping his voice low but still audible to his companions.

'Right,' Baker ordered. 'Fire at will.'

Dawson brought his rifle up to the aim, took a deep breath then exhaled part of it, sighted carefully and pulled the trigger.

The flat bang of the .303 cartridge firing – a sudden assault on the silence of the afternoon – seemed to act as a trigger for everyone else in the patrol. Almost immediately, Dawson was deafened by a volley from directly behind him as the three remaining soldiers covering the field opened up on the line of advancing men, and then both Richards and Watson fired as well. The thunderous noise of heavy-calibre rapid fire blotted out all other sounds, and the air filled with the unmistakable stench of burnt cordite.

Dawson had been right: the enemy *was* trying to out-flank them, and in fact they'd succeeded, approaching the patrol's position from four sides simultaneously.

He pulled back the bolt on his Lee-Enfield, hearing the metallic snicking sound of the well-oiled mech-anism. The brass cartridge case spun crazily out of the breech over to his right, and he immediately slid the bolt forward to chamber another round. All three of the approaching figures – including the man he'd shot at – were still standing. He aimed carefully and fired again, and then again and again.

But still the enemy came on, the shots having no

effect. Now they returned fire, the crack of their rifles joining the cacophony of noise as the patrol urgently fired shot after shot at their targets. Then there was a new sound, much louder bangs as explosives detonated all around them, adding to the noise and confusion.

Dawson fired the last of his ten rounds and pulled back the bolt to eject the spent cartridge case. Reaching into the ammunition pocket on his webbing, he pulled out a charger clip and pressed the five shells down into the magazine. A single glance showed him there was no time to use another charger to fully reload the weapon.

Dropping the charger and slamming the bolt forward, Dawson chambered a cartridge, looked up and searched for a new target.

Suddenly brown-clad figures filled the area, brandishing weapons.

Dawson fired off two of the shells he'd loaded, barely taking aim properly. And then one of the men was on him, his rifle aimed unerringly at Dawson's stomach.

Dawson furiously swung the barrel of his Lee-Enfield across and down, forcing the enemy soldier's rifle off aim, and rushed him with a body-charge that knocked the man off his feet. As Dawson pinned down the soldier's weapon, he swung his SMLE around and rested the coloured cap attached to the muzzle on the soldier's chest.

'Enough, Eddie,' the man gasped.

Dawson looked straight into his eyes and smiled broadly. Then he lifted up his rifle and punched the man lightly in the chest.

'You're dead, Fisher,' he said. 'In fact, you're dead three or four times over. I had you in my sights the

moment you stepped out of that fucking wood. I'd have dropped you twice if I'd had live rounds instead of these bloody blanks.'

'Yeah, yeah, yeah. Talk a good fight, don't you, Eddie?'

Then a whistle shrilled from somewhere nearby. All the soldiers fell silent and stood up, turning to face two approaching men. One wore the rank badges of a lieutenant, and the other – a short, red-faced and angry-looking man – a sergeant's stripes. He'd had an entertaining few minutes lobbing thunderflashes as close as he could to the men as the exercise had drawn to a close.

'Well, that was a bloody shambles, wasn't it?' Sergeant MacKenzie bellowed without preamble, which probably meant he thought it had gone quite well. He was the training sergeant for the platoon and, in the unanimous opinion of its members, had brought a whole new dimension to the expression 'short-arsed Scottish bastard'.

The platoon's day had started at six-thirty that morning with a briefing from MacKenzie, and in many ways that had been the high-point. At least for that fifteen-minute period they'd all been warm and dry – or at least dry – and pleasantly full of a hot breakfast washed down with numerous mugs of strong tea.

Like all Royal Engineers, they had been fully trained in the basic skills of the profession of war but also specialized in one of several engineering disciplines when they'd transferred to the Corps. Most of them were more used to building bridges or pillboxes – or blowing them up – than playing at being soldiers, but all had been selected by their respective units to take part in this

particular combat training course. Following twelve weeks of intensive training at Catterick, the exercise on the moors had been almost a final examination for them.

They'd marched out of the camp, climbed into the back of a Morris CS truck and been driven to the training ground. Divided into two groups – Red and Blue Platoons – they'd gone their separate ways, Blue Platoon with orders to secure and then defend one particular patch of woodland, and the larger attacking force – Red Platoon – to wrest this dubious prize from them. The ditch in which Dawson had been lying, accompanied by the five other members of Blue Platoon, had been directly in front of the wood they'd been told to guard and had been the first, last and in fact the *only* line of defence.

'I'll debrief all you dozy bastards when we get back to the camp,' MacKenzie shouted – he was one of those men who always shouted – 'but in the meantime the lieutenant here has an announcement to make. Sir?'

'Thank you, Sergeant,' Lieutenant Jayston muttered, and took a couple of steps forward. 'Gather round, please. Can you all hear me, men?'

There was a chorus of muttered 'yes sirs' as the soldiers formed a rough circle around the officer.

'Right, as you all know, we've been training hard here at Catterick for the last three months, hoping for the best while preparing for the worst, and I'm sorry to say that the worst has now happened. At eleven-fifteen this morning, Great Britain formally declared war on Hitler's Germany. Since that time, France and three of the British Dominions – that is to say, Australia, India and

New Zealand – have followed suit. Gentlemen, as of today, we are at war with Germany.'

The lieutenant stopped speaking and looked around at the group of soldiers. In the silence that followed, a single anonymous voice somewhere in the platoon muttered, 'Oh, fuck.' Several of the men laughed and were immediately silenced by Sergeant MacKenzie.

'Silence in the ranks,' he roared. 'This is *not* funny.'

A brief smile flitted across Lieutenant Jayston's face, then he resumed his serious expression. 'As you're all aware, the Corps has spent the last eighteen months or so involved in a busy programme of national defence building – everything from establishing depots for vehicles to creating anti-aircraft gun sites. I've no doubt that this level of activity will now increase substantially, and we'll probably also become involved in the construction of other defensive works. But because of the extra training you've been given, you men may well find that your skills are in demand for rather less conventional types of operations.'

Jayston paused and again looked round the group of expectant men.

'In fact, I've already received separate orders for two of you. Dawson and Watson, report to my office when you get back to the camp. Right, Sergeant, carry on.'

The lieutenant acknowledged the sergeant's salute as he turned away, heading towards the small clearing at the edge of the wood where his staff car was parked.

'Right,' MacKenzie shouted. 'Form up in three ranks. Attention! By the right, dress. Shoulder arms, two, three. By the left, quick march!' The last word emerged from

MacKenzie's mouth at full volume. He was a man with an impressive lung capacity.

As the men marched away into the gloom, their boots making a squelching sound as they strode over the muddy ground, Dawson and Watson, in the rear rank as usual, glanced uncertainly at each other.

'Looks like we drew the bloody short straws again,' Watson muttered.

'No fucking surprise there, Dave,' Dawson replied.

MacKenzie, marching along beside the squad, turned and bellowed at them. 'Silence in the ranks. Eyes front.'

'At least if we get posted we'll lose that Scottish bastard,' Watson muttered, lowering his voice.

Dawson grinned, but didn't reply, saving his breath for the march along the rough track. In fact, they hadn't got that far to go. In a clearing in the wood about a mile away, close to the road, the Morris truck was waiting to transport them the seven or eight miles back to the camp.

CHAPTER 2

3 SEPTEMBER 1939

Just under an hour later, Dawson and Watson – now both wearing clean battledress and their best, highly polished parade-training boots – walked into the Catterick administration building, strode down a succession of corridors and finally stopped outside a somewhat faded cream-painted door bearing the name 'Lt J. G. T. Jayston'.

Watson pointed at the name-plate and muttered to his companion. 'I manage with "Dave" and you with "Eddie", so how come bloody officers always have so many Christian names?'

'Buggered if I know. Tell you something else.' Dawson pointed at the first initial. 'I'm bloody sure that don't stand for "John" or "Joe". It'll be "Jeremiah" or "Julian" or something. Come on. Let's get this over with.'

He knocked briskly, waited until he heard 'Come' from inside the office, then pushed open the door and stepped inside, Watson right behind him.

The two men marched smartly into the room and, with a simultaneous crash of their leather-soled boots on to the wooden floor, halted right in front of Jayston's desk.

'Lance-Corporals Watson and Dawson, sir. Reporting as ordered,' Dawson snapped.

Jayston nodded. 'Very good. Stand at ease. And stand easy.'

The two NCOs relaxed slightly, standing with their legs apart and arms behind their backs.

Jayston picked up a sheet of paper bearing a few lines of text typed in capital letters, the standard format for military messages, glanced at it briefly, then dropped it back on to the desk.

'Right,' he said, looking up at the two men in front of him. 'As I said at ENDEX up on the moor, I've already received movement orders for the two of you. You'll both be leaving here in a couple of days.'

'Together or separately, sir?'

Jayston shrugged. 'Both, really,' he said. 'I've been sent separate sets of orders, but you're both going to more or less the same place.'

'Can you tell us where, sir? And what we've been volunteered for?' Dawson asked.

'I really can't tell you anything about it, Dawson, for operational reasons,' Jayston replied, 'but I can say that your tasking will involve a short sea crossing. And I hope you like snails,' he added, with a slight smile.

'France, then?' Watson muttered.

'I didn't actually say that,' Jayston said sharply. He picked up the sheet of paper and looked again at the typed orders. Then he glanced up at Dawson. 'I've been checking your personal file. You've had an interesting career. I didn't realize you were a Territorial before you joined the Corps.'

Dawson nodded. 'Yes, sir. Five years I was in the TA.

I really enjoyed it – most of the time. There was a lot of bullshit, of course, but that's the army, isn't it? Then I lost my job and joining up seemed like the right thing at the time. Didn't know Adolf bloody Hitler was going to foul things up so badly.'

'You were a demolition engineer?'

Dawson shook his head. 'Not exactly, sir. By trade I'm a quarry and mining engineer.'

'What's the difference?'

'The methods, really, sir. Demolition engineers here in Britain don't normally use explosives. If you're demolishing a house, see, the usual trick is to knock out a few bricks, stick wooden piles in the holes and set fire to them. That normally weakens it enough to make it collapse if you give it a good hard shove. What I was doing was a lot noisier, and a lot quicker. In my job, we drilled holes into coal seams or quarry walls, packed the holes with gelignite, lit the fuse and buggered off somewhere safe. A few minutes later there was a sodding great bang, and the miners spent the next few days picking up the pieces.'

'Colourful as ever, Dawson,' Jayston observed with a slight smile. 'So you're an expert with explosives?'

'I know my way round jelly – gelignite – sir, and dynamite and a few others.'

The lieutenant nodded thoughtfully. 'That's probably why you've been picked for this mission,' he said.

Dawson pricked up his ears. 'You mean I've got to go and blow something up, sir?'

Jayston smiled and shook his head. 'No,' he replied. 'If I'm reading this right, it's absolutely imperative that you *don't* blow anything up, and especially not what's referred to in this tasking order.'

'I don't understand.'

'You will, Dawson, you will. And you, Watson. You're an engineer as well?'

'Yes, sir, but I'm the real thing – I built stuff, not blew it up. Bridges, mainly, but anything with a steel frame or skeleton . . .' He hesitated. 'I hope you don't mind but I've got a question, sir, about this bloke Hitler and this war we've been dragged into, despite what Mr Chamberlain reckoned when he waved that bit of paper around.'

'I've got one bit of free advice for you, Dawson – never trust a politician or what he says.'

'Some of the lads was wondering if it might all be over by Christmas. What do you think, sir?'

'I've no idea, but I think you should be prepared for a lengthy conflict, at least as prolonged as the 1914 War, and maybe even longer. Hitler has shown himself to be a competent military leader, and I very much doubt we've seen the last of his territorial ambitions. I think his ultimate aim is a Europe forcibly united under a German flag, and even then he might have his sights set on America. Whatever happens, I think we're in for a few very hard and very bloody years.'

Jayston glanced at his wristwatch, then picked up two sealed brown envelopes from his desk and handed one to each of the two NCOs. 'These are your orders,' he said. 'If there's anything you don't understand once you've read them, come back and see me as soon as possible. Otherwise, go and get your kit packed. You can take two days' leave now – that's tomorrow and the day after – so go out and enjoy yourselves, if that's possible in Catterick. There'll be a truck here at five-thirty in the morning on the sixth to collect both of you. Dismiss.'

The two lance-corporals were almost at the door before Jayston spoke again.

'Oh, one other thing, Dawson.'

'Yes, sir?'

'It's "Jolyon", actually,' the lieutenant said with a smile.

'Of course it is, sir,' Dawson muttered as he pulled the office door closed behind him.

It was just after six in the evening of 3 September 1939, and what later came to be known as 'The Phoney War' had just begun.

CHAPTER 3

Four days later, Eddie Dawson hitched his rifle on to his shoulder, picked up his kitbag with his left hand and waited. In front of him, about half a dozen British soldiers made their unsteady way down the gangway of a small and rusty freighter that had been pressed into service as a troopship.

Dawson followed them down, stepped on to the stone-built jetty and marched about fifty yards towards the town of Cherbourg itself. He stopped and lowered his kitbag to the ground, glancing back at the troopship with a feeling of profound relief. The crossing had been one of the most uncomfortable twenty-odd-hour periods of his entire life, and hadn't been helped by the fact that he couldn't swim and was actually terrified of water.

He shrugged and looked around him. It was the first time he'd ever been out of England, and his initial sight of a foreign country wasn't particularly impressive. As far as he could see, Cherbourg didn't look a hell of a lot different from Dover.

Now he was on his own. According to the orders he'd been given at Catterick, he had to find a cavalry officer

17

– a Major Sykes of the Royal Scots Greys – and report to him. Then, perhaps, he might find out what he was doing in France.

The quayside was crowded with men – and just a handful of women – wearing uniforms and battledress and coats in a variety of designs and shades, different stripes and badges and colours indicating their nationalities, ranks and regiments. Some were standing in groups, others marching in formation to unknown destinations, directed by bellowing NCOs, while most of the remainder walked about with an air of purpose, several carrying clip-boards, pieces of paper or unidentifiable objects in boxes and bags. Numerous trucks and a few tanks flexed the muscles of their internal-combustion engines, the roar of their big diesel and petrol engines adding a deep bass counterpoint to the constant buzz of conversation, shouted orders and the sounds of marching feet, while their exhausts belched thick clouds of black and blue smoke that hung over the scene to form a persistent noxious miasma.

Around the edge of the dockyard area, several groups of civilians stood and watched the apparent confusion of organized chaos with a world-weary air. A number of them wore dark-blue berets, which immediately identified them to Dawson's wholly untrained eyes as obvious French locals.

A bellow from behind snapped him out of his reverie.

'You there! You, the lazy sod just standing about. Move yourself!'

Dawson spun round, grabbed his kitbag and stepped quickly to one side as a squad of men marched past, the

senior NCO in charge giving him a nasty look and another mouthful of abuse for good measure.

He shook his head and pulled a buff envelope containing a well-creased sheet of paper out of his pocket. He looked again at the brief typed sentences, a masterpiece of unambiguous military brevity that completely failed to suggest where Dawson might find Major Sykes, other than somewhere at the French seaport.

In fact, Dawson realized, reading the orders once more, all he actually knew was that Major Sykes was an officer in the Royal Scots Greys, a cavalry regiment. But obviously he had to start looking, so he slung the Lee-Enfield on his shoulder, grabbed his kitbag, glanced around again and selected a group of about half a dozen junior officers standing some fifty yards away.

He marched over to them, dropped his kitbag and snapped off the sharpest salute he could manage, encumbered as he was by the rifle.

One of the officers – Dawson could tell from his insignia that he was a lieutenant in an artillery regiment – lifted his swagger-stick to the peak of his cap in a lazy acknowledgement and looked at Dawson enquiringly.

'Yes, Corporal? What is it?'

'I'm looking for a Major Sykes, sir,' Dawson said, pulling the printed order from his pocket and offering it to the lieutenant.

'Regiment?' one of the other officers snapped.

'I'm a Royal Engineer, sir.'

'Not you, you idiot. I can see what you are. I mean, what regiment is Sykes in?'

'Sorry, sir. In the Royal Scots Greys, sir. That's a cavalry regiment.'

The lieutenant looked at Dawson to see if he was being facetious, decided he wasn't, and grunted. 'Well, what are you here to do? No work for a sapper around here as far as I know, or not yet anyway.'

A couple of the officers smiled slightly at his remark.

'I'm an engineer,' Dawson said. 'I've been sent here to assess something called the Marginot Line.' That was the only other piece of information his orders had provided him with, and it had left Dawson largely in the dark because he had never heard the name before. But he'd decided it was some kind of defence project because the name was followed by the word 'fortifications'.

'The what?'

'The Marginot Line, sir,' Dawson repeated. 'I think that's what it's called, and it's a group of forts.'

'He means the Maginot Line. The last great hope of the fucking Frogs,' the lieutenant said, with a sarcastic laugh. 'So why's a lance-corporal been sent to France to look at a static defence project, suggested by a "Marshal of the Nation", which probably won't work and cost the French government something like seven billion francs to construct?'

Dawson shrugged. 'I don't know anything about that, sir. My orders are only to look at these fortifications and assess them.'

'Assess what?'

'How easy it would be to demolish them, I suppose, sir. That's what I do – I blow things up, sir.'

'Well, take my advice, sapper,' the lieutenant said, glancing again at the typed order before passing the paper back to Dawson. 'If you think the Maginot Line fortifications aren't all they're cracked up to be, make

sure there aren't any French about before you tell anyone, because most of *les Frogs* think their *cloches* will be quite enough to stop the German advance in its tracks.'

'"Clutches", sir?'

'No – *cloches*. It means "bell" in French. They're the armoured steel bits of the Maginot Line that hold all the guns and stuff. There are about fifteen hundred of them altogether.'

'Right, sir. Thanks, sir. And Major Sykes?'

'I'm pretty sure that's him over there,' the lieutenant said and pointed at a short, dapper-looking officer with a small but perfectly trimmed moustache, a kitbag beside him, who was looking with interest at a couple of Morris trucks that had just stopped on the jetty, their engines rattling and wheezing into silence.

Dawson nodded his thanks, picked up his kitbag again and marched across to the officer. He saluted, and noted the officer's cap-badge – an eagle standing on a pedestal bearing the name 'Waterloo' and a scroll with the words 'Royal Scots Greys' below that.

'Major Sykes?' he asked, and the officer nodded. 'I'm Lance-Corporal Dawson, sir,' he added and proffered the typed orders he'd been given.

For a few moments, Sykes didn't respond, just took the sheet of paper and read it carefully, then looked at the man standing in front of him. Dawson was just under six feet tall, strongly built, with dark hair and features that at first glance appeared to have been hacked from something like granite by somebody using a fairly blunt chisel.

'You're late,' Sykes said, handing back the paper.

'I know, sir. The troopship was very late arriving here, and I didn't know where to find you. All I had was your rank, name and regiment, sir.' Dawson gestured meaningfully at the crowds of soldiers milling around them.

'You should have used your initiative.'

'I did. That's why I'm standing here now. Sir,' Dawson added, the final word a distinct afterthought.

Sykes stared at him for a moment, then smiled slowly. 'Good,' he muttered. 'I like soldiers with a bit of spirit. I think we'll get on well, don't you? Right, let's go.'

'Hang on a minute, sir,' Dawson said. 'I still don't have any idea what I'm supposed to be doing over here. All I've been told is it's something to do with this thing called the Marginot Line.'

'Maginot,' Sykes said, correcting Dawson's hard 'g' pronunciation. 'Named after the French Minister of Defence, André Maginot. It's a line of forts and gun emplacements the French built along their northern and eastern borders. They think it makes their country impregnable to attack by either the Germans or the Italians. It's our job to see if they're right, or if it's just the single most expensive and pointless mistake in the history of modern warfare.'

'Where is it, then, this line of forts?'

'Basically, it runs along most of the north-eastern borders France shares with other European nations, from Switzerland to Luxembourg. Obviously that includes Germany, but there's also a line along the Italian border, and in the north-west it links up with a similar set-up they've got in Belgium. Building it was a huge undertaking.'

'So which bit of the Maginot Line are we going to look at?'

'Oddly enough, none of it. We're heading for Lille, but the Maginot Line actually stops near a town called Montmédy, which is miles away, down near Luxembourg.'

Dawson's face reflected his confusion. 'So what are we . . .' His voice trailed off into silence.

'It's simple,' Sykes explained. 'The French built this line of forts that finishes at Montmédy, but the reason they stopped there was because the Belgians already had a defensive line that ran all the way from Montmédy to the Channel coast, and another one that ran up the eastern border it shares with Germany. The Maginot Line itself would be a tough nut to crack, but most of the forts along France's northern border are a relic from the Great War. They're obviously less secure, and it's those we've been sent here to inspect.'

'But why me, sir?' Dawson asked, sounding slightly over-awed. 'I know my way round gelignite, but I'm just a lance-corporal. I've only been in the Corps for a few months. There must be other people better qualified than me.'

Sykes shook his head firmly. 'Oddly enough, there aren't. You've been sent out here because as far as explosives and demolition work are concerned you're probably the most experienced person in the entire British army, entirely because of your work in civvy street. Your job is quite simple and straightforward. We want you to look at the way this defensive line has been built and see if destroying parts of it using explosives would be a viable

option for the Germans, and if that would allow them to breach the French defences. That's all. If you think it would be fairly easy to destroy some sections, then maybe the powers that be will try to reinforce the line, but that won't be our decision.'

'And will I be reporting to you, sir, or someone else?'

Sykes smiled. 'To me, Dawson, of course, because I'm the other half of the equation. You're the explosives expert; I'm the tactics man. My job is to work out if the Germans could bypass or neutralize these defences using some other method.'

'So it's just the two of us, then?'

'Can you drive?' Sykes asked, an apparent non-sequitur.

Dawson nodded. 'Yes, sir.'

'Right, then it *will* be just the two of us. Grab your kitbag and mine, and put them in the back of that truck over there.' Sykes pointed at the first of the two Morris lorries that had stopped a few yards away. 'Then get behind the wheel.'

Dawson nodded, picked up both kitbags and deposited them in the rear of the truck as Sykes had ordered, then climbed up into the cab. He stowed his rifle behind the seat, where it would be within easy reach, then glanced across at the major, who was already sitting in the other seat, a detailed map of France open on his lap.

'You'd already arranged for us to use this vehicle, then, sir?' Dawson asked as the engine spluttered into life.

'Perhaps "arranged" is putting it a little strongly,' Sykes replied, another smile on his face. 'Just get it moving, will you?'

Dawson nodded, engaged first gear and released the clutch. As he did so, he heard shouts from somewhere behind them, shouts that were audible even over the noise of the Morris's engine, and glanced behind him to see a large sergeant running towards the lorry, gesticulating and shaking his fist.

'Ignore him,' Sykes instructed. 'He'll just have to find himself another truck. Oh, and don't forget we drive on the right over here.'

Dawson changed up a gear and looked behind again, then smiled. He'd been in France for just over thirty minutes and already he was driving off in a truck that had been stolen – or at best borrowed without consent – aided and abetted by a senior officer who apparently seemed to think the entire process was perfectly normal.

It looked as if, no matter what else happened to him, his first mission of the war was, at the very least, going to be entertaining.

CHAPTER 4

It didn't take long to get out of the port area of Cherbourg, and in a few minutes they'd cleared the town limits and reached open countryside. Some distance ahead of them, a small column of British army trucks, perhaps five or six vehicles in all, was heading in the same direction. Dawson accelerated to match their speed, then glanced across at the major, who was still studying the map.

'This Maginot Line, sir,' he said, making a conscious effort to get the pronunciation correct. 'It's just a line of forts, then, is it? I mean, something like those big round buggers out in the sea near Portsmouth?'

Sykes lowered the map and looked up. 'I suppose it's a similar concept, yes,' he replied. 'The structures you're talking about are the Napoleonic Forts. They were intended to protect Britain's most important naval bases from attack by the French, hence the name. Britain's an island, and from a defensive point of view that's a huge advantage. It means that any attack has to be launched from the sea, and that severely limits the options for an invader. A lot of our coastline is completely unsuitable

26

for a landing – places like Dover, for example, apart from the port itself, because of the cliffs.'

'They could fly in, I suppose. Land troops from aircraft,' Dawson suggested.

Sykes nodded. 'Agreed, but you can't launch a successful invasion by air. Aircraft are too fragile and vulnerable to attack, and can't carry enough men and supplies to make them a viable option. The best you could hope to do with a purely airborne invasion is seize a specific objective for a fairly short time, and even then you'd need resupply and back-up quite quickly. To take control of another country you need troops on the ground, obviously, but you also have to have tanks and trucks and armour and a whole supply chain to support them. And you can't do that only using aircraft – it's just not feasible. So if we can protect our ports and beaches, we can always withstand any invasion attempt.

'But the problem the French have is different. Their country is virtually surrounded. It shares land borders with Belgium, Luxembourg, Germany, Switzerland, Italy and Spain. The chances of the Swiss or the Belgians invading are probably pretty slim, but they reasoned that Germany and Italy might well try their luck, especially after the Great War, and that was why they came up with this idea of a fortified border. And, of course, with Adolf the house-painter strutting about Europe in his shiny new jackboots, we now know that they were right.'

'Do you think it would be enough to hold off the Germans, then?'

'That's what we're supposed to find out,' Sykes replied. 'Personally, I doubt it, because it was conceived in the aftermath of the greatest land war the world had

ever seen. It might well stop a conventional frontal assault, but the people who planned it took no account of the rise of air power. Tactically, I think that when the Germans decide to invade France – and they will, there's not the slightest doubt about that – they'll identify the weakest point, parachute troops in behind it and hit it from two sides simultaneously. And when they've destroyed one section of it, they'll use that as an access point for their army and ignore the rest of the fortifications.'

'So the Frogs would have done better to have just strengthened their armed forces?'

'Perhaps. But it's not quite that simple. I've not seen any of the fortifications, but I know a lot about them. The French haven't just built a line of forts. In some places the Maginot Line defences are twenty kilometres deep, a proper layered defensive system that would be very difficult for any army, no matter how strong, to break through. Before they launch any attack, the Germans will send up reconnaissance aircraft, and maybe even infiltrate patrols into the border region, to assess the strength of the fortifications. They'll be able to identify the strongest and the weakest points, and that will give the French an obvious advantage.'

'Obvious, sir?'

'It's simple. There are sections of the Maginot Line that only an idiot would attempt to breach, and whatever you might think of Adolf, he's not an idiot, and nor are his commanders. Obviously the Germans will hit a weak point, and if they manage to break through that's where they'll send the rest of their troops. That means the French can predict where a German attack is

likely, and mass troops on their side of the border to counter it.'

'Got it, sir. An ambush.'

'Exactly. So even though the Maginot Line probably wouldn't stop an invasion, it might at least help slow down a German advance into the country. And this idea of a defensive line isn't unique to the French and the Belgians. The Germans have got one too. They call it the *Westwall*, though we've nicknamed it the Siegfried Line. It's a line of fortifications running along the western border of Germany from Switzerland north up to Luxembourg, intended to protect Germany from attack by the French.'

'So right now the French are sitting behind the Maginot Line looking at the Germans, who are sitting behind the Siegfried Line and looking straight back at them? Is that about right, sir?'

'In a nutshell, Dawson, in a nutshell.'

A few minutes later the convoy reached a small French town called Valognes. As the first of the lorries rumbled through it, inquisitive locals appeared on the streets, attracted by the unfamiliar sound of big diesel engines echoing off the stone-built houses. Somebody watching their progress apparently identified the vehicles as British, and loud cheers rang out. By the time Dawson's lorry reached the centre of the small town, the pavements were thronged with people cheering and waving, a few even clutching Union flags.

'They seem pleased to see us, sir,' Dawson remarked.

'Yes,' Sykes replied. 'It makes a change for the French to think of us as the good guys. They probably see the British as their saviours against the German hordes.

What they don't know is how ill-prepared we are to fight this war, and how stretched we're going to be for the next few months. The BEF is more of a token show of force than a serious attempt to counter the Germans.'

'Some of the lads on the way over told me we're sending a whole crowd of troops over here, and not just to Cherbourg.'

Sykes nodded. 'And they're quite right. In fact, the BEF will be using four separate ports to disembark troops in France – Brest, Nantes and St Nazaire, as well as Cherbourg. There's only a handful of soldiers here now, just the advance guard, as it were, and the rest will be arriving next week. As far as I know, they'll be assembling down at Le Mans, which is pretty central for those locations, before they move up to support the French forces in the Lille area.'

'Lille again.'

'Exactly. There's a perception that if the Germans decided to attack sooner rather than later, they'd probably send their invading armies through Belgium, avoiding most of the French Maginot Line. That's why the BEF will move up to Lille. But it wouldn't be anything like enough, Dawson. I know the German military and I know that, if Hitler's armies do somehow bypass the Maginot Line and invade France next week, the best we could hope to do is to delay them. In the end, his troops would roll right over us. It would be a disaster.'

'We'd all better make sure the Maginot Line does what it's supposed to do, and keeps the Jerries out.'

'Hope springs eternal, Dawson. Me, I've got my doubts.'

*

The trucks rumbled on through the afternoon. As soon as he was certain the vehicles were all heading the same way, Sykes abandoned his map and slumped back in the seat. Pretty soon his head fell forward, and the sound of gentle snoring filled the cab.

Just after six in the evening, when the convoy was approaching a village named Les Hayons, about five miles south-west of the town of Neufchâtel-en-Bray, Dawson saw the truck in front of him start to slow down and ease over to the side of the road. Moments later, he realized that the leading vehicles of the convoy were driving into an open field. He changed down and turned off to follow them, the Morris bouncing over the rutted ground as it left the road.

'Sir,' Dawson said, raising his voice and glancing at the slumped figure in the seat next to him. 'They're pulling over.'

'I am awake now, thank you,' Sykes murmured, stretching uncomfortably in his seat.

Dawson stopped the Morris beside the last vehicle in the group and switched off the engine with a sigh of relief.

Sykes pulled on his cap, climbed down out of the cab and strode away towards a group of British soldiers who'd just appeared from their vehicles. Five minutes later, he was back and walked over to Dawson, who was standing beside the Morris.

'We're all going to the same place, which is convenient. This lot are a kind of advance guard of the BEF and they're heading for Lille to liaise with one of the French regiments there, so we'll tag along with them. Right, food. Is there anything in the back of the truck – any rations, I mean?'

'No, sir. I've already checked. There are half a dozen jerry-cans of fuel, but that's all.'

'Pretty much what I expected, so it's just as well I told the officer in charge that we'd be eating with him and his men. Grab your mess kit and follow me. Oh, and Dawson – if you talk to any of these soldiers, don't tell them what we're doing in France. This is supposed to be a classified operation.'

About half an hour later, Dawson was looking at a portion of slightly lumpy stew that he'd just spooned into his mess tin from a large black cooking pot. But at least it was hot and, washed down with a couple of mugs of strong tea, didn't even taste all that bad. Sykes was sitting some distance away, with the handful of officers in charge of the convoy, and eating pretty much the same meal.

After they'd eaten, the soldiers around him started smoking and talking, but Dawson felt whacked – he hadn't slept for long on the troopship the previous night, and he'd been driving almost all day. He thanked his fellow soldiers for letting him share their meal, walked back over to the Morris, washed his mess tin and utensils, then pulled a sleeping bag out of his kitbag, unrolled it and laid it out on the floor of the loading area of the lorry, and climbed into it.

Despite the hard and cold steel underneath him, within a couple of minutes he was sound asleep.

CHAPTER 5

Dawson woke, cold and shivering in the grey pre-dawn light, to the sound of clattering mess tins and shouted orders. He sat up, his body stiff and aching from the unyielding steel that had formed his mattress for the night, and looked around. Major Sykes was lying in his sleeping bag at the far end of the truck, a rhythmic chorus of gentle snores showing that he was still asleep – an officer's privilege, Dawson thought briefly.

He pulled on his trousers and tunic – he'd slept in his shirt and underwear against the cold – and climbed down from the Morris, his mug and mess tin in hand. The other trucks were bulky black shapes that loomed out of the cold grey mist blanketing the field, reducing visibility to perhaps fifty yards. Dawson shivered and wandered over to the closest group of soldiers.

'Any chance of a brew, lads?' he asked.

'Yes, mate, just help yourself.'

Dawson nodded his thanks and filled his mug from their kettle. 'I thought France was supposed to be warm,' he muttered, as he took his first mouthful. 'This feels fucking cold to me.'

'It feels fucking cold because that's what it is,' the soldier said. 'This bit of France isn't that much further south than the Isle of Wight, and that's fucking cold too. I know – I've been there.' He glanced up at Dawson. 'You're with that officer, aren't you? That dapper little bugger?'

Dawson suppressed a grin – that was an entirely recognizable description of Major Sykes – and nodded.

'But you're a sapper and he's cavalry, chalk and cheese. He hasn't got his horse here, so you can't be in charge of the hay or shovelling its shit, so what the hell are you doing with him?'

'Right now,' Dawson said, Sykes's warning of the previous day ringing in his ears, 'I'm his driver and bag carrier, and probably his batman too. I'd better take him some tea now, I suppose. But what exactly I'll be when we finally get to Lille, I've no idea.'

Dawson washed out his mug, poured tea into it and added a dash of tinned milk. He walked back to the Morris truck and peered over the tailgate. Sykes was sitting up, running his fingers through his dishevelled hair.

'Morning, sir,' Dawson said. 'Tea,' he added.

'Thank you. Is that smoke or mist I can see outside?'

'Mist, sir. It's bloody cold and damp, and you can only see for a few yards. I think the lads have got breakfast going. Can I bring you something?'

'Thank you, no. I'll drink this tea, which is foul, by the way, then I'll go and see the convoy leader and find out what his plans are.' Sykes took another sip. 'I don't know what it is about tea in the British army. It's strong and thick and far too sweet, and tastes absolutely disgusting with tinned milk in it. In fact, it's probably one

of the most revolting drinks known to man, but every soldier seems to love it.'

'It keeps up morale, sir.'

'I don't know about morale, but it certainly keeps me up all night if I drink it late in the evening.'

After Sykes had left the truck, Dawson joined the others for breakfast, then did his best to wash, shave and clean his teeth – none of them particularly easy in the circumstances. Once he'd finished, he dragged one of the jerry-cans out of the back of the truck and emptied its contents into the Morris's fuel tank, and finished the process with about a quarter of another can. Then he climbed up into the cab of the truck and sat there, waiting for Sykes to come back.

It was another quarter of an hour before the major returned, looking pink and freshly shaved, so Dawson guessed the officer's ablutions had been rather more satisfactory than his own. Sykes glanced around him and then, when he spotted Dawson in the cab, he nodded, walked round to the passenger door and hauled himself inside.

'You've put some fuel in?' he asked.

'Yes, sir. The tank's full.'

'Good man. Right, the officer in charge reckons the convoy will head out in about half an hour, just to give this mist a bit of time to lift, so you can relax for a few minutes.'

Just over thirty minutes later, Dawson heard whistles blowing, then a clattering sound, and looked out through the windscreen. The visibility was noticeably better, and a puff of blue smoke close to one of the trucks showed

that the driver had just started the engine. Then another one fired up, and a third.

'Looks like we're ready to roll,' Dawson remarked, and Sykes nodded agreement.

As the last truck moved forward and headed towards the road, Dawson engaged first gear and followed it, the lorry bouncing and lurching over the uneven ground. Once they reached the tarmac, he accelerated to catch up with the last vehicle in the convoy, then held position about fifty yards behind it as the trucks headed east along the fairly narrow road.

'We should make Lille by early this afternoon,' Sykes stated, his head bent over the French map again. 'It's only about a hundred miles, so it shouldn't take us more than around three hours, even on these roads.'

'Do you speak French, sir?' Dawson asked.

Sykes nodded. 'Yes. That's one of the reasons why I'm sitting here now.'

The convoy drove through Neufchâtel-en-Bray, the large number of unfamiliar vehicles again the subject of curious scrutiny by some of the local residents. But this time there was no cheering, and no waving flags, just silent, almost unfriendly, stares.

'These Frenchies don't seem very pleased to see us,' Dawson remarked.

'That's because they aren't, and because this is not a simple situation. There's a large body of people here in France who don't see the Germans as their enemies. In fairness, they don't regard them as their friends either, but more as neutral partners. Some of them would be quite happy to see a French–German alliance, so they're probably not impressed that France has declared war on

Germany, or with the sight of British army lorries driving through their towns.

'They're deluded, of course. I'm quite sure Herr Hitler will have a list of priorities, and taking over France – and Belgium, of course – will be fairly near the top. An alliance with a neutral France wouldn't work because the Germans will have to launch their invasion of Britain from the French channel ports, so they have to defeat the French first.'

'You think Hitler will invade us, then?'

'He'll certainly try, Dawson, there's no doubt about that.'

Dawson absorbed that unwelcome information in silence, then changed the subject. 'What do we do when we get to Lille, sir?'

'We find the appropriate senior Frog and ask him to show us where the nearest fort is.'

'And they do know we're coming, sir?' Dawson asked. 'I mean, they *are* expecting you?'

'Not exactly,' Sykes replied, with a grin. 'My boss sent an official request to his French opposite number, or at least to the officer he thought might fit the bill, but he hadn't had a reply by the time I left. So you could say the French have been advised about our visit, but they haven't actually approved it.'

Dawson nodded, wondering how much of a problem that was likely to be. Major Sykes, he decided, was the kind of officer who got things done by sheer force of personality and his obvious willingness to bend whatever rules were in force at the time – the fact that they were still driving around France in a truck that was technically stolen was proof enough of that. It would be

interesting to see just how his particular brand of improvisation fared when he was confronted by a bunch of French army officers, who might regard Sykes and his mission in a very different way.

CHAPTER 6

'Make a right turn here, Dawson,' Sykes ordered, as the convoy of lorries in front of them carried straight on at a crossroads on the southern outskirts of Lille.

Dawson nodded and sounded the Morris's horn briefly as he turned the wheel. A couple of the soldiers in the back of the rearmost truck looked up and waved as their vehicle moved away.

'Right. Stay on this road, and keep your eyes open. We're looking for a village called Santes.' Sykes spelt the name aloud.

A few minutes later, the major pointed ahead. On the right-hand side of the road was a sign bearing that name.

Dawson slowed down as the Morris entered the village, and started looking for any sign of an army camp.

'Over there, sir,' he said, pointing to his left, towards a field that bordered the road.

A small cluster of tents occupied one part of it, and a handful of vehicles was parked on the opposite side. To Dawson, though he didn't recognize the make or model, the trucks looked unmistakably military.

'Pull over there,' Sykes instructed.

Dawson eased the Morris over to the opposite side of the road and braked the vehicle to a halt.

'Come with me.'

The major led the way through an open gate and into the field, then strode swiftly across to a couple of officers standing beside one of the larger tents, Dawson a few paces behind him. As they approached, the two Frenchmen stopped talking and turned to look at the new arrivals.

Sykes stopped right in front of them and just stood there, waiting.

The two Frenchmen were junior officers, probably lieutenants, Dawson guessed, from their insignia and rank badges.

They looked Sykes up and down, and then finally seemed to recognize his rank, even if they didn't know the man in the uniform. They both belatedly and somewhat casually saluted him – junior officers always salute their seniors – and Sykes acknowledged.

'*Bonjour, Major*,' one of them said – to Dawson the word 'major' sounded more like 'ma – shore'. '*Vous desirez quelque chose?*'

Sykes replied with a barrage of high-speed colloquial French, which was completely incomprehensible to Dawson. But the two French officers clearly understood every word. They stiffened perceptibly, pulling their shoulders back and straightening their spines. And when one of them replied, his manner was clearly deferential.

Sykes fired more French at them and was again rewarded with a snappy response from one of the men, and what sounded like a series of directions. The major

nodded and turned away, ignoring the two crisp salutes offered by the Frenchmen.

'We're in the right area,' he announced to Dawson, as they headed back towards the Morris truck. 'The officer I'm supposed to be meeting – or I think I'm supposed to be meeting – is actually over at one of the fortifications now. It's only a couple of miles away.'

Dawson started the lorry and pulled back on to the road. Following Sykes's directions, he took three turnings in quick succession, the road getting narrower and apparently less used with each change of direction, and moving deeper into a wooded area. Eventually, they started driving down a single-track lane where the branches of the trees on either side brushed against the cab of the Morris, and where the centre of the roadway was marked by a line of grass that had lifted and grown through the thin layer of tarmac.

The lane ran straight, like most French roads, with no signs of habitation on either side, but it wasn't all that long. Less than a mile after Dawson had taken the last turning, the lane ended in a clearing in the wood, a circular area wide enough for vehicles to turn round. A military vehicle – a kind of open scout car, Dawson thought – was already parked on one side of the road.

'Stick the truck next to that,' Sykes ordered.

Dawson hauled the truck to a standstill and switched off the engine. Once the diesel had rattled into silence, the two men climbed out of the vehicle and followed a well-trodden footpath that wound deeper into the wood.

About a hundred yards from the clearing, the path ended at a grey concrete structure that appeared to be half-buried in the undergrowth. As they got closer to it,

Dawson could see that the fortification was located in a commanding position right at the edge of the wood, the trees around it giving way to open farmland beyond. The land sloped away gently on both sides and more sharply to the front, which would provide a clear field of fire down the valley.

'This isn't a bad location at all,' Sykes muttered, as they stopped beside the left-hand wall of the structure and surveyed the terrain beyond it. 'What do you think of the design of the place, from a demolition point of view, I mean?' he asked.

Dawson looked critically at the square, box-like structure in front of them and shrugged. 'It looks to me like the walls are about two feet thick,' he said, 'and they'll be made from reinforced concrete, so it's pretty tough. But the design's old-fashioned, with all these flat surfaces, and it looks old.'

'It is,' Sykes agreed. 'This was probably built about twenty years ago. Is there a problem with flat surfaces?'

'Well, yes and no, really. A long straight wall is easier to make than one that's curved or has lots of corners, but it won't stand up to sustained fire as well as a curved structure. I did a course on fortification design earlier this year, sir,' he said, in answer to Sykes's quizzical look. 'The course dealt with how to build them, obviously, but we also covered the identification of weak points so we could blow them up as well.

'The front elevation of this place is an easy target from down there,' he continued, pointing into the valley below. 'If attacking troops could aim a howitzer or something similar at it, and were accurate enough, three or four shells hitting in about the same place on the front wall

would probably break through it. Job done. If they'd built it with a sharply curved front, that couldn't happen.'

'And if I told you to blow it up, to demolish it using dynamite or whatever, could you do it?'

'Dynamite or maybe gelignite, sir. Yes, no problem. I'd need to take a proper look inside first, just to see what the internal design was like, but I'd probably drill a line of holes along the back and both sides, because the front wall is probably the thickest, stuff charges inside and blow them all at once. That should take away the roof support on three sides, and the roof would just collapse on to the remains. But it would take a lot of jelly to do it.'

'Understood,' Sykes said, 'and that would obviously mean the place would have to be empty at the time. Suppose it was manned, and you had a group of soldiers with you. Could you still destroy it?'

'Probably, sir, but I'd need something like RDX to do it.'

'What the hell's RDX?' Sykes demanded.

'It's a German invention, actually. It's a pretty powerful explosive, and we've been playing with it for a while now in the Corps, and so have the Yanks – they call it cyclonite, just to be different. It's a kind of hard white stuff that'll go bang if you hit it with a hammer, which isn't a lot of use in most circumstances. But you can mix it with what's called an explosive plasticizer, and that turns RDX into a kind of high-explosive putty. You can mould it to shape and then fire it using an electric detonator. If I had to blow this place, I'd ignore the walls altogether and just mould some RDX around the door. It's made of steel, obviously, but that wouldn't be enough

to protect it. I'd fire the charge, the door would collapse and then I'd lob in a handful of grenades.'

Sykes nodded. 'It wouldn't be pretty, and it's certainly not an elegant solution, but it would obviously work.'

'What would work?' another voice asked. 'And just who are you two?'

Sykes and Dawson turned round to face the speaker: a tall, slim French officer wearing an immaculate uniform with three gold bars on the epaulettes, standing a few feet behind them, flanked by two soldiers, both carrying rifles.

Sykes made the introductions. 'I'm Major Sykes of the Royal Scots Greys, and this is my driver, Lance-Corporal Dawson, Royal Engineers. Are you Capitaine Marcel de St Véran?'

The French officer inclined his head slightly.

'My superiors sent a signal to your regiment, explaining that I would be coming to this part of France. Did you receive it?'

'I may have done,' the French officer said airily. 'I can't remember. I have been extremely busy recently. What did you want here?'

Sykes glanced at Dawson before he replied and managed to put a wealth of meaning into the look.

'Your English is very good, Capitaine,' Sykes replied, 'but I can speak French if you prefer.'

'My English is fluent, of course.' St Véran shrugged. 'I was unfortunate enough to have been sent to school in England for some years. So let me ask you again. What are you doing here?'

'If you'd read the signal, you'd know why we've come,' Sykes replied, his tone now noticeably sharper. 'My

superiors have instructed me to visit this part of the border to look at the existing fortifications.'

'Why?'

'So that we'd have a good idea of the likely strength of this border in the event that the Germans decide to invade France from Belgium.'

St Véran's reply was a snort. 'Why should you or your superiors make such a stupid assumption? Why do you think the Germans have any designs on France?'

'The fact that the French government declared war on Germany five days ago might be a clue,' Sykes replied mildly.

'Let me tell you this,' St Véran said, stepping forward and tapping Sykes's chest lightly with the end of his swagger-stick. 'Paris may have declared war on Germany, but that doesn't mean we actually have to *fight* a war. I am confident that reason will prevail, and that we'll soon reach an accommodation with Berlin. We have much more in common with the Germans than you might imagine.'

'Don't do that,' Sykes said, knocking the stick to one side, his voice rising in anger. 'I note your opinion, but I have my orders, as you will no doubt also have yours, if you can be bothered to check. Now, in accordance with *my* orders, we'll inspect this fortification. Get out of our way, Capitaine. And kindly remember your manners. I'm the senior officer here, and you will accord me proper respect.'

For a few seconds, the two officers stared at each other, then St Véran stepped back and gestured towards the concrete bunker. 'If you must,' he murmured, giving a somewhat casual salute, and then added 'sir'.

Sykes nodded, and waved for Dawson to follow him.

'What an arrogant, self-important little shit,' Sykes muttered, as they walked towards the entrance to the concrete fort. '"Unfortunate enough to have been educated in England", indeed. That's one of the problems we're going to face, Dawson. A lot of French officers have a strong dislike of the English, and quite a few of them would far rather see France uniting with Germany than joining us to fight against Hitler. Some of them are openly pro-German and even pro-Fascist. If he's typical of the officers in this area, we could have problems.'

The steel door at the rear of the bunker was open, and they walked over to it and peered into the darkness inside. There was a bank of light switches beside the door, and Sykes reached out and turned them all on. Bulbs flared into life throughout the structure.

It wasn't that big. There were three small rooms at the front, separated from each other by thick concrete dividing walls, but no doors. The centre one had an opening for a fifty-millimetre mortar, and the weapon itself was located directly in front of the opening in the concrete front wall. The two side rooms each had a couple of narrow slits through which rifles or machineguns could be fired down the valley.

Behind these three firing rooms were six even smaller rooms – a basic kitchen, two bunk-rooms, each with six bunks arranged in two tiers of three, a lavatory and a wash-room, plus an ammunition store and armoury protected by a thick steel door.

Sykes looked into the latter and scowled. 'Equipped for, but not with,' he said cryptically as he stepped outside again.

'What do you mean, sir?'

'I mean, Dawson, that France is at war with Germany and has been for nearly a week, but that armoury hasn't got a single mortar round in it, and I could only see a couple of boxes of machine-gun ammunition and, predictably enough, no machine-guns. I know this is the French border with Belgium, I know France only just declared war, and I know that Hitler's so far made no move against either country. But I also know how devious that little Austrian bastard is, and how quickly his forces can move, so I really would have expected this fort to be not only fully prepared for battle, but fully manned as well.'

Sykes stopped just outside the concrete bunker and turned back to look at it again. 'It might just as well not even be there,' he said, his voice low and angry. 'Typical of the bloody French, and especially of Kraut-loving bastards like St Véran over there. He's supposed to be in charge of the preparations and readiness in this sector. If this is the best he can do, we might as well all just give up and go home right now.'

Dawson nodded.

'Now you've seen inside it, what do you think about the structure?' Sykes asked. 'Could you destroy it using charges – RBX or whatever you called it?'

'That's RDX, sir, and yes, I could. The design's not that good. If I had time to do a proper job I could turn it into a pile of rubble, but with plastic explosive I could sneak up and blow a big enough hole in it to take it out of commission.'

'Right.'

'Satisfied?' St Véran sneered when they walked back to rejoin him.

'That's not the word I'll be using in my report,' Sykes retorted, 'and I *will* be reporting this to both your superiors and to mine, Capitaine. That report will discuss both your attitude and the complete lack of proper preparedness here.'

St Véran gave an expressive Gallic shrug of his shoulders, but didn't respond.

'There's not the slightest point in having a place like that unless it's fully manned and properly equipped, and that's neither. Why is that, Capitaine?'

'We have plenty of time to move men up here – they're based only five kilometres away. And the ammunition and weapons are on their way. We should have them here later this week, so there's no need to worry.'

'*I'm* not worried, Capitaine, but you should be. Are all the fortifications in this sector as poorly prepared as this one?'

St Véran stood in silence for a few moments. 'I don't accept that we *are* poorly prepared, Major. But even if there is some substance in what you're saying, I still don't see what it has to do with you.'

'If you bothered to read your orders, perhaps you'd find out,' Sykes hissed. 'Apart from this place' – he jerked his thumb towards the concrete bunker – 'what other defensive measures do you have here?'

'None,' St Véran said sharply. 'We're satisfied that this fortification would be entirely adequate to halt any German advance, unlikely though that scenario is, as I've already pointed out to you.'

'Tell him, Dawson.'

'With respect, sir, that's total bollocks,' Dawson said, 'and you've no idea what you're talking about. I could blow this place apart with a few pounds of plastic explosive, and any competent gunner with a howitzer could take it out from way down there in the valley with half a dozen rounds. It's over twenty years old and the world's moved on a bit since then. This is all show and no substance. It wouldn't hold up a German advance for more than about half an hour, tops.'

St Véran's eyes widened slightly. He stared at Dawson for a few seconds, then switched his gaze back to Sykes. 'Who is this, this person standing beside you? And how dare he speak to me in that manner?'

'That person, as you put it, is Lance-Corporal Dawson' – Dawson gave an ironic half-bow as Sykes said his name – 'and he's an expert in explosives. If you had the slightest bit of sense, you'd listen to what he tells you. But somehow, I don't think you will.'

'You're clearly both ignorant and insubordinate, *Corporal* Dawson. Now you will apologize to me.'

Dawson shook his head. 'No fucking chance. I'll stand by what I said. If you don't like it, tough.'

St Véran looked as if someone had slapped his face, his furious gaze shifting between the two British soldiers.

'Major Sykes,' he began, when he found his voice. 'You will order that man to apologize.'

'I won't, and don't you dare stand there and try to give me orders, Capitaine. I think Dawson said it quite well. "No fucking chance" seems to about cover it. Now piss off out of my sight, you incompetent piece of crap.'

For a moment, the French officer just stared at Sykes

and Dawson, then he turned on his heel without another word, gestured to his two men and stalked away.

'That went well, I thought,' Dawson said, as he and Sykes followed the trio of Frenchmen – at a distance – back towards the clearing where they'd left the Morris truck. 'So what do we do now, sir?'

'We're obviously wasting our time here,' Sykes muttered. 'These defences are just a joke, and that French idiot has no idea what's going on. We'll try and find where that convoy of soldiers has been billeted and see if we can stay with them overnight. I'll have to find a radio or telephone and contact my boss to explain the situation. And then, I suppose, I'll do whatever he tells me. As for you, I've no idea, but I'll ask.'

CHAPTER 7

9 SEPTEMBER 1939

Eddie Dawson cautiously opened one eye and groaned. Then he opened the other one, which didn't materially improve the view, though he could make it out more clearly. Through the opening above the tailboard of the Morris he could see trees. Lots and lots of trees. He thought they were firs or maybe pines, something like that, though his knowledge of botany was virtually nil. But their straight trunks were familiar to him from the woods and forests in some of the remoter parts of Yorkshire and Northumberland, where he'd worked before he joined the Corps.

He and Sykes had found the convoy the previous afternoon, and Dawson had scrounged an evening meal from the soldiers. It was another dollop of stew, the meat just as unidentifiable as it had been in the previous version he'd tried, accompanied by half a dozen slices of bread and the inevitable mugs of hot strong tea. Afterwards, he'd sat with the soldiers round the dying embers of the fire they'd built, talking and smoking.

He'd refused the half-hearted offer of a space in one of the soldiers' tents and returned to the Morris for the

night, because he didn't relish the prospect of dossing down in a tent surrounded by a group of hairy-arsed men, probably with sweaty feet and almost certainly snoring throughout the night. The downside was that his back was really beginning to suffer because the steel floor of the lorry was hardly comfortable, but the ground under the tents wouldn't have been a hell of a lot better.

And at least he'd been warm enough – unlike the previous night – because the weather seemed to have changed for the better. The overnight temperature had been pleasantly warm, and there was no sign of the bone-chilling mist that had so delayed the convoy's departure the previous morning.

Dawson squatted down on the floor and pulled on his boots, then grabbed his jacket and helmet. But before he could climb out of the Morris to go and find something to eat, there was a sharp rap on the steel tailgate.

'You're up, then,' Sykes stated, his voice unnaturally cheerful for the early hour, Dawson thought. The major had found a billet with the convoy officers the previous night.

'Yes, sir. Can I help you?'

'Not really. Now, I've been ordered to go back down to Abbeville to brief some of the British General Staff. There will be a big Anglo-French meeting there in a few days, and several of our top brass are already on the spot.'

'And me, sir?'

'You're a Royal Engineer, so they'd like you to get engineering. There'll be another group of men from the Corps arriving here later today, and the idea is for you to start doing something useful to fortify this area –

something that might actually slow down or stop a German advance, that is. A few concrete pillboxes, some decent tank-traps, that kind of thing.'

'So you don't want me to drive you to Abbeville then, sir?'

'No thanks. Much as I've enjoyed your company for the past couple of days, the prospect of spending another ten hours rattling around in the cab of that blasted truck isn't particularly enticing. There's a staff car on its way here now to pick me up.'

Dawson nodded. 'Understood, sir. What should I do about this lorry?'

Sykes considered the question for a few moments. 'Keep it,' he replied. 'I don't mean as your personal property, obviously, just as a spare vehicle for this convoy. I'll go and tell the OIC that he's acquired an extra truck.' The major glanced round. 'Right, the troops seem to have got breakfast on the go, so I'll leave you to it. Good luck, Dawson.'

Sykes lifted his arm in a somewhat half-hearted manner as Dawson saluted him awkwardly from the back of the Morris truck, then strode away.

Five minutes later Dawson walked across to the nearest cooking fire, clutching his mess tin hopefully.

'The galloping major buggered off, has he?' one of the soldiers greeted him, as Dawson dug his fork into the pile of brownish beans, studded with pale sausages and strips of fatty bacon, sitting in his mess tin.

'Yes. He's off to talk to a bunch of big-wigs somewhere. I doubt if I'll see him again.'

But only a few minutes later, as he was mopping up the remains of his breakfast with a slice of pappy white

bread, Dawson looked up to see Sykes walking quickly towards him, and stood up as the major approached.

'Change of plan, Dawson,' he announced briskly, as whistles started shrilling somewhere behind him and other officers began striding about with a sense of purpose, barking orders.

'You're not going to Abbeville, then, sir?' Dawson asked.

'No, I meant a change of plan for you. God knows why, but we've just been told that the French started an offensive thrust towards Germany on the fifth, and entered enemy territory yesterday. It wasn't a full-scale attack – it really couldn't be because they only started their general mobilization a week ago, and we were told no attacks would be made on Germany until the sixteenth at the earliest – but I gather they have managed to punch through the German lines towards a place called Saarbrücken.'

'Where's that, sir?'

'It's only just inside the German border, fairly close to Luxembourg, down to the south-east of here.'

Sykes gestured behind him at the soldiers, who were now rapidly breaking camp, packing up their gear and stowing it in the backs of the lorries.

'These men have been ordered to head down there, to the Rhine area, in support of that offensive, and you've been ordered to go there as well. If the French military leaders decide to tackle the German Westwall, you might find your demolition skills are much in demand. Anyway, just tag along with these troops and see what happens.'

Sykes glanced over towards the road outside the encampment, where a staff car had just appeared, the

driver peering around him, obviously looking for someone or something.

'That's probably my ride now,' the major said, 'so I'd better be off.'

Dawson watched the officer striding quickly across the field towards the staff car, which had stopped beside the gate, the driver obviously having seen the major.

'Bugger,' Dawson muttered. 'Another bloody day on the road, in another bloody truck.'

CHAPTER 8

9 SEPTEMBER 1939

Dawson's prediction had been absolutely right – he *had* spent all day on the road in a truck. But this time he wasn't driving, which was something of a relief. He'd slung his kitbag and Lee-Enfield into the back of one of the other lorries and then hopped in himself, to join a handful of other soldiers.

The distance from the army encampment just outside Lille to a village named Dalstein was about 250 miles, and it took them most of the day to cover the distance. It was a far from comfortable trip as the truck bounced and rattled over the uneven and rutted roads.

'Hell of a way to go to war,' one of the soldiers complained, as the truck lurched over a particularly savage bump in the road. 'By the time we see any Jerries, we'll be so battered and bruised from all this lot we'll be too buggered to shoot straight.'

'Maybe we won't have to shoot at all,' another man suggested, clinging on to the wooden seat with both hands. 'I heard the French army's pushed miles into Germany, about a dozen divisions, rolling right over the

Jerries. They could be in Berlin inside the month, and this lot might be over by Christmas.'

'No fucking chance,' another voice replied. 'If the bloody French *have* managed to stagger into Germany, they'll surrender the moment they meet any serious opposition. No stomach for a fight, your average Frog.'

'What about you, sapper?' the first soldier asked Dawson. 'You've been with that cavalry major for the last few days. Did he know what's going on? And what are you doing with him, anyway?'

Dawson shook his head. 'Right now, mate, I don't think *anyone* knows what's happening. Back at Catterick an officer I spoke to reckoned it was going to be a long haul, this war, said Adolf was a pretty good tactician. After all, they've already occupied Austria and Czechoslovakia with hardly a shot being fired, while that bloody idiot Chamberlain was waving his bit of paper around – "peace in our time" and all that crap. That didn't stop Hitler invading Poland, did it?'

'What about the galloping major? What did he think?'

'He thinks Hitler wants to invade the whole of Europe, including Britain. He reckons what's happening now is only the first step, and it's going to be a bloody long, bloody hard fight.'

That remark silenced the other soldiers for a few moments.

'Bit of a fucking depressing thought, that. I hoped we might be back home pretty soon.'

'Don't count on it.'

'You never said what you're doing over here, sapper.'

'That's right,' Dawson said, 'I didn't. In fact, I can't

tell you what I was sent here to do. The major told me it was confidential.'

The other soldiers looked at Dawson with varying degrees of interest.

'Not a bloody spy, are you?'

Dawson smiled and shook his head. 'No. Just a soldier, same as you lot. But I used to be a mining engineer. That's why I got volunteered. But that's all I can tell you.'

The convoy finally pulled off the road into an open field outside Dalstein late in the afternoon. The lorries stopped in a curving line, spaced widely enough apart that any of the vehicles could drive away without another truck having to be moved.

Dawson climbed down and looked around him. They were obviously some distance from the village, because he could see no signs of habitation at all. Rolling hills extended in all directions, separated by wide, shallow valleys and open fields, most of the landscape heavily forested. If he hadn't known that the German border was about ten miles away, it would have seemed a pretty pleasant place to have a picnic.

Within an hour the soldiers had erected their tents and were sorting out the rations for their evening meal. As Dawson was now more or less attached to them, he was given a bed-space in one of the tents, so he stowed his kit and helped out with the cooking.

Shortly after they'd eaten, a small group of French officers appeared in the field and spent half an hour talking to the officers in charge of the convoy. When they left, the British officers had a brief discussion, then one of them blew a whistle and ordered the soldiers to gather round.

'Right, men,' Lieutenant Charnforth began, when they were all assembled in a rough semi-circle around him. 'We now know a bit more about what's been happening in this area. Three days ago, on the fifth of September, just forty-eight hours after we and the French declared war on Germany, units of the French army started a limited offensive towards Saarbrücken.'

The lieutenant paused. A ragged cheer went up, and someone muttered, 'Bloody good!'

'Yesterday, about nine French divisions crossed the German border and began advancing into the Saarland region – that's the area between the border itself and Saarbrücken. This advance has been on a broad front, nearly twenty miles wide, and the French have met with very little German resistance so far. The intention is for the French forces to occupy the area between the French border and the enemy lines, and then try to probe the strength of the German First Army defence sector there.'

'Why don't they just launch a full-scale attack, sir?' someone asked.

Charnforth shook his head. 'That's not their objective. The purpose of this attack is to assist Poland. As you all know, Hitler invaded Poland at the beginning of September, and the French offensive is intended to divert German troops from that country and force the Germans to strengthen the Westwall – the Siegfried Line – in this area. So it's not a serious and committed advance, or not yet, anyway. I gather that there are plans in hand for a full-scale assault, but that won't happen for probably a couple of weeks, if then. And the reason the French have met very little resistance so far is

because the German troops seem to be spread pretty thin around here.'

'What are we here for, sir?'

'Support only at the moment,' the lieutenant said. 'The French officers will request our help if they need any assistance, but there are so few of us that it's unlikely we could do that much. For the moment, we'll just stay here. But we're only a few miles from the border, so keep your rifles loaded, and with immediate effect we will be posting sentries: two permanent two-man patrols, starting at twenty hundred hours today. The sergeant will draw up a roster.'

He paused and looked around. 'Dawson, show yourself,' he ordered.

Dawson moved forward and raised his hand.

'You're a sapper, and you might be needed sooner than the rest of us. One of the strategic objectives of the French advance is an area called the Warndt Forest. That's quite a large area of woodland that actually straddles the border region, and we understand that one section of it, about three miles square, has been heavily mined by the Germans. It's possible you might be ordered to assist with mine-clearance operations if the French decide to consolidate their advance in that area.'

Lieutenant Charnforth glanced around at the soldiers standing in front of him. 'Right, men. That's all for now. Dismiss.'

CHAPTER 9

10 SEPTEMBER 1939

The following morning Dawson was rudely awakened by someone shaking him roughly by the shoulder.

'Wake up, Eddie. Officer wants to talk to you.'

'Bugger,' Dawson muttered. 'What time is it?'

'Dunno, mate. About seven, I think.'

Dawson rubbed his eyes and staggered to his feet. He quickly pulled on his clothes and stepped out of the tent. A few yards away, Lieutenant Charnforth stood waiting, the sergeant alongside him.

'Morning, sir,' Dawson mumbled, whipping off a salute that wasn't anything like as crisp as it should have been.

'Morning. When I met Major Sykes, he told me you were a demolition specialist. Is that true?'

Dawson nodded. 'Yes, sir, sort of. My job in civvy street included demolition.'

'And you are qualified in mine-clearance?'

Again Dawson nodded.

'Good. I've just had a request from the French commander in this area. As I suggested when I briefed everyone yesterday evening, they do need a sapper to assist

with clearing the mines the Germans have laid in the Warndt Forest.'

'Don't they have their own people, sir?'

Lieutenant Charnforth nodded. 'Of course, but this operation, this invasion of German territory, was mounted at very short notice. They have their own specialists on the way, but they won't get here for at least two or three days. As far as I can gather, you're the only qualified sapper anywhere near this area at the moment.'

'To shift the mines,' Dawson pointed out, 'I'll need specialist equipment that I haven't got here. I'd like a detector to help find them, and then explosives – something like RDX – to blow the buggers up, if there's no way of making them safe. And there should be two of us involved – one to locate and remove the mine, the other taking notes and watching.'

The lieutenant nodded. 'I realize that. There's a truck arriving here some time today or tomorrow latest from Cherbourg. It should be carrying everything you want, and there's another sapper driving it, so there will be two of you to do the work.'

That sounded better, Dawson thought. 'So when do I start, sir?'

'As soon as the truck gets here. I just needed your confirmation that you're able to do the work, so that I can tell the French. Once the lorry's here, I'll brief the two of you, then you can head east.'

Twenty minutes later Dawson had washed and shaved and was sitting on a fallen log, his mess tin half-full of a brown mass predominantly consisting of beans. He

spooned the food into his mouth without any particular enthusiasm as he contemplated the unpleasant prospect of mine-clearance for real.

He'd done the job often enough back in England, on Salisbury Plain and other training grounds, but that was in an exercise scenario, where the 'minefield' was clearly laid out in front of you, marked by pegs or stakes and tape, where you knew how many deactivated mines there were to be located and what type. And, of course, where there were specialist observers watching every move, able to stop proceedings with a single order or a blast from a whistle if things started going wrong. But here in the Warndt Forest, actually inside German territory, there would be no observers, no markings to show the extent of the minefield, no safety precautions at all. If he got it wrong, Dawson knew, he'd probably lose his legs, or even his life.

It wasn't a prospect that did anything to improve his appetite, and he threw away the last few mouthfuls of his breakfast, then washed away the taste of what he'd been eating with a mug of strong tea.

The promised lorry arrived just after four-thirty that afternoon, and the first person Dawson saw when he walked across to meet it was Dave Watson, climbing out of the cab of the vehicle.

'Dave!'

Watson spun round, then his face broke into a smile. 'Bloody hell, Eddie, you get around, mate, don't you? I thought you'd buggered off with that major you told me about. What are you doing here?'

'Long story. I've spent the last few days driving all over the bloody place, but now I'm stuck here. When did you get to France?'

'We got in to Cherbourg yesterday, and I was ordered over here straight away, because of this French advance. I suppose they've found a minefield?'

'You got that right.'

Dawson explained what he knew about the German advance towards Saarbrücken, and the problem of the Warndt Forest.

'So the bloody Frogs want us to shift mines for them? Fucking typical.'

Dawson grinned, though frankly there wasn't much about the situation that was humorous.

At that moment, Lieutenant Charnforth walked around the corner, spotted Dawson talking to Watson and strode over to them.

'Right,' he began, as he returned the salutes of the two soldiers. 'What's your name?' he asked, looking at Watson.

'Watson, sir, David Watson.'

'And you're qualified in mine-clearance, like Dawson here?'

'Yes, sir. I've done the course, anyway.'

'Good. Now, both of you come with me.'

The lieutenant led the way towards the officers' tents, which stood a short distance away from those occupied by the soldiers. He crossed over to the largest of these, opened up the flap on the end, ducked down and stepped inside, Dawson and Watson following behind him. At one end was a large vertical board on which was pinned a large-scale map of the area, covered in various coloured

markings and with numerous different-coloured pins stuck into it.

Charnforth picked up a pointer and turned to face the map. 'Right,' he began, 'this is the situation. We're based just here, on the outskirts of Dalstein, about ten miles from the German border. This' – his pointer traced a meandering line that ran more or less from the northwest to the south-east – 'is the frontier between France and Germany. Further over to the east, in fact about fifteen or sixteen miles almost due east of where we are standing right now, is the town of Saarlouis. There are several towns and villages running in a line alongside the River Saar from Saarlouis down to the south-east, finishing up here at Saarbrücken.

'That town is the stated objective of the present French advance, but their forces are still quite some distance away, probably four or five miles at least. In fact, although the French have advanced on a broad front, the depth of their penetration into German territory is quite shallow, probably only about a mile in most cases and up to a maximum of five miles. They've reportedly captured about twenty villages that had already been evacuated by the German army, and they've met almost no resistance.'

'Major Sykes told me about the Siegfried Line, sir,' Dawson said. 'Have the French reached it yet? Is that why they haven't been able to advance any further?'

The lieutenant shook his head. 'You mean the Westwall, Dawson. No, I don't think the French forces have got anything like that far. In fact, the main Westwall defences in this region are located to the east of Saarbrücken itself. I gather you've seen some of the Maginot Line forts?'

'Just the one, sir, up at Lille, but it was pretty old and basic and dated from the Great War, so it wasn't really a part of the Maginot Line proper. The major told me the main Maginot Line forts are actually quite impressive.'

'They are, but I still don't think they'll stop a German advance. The Westwall defences were built for a similar purpose to those of the Maginot Line, but probably not as well. The majority of the French *cloches* are well designed and capable of accommodating heavy weapons, but we don't think that most of the Westwall forts are anything like as strong.'

Lieutenant Charnforth turned back to the map. 'As I said, the French forces have been making fairly slow progress, but they have now established a presence here.' His pointer circled an area marked in green on the map, lying just to the east of a town called Creutzwald-la-Croix. 'This is part of the Warndt Forest. As you can see, this area is heavily wooded, but it's important from a strategic point of view, because any major advance in this sector would have to pass through it. The Germans have heavily mined the forest, and that's why the French want you to go in there.'

The lieutenant turned to look at Watson. 'Did you bring all the equipment you need?'

The sapper nodded. 'Yes, sir. Everything's in the back of the truck.'

'Right. You'll be going into the forest first thing tomorrow morning, with six of my men as an escort. There'll be a group of French soldiers waiting there to show you which sections they need clearing. Any problems, send one of the soldiers back here with the truck. Finally, do either of you speak French?'

Dawson and Watson both shook their heads.

Lieutenant Charnforth smiled. 'I'm not surprised, but it shouldn't matter. A lot of the French officers speak a bit of English, and what you're doing won't require too much conversation. One of the soldiers I'll be sending with you speaks some French. All you have to do is clear a path through the forest where the French tell you to. Now, any questions?'

'No, sir,' Dawson said. 'We'll just need to check out the gear, then we're ready.'

CHAPTER 10

11 SEPTEMBER 1939

A little after nine the following morning, Dawson and Watson climbed into the back of one of the Morris lorries and sat down opposite each other on the wooden bench seats that ran along either side. Four other soldiers jumped up after them and sat down.

Between them lay half a dozen dark-green ammunition boxes filled with packets of RDX plastic explosive. In another box were a couple of dozen detonators, little more than slightly modified blasting caps, and in an open wooden crate several rolls of cable and a couple of hand-cranked generators that would produce the electric current needed to fire the detonators. Beside them lay a smaller wooden case marked 'fragile' and secured by two metal clasps. Inside that was a mine detector – a flat plate that would be attached to a wooden handle and powered by a battery – together with its various cables and headset. Two slightly modified Tele Set Mark V field telephones in their metal cases, a couple of spades, three hammers, pliers of various sizes, fifty or so wooden posts, flags, warning signs, small red-painted wooden crosses,

and balls of white tape to mark out areas cleared of mines completed the outfit.

A few seconds later the truck engine started, and the vehicle lurched forward, the driver swinging it in a wide circle to clear the other lorries, and bounced over the rutted field towards the road. The men in the back clung on, then relaxed slightly as the truck reached the tarmac surface.

'I knew I shouldn't have bloody volunteered, Eddie,' Dave Watson said.

Dawson smiled, though Watson's view wasn't dissimilar to his own. 'But look on the bright side,' he said. 'At least all we have to worry about is finding and destroying a few mines. With any luck the Germans won't be shooting at us as well.'

It wasn't a long drive. Less than half an hour after the Morris lorry had driven away from the British army camp, the vehicle left the road and began making its way down a track, the driver reducing his speed considerably. And a few minutes after that he pulled the lorry to a stop and switched off the engine. One of the soldiers dropped the tailboard, and they all climbed down.

Dawson looked around. The area seemed to be almost deserted, with just a small number of French soldiers standing in a group at the edge of the large clearing where the Morris had stopped.

'Are you sure this is the right place?' he asked the driver.

The soldier gestured in front of the truck, where a barrier had been placed across the track, bearing a round sign with the word 'Halt' printed on it. 'This is definitely as far as we could go, mate,' he said.

'This is a bit odd,' Dawson muttered to Watson. 'I wonder why those Frenchies are just standing about.'

As he spoke, two French officers appeared from a track that snaked into the forest and walked towards them.

The British soldiers saluted as they approached. The officers returned their salute and then one fired a sentence at them in high-speed French.

Dawson shook his head. 'We do not speak French, sir,' he said, enunciating each word slowly and carefully.

The French-speaking soldier who'd accompanied the two sappers – a lance-corporal named Tommy Blake – stepped forward and spoke to them, somewhat haltingly. The exchange continued for a minute or so, almost every word meaningless to Dawson, though he guessed that the repeated words *mine terrestre* and *mine dormante* probably meant landmines and unexploded mines.

Finally, Blake turned to Dawson and Watson. 'It seems clear enough. The French have already lost a couple of men – one killed, the other badly injured – as they started to advance through the forest. It looks as if the Germans mined that bit over there' – he pointed to the east of where they were standing – 'because that's the obvious route for an invading force to use. The slopes on either side of it are pretty steep and covered in trees, so it'd be difficult to move trucks or tanks along them.'

'That's why the French troops aren't doing a lot,' Watson commented. 'There's no point in them digging in if they're going to keep advancing, but they can't actually do that until the mines are cleared. That *does* make sense.'

'Right. So what do they want us to do?' Dawson demanded.

'They'd like you to start clearing a track through the centre of the forest, wide enough for a truck to get through. That'll save the French forces from having to go around the perimeter of the woodland.'

'Starting from where?' Watson asked.

'At the edge of this clearing, just over there.' Again the soldier pointed.

'Right, Dave,' Dawson muttered. 'Best we get going then. Do you want to start with the detector?'

'Might as well.'

The two sappers removed their webbing and battle-dress tops – for what they were going to do, they needed to be as unencumbered as possible – and retained only their bayonets. The two French officers and the British soldiers stood in a half-circle and watched while Watson opened the wooden box, removed the components of the electric mine detector and began assembling it. Meanwhile, Dawson grabbed one of the shovels, a hammer and a handful of the wooden stakes and walked over towards the point that the French officers had indicated. A post had been driven into the ground bearing a skull and crossbones symbol and the written words *'Danger – mines terrestres'*.

He saw immediately where at least one of the mines had been positioned. Just to one side of the track, perhaps twenty feet beyond the warning sign, was a small hole in the ground and a large red stain that showed where the French soldier unfortunate enough to have stepped on the weapon had fallen.

Dawson stopped about twenty yards away and studied the area carefully. He was looking for any signs that the ground had been disturbed, but there was nothing

immediately obvious. The probability was that the mines had been placed some months ago, maybe even longer, and the undergrowth had by now completely obscured their positions. There were several small glistening fragments scattered around, and he bent down and picked up a few of them. They were ball bearings – the shrapnel from the mine – together with a few small shards of steel that Dawson guessed had probably come from the casing of the mine itself.

He turned his attention to the site of the explosion, staring at the area directly around the hole. Something about it bothered him, quite apart from the fact that a man had either died or been seriously injured there, but it took a few seconds before he realized what it was.

All the mines Dawson had worked on before had been designed to explode on contact, the force of the detonation erupting from the ground and creating a funnel-shaped blast wave centred on the weapon. But what he was looking at seemed to be very different. The foliage had been shredded and torn at about waist-height, with almost no damage above or below that level, and he had no idea what kind of mine could have caused that pattern of destruction.

It was obvious he'd have to wait for Dave Watson before he could get any closer. They'd need to scan the area using the mine detector, because there was no other way of telling where the minefield actually began, or how wide it was. The French soldier who'd triggered the weapon might have walked past a dozen of them before the weight of his foot caused that first mine to detonate, so there was no way Dawson was going to take even a single step forward.

Watson walked up beside him and stopped.

Dawson glanced back to see the soldiers and the French officers waiting some distance away, now using the Morris truck as a shield. 'That's the first one, Dave,' he said, pointing. 'That bugger caught one of the French soldiers – you can see the blood on the ground near the hole. And look at where the blast hit the trees and bushes.'

Watson peered at the shredded undergrowth for a few seconds. 'Christ, yes. Looks like it exploded about three feet off the ground. What the hell kind of mine could do that?'

'I've no idea,' Dawson said, and opened his hand to show Watson the ball bearings he'd picked up nearby. 'This looks to me like pretty standard anti-personnel shrapnel to me, but that explosive pattern is new. Do you suppose the mine was fired into the air first, then detonated?'

'A kind of air-burst, then,' Watson mused. 'Mines are nasty bastards anyway, but that's a bloody devious twist. Typical of the fucking Jerries.'

He paused and looked at the woodland around them, deceptively peaceful in the early morning, the sunlight streaming through the trees that fringed the clearing, and transforming the grass into a bright emerald carpet.

'Right, then. We're doing bugger-all standing here looking around. Let's get started. Where's the safe zone? Is there one?'

Dawson shook his head and pointed at the warning sign the French had erected. 'It looks to me as if once that mine went off, they just dragged the body away, knocked that sign together and stuck it in the ground.

Bloody lucky they didn't hammer it down on top of another mine.'

'So they didn't do any sort of clearance or checking?'

'Not that I can see, no. There are no tapes or stakes anywhere.'

'Well, at least that means we don't have to check that they've done it right.'

Watson put the headphones of the mine detector around his neck. He checked all the connections, then switched on the unit. He placed his bayonet on the ground, ran the head of the detector over it, and nodded when he got a good strong signal from the unit.

'I'll start right here,' he said. 'That'll establish a base line and then we can move forward.'

'Got that,' Dawson replied. 'I'll mark it both sides.'

Watson nodded, and pulled the headphones up to cover his ears. He moved the detector slowly from left to right and back again as he walked to the right-hand side of the track leading through the forest.

'That's far enough, Dave,' Dawson said, raising his voice so that Watson would hear him through the ear-phones.

The other man nodded and waited while Dawson took a wooden stake and hammered it home close to where he was standing. Dawson attached a length of white tape to the stake and let it dangle on the ground. That established the right-hand side of the cleared lane they would drive through the woodland.

Watson continued scanning the ground as he walked back to a position on the left-hand side of the track, where Dawson repeated the process with another stake. Those two stakes formed the base line, and would give

them a distinct starting-point for the remainder of the cleared lane.

Watson waited for Dawson to attach the tape, then started covering the ground towards the wood along the left-hand side of the track. He checked about six feet, then nodded to Dawson, who drove in another stake and tied the tape around it. Then Watson crossed to the opposite side of the track, checking the ground all the way, and again Dawson drove home a stake.

The two men quickly established a routine, and within half an hour they'd extended the cleared lane to a length of about fifty yards, and Watson hadn't detected a single mine. But all that meant, of course, was that the Germans had buried them further into the woodland, because there was no doubt they were there.

'Your turn,' Watson said, pulling off the headphones at the right-hand side of the lane.

'Right.' Dawson took the mine detector, checked that it was still switched on, then settled the headphones comfortably over his ears. He stepped forward, swinging the instrument left and right, but taking care to keep the sensitive head – the flat plate – parallel with the ground and only a couple of inches above it. That was essential to give the coils embedded in the head the best possible chance of detecting any metallic objects buried in the ground.

The first two passes he made across the lane were negative, the detector registering nothing at all. But half-way across the track on his third pass, as he swung the instrument to his left, the noise in his earphones suddenly increased dramatically and he stopped immediately.

'Dave,' he called out, 'I've got something here.'

CHAPTER 11

'Hang on there for a second,' Watson said. 'I'll get the gear.'

Dawson swung the detector slowly to his left, then back the other way to pinpoint exactly where the buried mine – or whatever the sensitive head had detected – was. The signal was strong and consistent. There was definitely something there, not too far below the surface and made largely from metal.

He identified where the signal appeared to be centred. Keeping his eyes fixed on the spot, he stepped back slightly, then took a small red-painted wooden cross from his belt and placed it gently on that precise position.

He looked around. Watson was approaching, careful to keep inside the safety lane, between the two lines of stakes linked by tape. He carried a shovel and one of the field telephones. 'Right there, is it?' he asked.

'Yes,' Dawson said. 'A good strong signal. For fuck's sake be careful, mate.'

'You know me, Eddie. Slow and steady, those are my middle names.'

'Yeah, right.'

Watson put the field telephone on the ground, unclipped the lid and checked it, then attached the ends of the wires.

Dawson picked up the mine detector: it was an expensive and fairly fragile piece of equipment, and he needed to get it well away from the position of the mine. He ran the spool of wire to a position close to the Morris truck, a safe distance from the mine, prepared a second field telephone he took from the back of the lorry and attached the wires to it.

Watson glanced over his shoulder to check that Dawson had got the unit connected, then picked up the handset and pressed the microphone switch.

'You there, Eddie?'

'Loud and clear, mate.'

'Right. I'm switching to the headphones and starting now.'

Watson knelt down on the ground, pulled on the headset and slowly inched his way towards the red wooden cross his colleague had placed over the buried object.

All anti-personnel mines require a certain minimum pressure before they're triggered, for obvious reasons – it would be pointless laying mines if every rabbit or fox that walked over them could fire them – so generally a downward force of at least fifteen or twenty pounds was needed. Watson knew that he was safe as long as he didn't lean directly on the trigger, or hit it, but he still exercised extreme care.

First, he just looked at the ground directly in front of him, trying to spot any signs of previous disturbance or digging, but he could see nothing. And, exactly as he'd

been trained to do, he kept up a continuous running commentary to Dawson, who waited nervously beside the Morris truck, making notes as the operation progressed – again, standard procedure when dealing with unexploded ordnance of any sort.

'No sign of recent digging,' Watson reported. 'The grass has grown over the object, so I'm guessing that whatever it is has been buried there for at least a year. No sign of exposed metal parts or triggers, so it's presumably pressure-activated by a sensor just below the surface. A question, Dave. When the detector registered it, how big was the object? I mean, are we looking at something six inches across, or a foot, or what?'

Dawson thought for a second. 'Quite small, certainly less than a foot.'

'OK. In that case I'm going to start loosening the soil in a circle about two feet in diameter all around it, starting from the outside.'

'Go gently, Dave,' Dawson muttered.

Watson eased up into a crouch, pulled out his bayonet and slid the end of its blade gently into the earth some twelve inches from the red wooden cross, at a diagonal angle. He drove it in about six inches, felt no resistance, pulled it out and moved the blade closer. This time, he felt the tip touch something solid. That gave him an indication of the dimensions of the buried object.

He left the bayonet in position, picked up the shovel and drove it a couple of inches into the ground to scoop up the top layer of soil. He lifted the shovel, tossed the turf and earth behind him, away from the mine, then repeated the process slightly further over to his right, moving slowly around the buried object.

'Right,' he said into the microphone, as he lifted the last sod from the ground in front of him. 'I've just completed the circle. The cleared area runs around the object at a distance of about a foot. I'm now going to start shifting the top layer of soil directly over the mine.'

Watson removed the wooden cross that showed the position of the buried object, and discarded the shovel. He pulled out the bayonet and slowly, with infinite care, started removing the grass and soil that covered the mine.

He'd shifted about half of it when he suddenly saw a slim metal object protruding from the soil, and instantly stopped moving.

'Dave, I've spotted something,' Watson said.

'Keep talking,' Dawson replied, still making notes. 'Tell me what you can see.' If Watson didn't survive, the information Dawson would glean from his actions would help when he tackled the next one – as he would certainly have to do – and would hopefully allow him to avoid making the same mistake.

'OK. It looks like a thin black metal tube, angled downwards into the ground at around forty-five degrees, and about half an inch below the surface. It has to be some kind of a trigger, but it's not a type I've seen before.'

'Hang on a second, Dave,' Dawson said, doing a rough sketch on his pad of the object Watson had just described. 'Unless the mine's been installed at an angle, that sounds like just a part of the trigger. You could be looking at a three- or four-prong assembly. Can you try clearing the soil around it – carefully, of course – and just check it out.'

'I'm doing it right now, mate,' Watson said.

There was a short pause, then his voice sounded again in Dawson's ear.

'You're right,' he said. 'It's a three-pronged trigger, like an inverted tripod. I've found two other prongs just the same, pointing in different directions. So I know exactly where the mine is. You were pretty much spot on with the cross. It was right over the trigger.'

'I'm a professional, mate. What else would you expect?' Dawson's comment was light and humorous, but there was no disguising the tension in his voice. 'What are you doing now?'

'Keeping well away from that fucking trigger for starters. I'm probing with the bayonet to find out just how big this bastard is.'

There was another pause, and Dawson watched his friend closely.

'OK, Eddie. I've found nothing at a distance of six inches from the trigger, and I've gone down around a foot, so it can't be a flat mine. I'm guessing it's tall and thin.' Watson paused for a few seconds as he explored further. 'Right, now I've got it. It's not shaped like a conventional mine. It's more like a can of beans, quite small. I've never seen one anything like this before.'

'Copied that, Dave. What are you doing now?'

'I'm shifting the earth from all around it. Once I've got it free, I'll lift it out and we can take a proper look at it.'

Again there was silence over the field telephone circuit, and Dawson just stood and watched because there was nothing else he could do.

'Right, Eddie. I've managed to shift all the earth. I'm

going to lift it out of the hole. But before I do, I'll just describe it to you, in case there's any kind of an anti-handling device I haven't spotted. The mine's about six inches high and four inches in diameter, a thick black cylinder. On the top of the cylinder are four round plugs or something similar, and sticking out of the centre is a kind of rod that's about three inches high, and on top of that are the three prongs. As far as I can tell, that's the trigger. I guess pressure on the prongs would trigger a spring-loaded release, and that would detonate it.'

'OK, Dave. Just do me a favour and check all around it first, before you lift it out of the hole.'

'You bet. Wait, I've just noticed something else. That vertical rod I described has two thicknesses. It's fatter at the base, and there's a thinner section on top. I think *that's* the trigger. It looks like the thin section slides into the fatter part.'

'Got that, Eddie. Let me know when you've lifted it out of the ground.'

Less than thirty seconds later, Dawson watched Watson stand up and back away from the hole, and as he moved backwards Dawson saw the mine for the first time. At that distance, it looked remarkably insignificant, just a small black can with a rod on the top, but he had no doubt about its lethal power.

'That's it, Eddie,' Watson said. 'You can come over and take a look at it.'

Dawson placed his notebook in the back of the Morris truck and walked across towards Watson. When he reached his friend, the two men stood in silence for few seconds, just staring down at the mine Watson had

recovered. It appeared to be black-painted, but it was covered in earth so any markings on it were invisible.

'It doesn't look like much,' Dawson commented.

'No, but if it's the same type as the one that Frog soldier stepped on, we know it's a dangerous bastard.'

Dawson bent down and looked closely at the weapon. Then he pointed at the top of it. 'Did you see that?' he asked.

'What?'

'There's a hole through the thinner part of the rod. I'll bet that's where a safety pin would go.'

'If you're right, that would make disarming it really easy. Just stick another pin through the hole, and you could probably play football with it.'

'Rather you than me,' Dawson said, 'but I think you're right. I think that's how you make the weapon safe. Hang on a minute. I'll see if there's anything in the truck we could use.'

A couple of minutes later he was back, a selection of bolts and nails in his hand. He checked the size of the hole in the rod carefully, then chose a bolt about two inches long and slid it through the hole. For safety, he screwed a nut on to the thread to hold it in place.

'You think that's it?' Watson asked.

'Yes, I do.' Gingerly, Dawson stretched out his hand, picked up the mine and looked at it closely. 'You were right – the thinner section of the rod slides inside the other, and that must be the trigger. I guess the detonator's directly underneath that.' He hefted it in his hand. 'It feels as if it weighs about ten pounds.'

He turned it over and looked at the base, but there appeared to be no markings on it anywhere. The mine's

body looked as if it had been forged from a single piece of steel, formed into a cup shape, with a waterproof seal round the top, through which the trigger assembly and the four caps Watson had mentioned protruded.

'There's no sign of anything on the base of the mine,' Watson remarked. 'No separate charge to make the bugger fly up into the air.'

'No, but that would probably be internal. This mine was designed to be left buried in the ground for a long time, so the Jerries would have wanted as few seams and joints as possible to make sure it stayed watertight. If there *is* a charge designed to launch it upwards, it'll be inside the casing, with a steel plate above it to direct the blast downwards. That would work.'

'Yeah, Eddie. OK. That's one down and Christ knows how many to go.'

'Right. Let's put this bastard somewhere safe, and then we'd better carry on,' Dawson said. 'Do you want to use the detector and I'll dig out the next one?'

'Yeah, fine.'

The two men walked back to the Morris truck, where a small crowd of people had now assembled, not only the six British soldiers who had come with them into the forest, but also the two French officers and a handful of French soldiers as well.

'Where's Tommy?' Dawson asked, looking round. 'We need him to explain what we've found.'

'Here, mate,' Blake said, stepping forward.

'Right. Tell these Frenchies that this is a new kind of mine, and that we're going to have to look at it carefully before we can work out exactly how it works. From the pattern of destruction we've seen, we think it probably

83

jumps up into the air before it explodes, so it's bloody nasty. We think we've made this one safe, so we're going to leave it over there' – he pointed off to one side of the track where there was a ditch – 'while we carry on searching for any others. Tell them that nobody should handle or even touch this – we don't want any accidents.'

'Got that,' the lance-corporal said. He swung round, converted Dawson's remarks into slightly hesitant and far from colloquial French and fired it at the officers and soldiers standing there.

As he did so, Watson carried the mine over to the dry ditch, knelt down and placed it carefully on its side in the bottom of it, and marked the location with a couple of red-painted wooden stakes.

Then the two sappers turned and walked back towards the minefield.

CHAPTER 12

11 SEPTEMBER 1939

'We need to establish the pattern,' Dawson said, 'so let's start by marking the spot where we pulled that one out.'

He took a small wooden stake and hammered it into the ground a few inches from the hole Watson had dug to remove the weapon, then retreated a few yards as his colleague donned the headphones and switched on the mine detector.

'I'm continuing the sweep you started,' Watson said, and began walking slowly, moving the head of the instrument over the ground, as he worked his way from one side of the track to the other.

He'd only covered about ten feet when he stopped abruptly. He moved the detector very slowly over a spot directly in front of him, then changed position slightly and repeated the process.

'I think that's another one,' he said, raising his voice. Mirroring Dawson's previous actions, he noted the spot where the signal from the buried object was strongest, and placed a red cross over that exact location.

Dawson prepared to remove the second mine and

make it safe, while Watson walked back over to the Morris truck to observe and make notes. Knowing the type of weapon they were dealing with made the task of extracting it a lot quicker. Once he'd established exactly where the trigger was located, Dawson was able to dig down in a circle around it, and within five minutes he'd removed the mine, inserted a bolt through the hole in the metal plunger and placed the weapon beside the first one in the ditch.

Watson drove another stake into the earth to mark the original position of the mine, and then resumed his clearance procedure.

It quickly became a routine and, within about an hour, Dawson and Watson had found and removed a further four mines, which they stored in the ditch with the first two. The cleared lane was now marked with half a dozen wooden stakes and white tape, and studded with other stakes that showed where the mines had been positioned. By then, the soldiers who'd accompanied them had brewed some tea, and the two sappers stopped working and sat down at the back of the lorry for a drink and a smoke.

'I can see the pattern now, Dave,' Dawson said, lighting another cigarette. 'They've laid them in groups of three, starting more or less on the right-hand side of the track and then angling across to the opposite side. Then they moved about twenty feet forward and repeated the line, this time from left to right, so it's a kind of open zig-zag that covers the whole of the track through the forest. You'd have to be bloody lucky not to step on one of them if you were walking through here. Any sizeable force would be cut to pieces.'

'Yeah,' Watson agreed, 'and, now we know how they were positioned, it should be a lot quicker to find the rest of them.'

'As long as the Jerries stuck to the same pattern, yes. If I was laying a minefield, I think I'd alternate them a bit, just to keep the enemy sappers on their toes.'

Watson looked at him. 'Thanks for that, you cheerful sod. But you're right – we mustn't make any assumptions. We'll take it slowly and carefully, and check everything.'

Dawson looked at the area they'd cleared so far, which looked pathetically small compared to the acres of forest that surrounded them.

'Just looking at that,' he said, 'and bearing in mind there are exactly two of us here, I reckon it'll take months to clear a path all the way through. And that's assuming that the bloody mine detector keeps on working.'

'Don't forget what that lieutenant said. The French are supposed to be sending some of their own sappers out here to help us.'

'I'll believe that when I see it. When I—'

At that moment there was a loud bang from somewhere well over to the right of the safety lane, almost at the edge of the clearing. Watson and Dawson spun round to look, and saw a sight that both of them knew instantly would stay with them for ever.

About seventy yards away, a French soldier had wandered towards the undergrowth, perhaps looking simply for a place to have a crap, and had clearly stepped on one of the buried mines.

As the sappers – and everyone else in the clearing –

watched, a black object shot out of the ground from just behind the soldier, reached about level with his waist and almost immediately exploded, the sound an echoing blast that dwarfed the first explosion.

CHAPTER 13

11 SEPTEMBER 1939

'Down! Get down!' Dawson yelled, and threw himself behind the Morris truck, Watson tumbling to the ground right behind him.

They covered their heads with their arms and lay as flat as they possibly could. Less than a second afterwards, the metal sides of the Morris truck rang with hammer-blows as the ball bearings from the mine crashed into it. Other missiles whistled past them, screaming over their heads and embedding themselves harmlessly in the ground beyond or smashing into the undergrowth around them.

'Fucking hell!' Watson muttered. 'Did you see that?'

'Damn right I did. That bloody mine popped right up out of the ground. What a bastard.' Dawson looked round cautiously. 'We'd better see if we can help that poor sod.'

Watson shook his head. 'He'll be cats' meat, but we'll have to go and check.'

'Yes, and head off the rest of the Frogs before they rush over there and step on another one. Come on, and bring the detector.'

The two men climbed to their feet and looked cautiously around the side of the lorry. The shrapnel from the mine had torn a devastating circular path through the clearing, and Dawson could see at least three soldiers writhing in agony on the ground, already being attended to by their comrades. Yells and shouts of pain echoed around.

And, as Dawson had feared, three French soldiers and a couple of the British lads were already running towards the site of the explosion.

'Oh, shit,' Watson said. Then he yelled out, 'Stop!' at the top of his voice.

Beside him, Dawson joined the chorus, bellowing, 'Halt! Mines!'

The two British soldiers stopped dead in their tracks, but the French carried on running. Then Tommy Blake, who'd been bending over one of his fallen comrades, stood up, took a couple of paces forward and shouted something, and the French soldiers stopped as well.

'Stand still, everybody,' Dawson yelled. 'You're all in the middle of a minefield. For Christ's sake, nobody move.'

For a few seconds there was no movement and total silence, then a piercing scream cut through the air, followed by a howl of absolute agony.

'He's still alive, then, the poor bastard,' Watson said, looking across the clearing towards the dark shape lying on the ground about sixty yards away.

'Be better if he'd died straight away, because I don't think we're going to be able to get there in time to do anything for him. I'll use the detector,' Dawson said. 'You mark out the path behind me.'

He switched on the instrument as they reached the edge of the safety zone they'd already cleared, and stepped forward cautiously, heading towards the nearest soldier.

'Everybody stand still,' Watson roared. 'Do not move. We'll get you out.' Across the clearing, Blake repeated his words in French.

Dawson was in a quandary. The injured French soldier was still yelling and screaming, but his cries were becoming weaker with every moment that passed. The only hope for him was if someone could reach him and administer immediate first aid, but there was no way that could be done safely. It was a classic 'for the greater good of the greatest number' situation – the French soldier was probably going to die no matter what anyone did, and Dawson's first responsibility was to find a safe path to allow all the soldiers who were standing in the minefield to reach safety. Only then could he try and get to the injured man.

But he still worked as quickly as he could, moving the mine detector from side to side as he advanced slowly, while behind him Watson drove wooden stakes into the ground every five or six feet, marking out both sides of a safe path around four feet wide down which the soldiers could walk.

'Stop!' Dawson yelled. 'I've got one right in front of me.' He pulled one of the small red crosses from his belt and placed it on the spot, then turned away – they didn't have time to remove or defuse the mine, so they'd just have to find a path around it.

Watson drove three stakes into the ground to clearly indicate the position of the mine as Dawson cleared the area to the right of it.

Ninety seconds later they reached the closest soldier, a young Frenchman, who was visibly quaking.

Dawson held up his hand, palm towards the young man, a universal gesture meaning 'stop' or 'don't move', and to reinforce the message Watson grabbed him by the arm. Dawson ran the head of the mine detector around the French soldier's feet, but received no hits at all.

'The area's clear,' he said to Watson. 'Send him back down the cleared lane.'

Watson pulled the French soldier towards him and pointed along the path he'd marked out with stakes. 'Walk down there,' he said slowly and clearly. 'Stay between the stakes.'

The young soldier nodded and swallowed nervously, then began walking gingerly along the path.

Dawson had already started moving forward, covering the short distance – only about fifteen feet – to the next man.

Once he was certain the first soldier was heading the right way, Watson began marking the next section of the path with stakes, and within a minute the two sappers had reached the second man, without encountering any more mines. They sent him back along the safe path, then looked around for the next one.

The French soldier who triggered the mine had fallen almost silent, his cries now reduced to barely audible moans of agony.

The two British soldiers were standing quite close together, and clearing a safe path to them took only another three or four minutes, but the third French soldier was some distance away, on the far side of the clearing.

Dawson looked across at him, then back towards the badly wounded man. 'Tommy,' he yelled, 'tell that French soldier to stay exactly where he is. We're going to check on the man who stepped on the mine. And get someone to come out here after us with a first-aid kit. Just make sure they stay on the cleared path. Got it?'

'I've got it,' Blake shouted back and yelled an instruction in French at the remaining soldier, still standing rigidly on the spot.

Dawson turned towards the wounded man and began checking the ground directly in front of him, moving as quickly as possible, Watson still using stakes to mark the edge of the path as the two men advanced steadily.

Behind the sappers, a British soldier walked slowly and carefully towards them along the cleared lane, a bulky medical kit in his hand.

About fifteen feet short of their objective, Dawson detected another mine. Again he marked the spot with a red cross and detoured around it.

And then they reached the injured man.

'Dear God,' Watson muttered, as he looked down.

Behind them, the soldier carrying the first-aid pack stared in horror at what lay on the ground in front of them, turned away and vomited copiously.

CHAPTER 14

The mine had detonated only about six or seven feet from where the French soldier had been standing, and he'd taken the full force of the blast.

Because it had exploded in mid-air, most of the ball bearings and shrapnel had torn into him at waist-level. He was still alive, just, but Dawson knew immediately that there was nothing anyone could do for him.

A virtual lake of blood surrounded his body like an obscene red halo; his left arm had been severed at the elbow and lay a couple of feet away, and his right hand was missing. But the worst injuries were to his midriff, and they were going to kill him, if he didn't die first from the massive blood loss from the ruptured arteries in his arms and torso. His stomach had been ripped open, his intestines shredded and torn, most of them lying outside what was left of his body.

The soldier was lying on his back, his eyes open, his breathing shallow and rasping in his throat. Blood caked his face and bubbled from his open mouth.

Not even the most talented team of surgeons in the

world, in the best-equipped and most modern operating theatre, would be able to save his life. In a field on the Franco-German border, three British soldiers clutching a basic field first-aid kit stood absolutely no chance of doing anything useful.

But still Dawson was determined to try.

'Fucking hell,' he murmured softly, the quiet grief in his voice making the expletive sound almost caressing. 'Poor bastard.'

He turned to the soldier standing behind him, who was wiping traces of vomit from his mouth. 'Give me that kit,' Dawson ordered. He grabbed the first-aid pack from him and pulled it open. There were bandages, pads, tape, tourniquets, scissors, sutures and a range of other medical supplies in it, barely adequate to cope with even one of the French soldier's multiple wounds.

'What are you going to do?' Watson asked, the shock evident in his voice.

'Put a couple of tourniquets on his arms. Try to slow down the blood loss. There's nothing I can do about his stomach wound.'

'He's going to die, isn't he?'

'Yes,' Dawson muttered, unconsciously lowering his voice so the fatally injured man wouldn't hear his words – though it was doubtful if he had the slightest awareness of his surroundings.

'Then do nothing, Eddie. That's the best thing. He's still losing a lot of blood from his arms. If you stop that, he'll just last longer, which means he'll suffer even more. The kindest thing you can do right now is just let him die.'

Dawson nodded his head slowly. 'You're right – I know you're right, Dave – but I can't just stand here and watch a man die and do nothing.'

Watson looked at the hideous shape – an object that just minutes earlier had been a fit young soldier – lying on the ground. Then he turned back to Dawson. 'I don't think you need worry now, Eddie. He's stopped breathing. It's all over.'

Dawson, too, looked down, but Watson was right. The man's chest had stopped moving, and there was a sudden stillness about his features that told the story. His eyes were still half-open, and Dawson bent forward and gently pulled the eyelids closed.

'Poor little sod,' he muttered.

'Come on, Eddie. There's nothing we can do now, but there's still that French soldier over there we need to sort out.'

Dawson tugged his gaze away from the dead body and turned round. 'Yeah. Let's go.'

He switched on the mine detector again and took a step forward, careful to keep within the safety lane Watson had marked out.

'We're coming to get you now,' Dawson shouted, and it looked as if the French soldier – who was about thirty yards away – understood his words because he nodded.

Then he took a single step backwards, probably just to change position after remaining in one place for so long, and looked down at his feet, a puzzled expression on his face.

Dawson caught the glance and in that instant guessed what had just happened. 'Down! Everybody down!' he

yelled, grabbed Watson by the shoulder and pulled him flat on to the ground.

'What the fuck?' Watson asked.

'That French soldier. I saw his face. He's just stepped on something. He's triggered another mine.'

'Eddie, why hasn't it blown up? It must be about three or four seconds since you—'

There was a bang from directly in front of them, and both sappers instinctively flattened themselves even more, hoping against hope that the main charge in the mine wouldn't ignite. Or that if it did, their steel helmets would offer their heads some protection.

Another massive explosion shook the trees, and a fusillade of shrapnel flew in all directions as the mine detonated.

CHAPTER 15

11 SEPTEMBER 1939

Two hours later Dawson and Watson were slumped, exhausted, behind the Morris truck, cigarettes in hand, their gear tossed into the back of the lorry. They were covered in mud and blood, none of it their own. Two of the soldiers who'd accompanied them into the forest had been hit by shrapnel from the explosion of the second mine, and had been taken away in an ambulance. The remaining four men – including Tommy Blake, the French-speaker – sat and lay nearby, in a similar bloodied, but uninjured, state.

The two sappers had been so committed to clearing the soldiers out of the minefield and getting to the wounded Frenchman that they hadn't taken too much notice of the other injuries caused by the first mine. These were comparatively light because the explosion had been some distance from where most of the soldiers had been standing, and were mainly flesh wounds where red-hot ball bearings had ripped through clothing and torn into the skin beneath. None of the soldiers injured by that blast had life-threatening wounds, but the second weapon had caused much more devastation.

When the mine had exploded, half a dozen men had still been standing at distances of between fifty and seventy yards from the epicentre of the blast, and they'd all been hit by shrapnel, mainly on their lower torsos and thighs, and some of these wounds were deep and serious. The soldier who'd stepped on the second mine had died instantly.

Three field ambulances had been summoned by one of the French officers after the first mine had exploded, and they arrived a couple of minutes after the detonation of the second weapon, which was providential. When the French medics climbed out and surveyed the scene, they immediately implemented a basic form of triage, ignoring those men with superficial wounds and concentrating on those with more serious injuries.

But somebody had to help the other men, and that task had fallen to Dawson and Watson and the four uninjured soldiers. They'd spent the previous two hours applying tourniquets, wrapping bandages round injured limbs and tying pads over gaping wounds, trying to do what they could until the doctor – only one had appeared in response to the French officer's request for help – could attend to the injured men. None of them had any proper qualifications for what they were doing, though both sappers had attended a field medicine course back in Britain, but stopping wounds from bleeding using dressings didn't take a very high degree of skill. They'd managed to cope, and the final ambulance had left the clearing ten minutes ago, carrying the last of the wounded men to hospital somewhere on the west side of the French border.

'What a fucking awful day,' Watson said, drawing deeply on his cigarette.

'Can't argue with that. We were bloody lucky, you know.'

'Thanks to you, Eddie. If you hadn't spotted that poor sod looking down when he stepped on the trigger, we'd probably both be dead now. I reckon it was being so close to the point of detonation that saved us. All the bloody ball bearings went right over us 'cause we were lying flat. If we'd been standing, we'd have been cut in two.'

'Maybe,' Dawson nodded. 'And now we know something else about these bloody bouncing mines. There's a three- or four-second delay between somebody stepping on it and the first charge detonating. We saw that with the second one, and when we were over by that first soldier I noticed he was lying about six feet clear of the hole where the mine had been buried, so he must have taken three or four steps after he triggered it.'

Watson nodded. 'Tactically, that makes bloody good sense. The designers of these bastards obviously want the victim to move away from the mine's location so that when the first charge fires there's clear air above it. That way the main charge can send the shrapnel the maximum possible distance and cause the greatest injuries. It's a foul weapon, but by Christ it's clever.'

Tommy Blake rolled on to his side and looked across at Watson. 'I was talking to one of the French soldiers earlier this afternoon,' he said. 'He spoke a bit of English, and my French isn't that bad. Anyway, according to him, the French have already given it a nickname. They call it "The Silent Soldier".'

Watson nodded. 'That's a pretty good name for it.

Any patrol trying to walk through this forest is probably going to trigger at least one or two of these mines. They've got a lethal radius of at least twenty yards, maybe further, and we know the shrapnel can still give you a nasty wound at nearly a hundred yards. The Jerries probably chose ball bearings because they'd travel further than just lumps of steel. One of these mines could wipe out a dozen men just as effectively as a squad of Jerry soldiers.'

'Yeah,' Dawson agreed. 'And that mine's a soldier that never sleeps, never needs relieving on duty and always reacts exactly the way he's supposed to. And they probably cost bugger-all to make, probably even less than a real soldier's uniform.'

He stubbed out his cigarette and stood up. 'You stay here, Dave. I'm going to take a look at one of the mines we pulled out of the ground.'

'We know what they look like,' Watson pointed out.

'I know, but I thought I'd try cleaning one up a bit, see if I can find a number or anything on it, something to tell us what it's called.'

'For fuck's sake be careful. I don't want the Frogs to have to carry you off in a coffin.'

Dawson nodded and walked away, heading for the ditch where they'd stored the mines they'd extracted. He bent down over the lethal pile and selected the one that looked the cleanest and picked it up, being careful to grasp it around the body and avoid touching any part of the stepped rod that formed the trigger.

He looked carefully at the mine, again surprised at how effective and compact a weapon it was, then started to rub the sides of the cylinder with his fingers, shifting

the earth that clung to the metal. It wasn't easy to remove, presumably because the mine had been buried in the ground for at least a year, but slowly he managed to clean the surface.

What he found under the compacted earth wasn't helpful. The outside of the cylinder seemed to be smooth and featureless black-painted steel, devoid of markings of any sort. But when he started clearing away the soil from the base, his fingertips felt something different, some faint incised letters. Dawson spat on the cylinder and rubbed harder, removing the last of the soil, and then held the object up in front of his face, the better to make out the words or designation.

At first, he simply couldn't discern what it was, but then he turned the cylinder slightly, and the last rays of the setting sun brought the letters into sharp relief.

'Dave,' he called out, 'can you write this down for me?' Letter by letter, he read out what he could see etched into the side of the cylinder, fairly close to the base. Then he gently replaced the mine in the ditch and walked back over to where Watson was sitting, looking at the notebook in his hand.

'So it's a "S.Mi.Z 35", whatever the fuck that is,' Watson said. 'Also known as a *Schrapnellmine*. A bloody nasty weapon.'

For a few seconds the two men sat in silence, their thoughts running over the events of the long and extremely traumatic afternoon.

Dawson spoke first. 'You ever seen a dead man before, Dave?'

'A few,' Watson admitted. 'Accidents happen all the time in my line of business. But I've never seen anyone

torn apart like those two Frenchies this afternoon. If I don't see another one for the rest of this bloody war, that'll be fine by me. A bit too much to hope for though, isn't it? What about you?'

Dawson nodded. 'I've seen lots. You should try mining and demolition. We had plenty of accidents in the mines. Quarrying's just as bad. Confined spaces and high explosives are a bad combination.'

Watson glanced round. The afternoon was slowly shading into evening, and the light was fading in the clearing. 'It's getting dark. There's nothing else we can do here now. Let's get back to camp.'

They stood up, but as they did so a pair of headlamps suddenly illuminated them when a staff car on French army plates turned into the clearing and stopped a short distance away from the Morris lorry.

The British soldiers stared at it as the door opened and a French officer climbed out.

'Oh, fuck,' Dawson muttered. 'That's all we need.'

'What do you mean?' Watson asked.

'You'll see.'

Immediately recognizable to the sapper in the twilight was the elegant figure of Capitaine Marcel de St Véran.

The French officer looked with distaste at the muddy ground around him, then walked slowly towards the silent British soldiers, who came somewhat raggedly to attention and saluted. He stopped a few feet away, lifted his swagger-stick in casual acknowledgement, and then sniffed disdainfully.

'You men are filthy,' he snapped. 'You look disgraceful. Where is your officer?'

For a few seconds nobody responded, so Dawson took a half-pace forward. 'There's no officer with us, sir.'

St Véran looked at him, his eyes widening as he immediately recognized the lance-corporal. 'So we meet again, Dawson. Your major – what was his name – Sykes? He isn't here?'

'No, sir.'

'What a pity. I wanted to discuss something with him. What are you men doing here?'

'Apparently the French army doesn't have any sappers, sir, so we were sent out here to clear a path through this forest. The whole area's been turned into a mine-field.'

'Sappers?' St Véran enquired.

'Engineers, sir. Mine-disposal specialists.'

'*Of course* we have people trained to do that.'

'Not in this part of France you haven't, sir,' Dawson replied. 'That's why we're here.'

'From what I've heard,' St Véran said, 'you haven't even done a very good job. There have been two deaths here today, and almost a dozen French soldiers injured.'

Beside him, Dawson could sense his fellow sapper stiffening with indignation, and, before he could reply, Watson started speaking. 'With respect, sir, since we arrived we've dug up six mines and made them safe. We told your soldiers not to wander around, but one of them did and managed to tread on a mine. When that blew up, several of your men started running towards him to try to help, and one of them stepped on another mine. I really don't see how either death is our fault. And if we hadn't been here, there'd still be six live mines buried in the ground. Sir.'

For a moment St Véran didn't reply, just stared at Watson, his expression hostile. 'I don't like the tone of your voice, soldier.'

'Yeah,' Watson snapped, 'well that's your problem, not mine. We've done a bloody good job here, whether you think so or not.'

'You insubordinate little bastard.' St Véran's voice was high and angry. 'I'm going to report you to your commanding officer. What's your name?'

Watson was steaming. 'If you're so bloody clever, you find out. Come on, lads, let's get the hell out of here.'

'All of you, stay right where you are!' St Véran ordered.

None of the British soldiers took the slightest notice, just climbed into the truck, Watson hauling himself up into the driving seat. He started the engine and swung the truck round in a tight circle.

St Véran had to jump out of the way as the heavy vehicle lurched forward, and seconds later there was a rending sound of tearing metal as the rear end of the Morris truck scraped along the front of the French staff car.

Dawson stuck his head out of the window and looked back. 'I think you might have scratched his paintwork a bit there, Dave.'

'Really?' Watson replied, grinning in the darkness of the cab. 'What a shame. I was hoping I might have written off the bloody car and then that bastard would have had to walk back to his lines. Who the fuck was he – obviously you'd met him before?'

Dawson nodded, and explained how he and Major Sykes had encountered the French officer up near Lille.

'He was in charge of the defensive fortifications up there. Sykes was bloody unimpressed with him. I mean, there were no troops, no ammunition and no weapons to use if the Germans suddenly steamed over the hill. In fact' – he paused for a moment – 'I wonder if the reason St Véran is down here now, on the front line, is because of the report Sykes made about him. Perhaps the Frog's on a punishment posting, sent down here instead of his cushy billet up north.'

'He wanted to talk to Sykes,' Watson suggested.

'Maybe you're right. Maybe he blames Sykes. Good for the galloping major, I say.'

'You should have been a *little* less aggressive towards him, Dave. I mean, he's a total arsehole, but he *is* an officer in the French army. He could make trouble.'

Watson glanced at him as he steered the truck down the track that led away from the clearing. 'You mean worse trouble than I'm in already, defusing German mines all day? How?'

Dawson nodded. 'Yeah, good point. Anyway, guess we'll find out tomorrow.'

CHAPTER 16

12 SEPTEMBER 1939

'Dawson, Watson. Atten-shun! Quick march!'

Word of what had happened the previous evening had obviously reached the British encampment, and the sergeant who was now escorting the two sappers to the lieutenant in charge didn't look at all happy with the situation. As the two men marched along, he muttered advice to them.

'That Frog's made an official complaint to the CO,' he said, 'and the lieutenant's already talked to the other four soldiers who were there. Oddly enough, they didn't seem to see or hear anything. My advice is just play dumb, and pretend it was all normal.'

'Thanks, Sarge,' Dawson replied.

They halted outside the lieutenant's tent and waited, standing at attention. After a few seconds, the officer emerged, wearing his cap and a serious expression, a sheet of paper in his hand.

'Off caps!'

Watson and Dawson obediently removed their caps and stood waiting. Lieutenant Charnforth stopped in

front of them, glanced at the paper he was carrying and then looked up at the two men.

'A very serious complaint has been made against you two. A French officer has alleged that you both, but particularly you, Watson, were insubordinate and rude. That is bad enough, but he also states that when you left the Warndt Forest yesterday evening you tried to run him down with the truck, and deliberately drove into his staff car. What do you have to say to that?' He stared expectantly at Watson.

The sapper looked puzzled, his face clouded. 'I do remember seeing a French officer there, sir, just before we left. He asked what we were doing and we explained about clearing the mines. I don't think we were rude to him, do you, Eddie?'

'Eyes front! Don't talk to Dawson,' the sergeant snapped. 'Talk to the officer.'

'So you admit you spoke to this French officer?'

'Oh, yes, sir, but neither of us was rude to him.'

Lieutenant Charnforth again looked at the paper he was holding. 'The officer said you told him it was his problem if he didn't like the tone of your voice. Do you remember saying anything like that?'

Watson again looked genuinely puzzled. Dawson repressed a smile.

'No, sir, I don't. Perhaps he simply misunderstood what we were saying. After all, he's French and we were speaking English. But when we were talking to the officer, I do remember saying to Corporal Dawson that the mines were a problem, so perhaps that's what he's talking about.'

Charnforth stared at Watson for a few seconds. 'Right,

I accept that there could have been a misunderstanding – a few words misheard – but there's no doubt about the damage done to the French staff car. I've seen it for myself. How do you account for that?'

'That probably *was* my fault, sir. We were all in a hurry to get back here – we'd had a pretty horrible day out there – and I just started the lorry and drove off. I think I remember a bit of a crash as we went past that French officer's car, but I didn't think anything about it at the time. The ground was very rough, and I just thought the truck had gone over a bump, or something in the back had fallen over. If I did hit his car, I'm really sorry. It certainly wasn't intentional.'

Lieutenant Charnforth looked from one man to the other, and prepared to accept the inevitable. The other four soldiers he'd already interviewed had all apparently been struck both deaf and blind during the incident in the forest, and had told him nothing. In the end, it was the evidence of six British soldiers against one French officer. And he was also well aware that the two sappers were the only people under his command who were capable of lifting the mines, so placing them under arrest wasn't a viable option.

'Very well,' he said. 'In the absence of any independent witnesses, there's no way of resolving this matter. Just think yourselves lucky you're not on a charge. But just let me say this. We're supposed to be working *with* the French, not against them, so just be a lot more careful in your dealings with them in the future. Language can be a problem, but try to remember we are on the same side. And, Watson, just watch your driving. The front of that staff car was badly mangled, and it had to be towed away.'

He paused. 'On a totally different note, you both did a very good job yesterday in lifting those six mines. You'll be going back to the same place today, and when you've finished this afternoon I want you to bring one of those mines back here. Make sure it's safe, obviously, before you put it in the truck. We'll need to get some experts to examine it and see exactly how it works. Anyway, well done, both of you. Shame there were so many casualties. Fortunes of war, I suppose.' Charnforth glanced across at the senior NCO. 'Right, Sergeant. Carry on.'

'Yes, sir. On caps. Left turn. Quick march.'

The two sappers marched about twenty yards from Lieutenant Charnforth's tent, then the sergeant halted them. 'Right, lads, you heard the officer. Sort your stuff out and then get yourselves back into that forest. There's still no word about the French sappers arriving, so it's down to you two again. We're sending Tommy Blake and another three squaddies with you, and this time let one of them do the driving. And if you see that French officer, Watson, try to keep out of his way. He's gunning for you.'

'Right, Sarge. We'll get moving.'

Tommy Blake pulled the truck to a halt and switched off the engine. The six men climbed out of the vehicle and stood in silence for a few moments, just staring around them. The sunlight streaming through the trees bathed the clearing, giving it a calm and peaceful appearance that was wholly at odds with the lethal power of the weapons that they all knew lay concealed beneath its grassy surface.

As before, there were a few – a very few, perhaps only

half a dozen in all – French soldiers there, sitting and talking in a group on the far side of the clearing. There was no sign of either of the officers who'd been there the previous day, and the French soldiers still looked somewhat lost and directionless.

'OK, Dave,' Dawson said. 'We know what we've got to do. If you want, I'll start with the detector.'

'That's fine with me.'

Watson picked up the hammer and stakes while Dawson swiftly assembled the mine detector. He checked it was working simply by putting on the headphones, switching on the unit and passing the head close to the hammer Watson was holding.

'OK?' Watson asked.

'Yeah. Bloody good signal. Let's get to it.'

The two sappers grabbed the rest of the equipment and headed off towards the safe lane they'd started marking out the previous day. Dawson already had the mine detector working and was carrying it loosely in his right hand as they stepped between the two lines of stakes and cord, but he'd barely taken a step inside when he suddenly stopped and raised his hand.

'Stop! Stop!' he shouted. 'I'm getting something.'

'What?' Watson demanded, coming to an abrupt halt. 'You can't be. We've already cleared this area.'

Dawson shook his head. 'No. I'm telling you I've got a strong signal right here. There's something in the fucking ground right in front of me. Here,' he added, 'you listen.' He took off the headphones but didn't shift his feet an inch, just continued to move the head of the mine detector slowly over the point where he'd detected the object.

Watson slipped the headphones on and listened for a couple of seconds, then nodded. 'Bugger me,' he said. 'You're right, but this is right in the middle of the cleared area. There's no bloody way I could have missed it yesterday.'

'We'll sort that out later,' Dawson said shortly, carefully placing a red wooden cross over the spot on the ground. 'For now, let's just lift the bugger and make it safe. Over to you, Dave.'

Dawson stepped back, away from the marker, and retreated to the truck to watch. The two sappers now knew enough about the mines that neither of them felt the need to use the field telephone.

Watson knelt down to start the removal operation. He dug his bayonet into the ground about a foot from the red cross and slid it forwards to locate the object, but then he stopped and stared at what he'd found. He swivelled round and looked back towards the truck where Dawson was waiting.

'Eddie,' he called out. 'You'd better come and take a look at this.'

'What?'

'Just bloody come here, will you?'

'OK, OK,' Dawson muttered, and walked across to his fellow sapper.

'I just dug the blade in here,' Watson said.

'I know. I was watching you.'

'And this is what I found,' Watson finished, raising the blade of the bayonet.

The turf was cleanly cut underneath and lifted easily, and Watson dropped it behind him.

'So what?' Dawson remarked. 'What did you want to show me?'

'You're missing the bloody point, Eddie. All I did was slide the bayonet into the ground. I didn't cut away the turf because I didn't need to. It was already cut. Some bastard's dug here very recently.'

The two sappers stared at each other as realization suddenly dawned.

'You mean somebody dug a hole since last night and put a mine in it? Some bloody Jerry soldier?'

Watson shook his head. 'I don't reckon there's any fucking Germans within five miles of here. And if there were, they wouldn't be buggering about planting mines. They'd be planning a full-on assault against the Frogs to drive them back across the border. No, this was some other bugger. Do me a favour, Eddie. Just go and check how many bloody mines there are in that ditch over there.'

Dawson walked back towards the truck, then crossed to the shallow ditch where they'd stored the mines they'd dug up the previous day. The count didn't take long, and Dawson's face was grim as he walked back over to Watson.

'There's one missing,' he announced. 'We lifted six, but there are only five there now.'

'I bloody knew it. Are you thinking what I'm thinking?' Watson demanded.

'Capitaine Marcel de St Véran?'

'Got it in one. That bastard was here after we left last night – we know that – and we really pissed him off.'

'Well, *you* fucking did. You shouldn't have driven into his car,' Dawson said.

'Yeah, Eddie, but that was just a public argument that

got a bit out of hand. This' – he pointed at the ground where the red cross marked the location of what both men guessed was the sixth mine – 'this is potential murder.'

Dawson shook his head. 'I can't bloody believe it.'

'What? That that fucking Frog would try to kill us by planting a mine in an area we've already checked?'

'Yeah. What a fucking extreme way to settle a score.'

Watson looked back at the ground. 'We'd never prove it was him, you know.'

'I know that. He'd just bloody deny it, same as we did over what happened out here last night. Fucking lucky I had the detector working when we walked over here, otherwise I'd probably have trodden on the bloody thing.'

Dawson walked back to the Morris truck and briefly explained to Tommy Blake what they'd found.

'You think that Frog captain put it there?' Blake demanded.

'Seems most likely, yeah,' Dawson replied. 'Dave really hacked him off last night, and I think he decided to pay us back in the worst bloody way he could think of. And if the mine had gone off, he'd be fire-proof. Everybody would just assume we'd missed it when we did our first sweep. Nobody would've bothered counting the mines we'd already lifted.'

Dawson turned back to see Watson walking over towards him, the mine held firmly in his left hand, the trigger pointed away from his body.

'Really fucking easy to get out,' Watson said. 'The others were a struggle, but this one popped right out, as if it had only been put there yesterday, which it bloody had been, of course.'

'So what are you going to do about it?' Blake asked, as Dawson slid a bolt through the hole in the trigger assembly to make the mine safe again.

'Right now,' Watson said, 'I don't bloody know. We can't accuse the Frenchie of doing it, because we've got no witnesses and no proof. And he's an officer and an aristocrat and we're just a couple of ignorant bloody squaddies. If we said anything, everybody would just think we were trying to get our own back on him. Probably best to just ignore it.'

'Bugger that,' Blake muttered. 'If it was me, I'd find a time when he was by himself somewhere and I'd ventilate him with a round from my Lee-Enfield. If anyone found out, I'd say it was an accidental discharge.'

'Too quick, mate,' Dawson snapped. 'A knife in the guts. That'd be my choice for him.'

Standing beside him, Watson nodded. 'I'll get rid of this,' he said, gesturing at the mine in his hand. 'I'll put it back in the ditch with the other buggers for the moment, but we should take all of them back to camp when we leave, just to make sure this can't happen again.'

'Good idea, Dave. And Tommy' – Dawson turned back to look at Blake – 'if St Véran shows up here again, keep your eye on him, and keep your bloody rifle handy – and loaded – just in case the bastard tries anything else.'

As soon as Watson had replaced the mine in the ditch, the two sappers walked back over to the cleared lane.

But before they started walking down it, Dawson switched on the mine detector and carried out a full sweep of the entire width, as if it was new ground, just in case, but didn't find anything.

CHAPTER 17

By the time Blake called them back to the lorry at just after eleven for a brew-up, they'd located and lifted a further three mines, which they'd found in more or less the locations suggested by Dawson's analysis of the pattern which had been used by the German troops who'd laid the weapons. As before, they'd been positioned in a kind of open zig-zag running down the main track through the forest, a layout that offered a high probability of successful kills against advancing troops.

The problem, as far as Watson and Dawson were concerned, was the time it would take them to clear the entire track. They were taking about twenty to thirty minutes to locate, lift and make safe each buried mine, and if the pattern they'd seen so far had been repeated throughout the Warndt Forest, there were hundreds, perhaps thousands, of mines buried there. Without help, they were looking at weeks or months of work, and the chances of the Germans not counter-attacking against the French invasion within a few days were probably fairly slim.

'I think we're just pissing in the wind here,' Watson said, accepting a light from Tommy Blake and cupping

the cigarette in his hand. 'If the French were mounting a really serious invasion, they'd just take a detour and go around this bloody forest, and forget about clearing the mines. Or else they'd bring in every French soldier qualified in mine-clearance and set them to work.'

'Yeah,' Dawson agreed. 'You're right. We're just wasting our bloody time.'

Watson took a long draw of his cigarette and leant back against the side of the lorry. 'Still,' he said, 'I suppose we should be grateful we're here.'

'Why?'

'Well, no bugger's shooting at us, are they?'

'No, not yet,' Dawson agreed, 'but I think that's only temporary. Once Adolf and his Nazi thugs have shafted the bloody Poles, which probably won't take them all that long, they'll come down here to give the French a bloody nose.'

'No bloody doubt about that,' Watson said, draining the last dregs of his tea. 'Right, let's get back to it.'

They found a further three mines quite quickly, laid out in the same pattern as before, and lifted all three of them. But the next section of the track appeared clear, or at least Dawson couldn't find any contacts where he'd expected to encounter them. That bothered him, so he checked the mine detector was still working properly – which it was – then scanned the whole area again, with the same result.

The two sappers moved on cautiously, and Dawson got his next hit some fifty yards further on, but on the extreme left side of the track, which wasn't where he'd expected it.

'It looks like they've changed the pattern, Dave,' he said, as Watson prepared to dig out the buried mine, 'so just be extra careful with this one.'

'I'm always careful, mate,' Watson muttered.

Dawson walked back about fifty yards down the cleared lane and crouched down to watch his partner extract the weapon.

Watson followed the same routine as previously, digging down vertically about a foot clear of the buried mine, then carefully removing the soil until he was able to see the weapon itself. Dawson's warning was ringing in his ears, and the change in the pattern of the minefield bothered him as well, so he took extra care as he started removing the soil from around the trigger assembly.

He was glad he did. As he brushed away the last of the earth, he noticed something different about it, and immediately stopped working on it.

'What is it?' Dawson called from behind him, seeing his friend freeze and then sit back on his haunches.

'This bloody trigger's different,' Watson called over his shoulder. 'It's a Y-shaped bastard, not like the three-pronged ones we've seen up to now. Hang on a minute – I'm still checking it out.'

For about a minute Watson just looked at the half-buried mine, trying to work out what the difference was. Then he saw it, and cursed under his breath. Attached to the right-hand arm of the Y-shaped assembly was a thin strand of wire, a wire that ran under the ground and away from the mine, towards the centre of the track.

'You'd better come and take a look at this, Eddie,' Watson called out, moving slightly backwards from the mine. 'And bring the bloody pliers, will you?'

The two sappers peered at the weapon Watson had partially uncovered.

'What do you think?' Dawson asked.

'That's not an electrical cable,' Watson said. 'It's not thick enough, so I don't think it's hitched to an electric detonator. It looks more like a single-strand wire, like a bloody tripwire, something like that.'

Dawson nodded slowly. 'That could make sense,' he said. 'If the Germans laid these mines right across the track, they could have linked them together. If they did, then anybody stepping on one of them would detonate the rest.'

'Could be,' Watson agreed. 'The sneaky bastards. But if you're right, and this wire does link them, then this bugger would have to be triggered by sideways pressure, not by someone stepping on it.'

'Yeah, I see what you mean. So there must be one or two of the pressure-activated mines here as well. Hang on, let me run the detector over the rest of the track.'

Watson stood back and watched as Dawson scanned the soil to the right of the exposed mine. By the time he'd reached the opposite side of the track, there were three more red crosses lying on the ground.

Dawson switched off the mine detector and placed it on the ground. The red crosses indicated two mines lying fairly close together near the centre of the track, and another one at the right-hand edge.

'I'll bet you the middle two are pressure-activated,' Watson said, 'and detonating either of those would trigger this bastard here or the one on the other side of the track.'

'Makes sense. Do you want me to lift those?'

'No, I'll do it. Just let me sort out this bugger first.'

Watson took the pliers and carefully cut through the wire close to the Y-shaped trigger, then continued removing the mine from the ground.

Once he'd got it out, he took a bolt from his pocket and slipped it through the hole in the trigger assembly to make the weapon safe. Then he cleaned off the earth from the body of the mine and stared at the inscribed number.

'This one's different, Dave,' he said. 'It looks like the number is "Z Z 35". All the others we lifted were "Z 35", so this is a variant.'

Then he walked over to the two red crosses near the centre of the track and quickly dug down beside the first one. In a few minutes he'd uncovered another mine of the type they were familiar with, one fitted with the three-pronged trigger. As they'd expected, the wire from the first mine was wrapped around the steel cylinder that projected from the body of the weapon.

'Just as we thought, Eddie,' Watson said, as he cut the wire and lifted out the mine. 'Tread on this bastard and as it jumps out of the ground it pulls the wire and that fires the second weapon.'

'Yeah. Twice as nasty, twice as deadly. Let's shift these next two and then go back to the truck and grab something to eat.'

'Good idea. Give me ten minutes.'

The other four soldiers were waiting for them, a fire already going beside the Morris truck. On the flames was a small dixie, and inside it Tommy Blake was stirring yet another anonymous stew.

'What the hell flavour is that, Tommy?' Dawson asked as he lowered the equipment he was carrying to the ground.

'Buggered if I know,' Blake replied. 'Could be anything – warthog, buffalo, whale, python, rat, anything at all. All I do know is that it was some kind of dead animal that the army's catering people could buy really cheap and turn into a barely edible meal for the British fighting man.'

Dawson and Watson sat down and waited for the stew to get hot enough to eat.

'Something that might interest you,' Blake said, and pointed his spoon across the clearing towards the group of French soldiers. 'I was having a chat with those lads earlier on. One of them claims he saw an officer doing something out here late last night, near the area you two had cleared.'

'Did he, by Christ?' Dawson muttered.

'That's what he said. The French have stationed sentries here round the clock, and his post was in the woods through there, over to the west. His orders were to move around, do a regular patrol, so he was walking up here towards the edge of the clearing, then going back to his original post. He said he saw an officer bending down somewhere over here, but the light was too poor for him to see what he was doing. He watched him for a few minutes, then went back to his route. The next time he walked up this way, the man had gone.'

'And he didn't challenge him?' Watson demanded. 'Why not?'

'Why should he?' Blake replied. 'He could see it was a French officer because of the uniform. The French

military's different to ours. A lot of the officers are real toffs, but most of the regular soldiers are peasants from the countryside, completely the other end of the scale. For any French soldier to challenge a French officer, he'd have to be absolutely bloody certain he was doing something completely out of order.'

'Christ, I thought it was bad enough in the British army,' Dawson said. 'He couldn't identify the officer?'

Blake shook his head. 'No bloody chance. I did ask him,' he added.

'We're no worse off than we were before,' Watson said. 'I still think it was that bastard St Véran who planted the mine, and what that Frog soldier saw pretty much confirms it. But there's still nothing we can do about it.'

'Not unless he walks in front of the barrel of my Lee-Enfield one night,' Dawson muttered darkly.

CHAPTER 18

Dawson and Watson moved deeper into the forest, steadily working their way down the track, finding and lifting the mines that had been buried there. By mid-afternoon they'd covered a total distance of about 150 yards from the Morris truck, which was still parked in the clearing.

The layout of the minefield varied, and there were some stretches with no mines at all. Sometimes they were finding the open zig-zag pattern they'd first encountered, at other times the lines of mines planted across the track and linked by wires, but they were able to lift each one and make it safe. They were making very slow progress, but they had no other choice. For obvious reasons, clearing a minefield wasn't something that could be hurried, and there were only the two of them to do the work.

They'd just had a brew-up and were walking back down the track when they heard the sound of a vehicle behind them and turned back to see what was happening.

A lorry had just driven into the clearing, and, as they watched, an officer climbed out of it and walked across

to the French soldiers waiting nearby. As soon as he stepped on to the ground Dawson realized it was Capitaine de St Véran.

'It's that French bastard again,' Watson observed, standing and watching what was happening.

'What's going on?' Dawson asked. 'What's he doing back here?'

For a few seconds they just stood and looked back. The French soldiers formed up into a short line and climbed into the back of the lorry, apparently preparing to vacate the site.

Watson shrugged. 'It looks like they're pulling out,' he suggested.

'No great loss. They didn't do anything while they were here, as far as I could see. Anyway, let's get on. We've still got plenty to do.'

'OK,' Watson agreed, and the two sappers turned away and walked on down the track.

Behind them, the French lorry turned round once all the soldiers had climbed aboard and then drove away from the clearing, heading back the way it had come, towards the road that led out of the forest.

Just over an hour later, Dawson suddenly stopped what he was doing and just stood there, listening. Beside him, Watson pulled off the mine-detector headphones.

'What is it?' he demanded.

'I don't know,' Dawson replied. 'I thought I heard something.' Then the noise came again. 'Listen. That sounds to me like vehicle engines. Not just a single truck, more like several of them.'

'Maybe the Frogs are moving their forces around,'

Watson suggested. 'St Véran ordered those troops out of the forest. They're probably just repositioning.'

'Perhaps. Just as long as it's not the bloody Germans arriving.'

'We'd have been told if that was happening,' Watson said.

Then they heard the noise of vehicles again, but louder and closer, though they still seemed to be somewhere outside the forest.

'I dunno, Dave. Maybe we should get back to the truck.'

As they looked back up the track, they saw two of the British soldiers trotting towards them, their Lee-Enfields slung over their shoulders.

'That's Tommy Blake and one of the other lads,' Watson said. 'Maybe they know what's going on.'

But before they could do anything, the air was suddenly filled with the crack of rifle shots, then the deeper, louder sound of sustained and very distinctive machine-gun fire – almost the same timing as a heartbeat, and quite unlike the ripping sound of a British Sten gun. Bullets tore through the forest.

'Oh, fuck,' Watson said. 'That's a bloody Schmeisser. Grab the stuff and get out of sight!'

The two sappers snatched up the mine detector and the bag of mines they'd lifted and ran a few paces back up the cleared track. Then they picked an area where the undergrowth was far too thick for mines to have been laid, and both dived off into it, burrowing deep beneath the bushes.

'It's the fucking Jerries,' Dawson muttered. 'They must be counter-attacking.'

'What the hell do we do now? Our rifles are up there in the truck. Shall we run back and get them?'

'Hang on. Where's Tommy and the other lad? They had their rifles with them.'

Dawson eased forwards to the edge of the track.

As he did so, a sustained burst of firing rang out from somewhere close by, followed by about half a dozen rifle shots, then more machine-gun fire. He dropped back into cover.

'Hell, they were close,' he muttered. But he moved forwards again. He had to know where Blake and the other soldier were, and what was happening on the track.

As he peered out cautiously from the undergrowth, more shots rang out, followed by a howl of pain. One glance was enough to show him all he needed to know.

Dawson pulled back to where Watson was waiting.

'We've got to move,' he hissed. 'Tommy's wounded and I think the other lad is dead. Tommy's just ducked into cover further up the track. We've got to help him.'

They started jogging through the trees, heading towards the spot where Dawson had seen Tommy Blake take cover. But they'd barely started moving before they heard more firing. A couple of Schmeissers opened up – a lethal melody and its hideous counterpoint – perhaps 100 yards away. And then came the crack of rifle shots.

'That was somewhere near the lorry,' Dawson said, and peered around a tree trunk to look up the track. 'Jesus.'

About 200 yards away, he glimpsed two British soldiers lying prone beside the vehicle, rifles at their shoulders, firing at an unseen enemy. Then his view was torn

apart by an explosion that rocked the Morris and obscured everything.

When he could see clearly again, one of the two figures lay unmoving, his Lee-Enfield silent. The other man – the distance was too great for him to make out which one it was – was writhing in agony, and Dawson could hear a thin, high-pitched scream.

'Oh, Christ,' he muttered, not taking his eyes from the scene in front of him. 'That was a fucking grenade.'

Suddenly, a gang of grey-uniformed figures appeared around the vehicle, weapons aimed at the men lying on the ground, and a handful of shots rang out. Instantly, the screaming stopped.

Beside him, Watson tensed as if to stand up, but Dawson grabbed him by the arm and ducked back into cover. 'Stay down,' he hissed. 'There's nothing we can do to help those poor bastards now. We haven't even got a pistol between us. If we stand up, the Jerries'll see us, and then we'll be dead as well.'

They'd just witnessed the brutal killing of two of the soldiers who'd driven into the forest with them, and there'd been absolutely nothing they could have done to prevent it.

'What the fuck do we do now, Eddie?' Watson whispered. 'Stand up and wave a white flag?'

'No way. We've just seen them shoot those two lads, and the one over there on the track. They'd probably gun us down as soon as we showed ourselves. We stay out of sight, keep our heads down and hope those bastards haven't seen us and don't know we're here. Then we find Tommy.'

Dawson slid the mine detector under a bush and picked up the bag of mines. 'Let's go,' he muttered.

'Why don't you dump the mines, Eddie? They're no good to us.'

Dawson shook his head. 'No. These are weapons – of a sort, anyway – and right now they're pretty much all we have.'

'Yeah.' Watson sounded doubtful. 'They go off with a hell of a bang, that's for sure, but I don't know how you'd trigger them, unless you plan to bury them and hope you can talk the Jerries into stepping on them.'

Dawson shook his head. 'No. There's a much simpler method than that. These mines have a delayed-action fuse. We saw it in action when that second one went off. We just remove the safety bolt, press the trigger and throw it like a big grenade. Then duck.'

Watson stared at him as if he was mad. Then he voiced what his face had already conveyed. 'You're bloody mad, mate. Ducking wouldn't work, would it? When you throw it, it could be in any position at all when the first charge goes off. It could even fire it straight back at us, and then we'd be totally fucked. And even if it didn't, we'd have no clue which way the cylinder would be facing when the main charge fired. We could get shredded by the shrapnel.'

'Look,' Dawson said, 'I agree it wouldn't be easy. They'd be our weapons of last resort, so I say we take them with us.'

Watson was silent for a few moments, then he nodded. 'OK, they *are* all we've got, so we might as well take them. But I hope to hell we don't have to use them, because that just sounds to me like a really messy way to commit suicide.'

CHAPTER 19

12 SEPTEMBER 1939

They reached Tommy Blake just minutes later. The soldier was lying with his back against a tree trunk, the front of his uniform sodden with blood. Both hands clutched his stomach, and his lips were drawn back in a silent snarl of agony. Beside him lay his Lee-Enfield, the fore-end smashed, the trigger missing and the guard bent badly out of shape.

'Oh, Jesus, Tommy,' Dawson muttered, looking down at the badly injured man.

'Took a few in the fucking gut, mate,' Blake murmured. 'Lost a finger as well.'

He lifted his right hand slightly to show Dawson the bloodied stump where his forefinger had been blown off by the round that had carried away the rifle's trigger.

'Luckier than Jock, though. He bought it on the track.'

Dawson reached out and gently lifted Blake's left hand away from the wound on his torso, but there was little to see – just a sodden red patch on his battle-dress – and even less he could do. And all three of them knew it.

'Your medical pack?' Dawson asked.

Blake shook his head, and blood ran from his mouth as he coughed. 'In the truck, mate. Wouldn't help if you had it. I'm fucked. Save yourselves. Get the hell away from here.'

Dawson crouched down beside the man he'd known only for a couple of days.

'Anything we can—' he started, then realized the futility of what he had intended to say.

'Just go,' Blake muttered. 'No – wait.'

'What, mate?' Watson said.

'You got any of them bouncing mines?'

Dawson nodded. 'Yeah. Half a dozen. Why?'

Blake summoned a semblance of a grin from somewhere. 'Leave me a couple. When those Jerry bastards come for me, I'll take them with me.'

Watson shook his head. 'We can't just leave you here, Tommy. Not like this.'

'You can't do nothing for me, Dave,' Blake muttered, coughing up another spray of blood. 'Just give me the mines and bugger off.'

Dawson stood up and nodded. He took two of the mines out of the bag and placed them beside the dying man.

'One either side of me,' Blake instructed.

Dawson repositioned one of the mines as he'd been asked. Both were base-down, with the trigger assemblies pointing upwards. 'You sure about this, Tommy?' he asked.

Blake nodded. 'Give me the rifle,' he said, and Dawson passed him the useless weapon. With his left hand, Blake laid the Lee-Enfield across his thighs, the two ends of the broken rifle resting on the triggers of the mines.

'Now arm them,' Blake said.

Carefully, Dawson extracted the bolts they'd inserted to make the mines safe, then stood up.

'Reckon I can just push down on this when the time comes,' Blake said, looking down at the improvised booby-trap. 'Good luck, Eddie, and you, Dave. Now go.'

Dawson nodded and turned away, not trusting himself to speak.

Watson hesitated for a moment, then bent forward and squeezed Tommy Blake's shoulder. 'You really will be going out with a bang, mate,' he said, tears in his eyes.

'Fuck off, Dave,' Blake said, summoning another smile.

Moments later, Dawson and Watson were nowhere in sight.

'Which way?' Watson asked. 'Back to the clearing?'

They'd moved deep into the forest, staying well away from level ground to avoid any mines, and had put as much distance as they could between themselves and Tommy Blake, just in case the German troops found him quickly.

'No fucking way,' Dawson said. 'That'll be crawling with Jerries by now.'

'So where do we go?'

'Right now, mate, I don't know.'

There was a sudden massive double-explosion from somewhere in the forest behind them, the two blasts separated by the briefest fraction of a second.

'That was Tommy, I guess,' Watson muttered, turning back to look in that direction. 'Hell of a thing to say, but he's better off dead.'

'With those wounds, you're right. He'd have died anyway. This way he might have taken a few of those Jerry bastards with him.'

For a few moments the two men stood there in silence, the appalling reality of their situation numbing their thoughts. They were alone, unarmed apart from the bayonets they'd used for lifting the mines, on German territory and probably virtually surrounded by enemy troops.

'I'll tell you something,' Dawson said, his voice low and bitter. 'That French bastard St Véran must have been ordered to collect his troops and withdraw, and he never said a word to Tommy Blake – just abandoned the four of us here in the forest, knowing the Jerries were on their way. If I get out of this alive, I'm going to track that fucker down and blow his bloody brains out.'

'You might find yourself in a queue, Eddie,' Watson said, his tone just as angry.

'Ready?' Dawson asked, his voice little more than a whisper.

'As ready as I'm ever likely to be,' Watson replied.

He and Dawson were each carrying one of the mines in their left hands, and their Lee-Enfield bayonets in their right. Over his shoulder Dawson had a haversack they'd brought from the Morris lorry, with the other two mines inside it.

'I really hope we don't have to try lobbing these at the Jerries,' Watson muttered.

'So do I, mate, so do I. Right, we're well away from the clearing now, so I think we should try and angle back towards the track through the forest and follow that. That'll make sure we don't end up going round in circles in this bloody wood.'

'Yeah, that makes sense.'

'OK, let's go.'

Dawson checked all around them, but saw and heard nothing that caused him any alarm. The two men moved cautiously through the undergrowth and took their first few silent steps down the hillside towards where they thought the track was.

They covered a couple of hundred yards down the slope, and Dawson felt his heart thudding in his chest with every step that he took. He kept on expecting a German soldier to appear in front of him every second, Schmeisser machine-pistol, rifle or pistol levelled at him, and knew that his life would end the moment that happened. Despite his suggestion to Watson about using the bouncing mine as a kind of improvised grenade, he had no illusions about how effective a weapon it was likely to be.

They moved slowly, their attention concentrated on the view ahead and to both sides of them, Dawson leading and Watson bringing up the rear. They were paying less attention to the wood behind them, because they guessed that most of the German troops would be closer to the track than deep in the forest.

That cosy assumption was violently shattered within another couple of minutes. They'd just crossed through a large open space in the forest when a sudden burst of machine-gun fire erupted – and it came from right behind them. Bullets whined past the two sappers, screaming through the undergrowth in front of them and to their right.

Dawson instinctively dived to his left, behind a tree,

and glanced back the way they'd come. About seventy yards behind them, a single grey-clad figure was standing right at the edge of the clearing. He was holding a Schmeisser machine-pistol and was just snapping a fresh magazine into place.

Instinctively, the two sappers dived into cover, burrowing deep into the bushes and shrubs that surrounded them.

But hiding wasn't going to be enough. The German soldier had missed with his first burst of fire, because, although the maximum range of the MP 40 was about 200 yards, it was rarely accurate even in trained hands at much over fifty. If he guessed his quarry wasn't armed – and he might even have seen that neither man was carrying a rifle – he'd be able to walk right up to them and shoot them at point-blank range.

And there was no doubt about his intentions. His weapon reloaded, he was now walking around the edge of the clearing towards the spot where they'd gone to ground. He was pointing his machine-pistol in front of him, his finger resting on the trigger, and Dawson had no doubt that he'd open fire the moment he saw any sign of movement.

'Shit,' Dawson muttered, looking around for inspiration and finding nothing. Their only chance was to use one of the mines.

Dawson slipped the haversack off his shoulder and placed it on the ground. He lifted up the mine he was still carrying, grasped the head of the bolt with his left hand, wrapped the fingers of his right hand around the nut he'd screwed on to it and spun it off. Then he extracted the bolt itself. The mine was now live, and

quite a gentle pressure on the trigger assembly would start the ignition sequence.

He looked up. The German soldier was now only about thirty yards away, still moving cautiously towards their hiding place.

Dawson knew he had just the one chance, a single opportunity to get this right. If his plan failed, both he and Watson would be dead in a matter of seconds.

'Wish me luck,' he muttered, took a deep breath and rammed the trigger of the mine straight down on to the ground.

Nothing happened, but Dawson knew that inside the weapon some kind of a delayed-action fuse had been triggered, and he had three or four seconds – at the most – before the weapon exploded. Immediately, he changed his grip slightly and then threw the mine, as hard as he could, towards the approaching soldier.

'Down, Dave!' he hissed, and dropped flat himself, waiting for the explosions.

From his hiding place, he had a fairly clear view of both the clearing and the German soldier. He watched as his improvised grenade sailed out of the undergrowth towards his target.

The German obviously saw the missile almost as soon as Dawson threw it, and swung his machine-pistol round to aim at it. But then he appeared almost to relax slightly as he realized that the canister wasn't the grenade he'd been expecting. He aimed his Schmeisser towards the edge of the clearing from which the object had appeared, and where the two men had to be hiding, and Dawson could almost swear he could see the man's finger taking up the pressure on the machine-pistol's trigger.

Then the mine hit, base first, perhaps thirty feet in front of the approaching German soldier. It started to bounce upwards, its momentum carrying it forward, then there was a sudden bang as the first charge detonated. When the explosive fired, the mine was about a foot off the ground and perhaps thirty degrees off the vertical, pointing away from where the two sappers had taken refuge. Without the weight of soil above it to restrict its flight, the mine shot about a further ten feet upwards and over towards the far side of the clearing. Then the main charge fired. There was a colossal bang, and suddenly the air was filled with red-hot flying ball bearings.

Dawson and Watson, lying flat on the ground with their hands over their ears, heard a cacophony of thuds and cracks and whistles as the tiny, lethal, missiles ripped through the trees over their heads, but the main axis of the blast was well above them.

The German standing out in the open wasn't so lucky. The first explosion had caught him by surprise, and he'd just watched uncomprehendingly as the small black cylinder had suddenly jumped into the air about thirty feet in front of him. When the main charge detonated a split-second later, his unprotected body was virtually shredded by the impact of dozens of steel balls travelling at enormous velocity. He was dead even before he hit the ground.

'Shit,' Watson said, a kind of awe in his voice as he stood up and looked out at the clearing. 'I'll never doubt you again, Eddie.'

'We were lucky that time,' Dawson replied shortly, 'but we aren't out of the wood yet. Come on.'

He handed the bag holding the mines to Watson, then dashed out into the clearing, over to where the body of the German soldier lay sprawled on his back. His injuries were horrendous, his stomach and torso ripped open, his face torn to pieces, blood and splatters of tissue spread all around his corpse and across the track. Dawson did his best to avert his eyes, knowing that his actions had caused the death of this anonymous soldier, but also knowing that if he hadn't done what he did, he and Watson would themselves now be dead.

He reached down and grabbed the Schmeisser machine-pistol. The leather strap for the weapon was around the dead man's shoulders, and Dawson had to roll the body over slightly to free it. Then he undid the belt buckle which secured the soldier's brown leather ammunition belt – fitted with two sets of three long green canvas and brown leather ammunition pouches, each holding a Schmeisser MP 40 magazine – and dragged it off the body. One section of the belt, and three of the magazines, were covered in blood, and there were a few cuts and scratches on it caused by the shrapnel that had ended the German soldier's life.

Dawson glanced all round the clearing. At that moment he saw no other enemy soldiers, but then he heard shouts from the far side and looked up to see two figures wearing grey uniforms appear and start running towards him. It looked as if both men were carrying rifles.

But now Dawson himself had a gun. He roughly aimed the machine-pistol and fired a long burst at the approaching figures, though at that range – probably about seventy yards – he had no hope of hitting either

of them. All he wanted to do was make them keep their distance, while he and Watson made their escape.

The two German soldiers stopped, but they didn't retreat, which was what Dawson had hoped they'd do. Instead, they both dropped to one knee and aimed their rifles towards him. Despite the machine-pistol, Dawson knew that at that range he was hopelessly out-gunned.

The standard German army rifle was the Mauser Karabiner 98k, a 7.92-millimetre rifle that was accurate at over 500 yards with iron sights, and at nearly 900 yards if a telescopic sight was fitted. At less than 100 yards, the type of sight was irrelevant – at that range anybody who'd ever fired a rifle would be able to hit a man-sized target with every single round. Dawson knew he had to move, and quickly.

He ducked down, then rolled sideways towards the edge of the clearing, keeping as low as he possibly could, just as the two German soldiers fired their weapons, almost simultaneously. He heard the bullets whining over his head, then the echoing crack of the two shots. The Mauser was a bolt-action weapon, so Dawson knew he had a bare second or so before either of the soldiers would be ready to fire again. He jumped to his feet and ran for the shelter of the undergrowth.

'Dave,' he shouted, 'let's get out of here. And bring those mines – we might need another one before this is over.'

The two sappers headed away from the clearing, deeper into the forest. Another couple of shots cracked out, but Dawson guessed the Germans had to be firing blind and neither bullet came anywhere near them.

After about 100 yards they stopped and took up

positions behind a pair of substantial trees. Dawson checked the MP 40. There was a bullet in the breach, and after a couple of seconds he found the release and dropped the magazine on to the ground. He dragged another one out of the soldier's belt and snapped it into place. If that magazine was fully charged, he knew from their briefings at Catterick a few weeks earlier, it had a total capacity of thirty-two rounds.

Ignoring the blood, which was now sticky to the touch, he quickly shrugged on the ammunition belt and secured the buckle. He picked up the discarded magazine and slipped it into one of the empty pouches. It felt as if there were still four full magazines, so ammunition wouldn't be a problem for a while.

The two men stared into the forest around them, looking for any sign of the two German soldiers.

'They won't follow us in here, mate,' Watson said, his voice little more than a whisper, 'not with you carrying a machine-gun.'

'I bloody hope not,' Dawson replied, equally quietly.

Watson nodded and lifted the bag holding the mines. 'You think we still need to lug these around?'

Dawson nodded. 'If it wasn't for those, we'd both be dead by now. We might find another use for one or two of them.'

'I still think we were bloody lucky the way that mine exploded.'

'We were, mate, but right then we were fresh out of fucking options. I hoped that when it landed it would bounce away from us when the first charge fired, and if it did, that would mean that the main explosion would blow the shrapnel over our heads. And pretty much

whichever way the mine fell or bounced, that soldier wasn't going to survive the blast.'

'If you say so.' Watson nodded. 'And thank Christ that Jerry opened fire too soon. If he'd got much closer, he'd have killed us for sure.'

CHAPTER 20

The two sappers stayed hidden in the forest for about fifteen minutes, watching and listening for any sign of the two German soldiers they'd seen in the clearing, but could detect no sign of them. Watson wasn't too surprised.

'It's one thing to shoot at a bloke with a rifle over open ground,' he said, 'but it's a bloody sight different when he's hiding in a wood and you know he's got a machine-gun. Buggered if I'd want to go in after somebody like that. And when they see what's left of that Jerry, they'll probably think we've got some new and really fucking powerful grenades as well.'

Dawson nodded. 'And they only saw me, so they're probably not going to want to risk their lives to chase down a single man.'

But they knew they had to move. If possible, they had to get hold of more weapons, but they certainly needed to find a way to cross the border and get back to their own lines. And the longer they waited, the more enemy troops were likely to be in the area as the Germans brought up reinforcements.

Dawson stepped out cautiously from his hiding place and looked around. Everything appeared peaceful, and nothing seemed out of place.

'The border's that way,' he said, pointing, 'so we'll head in the opposite direction. Let's go. Keep it slow and steady.'

Taking care to make as little noise as possible, the two men separated slightly and started moving through the forest, staying on slopes that couldn't have been mined. Dawson was in the lead, the MP 40 held ready, his finger resting lightly on the trigger. Watson followed him, the bag of mines slung over his shoulder. Both men checked all around them, looking for anything suspicious, anything that could indicate the presence of enemy soldiers.

The sound of firing had died away almost completely, just a few sporadic rifle shots occasionally audible at some distance, out to the west. They had no idea if they'd witnessed a full German counter-attack, or if the enemy troops they'd seen were part of a smaller unit, sent into the Warndt Forest to probe the strength of the invading French forces.

But whatever the truth of the matter, both the sappers knew they were now marooned inside German territory, probably with enemy troops all around them. Dawson hoped that, by moving away from the forest, they might manage to meet up with one of the French advance units. And all they had to fight their way through the German troops and back to their own lines across the border was a captured Schmeisser machine-pistol, about 150 rounds of nine-millimetre ammunition, three

rusting mines covered in earth and a couple of bayonets – not good odds, by any standard.

Dawson led the way, moving slowly and cautiously, taking only three or four paces before stopping for a few moments to look and listen again, Watson mirroring his actions a few steps behind. But they'd only walked about 400 yards when Dawson suddenly spotted the flash of a grey uniform in the trees, this time in front of them, maybe fifty yards away. He froze instantly and raised his right hand to stop Watson moving any further. Then he sank slowly to his knees, back into cover, and gestured to his fellow sapper to do the same. Was it a single soldier, or a member of a patrol searching for them? Until they knew that, he daren't open fire or even move.

Almost directly in front of Dawson was a large shrub of some sort – the undergrowth in the forest was fairly thick – and he knew he'd remain invisible to the German soldier as long as he stayed behind it. But he needed to see the opposition – he had to see what they were up against – so he eased silently to one side and looked through the lowest branches.

Standing among the trees, and almost hidden behind the trunk of one of them, he could just make out a grey-clad figure, a Mauser rifle held in both hands at port. The soldier looked alert and prepared for trouble – he would have heard the sound of machine-gun fire and the explosion of the mine just a few minutes earlier. At that moment he wasn't moving, just looking around him, and Dawson guessed there would be at least one other soldier with him.

'I see one man,' Dawson whispered to Watson, 'but there's got to be another one somewhere nearby.'

Watson nodded but didn't respond; he just pointed over to his right, away from the man they'd already seen.

Dawson looked in that direction. Another German soldier was moving slowly towards them, his head turning from side to side as he made his way cautiously through the forest, his Schmeisser held at the ready. Once again the two sappers were out-gunned. And this time they were virtually surrounded, with one enemy soldier on each side of their position.

'Stay down,' Dawson whispered, checking his machine-pistol once more. There was no chance that the German soldiers would fail to spot them, because they were already so close. So he knew that, no matter what they did, they were going to be involved in a fire-fight. Their only chance was to take down one of the enemy first, and use the advantage of the element of surprise.

The German carrying the Schmeisser was the most dangerous – the machine-pistol would prove to be a lethal weapon at close quarters – so Dawson knew that man had to be his target.

He eased back, lay flat on his chest and started to crawl away from the bush where Watson still lay hidden, holding the Schmeisser in both hands, keeping it clear of the ground. He'd practised the technique often enough in training, at Catterick and elsewhere, but that had always involved a Lee-Enfield rifle, a slightly easier weapon to handle doing that manoeuvre than the MP 40 with its long magazine sticking out at right angles from under the receiver. But he managed to move perhaps fifteen feet without, as far as he could see, either German seeing him. That brought him a lot closer to his target, the soldier armed with the machine-pistol.

Then he simply lay still, making use of what cover there was. He looked back, towards the second soldier, who had now started moving again, his rifle still held loosely in his hands. He checked the other man, now only about twenty yards away and still walking slowly towards him.

Dawson had never been a sportsman, had never even held a firearm of any sort before he joined the Territorial Army, but even he was familiar with the concept of never shooting a sitting bird. But in his present circumstances, the ideas of fair play and sportsmanship were as alien to him as they were irrelevant. It was quite simply a matter of kill or be killed.

He waited until the German soldier was no more than ten yards away from him, then eased the Schmeisser into the firing position, but turned through ninety degrees so that the magazine was almost flat on the ground. He daredn't stand up, or even kneel, to hold the machine-pistol upright, because that would immediately give away his position. He just hoped it would be reasonably accurate when he fired.

The German was continuing to scan his surroundings, and, as Dawson took up the pressure on the trigger, the man suddenly seemed to notice something. The soldier swung his Schmeisser around, the muzzle tracking towards Dawson's hiding place, and he opened his mouth to shout something.

Dawson fired. He squeezed the trigger and released it almost immediately, holding it for under a second. The machine-pistol jumped in his hands as the nine-millimetre bullets poured out of its barrel. The MP 40 fires only 500 rounds a minute, but Dawson guessed

that brief burst had probably been about half a dozen rounds.

The German soldier's tunic suddenly bloomed red as three or four bullets smashed into his torso, knocking him backwards. As he fell, his muscles went into spasm and his finger briefly pulled the trigger of his own weapon, sending a long burst of fire crashing into the trees around him.

Instantly, Dawson swung round, looking for the second enemy soldier. For a moment, he didn't see him, then caught sight of a flicker of grey as the man ducked into cover behind a tree some thirty yards away, lifting his rifle to the aim as he did so.

Dawson checked that Watson was still crouched down and well below his line of fire, then aimed the MP 40 and pulled the trigger, already starting to move. He had no hope of hitting the man, but the burst of machine-gun fire should ruin his aim. And once he'd fired his Mauser, the German would effectively be disarmed until he could work the bolt and reload the weapon. That was the best Dawson could hope for.

The crack of the rifle was a single loud bang, easily audible over the yammer of the machine-pistol. The bullet ploughed into the trunk of a tree no more than two feet from Dawson, who was sprinting to the left, trying to get into a position where he could see and shoot the German before he could reload.

As Dawson ran, he could see the enemy soldier already working the bolt of his Mauser, and fired another short burst at him. But all the bullets from the machine-pistol appeared to miss their target, and the man quickly

brought the rifle back up to the aim, moving slightly behind the tree trunk again to protect himself.

Dawson saw the muzzle swinging towards him and dived forward, rolling into cover as the second rifle shot rang out. The bullet missed him, but only by inches, and immediately Dawson was back on his feet and running.

He swung the Schmeisser towards his target again, and pulled the trigger. The bullets smashed into the tree trunk beside the German, but, before Dawson could alter his aim to the left, the machine-pistol fell silent as the last bullet was fired.

Dawson pressed the magazine release and scrabbled to pull another one out of one of the belt pouches, but he knew he was in a losing race. The German only had to work the bolt of his Mauser to chamber another round, and then there was no way he could miss – the two men were a bare twenty yards apart.

He pulled out a full magazine, slammed it into the Schmeisser and reached for the cocking handle. But even as he did so, the German aimed the Mauser straight at him.

Then another burst of firing echoed through the trees, and the German soldier toppled forwards, the rifle falling from his lifeless hands. Fifteen yards behind him, Dawson glimpsed Watson, standing with his legs apart, another Schmeisser MP 40 held firmly in his hands.

'Thank Christ for that, Dave,' Dawson said. 'I reckon he was about half a second from blowing me away.'

He trotted forward to the fallen soldier and checked for a pulse, but the man was clearly dead. Swiftly, he and Watson stripped him of his rifle and ammunition

belt, then ran over to the other German and grabbed his weapon and ammunition.

As they did so, Watson looked at the uniforms the dead men were wearing. He was by no means an expert on German army uniforms, but it looked to him as if both were regular Wehrmacht troops, the grey-green colour of the material quite distinctive, with the Nazi 'flying eagle' badge on the right side of the chest.

He pointed at the lapels of the man who'd been carrying the Schmeisser. On each was a black oblong with two white squared dots in it. 'I think that's a sergeant's rank badge,' he said, 'and that explains why he was carrying the machine-pistol instead of a rifle.'

One of their briefings at Catterick had emphasized that the Schmeisser was believed to be in short supply in the Wehrmacht, and the weapon was normally only issued to section or patrol leaders.

'Now that's better,' Dawson said, looking at their haul. 'One rifle, twenty rounds of ammunition, and two machine-pistols with about six full magazines. Now we really have got teeth, Dave.'

'Does that mean we can dump these bloody mines?' Watson asked.

'Not yet. They might still be useful. Now let's get the hell out of this area before any other Jerries decide to come out here to investigate all the shooting.'

CHAPTER 21

'The border's over to the west,' Watson pointed out, 'and we're still heading east.'

'I know, but I really don't think trying to go that way is a good idea. The area will be full of fucking Jerries, and we'd find it bloody difficult to sneak through their lines, and then we'd have to face a whole mob of French soldiers with itchy trigger fingers and watching out for anybody heading towards them. I think it'll be a lot safer if we try to cross the border somewhere else.'

'Where?' Watson asked. 'And do you have any idea where we are right now, bearing in mind we haven't got a map or even a bloody compass?'

Dawson looked around him. They'd already moved – jogging as quickly as they could over the uneven ground – perhaps half a mile away from the killing ground, where they'd left the bullet-riddled bodies of the two German soldiers. They'd finally stopped for a breather, and were sitting down high on a slope, their backs to another large fallen tree. They were deep inside the forest and had been working their way through the thick undergrowth that grew on the steeper slopes of the heavily wooded

valleys, where they hoped no mines would have been planted.

'We're in Germany,' Dawson said.

'I did know that,' Watson remarked.

'I remember the map that Lieutenant Charnforth showed us, or the rough lie of the land here, anyway.' Dawson reached into one of the pockets on his battle-dress tunic and pulled out a folded sheet of paper and the stub of a pencil. Smoothing out the paper on his knee, he drew a rapid sketch, beginning with a line running diagonally from the top left-hand corner of the page. Then he looped the line up in a curve to point upwards, then across to the right, then down again before extending it to the right. The finished shape was a gently curving line that ran from the top left of the page towards the bottom right corner, with a kind of n-shaped bulge in it.

Above the n-shape, Dawson drew an oval that he labelled with the letters 'SB'. Above and to the left of that, he drew a smaller circle which he annotated 'SL'. Finally, almost opposite the 'SB' oval, but to the left of the diagonal line and fairly close to it, he marked a dot and labelled it 'CLC'.

'Right,' he said, turning the sheet of paper so that Watson could see it clearly. 'The "SB" stands for Saarbrücken, the "SL" for Saarlouis, and the "CLC" for Creutzwald-la-Croix, which is on the French side of the frontier, close to where we were camped. That line' – he pointed – 'is the Franco-German border, obviously. Now, we crossed it just to the east of Creutzwald-la-Croix, about here. So right now we're somewhere in this area, between the border itself and Saarbrücken.'

'So the closest part of the border, apart from just over to the west, is either to the south or, if you and this sort of map are right, due east of here? So we're going to keep heading east? Or turn south?'

'Yes and no,' Dawson replied. 'You're right about where the closest border is, but I'm not happy about those two choices. If we head south, we're entering a kind of pocket of German territory, with a fortified border on three sides of us, and I'd lay money that it's going to be full of Jerry troops looking for trouble. And if we go east, we could miss the border altogether and just end up deeper inside Germany. We also need to think about pursuit. We've left three dead German soldiers behind us, and from what I've heard about the Jerries, they're not going to take that lying down. I think that, once they've sorted out the French and re-established their border defences, they'll send out a couple of patrols to hunt us down.'

'Full of fucking good news, you are. I hadn't thought about that. So what do you reckon we should do?'

'If I was the NCO in charge of a Jerry patrol, I think I'd expect us to try to get across the border as quickly as possible, which means he'd probably think we'd start heading south or south-east.'

'So we'll go north?' Watson suggested.

'Almost right. If we go north, we'll end up near Saarlouis, and that would be a really bad idea. I think our best bet is to follow the border up to the north-west, keeping to the west of that corridor of built-up areas that runs from Saarbrücken to Saarlouis. That way, we'll stay away from the more populated areas and hope to cross the border somewhere up here.'

Dawson pointed at the line he'd drawn on the paper up to the north-west of the circle labelled 'SL'. 'As far as I remember from the map the lieutenant had, there are only small villages and hamlets in this area, between the border and that corridor of towns running along the River Saar, so we should be able to sneak through there unnoticed.'

'We'll use the sun to navigate by?'

'Unless we can find a compass somewhere, yes.'

Watson nodded. 'So let's hope the weather stays fine. What about crossing the border itself?'

Dawson shrugged. 'We'll pick the best place when we get up there and find out what the defences are like.'

'OK,' Watson said. 'You talk sense, as usual, Eddie. Let's get moving.'

The two men stood up, hitched their weapons over their shoulders and prepared to move off. 'There's something else we need to think about,' Dawson said, as they started walking. 'Unless we're really lucky, we're going to be out here on the wrong side of the border for at least a day or two. We've got no rations, not even any water bottles, and we're going to need to find some food – or at the very least something to drink – if we're going to make it.'

They were well away from the obvious tracks through the woods, most of which ran along the lower, more level, sections at the bottoms of the valleys that characterized the area, but still they proceeded with caution, ever watchful that a sniper might be scanning the woods through the telescopic sight of his rifle, or a German patrol lying in wait for them somewhere. But for the first hour, as their route slowly took them further to the

north, towards the edge of the Warndt Forest, they saw nobody at all.

'You reckon we're clear of the Jerries now?' Watson asked, as they crested a ridge and started the descent on the other side. A basic rule of hill-walking is that you should never surrender height – climbing uphill is exhausting, so once height has been gained, walkers should do everything possible to remain as high as they can. Dawson and Watson were both well aware of the principle and were doing their best to adhere to it, so, although they were having to both climb and descend, they were trying to keep their descents to a minimum, walking across the frequent slopes rather than down them.

'For the moment, I think we are. They won't know which way we went after we left those two dead soldiers, and the further we walk, the wider the search area will become. Why?'

'Because I'm pretty much knackered, that's why.' Watson pointed over to the west. 'The sun's going down, and I think we need to find somewhere to hole up for the night. This country's too bloody rough to try walking over it in the dark. If one of us twists an ankle or breaks a leg out here, we're both buggered.'

Dawson nodded. What Watson had said was compellingly obvious and, in any case, he was really tired himself. It had been, by any standards, an extremely full day. They'd gone from the dangerous, but ultimately routine, clearance of a minefield to what amounted to a full-scale battle with the German army. They'd each shot and killed a man, and Dawson had blown another one to pieces with his improvised grenade. They were now deep inside enemy territory, where they were liable to

be shot on sight by any German soldiers they met and, most probably, they were also on the run from at least a couple of enemy patrols who would be looking for them somewhere in the forest behind them.

'Yeah, Dave. That's a good idea. Let's start looking for somewhere right now.'

About fifteen minutes later, the two sappers found a spot that looked as if it would do. It was close to the top of another ridge, where a couple of trees had fallen over, their collapsed trunks forming a giant X-shape. The area between the exposed roots and the point where the trunks crossed offered a concealed hollow that could easily accommodate both men.

'That'll do,' Dawson said, and climbed over the roots into the partially concealed opening, Watson following behind him.

When both men crouched down, they were completely invisible, except from directly above.

'What's on the menu for dinner?' Watson asked, as they settled down and dusk began turning the surrounding trees into dark and menacing monochrome shapes.

'That's the problem, mate. I've got one small bar of chocolate in my pocket. What've you got?'

'Sweet FA. Nothing,' Watson admitted.

'You're welcome to share this,' Dawson offered, pulling out a small foil-wrapped packet from a pocket. 'We'll have to find some food tomorrow.'

For a couple of minutes they sat in silence, chewing the chocolate, then Dawson spoke again.

'I don't think we can both go to sleep at the same time, Dave, not out here. It's just after eight now. If you

try and get your head down, I'll wake you up at two, and then we'll change over. Or would you rather take the first watch?'

Watson shook his head. 'No, I'm whacked, so I'll have no trouble getting to sleep now. But are you OK? I mean, can you stay awake for the next six hours?'

'I'll do my best, mate. If I don't think I can keep my eyes open any longer, I'll give you a shake – fair enough?'

'Yeah, no problem. God, what I wouldn't give for a brew-up right now,' Watson muttered, turning on to his side at the bottom of the hollow and closing his eyes. 'I'll probably dream about tea and scran, crap though it usually is.'

Dawson chuckled, then stood up and moved to one side of the hollow, where a protruding root offered a reasonable seat. He checked the Mauser rifle, ensuring that the magazine was fully charged and that there was a cartridge in the chamber, and did the same with his Schmeisser MP 40 machine-pistol. Then he placed both weapons so that they were within easy reach, took his seat on the root and leant back against the trunk of the fallen tree. He scanned all around him, glanced down at Watson, who was already snoring softly, then back out at the darkening forest.

It was going to be a very long and boring night, but, as far as Dawson was concerned, the quieter and more boring it turned out to be, the better.

CHAPTER 22

'What time is it?' Dawson asked, as Watson shook him by the shoulder.

'Just gone eight.'

'Breakfast?'

'Pull the other one, mate. But it's time we started moving, I reckon.'

Dawson stood up and stretched his aching limbs. He'd slept quite well, since Watson had relieved him at two in the morning, but the hollow was far from comfortable, and he seemed to have knots in every muscle. But once he started moving, he guessed he'd quickly work out the kinks.

He looked round to check the position of the sun, the light from which was visible, streaming between the trunks of the closely grouped trees. He glanced at his watch, looked back over to the east and nodded.

'We'll start with the sun at our backs,' he said, scanning the horizon in front of him. They were near the edge of the wood, a patchwork of fields and small groups of trees laid out across the wide valley that opened up before them. 'If we make for that copse over there' – he

pointed – 'that should be pretty much right: a bearing of about north-west.'

The two men picked up their weapons and the mines, made a careful check of the terrain in front of them, then stepped forward. As they made their way slowly down the slope, moving away from the forest, they kept under cover as much as they could, using the contours of the land to keep out of sight. There were trees and undergrowth and even ditches that they could see in front of them, all of which they could use as they made their way down the hill.

At the bottom of the slope that delineated the edge of the forest was a small stream, little more than a brook, the water trickling down a slope that wound its way through the remaining trees and bushes.

'God, that looks good,' Watson muttered. 'I'm parched.' He looked round carefully, checking for any danger, then lowered the bag of mines and his machine-pistol to the ground, trotted forward and bent over the clear, fresh water. He cupped his hands, filled his palms with water and drank greedily. Then he did the same again and finally splashed the cold water over his face.

'Fucking shame we haven't got a bottle or something,' he said, as Dawson bent over the stream and took a drink.

'We'll have to find something,' Dawson said. 'We can't rely on running across a stream every few hours. Keep your eyes open as we walk through the farmland. Perhaps we'll find a can or something down there that we can use.'

★

By mid-morning they were well beyond the copse Dawson had used for his initial navigation, and now heading in a more northerly direction, working their way through fields and along hedgerows. They were moving as cautiously as ever, checking all around them every few paces, but still they hadn't seen anyone – not a soldier, or even a farmer or farm labourer. The whole area seemed to be deserted.

They reached the corner of a field, where the hedgerow they'd been using for cover ended, and looked out over the fields in front of them. Most had clearly been cultivated over the year, but had now, at the end of the summer, apparently been abandoned until the spring. But there was still no sign of life, human or even animal.

'Fucking odd, this,' Watson commented, staring across the fairly level stretch of land lying to the north. 'You'd have thought we'd at least see a few cows or sheep or something. It's as if the whole area's been evacuated.'

Dawson nodded. 'You're right,' he said, 'and I've just remembered what Lieutenant Charnforth told us when he gave us that briefing on the tactical situation. He said the Frogs had advanced slowly, against almost no Jerry opposition, and that they'd captured a few villages that had already been evacuated. I think that's what happened here. The Germans must have seen that the French forces were gathering on the border and decided to pull everyone back a few miles for safety.'

'Farmers and other civilians as well as soldiers, you mean? And their farm animals too?'

'Maybe. Or perhaps all these farms just grew crops, not raised sheep or cattle. I don't bloody know. But I suppose from a tactical point of view a full withdrawal

makes sense. With everyone cleared out of this area, when the German army appeared to push the French back over the border, they wouldn't have to worry about any civilian casualties, because there wouldn't be any civilians here. And that's good for us.'

Watson nodded agreement. 'Definitely, because I'm bloody famished. Let's find a farmhouse somewhere and see what they've got in the larder.'

'That's a fucking good idea,' Dawson said. He looked ahead and all around them, then pointed slightly over to the right of their intended route. 'I think that's the roof of a building over there. Let's head across that way and check it out.'

There was no cover they could use as they crossed the open field, so the two men separated and followed as unpredictable a course as they could, just in case there were any snipers watching them. They weaved from side to side, and varied their pace so that they presented the most difficult targets possible. But there were no shots, no apparent threat, and they quickly reached the far side of the field and gratefully melted into the welcoming gloom and temporary safety of another small stand of trees.

They were then much closer to the building Dawson had spotted and crossed to the edge of the copse to check it out. Ensuring they remained hidden in the trees, the two men stood and stared at their objective.

What Dawson had seen was actually the roof of a small barn, the door of which was facing them and standing open. Inside they could see what looked like various pieces of farm machinery, ploughs and the like, none of them of the slightest interest to the two sappers.

But beyond and to one side of the barn was a farm-house, or a farm cottage, to be exact.

It was fairly small and square, constructed of stone under a tiled roof. It had a central wooden door in the wall facing the two sappers, flanked by one window on either side, with three windows in a line above. There was a second door and window, with two other windows above, in the side wall that they could see at an oblique angle.

'It looks to me like it's all locked up,' Watson murmured, shading his eyes as he looked across at the building. 'All the windows and doors are closed, and there's no sign of life.'

'I agree. That's good for us. OK, we'll go quickly but carefully. Leave the bag of mines here in the wood, where we can pick them up later, and we'll take the rifle and the machine-pistols.'

'What do we do if there's anyone inside the house?' Watson asked, as they got ready to move.

'We don't kill civilians,' Dawson said firmly. 'If the farmer or his family are in there, the Schmeissers should be enough to persuade them to keep quiet while we take what we need. And we'll only take food and drink – no looting. If we have to, we can tie them up or lock them in the cellar or something. But let's hope that the place is as deserted as it looks. OK, Dave. Keep your eyes open, and cover me with the rifle. If you see anything suspicious, when I stop and look back at you, just wave and point at it. But if it's a Jerry soldier, just shoot him and then we'll leg it.'

Dawson went first, sprinting across the seventy yards or so of level ground that separated the open barn from

the wood. He reached the side of the building opposite the farmhouse and stopped there for a few seconds to catch his breath. Then he crept along the side of the barn and peered around the corner. There was nobody in sight. He glanced back towards Watson, who remained motionless at the edge of the copse, the Mauser rifle held in his hands.

Dawson looked behind him, down the side of the building. Nobody in sight. Then he stepped around the corner and took six swift paces that brought him to the open door. He peered around the door into the barn, then stepped cautiously inside the structure, his machine-pistol held at the ready.

As he'd guessed when he'd studied the building from his vantage point among the trees, the barn was full of various types of farm machinery, almost none of which he recognized. More importantly, it was entirely empty of human beings, and had the indefinable air of having been deserted for some time.

Even though he was sure he was wasting his time, Dawson checked everywhere in the building, looking in every corner and behind every piece of machinery, before he relaxed, walked back to the open door and waved for Watson to join him.

'Empty?' Watson demanded, as he stepped inside.

'Yes. No sign of recent activity at all.'

Dawson walked over to one corner of the barn, where he'd spotted a cluttered work-bench. He rested his machine-pistol on the ground and started rooting through the tools he saw there. If both of the farmhouse doors were locked, they were going to need something to force one of them, and something a bit more discreet

than a stream of nine-millimetre bullets from one of the Schmeissers.

He found nothing suitable on the bench itself, but hanging on the wall behind it was a short crowbar, twisted and rusty, but still serviceable. That would be ideal. Dawson lifted it off its nail and slipped it into his belt.

'Right,' he said. 'Let's get over to the house. Same routine, right? I'll go first, while you keep watch. Then I'll cover you from the house.'

The farmhouse was only about forty yards away from the barn, but there was no cover at all between the two buildings, just a wide-open space, the ground rutted and marked with tracks made by wheels and the hooves of animals. In front of the house was a small garden, perhaps used for growing vegetables, bounded by a low hedge, but that was the only cover Dawson could see. And the hedge was very close to the house itself, and would offer only a measure of concealment for him. Anyone looking out of the windows on the top floor of the cottage would probably be able to see him clearly, even if he was crouched down behind it.

'I'll make a dash for that hedge,' he said. 'Keep your eyes on the upstairs windows, and yell if you see any movement up there.'

Watson moved over to a position from which he had a clear view of the house, lifted the Mauser to cover the building – if there was a soldier up there, he needed the extra accuracy the rifle offered – and nodded.

Dawson stepped out of the barn door, paused for a second to take a swift glance around him, then sprinted

towards the farmhouse, dodging and weaving from side to side as he ran.

He made it to the hedge, ducked down and glanced back. Watson was still standing in the doorway of the barn, rifle at the ready, but gave no sign that he'd seen anything to alarm him. Dawson eased up and peered over the hedge at the farmhouse. Everything still looked quiet, so he stood erect, dodged around the end of the hedge, crossed the few feet to the wall of the house itself and flattened himself against it.

Again he looked back at Watson, who simply gave him a thumbs-up sign. Dawson stepped to the corner of the building and glanced at the side door, then strode down to it. He looked round yet again, grasped the door handle, turned it and pushed his shoulder against the old wood. He wasn't surprised when the door refused to yield, and it was a further confirmation, of a sort, that the place was deserted.

Dawson walked back to the main door of the farmhouse. That, too, was locked, so he retraced his steps. Breaking open the side door would be less obvious than forcing the one at the front of the house, and might even be a bit easier.

He waved to Watson to come across to the house and then, while his colleague kept a lookout, he pulled the crowbar from his belt, rammed the point into the space between the door and the jamb, right beside the handle and lock, and levered. The old door creaked, but held firm, so Dawson changed the position of the crowbar slightly and pushed again. He did that three times and then, with a crack that seemed to echo around the valley,

the door gave, slamming open to crash back against the inner wall.

'Well,' Watson said, as Dawson tucked the crowbar back into his belt. 'If there *is* anyone inside, that should have woken them up, no problem.'

'The place is empty, Dave. It has to be,' Dawson said, picking up the MP 40 and leading the way inside. 'You take upstairs. I'll do the ground floor.'

Two minutes later, Watson rejoined his fellow sapper, who was standing in the kitchen, a canvas bag on the table in front of him, his machine-pistol next to it. Behind him, the door to the larder stood open.

'I've checked the larder and the store cupboards, and there's not a lot here, Dave. It looks like the occupants of this place cleared out most of the food before they left. But we will be able to eat. I've found three big dried sausages – though fuck knows what they've got in them – and a couple of jars of beans. It's not a lot, but it should keep us going for a day or two. And I've grabbed a couple of spoons and a sharp knife.'

'And we need something to drink out of as well,' Watson said. 'Are there any empty jars or anything in there?'

'Yeah. I picked up a couple of glass jars. They've got screw-on lids, so we can use those. Here,' he said, picking them up and passing them over to Watson. 'I haven't filled them yet, but there's a pump out there in the yard, so why don't you do the honours?'

Watson carried the two jars outside to a small pump close to the house, cranked the handle until water ran out of the nozzle, then filled the two jars and walked back into the kitchen.

'I reckon they only hold about a pint each,' he said, handing the jars to Dawson, 'but having them means we can refill them in streams or pools.'

Dawson packed the jars away in the canvas bag he'd found. 'We ought to drink more water right now,' he suggested. 'We've still got a long way to go, and we've had hardly any liquid for the last twenty-four hours.'

'Good idea.' Watson stepped into the larder and selected another couple of glass jars that looked reasonably clean. He was heading for the kitchen door with them in his hands when he glanced out of the window and froze.

'Eddie,' he said. 'Come here. We've got company.'

CHAPTER 23

13 SEPTEMBER 1939

Dawson strode the few paces across the kitchen to the window and looked out.

'There,' Watson said, pointing.

About a hundred yards away, a German soldier was walking through the field, his rifle held at the ready. Fifty yards further away was another soldier, and another one beyond him, a small patrol of men walking more or less in line abreast. It was obvious they were searching for something, and Dawson didn't need too much thought to guess what their object was.

'Shit!' he muttered. 'How many are there altogether?'

'I can see three, but I'll bet there are at least a dozen of them.'

'We can't fight that many,' Dawson decided immediately. 'Not just the two of us, with the weapons and ammunition we've got. I'll bet they're after us, and they've probably been ordered to check all the buildings in this area. We'll have to barricade the side door and hope they think the farmhouse is still locked up and deserted. Come on.'

Dawson grabbed the canvas bag and put it on the

floor, out of sight of the window, then followed Watson out of the room. The lock on the side door was still intact, but the strike plate had been ripped out of the jamb when Dawson had forced the door with the crowbar. They had no time to try and replace it – even if it had been possible to do so.

'Bugger,' Watson said, looking at the door. 'No bolts. That would have been just too bloody convenient. I'll get a kitchen chair. That should do it.'

He returned a few moments later, carrying a heavy wooden chair. Together, the two men held the door closed, then jammed the back of the chair under the handle and forced the legs as close to the door as they could. If somebody tried the door from the outside, it wouldn't feel quite as secure as if the lock was still in place, but the door certainly wouldn't open. All they could hope was that, if the German soldiers did check the security of the farmhouse, they'd be convinced that it was still locked up and empty, and just move on somewhere else.

'So where do we hide?' Watson asked. 'Upstairs?'

Dawson considered the suggestion for a few seconds, then nodded. 'Yes. If this does turn into a fire-fight, the extra height might be a help to us.'

Quickly, the two men climbed up the wooden staircase and went into the bedroom that was situated over the kitchen.

'Keep out of sight,' Dawson hissed. 'I'll just take a quick look outside and see what's going on.'

He crossed over to the window, where the curtains were closed, and gently eased one slightly away from the other, just enough to create a thin vertical crack that he could look through.

'I can still see three Jerry soldiers,' he said, his voice barely more than a whisper. 'They're moving across the fields, now passing in front of this house. Wait.' He moved the curtain very gently, reducing the width of the gap. 'I've just spotted another one, and he's heading straight for the house. No noise, and let's hope that bloody chair holds the door closed.'

Dawson stepped back from the window – even the slightest movement of the curtain would tell the approaching soldier that somebody was in the house – and stood still, his right hand seizing the pistol grip of his Schmeisser MP 40.

Both men stood in silence, listening intently. They couldn't hear the sound of the soldier's approach, but Dawson knew he now had to be very close to the farmhouse. Then there was a rattling sound from the floor below.

'The front door,' Dawson mouthed to Watson, who nodded agreement.

There were a few moments of silence, then they heard a similar sound from the side door, as the soldier obviously attempted to open it. Another brief silence, then the sound came again.

'I wish we could see down there,' Watson whispered.

'We'll know soon enough. He'll either bugger off or kick down the door, and we'll know which he's decided to do in a couple of minutes.'

The two sappers waited in apprehensive silence but heard nothing else. After a few minutes, Dawson crept over to the window he'd peered out of before and, without moving the curtains at all, looked out through the narrow gap between them. About ten yards away,

just beyond the hedge, a single German soldier was standing still, looking back at the house, a quizzical expression on his face. But as Dawson looked at him, barely breathing, the soldier visibly shrugged, then turned away and began walking across the fields towards his distant comrades.

'I think he's leaving,' Dawson said, remaining by the window and continuing to watch the scene outside.

'So we stay here, yes? For a while, anyway.'

'Yes. We don't know what route those Jerries are following. They could double-back, or they might have a second squad patrolling behind them. It looks as if they're happy with their check of this house, so I think we should stay here. At least for an hour or so.'

'Right, then,' Watson said. 'If I don't get something to eat soon, those Jerries won't need to see us to know where we are – they'll be able to hear my bloody stomach rumbling. So at least we can grab some scran. Fancy a bite of sausage?'

'Yeah, why not? But give it a few minutes before you go down, just in case. I'll stay here and keep watch.'

Five minutes later, Watson stood up from his seat on the edge of the double bed, walked over to the door and looked down the stairs.

'Just check the kitchen before you go in there,' Dawson said, 'and make sure there aren't half a dozen Jerries peering in through the window.'

'Right.'

Dawson heard Watson's footsteps going down the stairs, and a couple of minutes later the sapper re-entered the bedroom, carrying the canvas bag.

The sausage was tough and dry, but surprisingly tasty,

and each man wolfed down half a dozen thick slices.

'That's better,' Watson murmured, then belched contentedly.

'There's no sign of the German soldiers now,' Dawson said. He hadn't left his post by the curtained window the entire time they'd been eating. 'And I can't see any other Jerries following them, so maybe they've gone. But I still think we should wait a bit longer, just in case.'

A little over an hour later, having checked the scene outside from every window in the farmhouse – and having seen nothing to alarm them – Watson carefully and silently removed the kitchen chair from under the handle of the side door. Dawson was standing right behind him, his Schmeisser machine-pistol aimed at the door, his finger resting lightly on the trigger, just in case they were wrong and the German troops had been cleverer than they'd thought and had left somebody there.

Watson lifted the chair out of the way, then grabbed the handle, pulled open the door and stepped back.

Dawson moved forward, looked out and then stepped outside, his head swivelling from side to side as he checked for danger, his Schmeisser ready to fire, but the gentle rural scene seemed quiet – the loudest noise he could hear was birdsong – and appeared completely peaceful.

'I think we're OK, Dave,' he said quietly.

Watson stepped out of the house behind him, laden down with his machine-pistol plus the Mauser rifle and the canvas bag of rations.

'Which way do we go?' he asked.

'The Germans went that way,' Dawson said, pointing

to the north-east, 'so we'll head over there, towards the west, until we've put a good distance between us and this place, then we'll turn north-west again.'

After taking a further look around them, the two men jogged across to the barn, waited there for a minute making a further check, then made it back to the copse where they'd stashed the recovered mines, which Dawson was still reluctant to abandon.

'You *still* want to lug these around with us, Eddie?' Watson asked, looking down at the bag.

'We may yet need them, Dave.'

'If you say so.'

Watson bent down to pick up the bag, and as he did so there was a sudden crack from the trunk of the tree directly behind him, followed almost immediately by the sound of a distant shot.

Both men immediately dropped flat and crawled into cover.

'Those Jerries must have left a fucking sniper behind them,' Dawson hissed, staring towards the field through the undergrowth. 'There's nobody in sight out there.'

'Where the fuck is he?'

Dawson rolled on to his back and looked up at the tree which the bullet had hit. The mark of the impact was quite clear, a raw scar marring the grey-brown bark on one side. That gave him a rough idea of the direction from which the bullet must have been fired and that, in turn, located the approximate – but only the *very* approximate – position of the sniper.

'He must be somewhere over there,' he said, pointing towards the row of trees lining the opposite side of the large field that bordered the farmhouse.

'That's only about two hundred yards away,' Watson muttered. 'How the hell did he miss me?'

'I think you ducked at just the right moment, when you bent down to pick up the bag of mines. You should be grateful we decided to hang on to them.'

'Yeah, right,' Watson replied. 'So what the fuck do we do now? He's got us pinned down in this clump of trees, and his Mauser or whatever he's using will be fitted with a telescopic sight. So he knows where we are, but we don't know his location. He's got a better rifle and he's probably a better shot than either of us. To me, it doesn't look good.'

'Nor to me,' Dawson said. 'Somehow, we've got to get out of here, and quickly, before the rest of that Jerry patrol comes running back here to pick up our bodies.'

He looked round. The stand of trees where they were hiding was small and more or less circular, probably only about fifty yards in diameter, and Dawson knew that if they stepped out of it, even if they ran out of it, and then tried to cross the field, the hidden German sniper would cut them down before they'd covered even half the distance to the other side. That was simply suicidal.

Dawson glanced the other way, then nodded. 'We can't go north or west,' he stated firmly, 'because that would put us straight into the sniper's sights. But we can use this copse as a shield. If we head south-east, that'll keep these trees between us and that Jerry, and once we've gone about five or six hundred yards we'll be pretty much out of range. What do you think?'

Watson looked over the field in front of them, then back the way Dawson was indicating. 'Makes sense,' he said, 'as long as there's only the one sniper. If they left

one over there in front of us, and another one covering the fields on the south side, we're screwed.'

Dawson grinned mirthlessly. 'I doubt it,' he said, with a confidence he really didn't feel. 'If they thought we were hiding in that farmhouse or somewhere else here, I think they'd have broken down the door or swamped the area with troops. My guess is that they just left a sniper hidden in the trees over there as a back-up, just in case they'd missed us and we suddenly appeared. But whatever,' he added, 'I guess there's only one way to find out, because we sure as hell can't stay here. If that bloody sniper's got a radio, he might already have called the patrol leader and told him he's seen us. And even if he hasn't, there's a good chance at least one of the German soldiers will have heard that shot. We need to move, right now.'

Quickly, the two men grabbed all the weapons, their food and the mines, and slid backwards. Keeping as low as they could, and making sure there were trees in front of them to act as a barrier between their position and where they thought the sniper lay concealed, they worked their way through the stand of trees to the opposite side. Only then did they feel secure enough to stand up, knowing that, at least for the moment, the sniper couldn't possibly see them.

They stood side by side between two substantial trees and looked out across the fields on the other side of the copse. Over to the west, the tree-line continued along the edge of the field and that, they both knew, would be where a sniper would be positioned, if there was a second man out there.

'Let's assume there *is* a sniper there,' Dawson said,

considering. 'If so, he'll have heard that shot and he'll be looking for a target. He'll probably guess that we're somewhere near the farmhouse or this clump of trees, so that's where his rifle will already be pointing. So if one of us steps out there into the field, I reckon it'll probably take him no more than a second to see his target, another two seconds to aim his rifle and settle down for the shot, and then another second to pull the trigger.'

'So you think one of us will be dead four seconds after we leave these trees?'

'Yes. Or, rather, I think we should just test this idea. I'm going to take a step out there and stand still. I want you to start counting the moment I do that. When you get to "four", I'm going to drop flat and dive back under cover. If there's no shot, I'll do it again, if necessary for five or six seconds, and that'll pretty much prove that there isn't a sniper.'

'And if there is a shot?' Watson demanded.

'Well, I might be dead, I suppose, but I'm hoping I won't be. Just count quickly,' he said. 'If there *is* a sniper, we'll have to think again. If there isn't, we'll head south-east as quickly as we can.'

Dawson slid the Schmeisser off his shoulder and lowered it to the ground. He wanted to be as unencumbered as possible when he stepped out into the open, beyond the temporary safety of the trees.

'Ready?' he asked Watson.

'This is fucking risky, if you ask me, Eddie.'

'I know,' Dawson said, 'but it's a hell of a lot less risky than both of us walking out there. And keep your eye on the tree-line over to the west. If there is a shot, try and see where it comes from.'

'I can do better than that,' Watson said, and picked up the Mauser. 'I'll give the bastard a taste of his own medicine.'

He moved around to a position where he had a good view of the line of trees on the far side of the field, rested the Mauser over a branch that would provide a stable rest for him to shoot from, checked that the rifle was loaded with a round in the breach, then nodded his head.

'OK, Eddie,' he said. 'Good luck.'

Dawson took a deep breath and stepped a couple of paces clear of the trees.

Behind him, Watson started counting loudly and clearly. 'One – two – three – four.' As he said the last number, Dawson dodged back behind the trees.

'So what do you think?' Watson asked, looking at his friend.

'Maybe he's a bit slower than we expected,' Dawson said. 'But he must have seen me by now, so I'll do it again. This time, count five seconds, OK?'

Watson shook his head, but again aimed the Mauser rifle at the tree-line as Dawson prepared to step out into the field once more.

This time, as Watson said the word 'four', Dawson ducked down, took a step sideways, ducked again, and then stood still for another couple of seconds.

'Eddie!' Watson shouted. 'Get back in here, for Christ's sake.'

Dawson ignored him, and continued to stand in the open, quite literally inviting a bullet. But nothing happened. No shots, nothing.

Finally, after at least fifteen seconds, Dawson stepped back into the copse.

'You mad bastard,' Watson said, lowering the Mauser.

'Maybe, but now I think we can be pretty sure there's no sniper in the trees over there. So it's time we got the hell out of here.'

Watson nodded, handed Dawson the Mauser and grabbed the two bags. 'I'll carry this stuff,' he said. 'You keep your eyes open and keep that ready to fire.'

'OK,' Dawson replied, slung the Schmeisser MP 40 over his shoulder, where it wouldn't affect his handling of the Mauser, and again stepped to the edge of the copse. 'I reckon that first sniper is directly behind us,' he said, 'so we head over that way, towards that hedge, near those three tall trees.'

'Got it. Let's go.' Watson ran forward awkwardly: the bag containing the mines was heavy, and he was also carrying the canvas bag of food and drink, plus the machine-pistol slung across his back. And he wasn't following a straight course. Just in case there *was* a sniper hidden somewhere who was biding his time before he started shooting, Watson was jigging from side to side as he ran.

Dawson jogged out a few seconds behind him, checked that his friend was heading in the right direction, then spun round to check the territory behind him. There was nobody and nothing in sight, and he could tell that they were still shielded from the view of the sniper by the copse of trees. He turned again and started running to catch up with Watson, following an erratic path across the ploughed and rutted field.

The distance they had to cover before they reached the hedge and the trees was about 150 yards – a matter of no more than about thirty seconds for even an average

sprinter, but laden down as they were, and with the way they were changing direction every few seconds, it took them almost two minutes to cover the distance.

Watson dodged around the end of the hedge, carefully lowered both bags to the ground, then slumped forward, his hands on his knees, panting with the exertion. Moments later, Dawson jogged up and stopped beside him, then turned back to survey the field they'd just run across.

'I don't see any Jerries,' he said, 'so I think we're in the clear, at least for the moment.'

'Fucking good job,' Watson muttered. 'I don't feel much like taking on a German patrol right now.'

'Got your breath back?' Dawson asked. 'Because we need to keep moving.'

'Yeah, I'm ready.'

Watson picked up the bag of mines, but as he reached for the other, lighter bag that contained their food, Dawson beat him to it and grabbed it.

'I'll carry this one, Dave,' he said, slinging the bag over his shoulder alongside the Schmeisser. 'I can still use the rifle, if I have to.'

The two men started walking briskly along the edge of the field, keeping the substantial hedge – which was probably at least ten feet high – on their left-hand side. Once again, they were heading more or less north, and, as far as Dawson could see, there was no way that anyone over to the west would be able to see them. That was where the sniper had to be, and that was where they'd seen the German patrol. What they had to do was keep going and hope that they could either out-run – or simply avoid – any other patrols.

They reached the end of the hedge and stopped while Dawson checked the next few hundred yards. It all seemed clear, and they covered the distance as quickly as possible. They carried on like that, jogging for short distances, then stopping and checking the next section, for over an hour.

Then, at the end of one long field, where they'd again taken advantage of a lengthy and fairly straight hedge, they stopped in a small copse to have a drink of water and another couple of slices of the dried sausage they'd taken from the deserted farmhouse. When they'd eaten, Dawson took out his hand-drawn map, checked his watch and looked at the position of the sun.

'I think we must be somewhere down here, to the south-west of Saarlouis,' he said, pointing at a spot on his sheet of paper, 'so we shouldn't keep going too far north, or we're going to start getting close to the built-up areas. We really need to start heading further over to the west, to get closer to the border.'

'That shouldn't be a problem, as long as we don't run into another patrol,' Watson said.

'OK, let's move.' Dawson stood up, picked up his weapons and the bag of food, now slightly lighter after their snack meal, and stepped forward. As he cleared the trees and stepped out into the field he suddenly stopped, freezing into immobility.

Then he leapt back into the shelter of the copse, dropped the food bag on the ground and swung up the Mauser.

Less than 100 yards in front of them, a six-man German patrol was walking straight towards them, and, as Dawson ducked behind a tree, a volley of shots crashed into the copse around them.

CHAPTER 24

'Fuck, oh, fuck,' Watson muttered, taking cover behind a large tree trunk and swinging up his machine-pistol, though the weapon would be useless at that range.

Next to him, Dawson dropped to the ground and lay prone, his legs apart, and wrapped the sling of the Mauser around his left arm to steady the rifle as he took aim. The members of the German patrol had separated, and were pointing their weapons at the copse of trees. As far as Dawson could see, only one of the soldiers was carrying a Schmeisser, which meant that the other five had rifles, and that was bad news. The only advantage he and Watson had was that they were in the copse, which meant they had some sort of cover. The patrol, on the other hand, was caught out in the open field, so they were vulnerable.

Another volley of shots crashed out, bullets tearing through the undergrowth and smashing into the trunks of the trees around them, as Dawson picked his target and gently squeezed the trigger.

The Mauser kicked against his shoulder, and the crack of the weapon firing echoed around the copse. Eighty

yards away, one of the German soldiers tumbled backwards and lay still.

'That's one down,' Dawson muttered, working the bolt to chamber another cartridge and moving the rifle slightly to seek out a new target. Whatever happened, he knew they had to even the odds, because there was no way he and Watson would survive a close-quarter firefight against four or five German soldiers. He had to take down as many of the patrol as he could, while they were still out there in the field. And there was another reason why he didn't want to let the enemy soldiers get too close.

He picked a second target and squeezed the trigger. But this time he saw his bullet throw up a spray of soil just to the left of the crouching man. He cursed, worked the bolt again and brought the rifle back to the aim, concentrating on the sight picture. The German was also aiming his rifle with care, and Dawson wondered fleetingly if either he or Watson could be clearly seen from the field.

Well, he thought, he'd soon find out. He took a breath, released about half of it and then stopped breathing, just as the instructors at Catterick had taught him. Then he squeezed the trigger gently. Even at that range, the sudden scarlet bloom of the German's face as the 7.92-millimetre bullet from the Mauser K98k ploughed through his forehead was absolutely obvious, and Dawson shuddered involuntarily as the man slumped to the ground, killed instantly.

He swallowed, worked the bolt and scanned the field for the next enemy soldier. As he did so, another burst of automatic weapons fire raked the trees and undergrowth close to him. For a few seconds Dawson ducked

down flat, burying his face in the grass, praying that the Germans were just laying down suppressing fire – trying to make them keep their heads down – rather than actually aiming at them.

The bullets howled and whined above his head, shredding undergrowth and slamming into the unyielding trees, the hammering sound of the Schmeisser ripping the air apart.

Then a brief moment of silence. Dawson lifted his head again, to aim the Mauser, but his targets were on their feet and moving, running and weaving in different directions. The German NCO in charge of the patrol had obviously realized that his men were sitting targets out in the open and had ordered them to scatter.

Dawson tracked one man as he ran to the left and fired the rifle, but his shot clearly missed as the German soldier continued running, snapping off wild shots towards the copse from his weapon as he did so.

Then, from his right-hand side, he heard a short burst of automatic fire, then another. Watson had waited until his targets were closer – a lot closer – before he'd opened up with his machine-pistol. The Schmeisser, which fired the nine-millimetre Parabellum round that was also used in several types of semi-automatic pistol, was too inaccurate at long distances. If he'd fired the weapon before, he'd just have been wasting ammunition.

'Got one,' Watson shouted, satisfaction mingled with fear in his voice.

'But there are still three of them left,' Dawson yelled back. 'Where the fuck are they?'

'They're trying to out-flank us. And when they're close enough, they'll use their grenades.'

That was Dawson's worry as well. The two sappers were effectively holding the high ground – they were hidden in the copse of trees, and their attackers were out in the open and vulnerable – so for the moment they held the advantage, but only until the Germans could get close enough to throw their grenades. Grenades are a great force-multiplier.

'You cover to the right, Dave. I'll go left,' Dawson instructed.

He checked all round. The sound of gunfire was still loud in his ears, and coming from both sides as the German soldiers tried to out-flank them. Bullets were thudding into the trees around them, but he had to move. He could see none of the enemy soldiers in front of him, which meant they had to be moving around on both sides of the copse. They had to do something before they managed to get close enough to throw their stick grenades.

The German *Stielhandgranate* Model 24 grenade – known to British troops as the 'potato masher' – was a much more deadly weapon than the familiar Mills bomb, entirely because of the wooden handle attached to it. The Mills bomb could only be thrown perhaps fifteen or twenty yards, but the stick acted as a lever on the German weapon, allowing it to be lobbed for more than twice that distance.

The two sappers knew that once the German troops closed to about forty yards, the grenades would start coming. And then they'd die, because there was nowhere to hide from a grenade. They *had* to keep the enemy soldiers at bay.

Dawson rolled sideways, then pushed himself up on

to his knees and looked through the undergrowth over to his left. He saw nothing, then raised himself slightly higher.

A grey shape moved across his field of vision, a bare thirty or forty yards away, firing a Schmeisser towards the copse. Dawson didn't hesitate. He stepped to one side, keeping the man in sight, then brought the Mauser up to his shoulder and aimed the weapon. As he looked over the sights, the soldier stopped, lowered his machine-pistol and reached towards his belt. He had to be reaching for a grenade.

Dawson steadied his hands, rested the rifle on the branch of a tree and took careful aim. As the German swung his arm back to throw the stick grenade, he squeezed the trigger. Against a stationary target at such short range, the outcome wasn't in doubt.

The enemy soldier tumbled backwards, the grenade falling from his dead hand, and two or three seconds later the explosive charge detonated right under the man's body, momentarily lifting the corpse upwards. But Dawson didn't even notice. By then he was already looking for his next target.

Close behind him, he heard another burst of machine-gun fire as Dave Watson fired his Schmeisser.

Dawson crept forward towards the edge of the copse, keeping behind the tree trunks as much as he could. Somewhere in front of him he could hear the hammering sound of another Schmeisser firing, the bullets ripping through the undergrowth close to him. Then, as he neared the edge of the stand of trees, the firing abruptly stopped.

Maybe Watson had got him, Dawson wondered, and

then an instant later realized how badly mistaken he was, as he saw the sight he'd been dreading the most. A grenade came sailing through the air, the wooden handle cartwheeling wildly, almost directly towards him.

'Grenade!' Dawson yelled, and immediately stood up. He dropped the Mauser, ran a few paces to the nearest tree and dodged behind it, getting the thickness of the trunk between himself and the weapon. Then he closed his eyes and covered his ears with his hands, forcing his palms tight against the side of his head.

The stick grenade had, he knew, about a five-second fuse from the moment the thrower unscrewed the metal base cap and pulled on the porcelain ball and cord held in the hollow wooden handle. That dragged a roughened steel rod through the igniter, causing it to flare and start the delayed-action fuse burning – an unusual but actually very reliable method of triggering the grenade.

Dawson also knew that the Model 24 was an offensive grenade, relying upon the blast wave from the exploding warhead – a high-explosive charge inside a thin steel canister – to do the damage, rather than a defensive fragmentation type. He knew the tree trunk would protect him from the limited amount of shrapnel that the weapon would throw out, and he just hoped his hearing wouldn't be too badly damaged by the blast wave.

An instant later the grenade exploded, perhaps twenty feet away from him, a colossal explosion that seemed to tear the very air to shreds and blast it in all directions. His head felt as if it was going to burst but, as far as he could tell, nothing hit him.

Dawson dropped his hands from his ears and peered

cautiously around the tree trunk. A renewed burst of firing from outside the copse – sounding strangely muffled to him – told him that the remaining two Germans were still out there and still shooting at them.

He grabbed the Mauser and pulled back the bolt. The rifle had a five-round magazine, and Dawson knew he'd fired four or maybe five shots. A cartridge spun out of the breach and tumbled to the ground beside him, and when he looked down he could see that the magazine was empty.

An empty rifle was no use to anyone, so he felt in one of the pouches on his battledress and pulled out a clip of shells. Like the Lee-Enfield .303, the Mauser Karabiner 98k was loaded from five-round clips, from which the cartridges were stripped into the magazine from above, with the bolt pulled back. Dawson pressed down on the gleaming brass case of the top shell with his thumb and pushed all of them down into the magazine. He slid the bolt forward to chamber the first cartridge, then replaced the stripper clip in his pouch, along with the ejected round.

Only then did he turn round to look for Watson. 'Dave!' he yelled. 'You OK?'

Watson didn't reply, but a burst of firing close by showed he was still alive, and still fighting.

Dawson nodded in relief and headed over towards the edge of the copse from which the grenade had been thrown, the Mauser held ready in his capable hands and the Schmeisser slung over his shoulder. He stopped while he was still largely concealed in the undergrowth and looked out, searching for any sign of the soldier who'd thrown the stick grenade. But the enemy soldier

appeared to be nowhere in sight. Dawson pushed on, getting closer to the edge of the field, his head turning from side to side as he sought his quarry.

Then he reached the side of the copse, scanning in all directions, but still saw no sign of the German soldier. He stepped back behind a tree, intending to move further over to the left, to search in that direction, when a rifle cracked. Dawson's sudden movement saved his life. The bullet sang past his chest and thudded into a tree somewhere behind him.

Only then did he spot the enemy soldier. He was lying prone in the field, about forty yards away, and already frantically working the bolt of his Mauser to chamber another round. Dawson swung up his own rifle, sighted quickly and squeezed the trigger.

But his shot missed, and, as Dawson pulled back behind a tree, the German fired again, the bullet hitting the trunk so close to Dawson that he was showered with wood splinters.

He made an instant decision. They could trade shots, or he could finish it quickly. He dropped the Mauser, swung the Schmeisser around his body, pulled the skeleton stock into his shoulder, seized the pistol grip and sighted down the barrel.

As the German soldier moved the rifle to point at him again, Dawson squeezed the trigger of the machine-pistol. The first bullets struck the ground a few feet in front of his target, but the muzzle was already lifting as he corrected his aim. He released the trigger, then squeezed it again, pulling the weapon back to the aim each time as the recoil lifted it. When the bolt of the MP 40 slammed open as the last round in the magazine fired,

the German lay dead, two bullets from Dawson's bursts of fire having ploughed through his skull.

Dawson was suddenly aware of the silence. From the moment they'd first seen – and in their turn been seen by – the German patrol, bullets had been flying all round the copse, fired by both sides. Now, though, he couldn't hear anything. He slipped a new magazine into the Schmeisser and cocked the weapon. Then he picked up the Mauser carbine and headed back into the copse.

CHAPTER 25

13 SEPTEMBER 1939

Just under an hour later, Dawson and Watson were on
the move again. The sixth member of the German patrol
had fallen victim to Watson's MP 40 at almost the same
moment as Dawson had used his machine-pistol on the
soldier on the opposite side of the copse, which accounted for the last member of the six-man patrol.

And now the two men were much better equipped.
They'd stripped the bodies of all the ammunition they
had been carrying, and Watson had appropriated another
Mauser K98k carbine, so each man was now armed with
both a rifle and a machine-pistol, plus several stick
grenades. And when Dawson had examined the body
of the NCO in charge of the patrol, as well as his
Schmeisser the man had also been carrying a Walther
P-38 semi-automatic pistol in a belt holster, with a couple
of spare magazines. Dawson took the lot, and slipped the
holster on to his own belt. The Walther fired the same
nine-millimetre Parabellum rounds as the Schmeisser.

They'd also dumped their eighteen-inch Lee-Enfield
bayonets, which wouldn't fit on the German rifles, and
had each taken a Mauser bayonet and scabbard from

the corpses. And Dawson had picked up a trench knife – a short-bladed single-edged weapon that was fitted into a boot scabbard and issued to Wehrmacht infantry soldiers.

But it wasn't just weapons and ammunition that they'd taken. All of the German soldiers had been carrying metal water canteens – a much better bet than the fragile glass jars Dawson and Watson had taken from the farmhouse – and even a few bars of chocolate. They took two canteens each, topped them up from the jars, and all the chocolate that wasn't covered in blood. And Dawson finally decided to abandon the mines. They were heavy and unwieldy and, realistically, if the two men couldn't fight their way out of trouble with the weapons and ammunition they now had, a bag of German mines probably wouldn't make any difference.

'I know it'll take a few minutes,' Dawson said, 'but I think we should try and hide the bodies. If we just leave them out on the field, the first German patrol that comes along here is going to spot them straight away. If we can conceal them in the undergrowth, that might buy us a little time.'

Together, they dragged all the bodies into the copse and dumped them in one of the most overgrown sections. They knew the smell of decomposition would soon attract scavengers, but the stand of trees was fairly remote, and hopefully nobody would find the dead bodies for a while.

Then they set off, and now they had three other things they hadn't had before – a military map of the area, a pair of binoculars and a compass, all of which Dawson had removed from the sergeant's body.

'This map's going to be bloody useful,' he said, as they started walking, once again keeping close to a substantial hedge that ran more or less north–south. 'I still don't know exactly where we are, but as soon as we see some kind of distinctive geographical feature I'll be able to work it out. And once we know that, we'll be able to pick the best possible route to get across the border.'

Watson seemed somewhat subdued, and responded only with a grunt.

'You OK, Dave?' Dawson asked.

'Yeah, I guess so. It's just so bloody different to what I expected. I mean, back at Catterick on the range we were just shooting at a cardboard target shaped like a man. Then bayonet practice was against bags filled with straw. But between us we've just killed six men, and then there were the others in the forest earlier.'

'This is war, Dave,' Dawson said simply.

'I know that, mate. I also know that all those Germans were doing their best to kill us, and if we hadn't been fucking lucky and pretty good shots, it'd be our bodies lying rotting in a field somewhere. But it's not easy, Eddie. It's not easy at all.'

Dawson nodded. What Watson had said pretty much coincided with his own feelings. In the thick of the action, adrenaline took over, and he had acted the way he'd been trained to do, not seeing the enemy soldiers as living, breathing human beings, but simply as targets to be engaged with whatever weapons he had available.

But when he'd walked out into the field to recover the weapons and ammunition and other equipment they needed, he'd been appalled at the injuries he'd seen. He'd stared at the gaping holes torn in the bodies of the

German soldiers by the bullets they'd fired, and in two cases the sight of their skulls almost literally blown apart, and it had taken all his resolve not to throw up.

No, Watson was right. It wasn't easy, and war was hell on earth. But they had no option, and Dawson was sure that Watson realized that. It was kill or be killed, an old and perhaps trite expression, but in their circumstances none the less absolutely true. They were deep in enemy territory, where the hand of every man would be raised against them, where any German soldier would be perfectly entitled to shoot them on sight. The only way they were going to get out and back to the safety of their own lines was to stay out of sight as much as they could and, if they were spotted, to fight back with as much skill and ferocity as they could manage. Any other course of action would end in their deaths, and both men knew it.

'I know, Dave, I know,' Dawson said, trudging along beside the hedge and constantly checking all around them, 'but we've no option, mate, no fucking option at all.'

By the end of the afternoon, it was clear to both men that Dawson's plan to cut across to the west and somehow work their way over the border back into France wasn't going to happen – or, at least, it wasn't going to be as easy as they'd hoped.

Within a couple of hours of leaving the copse, Dawson had identified three geographical features that had suggested their location, and then a village named Kerlingen, which they'd studied through the binoculars and which had confirmed exactly where they were. They'd covered rather more distance than he'd expected, almost ten miles in a straight line from the Warndt

Forest, and were now lying up in a wood on a low hill, overlooking another village, called Rammelfangen.

The problem wasn't their location, which was a bare two miles from the Franco-German border, it was the fact that, between them and that border, the area seemed to be swarming with German troops.

Back at the British camp on the outskirts of Dalstein, Lieutenant Charnforth had told them that the French had mounted an assault across the border, covering a front that was wide but not very deep, and had met with little resistance from the German forces. The trouble was, all the troops they'd seen so far were German, not French.

'Any Frogs down there?' Watson asked hopefully, lying beside Dawson in the undergrowth on the edge of the wood.

'Fuck all, mate. Wall-to-wall Jerries as far as I can tell.' Dawson lowered the binoculars and rubbed his eyes. 'Here,' he said. 'Take a look.'

Watson took the binoculars and began surveying the narrow plain that lay below the hill.

'Charnforth told us the French had captured about twenty villages that the Germans had abandoned,' Dawson remarked. 'Looking down there, I reckon it's completely deserted. No sign of any French troops, and all I can see everywhere else is Germans.'

'The French probably buggered off as soon as the Germans arrived, which is what you'd expect. First sign of trouble and they're off.'

'They're not that bad, are they?' Dawson asked. 'I thought the French army was pretty tough.'

'You think about it,' Watson said. 'In Britain we

celebrate a string of military victories, but all the Frogs do is mourn a bunch of glorious defeats. And you don't see any of them down there now, do you?'

'Can't argue with that.'

'If you're reading that map right, we're a mile or so from the border, so if Charnforth's information was right, those should be French troops down there, not Jerries. So, like I said, if the Frogs ever were here, they've obviously buggered off now.'

Dawson nodded and looked back over the view below them. The ground sloped away gently from the hill to the level fields that lay to the west. A few scattered buildings – farmhouses and farm cottages and the occasional barn or machinery shed – studded the landscape, and roads and tracks meandered alongside the hedgerows. It could almost have been a view of England, perhaps somewhere in the West Country or Wales or even the Borders, except for the troops.

Most of them were too far away – moving about close to the woodland that lay on the opposite side of the wide valley – for Dawson to see them clearly, but through the binoculars the coal-scuttle helmets and grey-green uniforms of the Wehrmacht troops were completely unmistakable. They hadn't tried to do an accurate count, but at a rough guess Dawson estimated there were about 200 German soldiers in front of them, plus about a dozen lorries and a hell of a lot of horses, apparently being used both as pack animals and also to pull carts loaded with supplies. But the number was frankly irrelevant. There was no way he and Watson were going to be able to slip past that concentration of troops without being noticed. And shot, obviously.

Watson lowered the binoculars and rested his chin on his hands. 'We ain't going that way,' he stated.

'Damn right,' Dawson agreed. 'In fact, we ain't going anywhere any time soon. There are too many troops coming and going down there for us to risk leaving this wood in daylight. I think we'll just have to hole up here until dark and then try and slip away.'

'Which way?' Watson asked.

Dawson looked at the German map which he'd placed on the ground right beside him. 'I think we need to move further north. In fact, I think we need to try to get all the way up here' – his fingers traced a route on the map – 'to the border with Luxembourg.'

'And then cross into France?'

Dawson shook his head. 'No. I think our safest route might be to cross into Luxembourg itself. I doubt if that border's heavily guarded, because Luxembourg's neutral, and it's not really got a military machine. The Germans would hardly be worried about an attack from that direction, and once we're in Luxembourg I'd guess that crossing the second border, the one into France, would be a lot easier.'

Watson looked at the map, at the route Dawson was suggesting, and nodded. 'It's not even that far to go,' he said. 'I mean, we've covered about half the distance already. So as long as we can avoid the Jerries once we leave here, we should get to the Luxembourg border by tomorrow evening, something like that.'

'As long as we don't meet any more trouble on the way, yes,' Dawson agreed. 'Though with our present track record, that's probably not very likely. Anyway, we'll go slowly and quietly and hope for the best.'

'And we keep on heading north, I suppose?'

'Maybe north-east to start with,' Dawson replied, 'depending on what we find when we get out of this wood. What we have to do is avoid any contact with those troops, so we might even have to head east to get clear of the area, and then swing round to the north.' He glanced at his watch. 'I guess we'll find out in about three or four hours, when it's dark enough to move.'

CHAPTER 26

13 SEPTEMBER 1939

'OK, it's about time. Let's go,' Dawson muttered and stood up. He slung the Mauser over his shoulder and checked his Schmeisser – if they met anyone, it would probably be at very close range, and the machine-pistol would be a more useful weapon than the rifle in that circumstance.

'Ready,' Watson acknowledged, and stood ready to follow Dawson along the meandering path that led down the gentle slope from the hill to the level farmland below.

They'd watched the activity on the plain diminish steadily as dusk fell and the darkness approached. There had been progressively less movement of troops and supplies as the shadows lengthened, and by early evening most of the German soldiers had assembled in makeshift camps consisting of groups of tents, sentries posted on the outskirts of each encampment.

That was what Dawson had been hoping would happen. The wood they'd taken shelter in was to the south of an unmade road the Germans had been using to transport men and materiel. It would have been very difficult to cross it unseen if the movements had continued

through the night, and they had to cross it to make any progress towards the north-west and the border with Luxembourg.

In silence, the two sappers walked down the track that snaked through the trees. At the very bottom of the hill there was a small clearing. Just before they entered it, Dawson held up his hand, and both men stood in watchful silence, carefully checking the land ahead of them, in case the Germans had positioned sentries there. But the clearing appeared completely empty in the moonlight, the only illumination.

Dawson stepped forward, Watson a few steps behind him.

'The road's about a hundred yards over there,' Dawson whispered, pointing to the north. 'I know it all seems quiet at the moment, but I still think we ought to head east for a while.'

The two men walked around the edge of the clearing, and emerged through the trees on the far side. Beyond the wood and the hill, the land was more or less flat, a network of cultivated fields with lanes and tracks snaking around them.

'This way,' Dawson muttered, and began walking slowly down a narrow track that turned into a field through an open gate. They stepped through the gateway and carried on walking down the side of the field in the same direction, Dawson holding the compass in his left hand and checking it periodically.

After about half a mile, he stopped. In front of them just outside the field was another lane or track, unmade and continuing to the east.

'I think this is about far enough, Dave,' he muttered.

'We don't want to go very far this way or we're going to get too close to that town over there – Pachten, I think it's called. It's time we tried to cross that road.'

Dawson led the way out of the field, across the unmade track and into the next field. The whole time both men scanned in all directions for any sign of trouble. The field was perhaps 400 yards wide, and they kept close to one end of it, where the fence and hedge offered some cover. At the far side they stopped and looked over the fence into the adjoining meadow.

'Empty,' Dawson muttered, 'but we must be getting close to the road now. Keep your eyes open.'

'I'm like a tree-full of owls, mate.'

The two men followed the same routine, crossing the field at one end, walking about twenty feet apart.

At the opposite side they stopped and again checked over the hedge. But this time, they could actually see the track the Germans had been using, because beyond this hedge was an area of unfenced waste ground, and the rutted and unmade road was clearly visible on the far side of it.

Also visible were two intermittent faint red glows that periodically brightened and then faded, but always stayed just visible.

'Bugger,' Dawson muttered. 'Two sentries, both smoking cigarettes. And there might be more of them – non-smokers, maybe – that we can't see, posted at intervals along the road.'

'Do you want to try to take them out? Rush them and then run for it?'

'No. Far too risky. I'd rather try and slip across the road without being spotted. If we use the pistol or the

Schmeissers, we'll wake up the entire camp back there and we'll end up running with a couple of hundred fucking Jerry soldiers hot on our trail. A really bad idea. If we do have to make a kill, we'll have to use the bayonets, but I really don't want to do that. We've no idea when these sentries are going to be relieved, and if we did kill one, his body might be found within minutes.'

'So we need to sneak across that road, somehow and somewhere?'

Dawson nodded. 'Definitely, even if we have to go another mile east.'

Watson took a final look over the hedge at the silent sentries. 'Then we'd best get moving,' he whispered.

An hour later, that's where they were – about a mile further east – having back-tracked some distance away from the unmade road before they again started heading in the general direction of Pachten.

'Right,' Dawson said, 'let's try again.'

As before, the two men moved slowly and as quietly as they could in a northerly direction, creeping across the deserted fields towards the road they needed to cross. The geography was much the same – fields separated by hedgerows and tracks used for farm machinery – but this time they had to cross three meadows before they reached a point where they could see the unmade road.

'What do you reckon?' Watson whispered, peering through a gap in the hedge.

'I don't see any sentries,' Dawson replied quietly, studying the land beyond the hedge just as carefully as his companion, 'but that doesn't mean there aren't any out there. Let's give it another few minutes, just in case.'

They waited in silence for perhaps another five minutes, but saw nothing to suggest that the Germans had posted any sentries along that stretch of the road.

'Right,' Dawson decided. 'Time's passing, and we've got a long way to go. Let's do it.'

They stood up cautiously, backed away from the hedge and checked their weapons. They each had their Mauser rifles slung diagonally across their shoulders and the straps of the Schmeissers around their necks, allowing the machine-pistols to hang directly in front of their chests, within easy reach.

Dawson reached down to his belt and drew out the Mauser bayonet, and motioned Watson to do the same.

'Just in case,' Dawson said. 'No noise.'

He led the way to a break in the hedge perhaps twenty yards away, then paused and for a few seconds just stared towards the road, alert to any sight or sound. He still neither saw nor heard anything, so he stepped cautiously through and took a dozen silent steps that brought him to the edge of the unmade track.

He glanced behind him, checking that Watson was ready to follow him, then looked both ways again and stepped out. He was barely half-way across when he heard a guttural shout from his left. He stopped immediately and half turned towards the sound.

Clearly visible in the pale moonlight was a German soldier, striding down the track, his Schmeisser pointed straight at him.

CHAPTER 27

13 SEPTEMBER 1939

Dawson stood stock still, his heart pounding. His hope was that, in the darkness, the sentry wouldn't be able to properly see either the outline of his helmet or the colour of his uniform, and might even mistake him for another German soldier because of the unmistakable shape of the Schmeisser machine-pistol hanging round his neck. He held the Mauser bayonet down beside his right leg, where it would be invisible to the approaching soldier.

The man barked something else at Dawson and gestured with the muzzle of his Schmeisser. Dawson turned further towards him, still keeping the bayonet out of sight, but otherwise didn't react.

The German soldier stopped about three or four feet away, and shouted something else. Dawson had no idea what he'd said – the only word of the German language he knew was *Achtung*, and he wasn't even sure what that meant – but he guessed the soldier might be asking for his papers. If the situation had been reversed, and Dawson had been on sentry duty and spotted an unknown man approaching, that's what he would have demanded. So he reached towards the top right-hand

pocket of his battledress, undid the button and slipped his fingers inside.

He pulled out a piece of folded paper, and realized it was the original printed order he'd been given, instructing him to report to Major Sykes at Cherbourg, what seemed like months ago. He extended his arm towards the German, but at that instant everything changed.

The sentry suddenly noticed something about Dawson – maybe his characteristic British helmet, or perhaps the design or the colour of his battledress – and snapped the Schmeisser up and into the firing position.

Dawson dropped the paper and immediately swung the bayonet towards the German, but even as he did so he knew that he was too slow – a lifetime too slow.

But before the enemy soldier could pull the trigger of his machine-pistol, a dark shape materialized behind him, and Dawson saw a sudden flash of steel. A hand reached over the man's shoulder, wrapped itself around his mouth, jerking his head back, and simultaneously the gleaming steel blade of a bayonet ripped through his throat, tearing the life from his body as a spray of blood fountained upwards.

The German soldier slumped forward, his limbs twitching in his death throes. Behind him, Dave Watson lowered the man's body to the ground, the blade of his bayonet dripping blood on to the surface of the road.

'Thanks a lot, Dave,' Dawson said hoarsely, as he stepped forward. He'd looked death in the eyes, and hadn't much enjoyed the experience. 'I owe you one. Let's get him out of sight.'

While Watson cleaned the blood off the blade of his

bayonet on the dead man's clothes, Dawson picked up the sheet of paper – he knew that leaving that piece of evidence behind would be a really bad idea. And then, together, the two men lugged the body of the German soldier off the side of the road and into the adjoining field to the south. They dragged him about thirty yards, then dropped the corpse behind a clump of low bushes.

'Somebody's bound to find him pretty soon,' Dawson muttered. 'When the watch changes and another soldier arrives to relieve him they're going to know he's missing. All we can hope is that maybe they'll think he's gone AWOL.'

'Maybe,' Watson agreed, 'but we'll need to get rid of the blood on the road right now or it'll be obvious someone killed him. I never thought he'd bleed that much.'

'You must have cut through one of the arteries in his neck.'

There was a substantial dark stain marring the surface of the unmade road where the German sentry had met his untimely end, clearly visible in the light from the moon, but it was an easy job to toss a few handfuls of loose soil over it. That, Dawson knew, probably wouldn't be enough to hide what had happened when dawn broke, but hopefully in the darkness it would be enough to conceal the stain. And, at the very least, even if the Germans discovered the dead body, they would still have no idea who'd killed the man or which way his attacker or attackers were going.

The two men checked in both directions that there were no more enemy soldiers in sight, then strode swiftly

across the road and vanished through a gate and into the field that bordered the northern side.

The moon chose that moment to disappear behind a cloud, plunging the landscape into full darkness and, moments later, Watson tripped on the uneven ground and fell heavily, his equipment clattering and banging.

Almost immediately, there was a challenge in German from somewhere behind them.

'Fucking hell,' Dawson muttered, as he and Watson automatically ducked down into cover behind a low mound in the field.

'They must have heard,' Watson said.

Dawson risked a quick glance around the side of the mound, keeping his head pressed well down into the long grass that covered it.

The moon was emerging fitfully from behind one of the clouds that partially covered the sky. On the road, no more than thirty yards away, two German soldiers were standing and staring in their direction, their faces pale and anonymous blobs in the semi-darkness, their weapons – both were armed with rifles – held across their bodies. They'd obviously heard the two men, or at least heard the noise Watson had made, but didn't know exactly who or what had caused it.

'There are two of them,' Dawson whispered. 'Stay really still. They might just go away.'

But somehow that didn't look likely. The two German soldiers remained immobile but obviously alert, clearly highly suspicious of the noise they'd heard, but apparently unwilling to venture off the road to investigate it.

'If we move, they'll see us,' Dawson whispered, 'and if they see us, they'll shoot.'

'Bugger,' Watson muttered.

The two German soldiers held a muted conversation, then one of them moved slightly to one side and brought his rifle up to his shoulder to aim it into the field, while the other stepped forward, heading directly towards the mound behind which the two sappers had taken refuge.

And right then Dawson realized they were fresh out of options. They couldn't use their bayonets or the trench knife, because the enemy soldiers had separated – they might be able to kill one of them that way, but certainly not the other. They'd have to use their guns, and use them now, while they still had the element of surprise. And then they'd have to run for it.

Dawson watched the approaching German soldier as he strode closer to the mound of earth they were using for cover. When the man reached a point about ten yards away, Dawson tensed and rested his finger on the trigger of the Schmeisser – the machine-pistol was the obvious weapon to use at such close quarters.

But then the German stopped. He stood on one spot for a few seconds, scanning the ground in front of him and all around. Then he shrugged, turned away and walked back to the road to rejoin his companion.

Again, the two Germans exchanged a few sentences, and this time both men heard a couple of the words clearly.

'He just said something about *Geräusche*,' Watson said quietly – he'd done a basic German course the previous year. 'That means "noises", and then he used the word *Schlachtrösser*, which means "horses". Maybe he thinks that noise was made by some of the horses they've been using to pull the carts.'

'Christ, I hope so. I don't want to kill anyone else unless it's unavoidable.'

For another few seconds, the two German soldiers chatted together on the road, then both lit cigarettes and walked away, side by side, heading west and away from the two sappers.

Dawson and Watson waited a couple of minutes after the two enemy soldiers had vanished from sight, then both stood up slowly and carefully.

'Right,' Dawson said quietly. 'Let's get the hell away from here before they come back, or start wondering where the sentry is.'

'I'm right behind you.'

Dawson made a very quick check of his compass, the illuminated pointer and cardinal markers dimly visible, then led the way through the field to the north. Just as they reached the far side of it, both men stopped. They'd heard a sudden noise from directly in front of them, on the opposite side of another hedge, a deep snort, like a man with a really bad cold.

'Fuck me, not again,' Watson muttered, as he seized the pistol grip of his Schmeisser MP 40.

'Wait,' Dawson whispered and crept over to one side, where he could see a narrow gap in the undergrowth. Holding his machine-pistol ready, he looked through the space he'd found. For a few seconds he just stared at the sight beyond. Then he stood up and turned back to Watson, a grin on his face.

'That German was right,' he said. 'This field's full of horses.'

'Thank God for that. Let's move.'

The two men squeezed through the gap and started

walking. There were about twenty horses in the field, big friendly shapes, tethered in lines. Some were standing and eating, others lying down, and all looked inquisitively at the two men as they made their way past them.

'Shame we can't borrow a couple of them and ride off into the sunset. Or perhaps the sunrise, in this case,' Watson said.

'Yeah, I was just thinking about that. But there are no saddles or bridles and – I don't know about you – but I don't know how to ride a bloody horse. We're much better off on foot.'

About an hour later, they came to a stop again, this time because they were standing on the southern bank of a river. Dawson pulled out the map and used his small torch to study it for a few moments.

'Right,' he said, 'this section of the river looks fairly straight and it's lying north-east to south-west, so I think we must be somewhere here.' He pointed at a position on the map close to a town named Rehlingen. 'This river branches off the Saar just to the north-east of here, and runs all the way down to the border near another town named Niedaltdorf.'

Knowing where they were helped, but what they had to do was get across the river, which was wide and looked deep.

'Is there a bridge somewhere?' Watson asked hopefully.

'Yeah, several of the bastards, but I think our best bet would be to head north-east and cross it here.' He again pointed at the map.

'That'll take us pretty close to Rehlingen, and that

looks to me like a main road as well,' Watson said, peering at the map. 'Sure that's a good idea?'

'I'd prefer to cross the river somewhere else, but we already know that the area closer to the border is well guarded, so going in that direction might be a worse option. I'm just hoping that the bridge near Rehlingen won't be guarded.'

Dawson replaced the map in his pocket and the two men started walking along the bank of the river, keeping a sharp lookout, as they had been ever since the Warndt Forest. The ground was sloping gently upwards, but the going was fairly easy, and the moonlight was sufficient for them to see.

Ten minutes later, Dawson held up his hand and stopped. 'There's the bridge,' he whispered, pointing ahead of them.

In the monochrome moonlight, they could see a structure of stone and steel that spanned the river about 200 yards ahead, a coat-hanger-shaped bridge that obviously carried a road from one bank to the other. They could also see an army truck – it looked like about a three-tonner – parked at the nearer end of it, and dimly visible were the shapes of several soldiers standing near the vehicle.

'Bugger,' Watson whispered. 'What do you reckon? Has the truck broken down, or is that a checkpoint?'

Dawson didn't reply, just ducked into cover and stared at the scene through his binoculars. After a few moments he lowered them and glanced at his companion.

'It looks to me like a road-block,' he said. 'I can see what looks like a wooden barrier across the road beside

the truck. And that,' he added, 'just might be good news for us.'

Watson looked quizzically at his companion. 'Explain that,' he said.

'Those troops will probably have been ordered to stop and check the papers of any pedestrians or drivers who want to cross over that bridge. It's just about midnight now, so they're probably also quite tired if they've been there for several hours, so maybe their concentration will be starting to go.'

'So what?'

'So all their attention will be focused on checking people crossing over the bridge, and they probably won't be quite as alert as they should be, so hopefully they won't notice us crossing *under* the bridge.'

Watson looked from Dawson to the bridge, and then back again.

'Oh, shit,' he muttered.

CHAPTER 28

14 SEPTEMBER 1939

Watson took the binoculars from Dawson and stared through them for a couple of minutes. Underneath the roadway that spanned the river was a lattice of steel girders that supported the structure. Crossing that way looked difficult, dangerous and possibly even less likely of success than simply trying to swim across. He lowered the binoculars and glanced back at his companion.

'Fancy yourself as a monkey, then, do you? I don't like to remind you, but we're both carrying two weapons. We've got webbing belts stuffed full of ammunition and a few grenades, plus all the rest of the gear we've picked up along the way. Laden down like this, I don't think we're really in a position to swing along under that fucking bridge like a couple of chimpanzees. I'd rather take my chances, shoot the sentries and then run over it. Aren't there any other bridges we can use?'

Dawson pulled out the map again, checked that they were completely invisible to the German soldiers manning the bridge and turned on his torch for a few seconds. Then he switched it off again.

'There's nothing else marked until you get really close

to the border, back the way we've come,' he said. 'I don't think we've got a lot of options, mate.'

'Bugger,' Watson muttered. 'What about swimming across?'

The two sappers glanced to their left, at the wide river that glinted in the moonlight. As they'd thought before, it looked deep, and seemed to be quite fast-flowing. It would probably be a challenge even in daylight for a powerful swimmer wearing nothing but a costume.

'With what we're carrying,' Dawson said, 'I think we'd drown before we got ten feet from the bank. And there's another reason – I can't actually swim.'

'I could try and teach you, really quickly,' Watson suggested with a grin.

Dawson shook his head. 'No, I think we've either got to use the bridge, or go even further east and look for another way over. And that would take us too close to Rehlingen for my liking.'

'Bugger,' Watson said again. 'So how do we do it?'

Dawson stared down the riverbank towards the bridge for a moment or two. Trees, bushes and undergrowth lining the south bank of the river would offer reasonable cover as they approached the structure.

'I think we can get pretty close without any chance of them seeing us,' he said, 'just by following the bank of the river through those trees. Then we'll have to wait for a vehicle – any vehicle – to approach the checkpoint, because, while they're looking at that and checking the driver's papers and stuff, they won't be looking over the side of the bridge. That'll be our best chance.'

Watson shook his head. 'Bloody risky, but we don't have any other choices,' he said.

The two sappers checked that none of the weapons and equipment they were carrying would rattle or make any other noise, and set off, working their way as quietly as they could through the sheltering undergrowth. For the first 100 yards or so, there was no problem in staying completely hidden from the view of any of the enemy soldiers on the bridge, but the closer they got to the structure, the more sparse the vegetation became, and the more difficult it was to remain under cover.

They stopped about fifty yards from their objective and studied the ground ahead of them, which didn't look that promising. Once they got to the bridge they'd be completely out of sight of the soldiers manning the checkpoint, because there was a pathway that ran underneath it, along the riverbank. If they could reach that point, they'd be able to climb up on to the framework of steel girders and make their way across the river undetected. They hoped. The trick was getting to the bridge itself.

The heavy undergrowth had largely petered out, to be replaced by clumps of low bushes that would hide them, certainly, but which would provide very little cover while they were actually moving.

And that presented them with something of a dilemma. If they moved slowly between the bushes, they'd be exposed for quite a long period each time they changed position, but moving faster meant they would be more likely to be seen by the German soldiers, because the human eye is very well adapted to detect movement.

'Bit of a bugger, this,' Watson muttered.

Then, from some distance off to their right, they saw a sudden loom of light. It looked as if a vehicle of some

sort was heading towards the bridge, along the road that led past Rehlingen and on to Saarlouis.

Dawson glanced up at the soldiers manning the checkpoint. They'd hitched up their weapons and were obviously getting ready to stop whoever was driving down the road.

'This could be the best chance we'll get,' he whispered. 'They'll all be staring towards the headlights, and that'll bugger up their night vision. We'll wait until the truck or whatever it is gets a bit closer, and then we'll make a run for it.'

The two men crouched down, watching the headlights – the illumination from which was actually little more than two thin slits of light, because the headlamps had obviously been fitted with blackout screens – move closer. The vehicle slowed perceptibly as it approached the bridge, the driver clearly having seen the armed men and the road-block in front of him.

On the bridge, the German soldiers fanned out, moving around behind the barrier and preparing their weapons so that each of them would have a clear field of fire towards the incoming vehicle if the driver failed to stop. But clearly that wasn't going to happen, because the truck was already almost at a standstill. Dawson could now see that the vehicle was a small six-wheeled military truck, with a low, sloping bonnet, an open cab behind it and a passenger or cargo area behind that. There were at least two people sitting in the cab, but there appeared to be nobody in the rear section, so possibly it was taking supplies from Rehlingen to the German lines close to the border, or maybe heading over that way to pick up some troops.

Dawson frankly didn't care why the truck was on the bridge – he was just grateful that it was, because the vehicle's arrival gave them the opportunity they so desperately needed.

'Get ready, Dave,' he said and started moving around one side of the bush where they'd taken refuge. 'OK, let's go.'

The two men walked – not ran – to the next piece of cover and ducked down again. No shouts of alarm greeted them, no challenges of any sort.

'And again,' Dawson said shortly and immediately started moving.

They were now less than twenty yards from the bridge, but as they stepped out from behind the scrubby bush, there was nothing else in front of them, between them and their objective, apart from grass. Nothing that offered any cover at all. They just had to hope that the soldiers were concentrating all their attention on the truck, and that nobody was peering over the edge of the bridge into the fields surrounding it.

But one of the German soldiers obviously *was* looking their way, or perhaps he'd caught sight of them in his peripheral vision, because as the two sappers dived for cover under the bridge, there was a sudden shout of alarm from above them. The shout was followed instantly by a burst of fire from a Schmeisser machine-pistol, the bullets raking the ground behind them.

'That's fucking torn it,' Watson said, unslinging his Schmeisser and swiftly checking it.

'Another good idea down the pan,' Dawson agreed. He pulled a stick grenade from his belt and unscrewed the metal cap from the end. 'Wait here,' he said, heading

for the far side of the bridge. 'With any luck, they'll be looking for us on that side, where they saw us running, not over here. I'll lob a grenade up there. Once it goes off, you do the same from that side.'

He ran to the far side of the bridge, took a couple of paces out from under its protection, and glanced up. He saw nobody looking down, so he held the weapon in his right hand, pulled down the ceramic ball to arm the grenade with his left, and then lobbed it as hard as he could upwards and backwards, trying to deliver the weapon as close as possible to the spot where they'd seen the sentries standing.

He heard shouts of alarm from above, as at least one of the German soldiers saw the stick grenade spinning towards them. Then there was a colossal blast that seemed to shake the very bridge itself. A moment of silence, and then a man started screaming.

Dawson knew they had to take advantage of the situation. This was no time for sentiment or mercy – they had to finish the job before any of the German soldiers still alive could recover their wits. Despite the damage the grenade had obviously inflicted, he and Watson were still heavily outnumbered. They had to kill or incapacitate the rest of the enemy soldiers, and as quickly as they could.

Dawson took another grenade from his belt, removed the end cap and stepped over to the side of the bridge again. But as he prepared to throw the weapon, a rifle cracked above him and a bullet buried itself in the ground a mere foot or two away from him.

Then another blast echoed from above him, as Watson's grenade detonated somewhere on the other

side of the bridge. Dawson took advantage of the timing. He stepped out into the open again, pulled the ceramic ball of the second grenade and threw it up and backwards, then stepped back under the bridge just as the third blast tore through the air. The screaming stopped in that instant.

'You OK, Dave?' he shouted.

Watson was standing close to the far side of the bridge, his machine-pistol in his hands. 'Yeah. Now we go and finish this, right?' he asked.

Dawson nodded. 'No other option, mate. And quick as we can before a Jerry patrol comes looking for trouble. You go this side. I'll take the other.'

Watson nodded, peered upwards at the balustrade of the bridge above them, then stepped forward, turning left to run towards the road that led to Rehlingen, to find a place where he could climb up on to the road itself and get on to the bridge.

On the other side, Dawson mirrored his actions, and seconds later both sappers were striding down the road towards the carnage on the bridge, their machine-pistols held ready, their fingers resting on the triggers, ready for instant action.

Most of the German soldiers had been caught out in the open when the first grenade exploded, and it looked as if the only men who had survived that blast had been those who had been standing on the opposite side of the bridge, to the left of the six-wheeled truck. That had shielded them from most of the effects of the detonation, but when Watson's grenade had exploded behind them, the situation had been reversed, and they'd been cut down as well.

Looking around, Dawson realized the effects had been simply devastating in the relatively confined space of the road bridge. Four German soldiers lay close to the right-hand side of the bridge parapet, and he guessed that three of them had most likely been killed by the detonation of his first grenade, and the fourth had probably been the soldier who'd fired his Mauser over the side of the bridge at him. On the left-hand side, two other unmoving bodies lay sprawled across the road surface.

The six-wheeled truck had stopped at the drop-down barrier, more or less in the centre of the road, and the two shapes slumped in the cab suggested that they hadn't survived the blasts either.

'Jesus, Eddie,' Watson muttered, as they walked around the bodies that lay scattered over the road.

Then Dawson saw a slight movement over to his right, as one of the German soldiers – clearly badly wounded, the front of his uniform soaked with blood – attempted to swing his Schmeisser towards them.

Dawson didn't hesitate for even a second. He aimed his machine-pistol and squeezed the trigger, and the burst of half a dozen nine-millimetre bullets mercifully ended the life of the wounded man.

'Check them all, Dave,' Dawson ordered tersely, 'just in case any of them aren't quite as dead as they look. And it'll be a mercy killing if you do have to finish one off.'

Watson nodded and walked over to the left-hand side of the bridge, while Dawson checked the other bodies on the right. Then he looked at the two men in the cab of the truck. They'd had nowhere to run, and nowhere to hide, and the blasts from both sides had done horrendous damage to their heads and upper bodies.

The engine of the truck was still running, and for a few seconds Dawson just looked at the vehicle. Then he leant forward, grabbed the arms of the dead soldier sitting in the passenger seat and started hauling him out of the cab.

'What're you doing?' Watson demanded

'I'm getting fucking fed up with walking,' Dawson snapped, 'and I reckon this truck will take us a good few miles closer to the border before we have to abandon it. Here, give me a hand getting these two out.'

'You don't think any Germans we meet might be suspicious if they saw a German army truck being driven around on this side of the border by a couple of British squaddies?'

'They might,' Dawson agreed, 'but if we borrow a pair of these coal-scuttle helmets I reckon we'll look the part.'

'Isn't that against the Geneva Convention or something?' Watson asked.

'Right now, I don't give a flying fuck about the Geneva Convention or anything else. I just want to get the hell out of Germany as quickly as possible, and if wearing a couple of German helmets is going to help us do that, then I for one will bloody well risk it.'

'OK,' Watson said. 'And we might be able to shoot our way out of trouble anyway. We seem to have been getting quite good at that,' he added.

CHAPTER 29

14 SEPTEMBER 1939

Together, they half dragged, half lifted the two bodies out of the truck and lowered them to the road. Then they picked out a selection of weapons from the dead soldiers – the Schmeisser MP 40 was particularly prone to jamming and stoppages, so having a couple of spare machine-pistols each, plus all the magazines they could find, seemed like a good idea and, as they now had a form of transport at their disposal, the extra weight wouldn't be a problem. They also took all the grenades the soldiers had been equipped with, and two more Mauser K98k rifles.

Finally, they removed a couple of the German coal-scuttle helmets from the bodies and tucked their British versions away in the cab of the truck.

'It's what people think, not what they know,' Dawson said as he adjusted the chin strap. 'And if we drive past them in Germany, in a German truck, both of us wearing German helmets, people will automatically think we're Germans, despite the different-coloured uniforms. They'll probably assume we're just from a regiment they've not seen before. That's what I hope, anyway.'

'Yeah, likewise. You want to drive, or ride shotgun?'

'You drive,' Dawson said. 'I'll map-read and keep my eyes open.'

Watson climbed behind the wheel and spent a few minutes locating all the controls. Then he pushed the gear lever into first and eased the heavy truck forward as Dawson lifted the drop-down barrier, which had still been in the lowered position. He stopped just beyond the barrier, waited for Dawson to climb into the passenger seat and then released the clutch. The truck lurched clumsily and the engine stalled, but his second attempt was better, and the vehicle juddered off down the road.

'Which way are we going?' Watson asked.

Dawson was bent forward, looking at the captured map, which he'd spread open on his knee, and the compass, by the light of his torch.

'We're heading north-west, and we're on the main road that runs past Saarbrücken and Saarlouis and then goes through Saarburg and all the way up to a place called Trier, which is a long way further north than we want to go. I think it would be a bloody good idea to try and get off this fairly soon. The Germans are bound to be using the main roads to move their troops and supplies around, so we need to try and find some country roads we can travel along instead. Just give me a minute and I'll see what other options there are. How's the fuel level, by the way?'

Watson scanned the dimly lit and very basic instrument panel in front of him and finally thought he'd found what he was looking for. 'If that *is* the fuel gauge,' he said, 'it looks like there's about three-quarters of a tank.'

'No problem. And even if the thing does run out of

fuel, we'll still be a lot closer to the Luxembourg border than we were before, so it's a no-lose situation.'

The German truck lumbered on for about five minutes while Dawson studied the map, trying to choose the best route to get them as close as possible to the Luxembourg border before they tried to cross it. They knew the crossing itself would have to be on foot – trying to drive a German truck into neutral Luxembourg was never going to work, for obvious reasons, but if they could get to within about a mile or so, they should be able to cross back into France within days, maybe even that very day.

'OK,' Dawson said. 'If we keep on going, we'll have to drive right through a town called Fitten, and there might well be other road-blocks there. Now, there's a junction coming up any time now. There probably won't be any signposts, of course, but what we're looking for is the road to either Biringen or Hilbringen. That'll take us off this road and a bit closer to the German border, but that's still a better option than staying on it.'

Less than five minutes later a junction loomed up on the left, and in the distance over to the west they could see a peak rising in the moonlight.

'That high-point should be the Alte Berg,' Dawson said, 'so that's definitely the right direction. That road might not be the one we're looking for, but it'll do. Take it.'

Watson swung the truck across to the other side of the main road and then drove down a much narrower road, actually more like a farm track, albeit one that had been covered in tarmac at some point in the past.

Dawson temporarily abandoned the map and just

concentrated on studying his compass. 'We're going the right way,' he said. 'We're now heading north-west, and that's more or less the right direction, and I think I know which of the roads marked on the map this one is. Well, which one of two roads, actually.'

'You know we're in a moving vehicle made of steel,' Watson pointed out, 'so the reading you're getting on that compass might not be entirely accurate?'

'I know, and the metal around us probably is having some effect on it, but I still think it's about right. Anyway, keep on going for the moment.'

The minor road swung left and right, the surface quality ranging from bad to poor, but the overall direction stayed fairly constant, which pleased Dawson, who now thought he knew exactly which road they were following.

'I reckon we're around half a mile south of Hilbringen,' he said, 'so just carry on. We should come across a main road – a crossroads – in about two or three miles, and that'll be the road running from Fitten due west to Scheuerwald. We need to cross over that and carry on heading north-west, but the moment I think we're getting close to the crossroads we'll stop and check out the lie of the land. I definitely don't want us to drive straight into another road-block.'

'Amen to that,' Watson muttered.

Ten minutes later, they saw a few lights some distance ahead of them. Watson immediately slowed and stopped the truck, killing the vehicle's headlights and turning off the engine as he did so. For a moment, they sat in silence, the only sound the ticking of the truck's engine as it started to cool.

Dawson took out the binoculars and studied the scene. 'OK,' he said. 'From what I can see, it looks like that's the main road. There are a couple of vehicles – they look pretty big, so they're probably army lorries – driving along it, and heading west, towards the border.'

'What about road-blocks or troops?' Watson asked.

'None that I can see right now,' Dawson replied, still staring through the binoculars. 'Hang on a second. Let me just take a look down the road we're on, see if there's any sign of anything there.'

Bracing his elbows on the dashboard in front of him, Dawson focused the binoculars on the road, and as far as he could he covered the whole length of it from where they were parked at that moment right up to the main road itself. The moonlight helped a lot, because the tarmac surface was clearly visible, and the only sections he couldn't cover were those where the ground dipped down or the road moved behind clumps of trees or bushes. But what he didn't see were any German soldiers, or any stationary vehicles that might indicate the presence of a road-block.

Dawson waited until the two vehicles he could see had moved well out of sight, then nodded to Watson.

'OK, Dave. I think we're clear. Let's get moving, but keep the lights switched off, just in case.'

Watson started the engine, engaged first gear and got the vehicle moving again. He was now more used to the fierce clutch, and the truck hardly lurched at all as he accelerated away. The moon was still out, and the winding road clearly visible, but Watson kept the speed down to little more than walking pace, to ensure he'd be

able to stop well before any potential danger they might encounter.

The last section of the minor road, before it climbed up a gentle slope to intersect the main road that crossed it at right angles, was almost straight, and again Dawson told Watson to stop the truck while he checked the land ahead through the binoculars.

After a couple of minutes he lowered them and shook his head. 'If there *is* a checkpoint up there, I'm buggered if I can see it. The junction looks clear, and there's no sign of any traffic moving along the road in either direction.'

'So we go?'

Dawson nodded. 'Yes, let's go. But get ready just in case I've missed something.'

Watson nodded, reached down into the cab beside him and picked up a Schmeisser. He checked the magazine was fully loaded, a round ready in the chamber, then slung the weapon around his neck. It might interfere with his driving, but it would be ready for immediate use, which was far more important.

Dawson placed one machine-pistol on the seat right beside him, between him and Watson, then took another one, checked that as well and held it ready to fire. Then he again nodded to his companion. 'Let's go.'

Watson accelerated away, up the slope towards the main road, looking all around him for any signs of danger, while beside him Dawson did exactly the same, his machine-pistol aimed over the front of the truck.

They reached the edge of the main road. Watson drove up on to the much better surface. 'Which way?' he asked, looking ahead and expecting to see another road heading north. 'I thought you said this was a crossroads.'

Dawson glanced in both directions. 'It is on the map,' he said. 'Hell, just go left, and put the bloody lights on. If anyone sees us driving without lights in the middle of the night on this road they're bound to try to stop us.'

Watson hit the light switch, then swung the wheel and accelerated, moving the truck over to the right-hand side of the road, looking ahead for any sign of a junction.

Dawson used his torch to check the map again, but the scale was too small to show the exact shape of the road junction. It *looked* like the road they'd driven up connected with an almost identical minor road going north, but there was no sign of it that either of them could see.

'I think we're getting too close to the border,' Dawson said, after a couple of minutes. 'Do a U-turn and we'll try the other way.'

Watson obediently swung the truck round – the road was just wide enough to allow him to turn the vehicle in a single manoeuvre – and headed back the way they'd come.

'That's where we drove up,' Dawson said, pointing to a junction on the right, 'so the other road should be somewhere on the left.'

Watson steered the truck over to the left-hand side of the main road and slowed down slightly as both men stared ahead.

'There it is,' Dawson said, pointing with the barrel of his Schmeisser.

Just coming into view was a narrow road that led away somewhere to the north.

'Got it.' Watson swung the truck out towards the centre of the main road, to give him enough room to

make the turn, then steered to the left. The truck lurched and bounced as it left the comparatively smooth surface of the main road and on to the rutted and uneven minor road, but that didn't bother either man.

'Thank God for that,' Dawson said. 'I felt really exposed up there on that road. I was expecting a road-block or a truck full of German soldiers any second.'

Watson grinned at him, then turned his attention back to the twisting and poorly surfaced road in front of them. 'Here,' he said, 'take this, will you?' He lifted the Schmeisser from around his neck and passed it over to Dawson, who checked that the safety catch was on, and then stowed it between them in the cab.

Dawson checked the map again. 'If this map is accurate,' he said, 'that road was the biggest problem. We shouldn't have to cross or go along any other main routes, so with any luck we won't run into any road-blocks. But we're almost bound to see German troops somewhere around here, because we're still pretty close to the French border.'

'So where are we heading for now?' Watson asked.

'This road swings round further to the north pretty soon,' Dawson said, again looking at the map, 'and it goes through a village or town named Nohn. With any luck, that'll be deserted, just like that other village we saw a while back, Rammelfangen. It was full of Jerry soldiers, but all the local inhabitants had buggered off.

'Anyway, from Nohn, the road turns back towards the north-west and goes through Orscholz, Kesslingen and Münzingen.' He stumbled slightly over the unfamiliar German names. 'Or there's another road – it's a shorter route – that we could use, but it's probably going to have

more enemy soldiers on it because it's closer to the French border. That runs almost due west from Orscholz through Borg to Wochern.'

'I'd rather take the pretty route if we're less likely to meet any Jerries,' Watson said, steering the truck around a bend.

'Good thinking. Me too. So just keep going along here for the moment.'

'How far is it to this Nohn place?'

'A couple of miles. We should be there in a few minutes.'

In fact, the road surface started deteriorating considerably almost as soon as Dawson spoke, and Watson was forced to slow down the truck to little more than walking pace as he drove over the worst of it. The truck was built for hard work, but they really didn't want to have to cope with a puncture or a breakdown, so taking it slowly seemed like their best option.

Minutes later, and almost without realizing it, they were driving through the silent and deserted streets of Nohn. One moment they were in open country, and then what Dawson thought was a barn appeared on the right-hand side of the road. They drove past it, followed the road around to the right and found they'd entered the village itself.

'Bloody good job there wasn't a Jerry road-block,' Watson muttered. 'We'd have driven straight into it.'

'Or gone straight through it,' Dawson suggested, 'but you're right. I thought we were still way out in the country-side. It just shows we need to keep a sharper lookout. If there had been enemy soldiers waiting there, we'd have been sitting ducks in this tin can.'

They drove out the other side of Nohn without incident, without seeing a soul, not even an animal. The truck lumbered on through the night along the road that still, as far as Dawson could tell from his compass, was heading roughly north-west. Orschloz was, like Nohn, totally deserted, though this time they stopped a couple of hundred yards from the edge of the developed area and checked it with the binoculars before they drove in.

At the far end of the village Watson pulled the truck to a stop at a fork in the road and looked across at his companion.

'Right,' Dawson said, holding the map so that Watson could see it. 'It's time to make up our minds. That road' – he pointed at the left-hand branch of the forked junction – 'is the most direct route. That's the one that goes due west, through Borg to Wochern. The other one is the long way round; that'll get us to Luxembourg about five miles north of the French border.'

Watson glanced at the map, then at the two choices in front of them. 'What do you think? I mean, we've seen nobody since we crossed that main road. This whole area seems to have been completely abandoned.'

Dawson nodded. 'I know, but we're about five miles from the border here. I'm pretty bloody sure that if we get very much closer to it we'll start running into Jerry patrols. I vote we take the right-hand fork and head north-west through Kesslingen and Münzingen, and stay a good few miles clear of the border. It'll add a bit to the journey, but I still think it'll be safer.'

Watson didn't reply for a few seconds, then nodded. 'Yeah. Let's keep on the pretty route. We've got all night, and all day, come to that.'

'Actually,' Dawson said, looking over to the east, 'there's not much of the night left. It looks to me like dawn's about to break. We need to get a move on. We can't risk moving in daylight once we're near the border, because there'll certainly be more patrols. We need to find somewhere to hole up for the day.'

He looked back at the map. 'We're at Orscholz now. Kesslingen's only about another couple of miles away, so let's get there as quickly as we can. We can either find somewhere to hide there, or forge on to Münzingen. OK?'

'OK,' Watson replied, put the truck into gear and swung the steering wheel to the right.

Because of what they'd found in Nohn and Orscholz, they weren't surprised when they drove into Kesslingen to find that village, too, was deserted. 'I think this is as far as we go tonight,' said Dawson. 'There's another main road just this side of Münzingen. I'd rather try and cross that at night. I don't want us to get half-way down the road and find ourselves looking at a bunch of Jerry trucks heading straight towards us, and us with nowhere to go. Let's find a barn or something and get our heads down.'

On the northern outskirts of the village, down a side street that was little more than a well-trodden track across the rutted ground, they spotted a farm out-building with sagging double doors secured with a rusting chain and an equally rusted padlock.

'That'll do, I think,' Dawson said, picking up his Schmeisser. 'I'll go and check it out. Turn the truck round, so you can back it in if there's room inside.'

Dawson strode down the track towards the out-building, the machine-pistol held ready in his hands,

glancing in all directions as he walked and listening intently for any sound that seemed out of place.

The small barn, or whatever the building was, was about twenty feet wide and forty feet long, the rear of it separated from the side of a small house or cottage by an open yard. There were other houses nearby, but none of them closer than about fifty yards. Dawson first checked the house, trying both doors – which were locked – and peering inside through the ground-floor windows. There was no sign of life, and the property had an indefinable air of emptiness, of abandonment.

He checked the rear and both sides of the barn, then walked around to the front of the structure to examine the doors. Watson sat in the truck, the engine idling, the rear of the vehicle facing the barn, ready to reverse inside. Dawson slung his Schmeisser over his shoulder and carefully examined the chain and padlock. It only took a couple of minutes to break in using his trench knife, and he pulled open one of the double doors and looked inside the building.

Even in the faint light of the early dawn, he could see that the structure was almost empty. The floor was covered in straw and dirt, and a few straw bales were visible at the back of the building. The walls were hung with a variety of tools and equipment, with other tools – spades, forks, hoes and scythes – leaning against them. He guessed that the building might have been used to store produce, because he couldn't detect any smell of animals. But whatever its function, it would do very well for what they needed.

Dawson turned back, pulled both doors wide open and beckoned to Watson. In minutes, the truck was

inside the barn, engine switched off, and the two sappers had pulled the doors closed.

'I'm knackered,' Watson said.

'You're not the only one, but we can't afford to both fall asleep together. Let's grab a bite to eat, and then I'll take the first watch, OK?'

They had some of the hard dried sausage left and split it between them, washed down with water, and finished their meal with half a bar of German chocolate each. High-class grub it wasn't, but it was food, and that was all that mattered.

'What I wouldn't give for a hot meal and a mug of tea,' Watson muttered, as he finished the last piece of chocolate.

Dawson nodded. 'I'd even pay money for a bowl of that fucking awful stew back at the camp. And for a hot bath. Christ knows what we smell like after – however long it's been – wearing this stuff.'

'No,' Watson said, 'but we're alive, and that's a hell of a lot more important. Right, you'll stay awake, then?'

'Yeah. I'll take a walk around the village first, just to get the lie of the land, then I'll come back here. If I think I'm falling asleep I'll just walk around the barn, or step outside again. But if I know I'm falling asleep, I'll wake you up. OK?'

Watson nodded. 'I'll rack out on those straw bales in the back there.' He walked over to the truck, picked up one of the Schmeissers and walked over to the rear wall of the barn, took off his German helmet, webbing belt and his battledress jacket and lay down.

Dawson crossed over to the doors and peered outside. He had to keep moving if he was going to stay

awake. He pushed the door open just enough to step through the gap. Then he stopped and listened to the silence. Apart from the birdsong all around him, there was no other sound at all, or none he could detect. It all felt empty and deserted. And that, he reflected, as he walked along the track back towards the largely unmade road that ran through the village, was just what they wanted.

But he still took infinite care, checking everywhere, using his eyes and ears. But within ten minutes he knew absolutely that he and Watson were the only two human beings in the village.

It was small, just a collection of perhaps forty or fifty properties scattered along both sides of the narrow country road. There was a kind of village square off to one side, with a couple of small shops so completely shuttered and barred that he couldn't even tell what they sold, and a village water pump. Many of the houses had official-looking notices displayed, which Dawson guessed might be warnings against looting. He checked the doors of a few of the houses – not to go inside, just to make sure they were empty – but every one was locked.

He walked all round the village, then retraced his steps to the barn, checking all around him as he did so. While Watson slept, Dawson would take the opportunity to refill their water bottles at the pump, which would give him something to do, and help to keep him awake for a little longer. He might even try and find a bucket or tub or something and take the opportunity to strip off and wash some of the grime from his body while he was at the pump.

CHAPTER 30

14 SEPTEMBER 1939

Just after two that afternoon, Dawson gave Watson a shake and handed him a tin mug of a thick black liquid from which clouds of steam rose agreeably.

'Bloody hell, mate,' Watson said. 'What's that?'

'Coffee,' Dawson replied shortly. 'There are a couple of shops in the village near the pump, and I kind of leant on the side door of one of them. It's a sort of village store, so I borrowed some coffee. There wasn't much else there, frankly. It looked like they emptied all the shelves before they left. All I found were a few packets of stuff that had already been opened, and the only one of those that was any use to us was the coffee.'

'So how did you heat the water?'

'I found a couple of saucepans, half a dozen tin mugs and a kind of Jerry solid-fuel stove in the back of the truck. It took me a while to figure out how to light it, but I finally got it going. And . . .' Dawson paused for a moment to make his dramatic announcement, 'I also found a ration pack there. Somebody had already eaten some of the stuff, but there were a couple of bars of chocolate there, and a tin of something.'

'You said there *were* two chocolate bars. How many are there now?'

'Just the one,' Dawson said with a smile. 'I ate the other while I had my coffee. Now, we can't leave here until it gets dark, so why don't we open that tin of whatever it is this evening and share that before we leave? I'm hoping it's meat or a stew or something. And I think it's perfectly safe to use the stove here in this barn, but in the back of the truck, obviously, because all the straw that's lying on the ground.'

'And you look clean. Or a bit cleaner, anyway,' Watson observed.

Dawson explained about the village pump. 'This place is completely deserted,' he said, 'so there's no danger. I've left the bucket there for you if you want to use it. Now I'm going to try and get some sleep.'

Dawson woke suddenly as a hand closed roughly over his mouth. He opened his eyes and stared up into Watson's face.

'Engines,' the sapper said shortly, his voice low, barely above a whisper. 'Vehicle engines and getting closer.'

Dawson nodded and sat up, reaching for his battle-dress jacket. He pulled it on swiftly, then his boots, his webbing belt and all his other equipment. Vehicle engines meant Germans, obviously, and that was bad news. If it was a patrol, they might have to fight their way out of the village.

He glanced at his watch – it was just after four in the afternoon, still broad daylight – and looked around the barn. Watson had already stowed everything in the truck, and was ready to leave immediately.

'Looks like our stew or whatever it is will have to wait,' Dawson murmured.

'I looked at the label on the tin,' Watson said, 'and you were right – it is a stew, or goulash, actually.'

The sound of an engine, perhaps two engines, was now very obvious.

'Sounds like a truck to me,' Dawson said. 'Have you looked outside yet?'

Watson shook his head. 'I already had everything ready to leave, so I just woke you, in case you wanted to make a run for it straight away.'

'Not without knowing what we're facing. I'll go and check outside.'

Dawson pulled the coal-scuttle helmet on to his head, picked up a Schmeisser and checked it, then gently pushed the barn door open. He looked all round, saw nothing to alarm him, then slipped through the gap.

Watson remained behind, watching through the partially open doorway, his machine-pistol ready.

For a few moments, Dawson stood just outside the barn, listening intently, trying to work out exactly where the noise of the truck engine was coming from. The vehicle had to be on the road, obviously, but the surrounding buildings meant that it was difficult to locate the source of the noise and the direction from which it was approaching.

Dawson ran a few paces forward down the track until he could see a short distance both up and down the road. Now the sound was much more distinct, and he knew the truck was approaching them from the direction of Münzingen. Not a particularly helpful piece of

information. What they needed to know was the type of vehicle and who was in it.

He ducked into cover at the side of the track and looked down the road, waiting for the truck to come into view.

Moments later he saw it, perhaps fifty yards away, as it swung round a gentle bend at the edge of the village. Clearly military, it looked like a three-tonner, the back covered by a kind of canvas hood. Dawson could see three figures sitting in the cab – the driver and two passengers – but there could be a whole squad of soldiers travelling in the back of the vehicle.

Then Dawson noticed something else. One of the passengers in the cab was wearing a cap rather than a helmet, which probably meant he was an officer. His presence almost certainly meant there was a group of soldiers in the back. The truck might even be the lead vehicle of a small convoy. Usually, a squad of soldiers – typically between about eight and sixteen men – would be commanded by a corporal or sergeant. The presence of an officer suggested a platoon-sized unit, upwards of twenty-five soldiers.

Everything depended, Dawson realized, on what happened next. If the truck carried on through the village, then presumably it was just a platoon being driven somewhere. If it stopped, then the chances were that the soldiers had been ordered to join the search for them. If so, he and Watson really were in the shit.

He lowered himself flat to the ground, taking advantage of the vegetation that lined the side of the lane, and pressed his head down on to the leaves – he didn't want the pale oval of his face to be visible as the truck drove past the end of the track.

Then he just listened. About ten seconds later he heard a squeal of brakes, then the noise of the truck's diesel engine rattled into silence. The vehicle had obviously stopped somewhere near the centre of the village.

'Oh, fuck,' Dawson muttered to himself, stood up cautiously and crossed to the other side of the lane. He worked his way forward until he could just see the village square and, parked close to the pump, the back end of the German army truck. As he watched, about a dozen soldiers wearing grey-green uniforms clambered down from the vehicle, weapons in hand.

It was just possible, Dawson hoped, that they'd simply stopped for a break on their journey, to refill their water bottles at the village pump and have a cigarette. But even as this thought crossed his mind, he knew he was being ridiculously optimistic. Seconds later the officer walked around from the front of the vehicle and started barking orders, his arms gesticulating as he detailed the soldiers. They'd obviously arrived to search the village.

Dawson could see the officer clearly, could see the Death's Head – the *Totenkopf* or 'skull of a dead man' – badge on his cap and the SS flashes on his right-hand lapel. This was the worst news of all.

'Oh, fuck,' he muttered again, and cautiously backed away from his vantage point. As soon as he was shielded from view by the adjacent buildings, he broke into a run back to the barn.

Watson pushed open the door as he approached, then pulled it closed behind him.

'It's a fucking SS patrol,' Dawson said, 'with an officer in charge. I think they're going to search the village.

They'll see that broken lock on the door, and then they'll bust in. We've got to get the hell out of here right now.'

'Right.' Watson ran over to the truck and prepared to start the engine, while Dawson peered out through the gap between the two barn doors. Even as he watched, two German soldiers reached the end of the track and turned down it, heading straight towards the barn.

'Now would be a good time, Dave,' Dawson said, watching the two men approach.

Behind him, the truck's engine sprang noisily into life, the sound unmistakable in the quiet afternoon air. The two German soldiers stopped and stared towards the barn, puzzled looks on their faces, then raised their weapons and started walking slowly forward.

Dawson abandoned his post by the doors and ran back to the truck. 'Now, Dave,' he said.

'But the bloody doors are still closed,' Watson pointed out.

'They won't be when this fucking truck hits them. Now go.'

Dawson jumped into the passenger seat, grabbed one of the Schmeissers and dropped the strap around his neck, then put two stick grenades on the seat beside him and removed the caps from the ends, ready to trigger them.

Watson let out the clutch, and the truck surged forward, accelerating swiftly. The front of the vehicle hit the barn doors hard, the impact forcing one back on its hinges. The other toppled forwards, the hinges torn away from it completely, to crash to the ground outside as the truck's wheels ran over it.

Dawson stood up in his seat and aimed the machine-

pistol at the two German soldiers, who had dodged to the side of the track as the vehicle had erupted from the closed barn.

As both soldiers raised their rifles, Dawson pulled the trigger, sending a steam of nine-millimetre bullets crashing into their bodies at almost point-blank range. They never stood a chance.

'Go right at the end,' Dawson yelled, as Watson changed up into second gear.

As the truck continued to accelerate, half a dozen more German soldiers appeared at the end of the track. For an instant they stared, puzzled, at the sight of a German army truck being driven by two men wearing German helmets and emerging from a barn. Then they obviously also saw the bodies of the soldiers lying behind the vehicle, aimed their weapons and opened fire.

The thick glass of the windscreen cracked as a couple of bullets smashed into it. Dawson could heard the thuds as other rounds impacted the heavy steel bodywork. The truck wasn't armoured like a tank or personnel carrier, but it was still pretty tough.

While Watson's steering weaved the truck from side to side within the confines of the narrow track, trying to throw off the aim of the German soldiers, Dawson reached down and picked up one of the grenades. He pulled the cord, counted a slow 'one, two', then lobbed it as hard as he could towards the approaching men. It exploded in the air, before it even reached them, and cut an immediate swathe through their ranks. But even before the weapon detonated, Dawson had already armed and thrown the second grenade.

Other soldiers tumbled to the ground as the grenade

exploded near them. Even the truck lurched with each explosion, though the grenades had exploded about twenty yards away, and the two sappers were well protected by its steel from the effects of the blasts.

Dawson let fly another couple of bursts with the machine-pistol, to make sure any of the German soldiers who'd survived the explosions wouldn't cause them any trouble.

But, actually, those soldiers weren't the problem, as both Dawson and Watson realized as the truck swung out of the track and on to the road that ran through the village.

Dawson glanced to his left, and swore loudly.

The German SS officer was running down the road towards them, a pistol in his hand. Behind him were another dozen or so soldiers, most armed with rifles. They were the problem because the road out of the village was straight and there was literally nowhere else they could go. Once the Germans started firing at them, from behind, they'd be sitting targets. The only thing that might save them was the thickness of metal in the cargo area directly behind the cab of the truck. It wasn't much to rely on.

Dawson grabbed another two stick grenades, and armed and threw each one towards the soldiers. But, even as he did so, he guessed most of the Germans were beyond the lethal radius of the weapons.

Watson pressed down on the accelerator as hard as he could, trying to accelerate out of trouble, but the truck gathered speed terribly slowly.

Dawson stood up in the seat and fired another long burst from the Schmeisser at the enemy soldiers, barely

even bothering to aim. The machine-pistol jammed after a couple of seconds, and Dawson dropped it back on to the seat.

He grabbed one of the Mauser rifles, pulled back the bolt to chamber a round, then aimed it back down the road and pulled the trigger. Again, trying to aim it was pointless because the truck was bouncing and jolting as Dave Watson powered it down the road.

Then he heard the first few rounds fired by the Germans smash into the back of the vehicle, and dropped down into his seat. There was nothing he could do now – it all depended on getting away. If the truck stopped or Watson crashed it, they were done for.

Dawson glanced behind and saw that the truck was creating quite a trail of dust from the poor road surface. 'Weave about a bit more,' he instructed. 'Try and kick up a bit more dust. Make us a more difficult target.'

The vehicle lurched across the road as Watson swung the wheel to the left, then back again to the right.

But Dawson could still hear the thuds as bullets smashed into the back cargo area of the truck. The steel was stopping them – or at least, none of the bullets had come through into the cab – but the tyres were vulnerable to a stray round. But with six wheels, unless the Germans managed to shoot out two tyres on the same side, or hit one of the front tyres, the truck would keep going.

The distance between the vehicle and the German soldiers increased with every second. Beyond about 700 yards, he reckoned they should be safe.

Suddenly, the sound of the bullets hitting the back of the truck stopped.

Watson glanced at Dawson. 'You think we're out of range?'

'Not yet. Let me take a look.'

Gingerly, Dawson stood up in the cab of the truck and looked back the way they'd come, but the dust cloud made it almost impossible to see. 'Stop weaving, Dave,' he said. 'I can't see a fucking thing.'

'Maybe that's why they stopped firing,' Watson suggested. 'If they couldn't see us any more, they'd just be wasting ammunition.'

As Watson straightened up and started driving down the centre of the road, the dust being thrown up by the vehicle diminished considerably, and Dawson could finally see back as far as the village.

'It wasn't the dust, Dave,' he said, slumping back into his seat.

'What was it, then?'

'They've turned their vehicle round, and they're following us. That fucking truck is full of SS troopers and it's only about a quarter of a mile behind us.'

CHAPTER 31

Watson glanced in the small side mirror, mounted on a steel rod on the front wing, and shook his head. 'I suppose our luck had to run out some time,' he said, raising his voice over the roar of the truck's engine and rattling of the suspension over the uneven surface of the road. 'What the hell do we do now? Can we outrun them?'

'Bloody unlikely,' Dawson replied, again lifting himself out of his seat to look behind at the pursuing vehicle. 'Not on these roads. This truck might be a little bit faster on flat tarmac, but I doubt if we'll be able to drive quickly enough to lose them on this kind of cart-track. That doesn't stop you trying to go quicker, though,' he added, as Watson swung the truck round a bend in the road.

Dawson glanced back again, then ducked down into the cab of the truck, moments before a shot ricocheted off the road surface somewhere beside them, and then another hit the back of the vehicle. They heard three more shots, but had no idea where the bullets went.

'One of the Jerries is leaning out of the passenger door, firing his Mauser,' Dawson said, 'but we're

bouncing around and so are they, so it'd be a miracle if they did any damage.'

'Why don't you shoot back?' Watson suggested. 'They're a bigger target. You might make them drop back a bit.'

Dawson nodded agreement, picked up one of the Mauser K98k rifles and turned round in his seat.

'I'll climb into the back,' he shouted. 'Give me sixty seconds. Then try and keep the truck as straight as you can for about half a minute and I'll fire off a few rounds.'

Dawson stared at the lorry for a few moments, checking that the German soldier wasn't still hanging out of the pursuing vehicle aiming his rifle at them, then clambered into the rear cargo and passenger area of the truck. Holding on firmly to the seats that lined both sides, and bracing his body against the violent and unpredictable motion of the vehicle, he moved unsteadily to the back.

Whatever he did and however carefully he aimed the Mauser, he knew his chances of even hitting the lorry lay somewhere between nil and slim, but Watson was right – if he could frighten the driver and make him back off, even a little, maybe a hundred yards or so, that would give them a bit of breathing space.

There was blanket lying on the floor in the back of the truck, and Dawson scooped it up. A sandbag would have been better, but the blanket would do at a pinch. Resting his rifle on the seats, he quickly folded it to form a bulky pad. Then he placed the blanket on top of one of the steel rear doors of the truck, picked up his weapon and rested the barrel of the Mauser on it. Hopefully, the fabric of his makeshift pad would help to cushion the

rifle against the movement of the truck and improve his accuracy a little.

He sat down on the seat, pulled the butt of the Mauser back into his shoulder and tried to bring his sights to bear on the following vehicle – an almost impossible task. Every time his finger started to squeeze the trigger, the truck hit a pothole or a lump in the road and threw him off his aim. Dawson knew he was just wasting his time, and if he started shooting he'd just be wasting ammunition.

But he had to do something.

He turned round to look at the road in front of the speeding truck. It ran straight for about another hundred yards, then bent sharply to the left, and about fifty yards beyond the curve was a large stand of trees and undergrowth.

An idea began to form in Dawson's mind, and he lowered the rifle and staggered across to the driving cab. He grabbed hold of the steel back of the cab and leant over it, towards Watson.

'There,' he shouted, 'just around the bend. When you get to that clump of trees, stop the truck.'

'Stop it? Are you out of your fucking mind? They'll be all over us.'

'No they won't. Just do it. The moment you've stopped, grab a Schmeisser and get ready. As soon as they come around that corner, we open up at them with everything we've got. We'll be stationary, so we'll be able to make every shot count. OK?'

'Fucking last-gasp plan if I ever heard one,' Watson grumbled.

It sounded slightly desperate to Dawson as well, and

it was his idea. But it was about the only option they had, as far as he could see.

He leant further over into the cab and grabbed a couple of the stick grenades as well. If his estimate of the distances involved was right, when the German army lorry came round the bend, he'd be able to lob the grenades with some chance of reaching the vehicle. And with Watson firing a machine-pistol to make the soldiers keep their heads down, Dawson reckoned they could do some serious damage to their pursuers, with any luck.

He looked behind. The German lorry was a little further away now, maybe 500 yards or so back: Watson had been driving noticeably faster and had slightly increased their lead. Then Dawson looked ahead. The bend was now only about twenty yards away, and he could see Watson was already altering his grip on the steering wheel, preparing to turn the truck to the left.

Dawson transferred the Mauser to his left hand, took a firm grip on one of the seats with his right and braced himself for the change in direction. He leant sideways as the truck started to swing around the curve and transferred his gaze to the road behind them. The Germans were still lumbering after them, but moments later they were lost to sight behind the shrubs and trees on the inside of the curve.

'Now, Dave, now!' Dawson yelled. 'Hit the brakes.'

Watson complied, knocking the truck out of gear and slamming his foot on the brake pedal. The truck bounced and shuddered as the wheels locked, slewing slightly sideways across the road. Dawson stepped to the rear of the cargo area – the steel doors at the end should, he

hoped, provide both partial concealment and some protection for him – placed the Mauser on the seat beside
him and picked up the first grenade. He unscrewed
the cap on the base of the wooden handle and took the
ceramic ball in his left hand, ready to pull it so that
the moment the German lorry appeared he could arm the
weapon and immediately throw it.

'Get ready, Dave,' he said. 'We should see it any
second.'

Watson had climbed out of the driving seat, leaving
the engine running, and had moved round to the side
of the vehicle. He had one Schmeisser in his hands and
another leaning against one of the rear wheels, ready for
immediate use should the first weapon jam.

The two men waited, tense with anticipation.

'So where is it?' Watson asked. 'We should have seen
it by now.'

'I don't know. It was only about five hundred yards
behind us.'

Dawson stared back down the track, but he could
neither see the German lorry nor hear the sound of its
engine. Where the hell was it? Had it broken down in
the last few seconds? Had the driver lost control and
crashed into the ditch beside the road?

Neither seemed likely in the circumstances. There was
still no sign of the lorry.

Dawson looked round, seeking inspiration. And then,
suddenly, he made an intuitive leap.

'Oh, fuck, oh fuck,' he muttered. 'Back in the truck,
Dave. Get us out of here!' he yelled. 'I know what these
bastards have done. Get us moving, right now!'

Watson didn't argue, just grabbed his spare machine-

pistol, ran back to the still-open driver's door and jumped back behind the wheel. He slammed the gearbox into first and dropped the clutch, sending the truck lurching down the road.

At the same moment, Dawson took aim with his Mauser and fired, but not at something behind the vehicle. Instead, his target was off to one side, beyond the clump of trees they'd used to stage their impromptu ambush.

'What is it?' Watson shouted, over the noise of the truck's engine, as Dawson fired a second, and then a third, round.

'That bastard of a German SS officer,' Dawson shouted back, searching for a new target. 'He obviously saw we didn't appear on the other side of that patch of cover, and must have guessed what we were doing. Then he sent his troops overland to cut the corner and attack us from the side.'

Dawson stopped and fired again, then ducked as three shots echoed from beyond the trees to the side of the track, two bullets slamming into the truck.

He put down the Mauser, grabbed one of the Schmeissers and pulled the trigger half a dozen times until the magazine was empty, spraying the bullets into the area on the inside of the bend, where the SS troops had cut across the corner.

'That should make those Jerries keep their bloody heads down,' he muttered, clipping a fresh magazine into place and firing another couple of short bursts.

Watson had got the vehicle up to speed and was weaving from one side of the road to the other, chucking up a cloud of dust as he did so. The truck had already

covered a couple of hundred yards from the place where they'd stopped. Another bend was ahead, and another stand of trees, and the two men knew they'd be invisible to their pursuers once they got round it.

They'd now moved well out of the effective range of the Schmeisser, so Dawson picked up his Mauser and fired twice more, emptying the magazine. Then he picked up another rifle and fired five shots, rapidly, from that, not aiming at specific targets, just into the area where he'd spotted the grey-green shapes of SS soldiers.

More shots rang out, and three more smashed into the side of the truck. As he returned fire, Dawson wondered just how much more punishment the vehicle could take.

Then they rounded the bend. Watson concentrated on putting as much distance as possible between them and the Germans.

Dawson picked up the end cap for the stick grenade from the floor and replaced it on the end of the wooden handle – the last thing he wanted was some jolt of the truck trapping the ceramic ball under a seat or something and then arming the weapon – then he climbed back into the cab and sat down beside Watson.

'So that Jerry officer must have guessed we'd stopped to ambush him?' Watson suggested.

'Exactly.' Dawson nodded. 'Whoever he is, he's one bloody clever bastard.'

'Fucking lucky you guessed when you did, then.'

Dawson picked up the map and glanced at it. 'Yeah, but we're not out of the woods yet. Those Jerries will be back in their lorry by now and steaming along behind us, desperate to try and catch us up. And that's not all:

somewhere right in front of us there's another main road that we've got to cross.'

'How far away do you reckon that is?'

'I don't know, mate. I don't know my arse from my elbow now. Let me try and work it out. Hope it's not too close, because if they've got guards on the road, they'd have heard all the shooting and will be expecting us.'

The truck swept round another bend and there, just over 200 yards in front of them, was the road itself. Even at that distance, both men could clearly see the steel barrier across the road, the two motorcycle combination outfits and the four German soldiers looking straight at them.

CHAPTER 32

14 SEPTEMBER 1939

'Bugger. What the hell now?' Watson asked.

'Keep going,' Dawson said, reaching down and picking up two stick grenades, 'but drop your speed down. Make it look as if we're just a couple of German soldiers on some routine mission.'

'You're going to try and fight our way through?'

'We've got no bloody option, just for a change. We've got a truck-load of angry Jerry soldiers hot on our heels and a German road-block right in front of us. We can't talk our way through, because we're wearing British uniforms and neither of us can speak enough German to convince anyone.'

'We could surrender, I suppose,' Watson suggested, easing his foot off the accelerator pedal.

'After the trail of carnage we've left behind? They'd shoot us out of hand. No, mate, I'm sorry, but it's do or die. Either we fight our way through this or we die right here, right now.'

Watson glanced at his companion, then back towards the road-block, now perhaps only 100 yards away. 'Right,

then,' he said. 'Give me one of those Schmeissers and make sure the fucking thing's fully loaded.'

Dawson picked one up, snapped a fresh magazine into place and handed it to Watson. Then he checked another machine-pistol for himself and slung it ready for instant use. Finally, he removed the safety caps from the two grenades and laid them gently on the seat beside him.

'Ready?' Watson asked.

Dawson nodded. 'I'm ready. Start slowing down when you get close to the road-block, just as if you were going to stop, but don't lose too much speed because we'll need enough momentum to smash through that barrier. Hopefully the soldiers will see our German helmets and recognize them before they spot the colour of our uniforms, so that might put them slightly off-guard.'

'The grenades?' Watson asked.

'I'll wait until we get to about thirty yards away, then throw them. The moment I do, you floor the accelerator pedal and crash through that barrier. And when you get to the junction, just take any bloody road you can see on the other side and get us out of here.'

Watson's right hand strayed nervously to the pistol-grip of the Schmeisser, to check it was within easy reach. He put both hands back on the steering wheel and looked straight ahead.

The soldiers manning the road-block were all armed with machine-pistols. Dawson also noticed that the four men had moved apart slightly, to give each of them a clear field of fire, and each soldier was holding his machine-pistol at the ready, pointing at the approaching truck, which was clearly the subject of their interest. One

of them took a couple of steps forward and raised his left arm in the universal signal meaning 'stop'.

Dawson held the first grenade in his right hand, below the level of the dashboard of the truck and well out of sight, clutching the ceramic ball in his other hand.

Watson dropped the gearbox down into first as the truck reached about forty yards from the barrier.

As he did so, Dawson pulled the cord on the stick grenade, priming the weapon. But he didn't immediately throw it.

Watson glanced at him in alarm as he held the live grenade in his right hand.

Dawson counted one, two, and only then did he stand up in his cab and throw the weapon as hard as he could towards the four German soldiers.

'Now, Dave. Hard as you can through the barrier,' Dawson shouted.

One of the Germans squeezed the trigger of his Schmeisser, but his burst of fire was poorly aimed because he ran for cover at the same time. The other three men scattered, shouting in alarm and diving towards the only place that offered them even the possibility of safety – the motorcycles and sidecars parked just behind them.

As the truck started accelerating, the grenade exploded with a deafening blast, still in the air and close to where the four soldiers had been standing. Screams of pain filled the air. Dawson had already primed the second weapon and immediately threw that towards them as well. Then he grabbed his machine-pistol and aimed the weapon at the area where the Germans had dived for cover.

Watson wrenched the gear lever into second and again stamped his foot on to the accelerator. The truck swept past the two motorcycles, and as it did so Dawson fired three bursts, but at the motorcycles themselves, not the soldiers. Petrol poured from ruptured fuel tanks and two of the tyres blew under the impact of the bullets. Seconds later there was a dull 'whump' as the spilt fuel was ignited by some spark, turning the machines into a blazing inferno.

Then the front of the truck hit the steel barrier, a single red and white painted pole, the base mounted on a concrete plinth, the other end resting in a Y-shaped steel fork on the opposite side of the narrow road.

The truck probably weighed over two tons and at the moment of impact was travelling a little over twenty miles an hour. The barrier stood no chance at all. The pole was smashed to one side, the free end torn out of the steel fork, and the base twisted completely clear of the mount on the plinth. Both the truck's headlamps shattered, but otherwise there was no real damage, the heavy steel bumper taking the brunt of the impact.

'Keep going, keep going,' Dawson yelled, swivelling round to check the scene behind them, his Schmeisser covering the area.

There was no sign of any of the German soldiers, no shots, so the grenades had done their work as bloodily and efficiently as ever. But just coming around the final bend, beyond the blazing motorcycles, was the German army truck that had chased them all the way from Kesslingen that afternoon.

He dropped back into his seat just as the truck roared up the gentle slope that led to the main road directly in front of them.

There were vehicles moving in both directions along it. He could see two lorries and a staff car heading south-west, towards the French border, and several lorries – perhaps eight or ten in all – were driving along in a well-spaced convoy, crossing in front of them from left to right. Somehow, they had to get through and find the road they needed.

As they reached the junction, one of the convoy lorries started to slow down and pulled across. Dawson could see the driver and passenger looking in shocked horror at the blazing motorcycles and scattered bodies beside the road-block. They were obviously going to stop and help.

Watson powered the truck on to the tarmac surface, swerved around the front of the slowing vehicle and swung left, cutting directly in front of the staff car with four soldiers sitting in it – two officers in the rear seats and a driver and escort in the front. The driver sounded his horn angrily, and the escort stood up, bringing his machine-pistol to bear.

Dawson stood up and spun round. He was in no mood to mess about. Before the German could fire his weapon, a stream of nine-millimetre bullets from Dawson's Schmeisser smashed into his chest, throwing him backwards and sideways out of the vehicle. He fired another burst at the front of the staff car, rupturing both front tyres and blasting holes through the radiator.

Watson stood up in his seat as well, clutching his Schmeisser and looking for a minor road away to the north-west, towards the border with Luxembourg.

Another soldier stepped from behind the now stationary convoy lorry and lobbed a stick grenade towards

the truck, but Watson saw him immediately, dropped back into his seat and accelerated hard.

Dawson swung round and fired at the soldier with his machine-pistol, but after a second or so it jammed and his bullets all missed.

'Fucking German junk,' he muttered, dropped it and grabbed another one.

The grenade exploded some thirty yards behind them, and they felt the blast, but the steel body of the truck protected them from its effects.

'Up there,' Dawson snapped, pointing at a junction about 100 yards in front of them.

Ahead of them, another of the lorries in the north-east-bound convoy had obviously seen what had happened and decided to do something about it. The driver swung his heavy vehicle across the road, barely twenty yards away, clearly aiming to ram them.

Dawson aimed the Schmeisser and fired a long burst. The windscreen of the oncoming lorry shattered, but the vehicle still hurtled towards them.

'Go left,' Dawson yelled. 'Go around it.'

He fired another two bursts at the lorry, aiming lower, at the engine and tyres, trying to do some serious damage, but the vehicle didn't stop.

Watson braked hard and wrenched on the steering wheel. The truck swung left, just missing the wing of the approaching lorry, which rumbled past them without stopping. Dawson's shots had obviously hit the driver, because the vehicle careered off the road and crashed in the ditch that ran alongside it.

Watson turned the steering wheel back again to the right-hand lane and pressed the accelerator, crunching

his way through the gearbox once more. Another lorry in the convoy was heading towards them, but the driver showed no inclination to swing over from his side of the road. But Dawson could see the muzzle of a weapon poking out of the window beside him. He fired another couple of bursts as the two vehicles closed on each other. Bullets peppered the steel of the cab and engine compartment, and with a sudden bang the lorry stopped dead, clouds of steam pouring from under the bonnet.

They were clear. In a few seconds they reached the junction, and Watson swung the wheel to the right, sending the truck surging off the main highway and down the narrower road that curved away to the northwest, scattering stones and debris behind them.

Dawson looked back again as the truck bounced over the uneven surface. The other lorries in the convoy had slowed, several had already stopped. Grey-clad figures ran down towards the road-block, but three others headed towards the north side of the road. And they all carried rifles.

'Keep your head down,' Dawson ordered, 'get the speed up and start weaving. There are three riflemen behind us.'

As he said the words, a bullet smacked into the rear of the truck somewhere, and another ploughed through the right-hand side front wing.

'If they hit one of the front tyres, we're buggered,' Watson shouted.

'Just keep going. They're on foot. We'll be out of range soon.'

Other shots rang out. Several bullets hit the rear of the vehicle, and one smashed through the windscreen,

but neither man was hit. The truck kept going, and that was all that mattered.

'I think we're clear now,' Dawson said, risking another glance behind them, back towards the road.

'I bloody hope so.'

Then there was a massive bang from the right-hand side of the truck.

'Oh, fuck,' Watson said. 'That's one of the bloody tyres.'

Dawson leant out of the cab, over the side of the vehicle, and looked down. 'It's the middle axle,' he said. 'Keep your foot down.'

The truck had three axles and six wheels. Dawson couldn't see any reason why it shouldn't keep running as long as at least four of the tyres remained intact.

'Was it a bullet?' Watson asked, raising his voice over the increased noise level. Bits of tyre were flapping and banging against the wheel arches as the truck rushed on.

'Probably, or the punishment we've inflicted on it. Either way, we've still got five fucking tyres, so there are a good few miles left in it yet.'

Dawson looked back again. What he saw on the main road, about half a mile behind them, wasn't entirely unexpected, but it still caused him to curse.

A German army lorry was just making the turn to follow them. It was too far away for him to identify it positively, but he had no doubt, no doubt at all, it was the one that had been chasing them all afternoon.

Watson heard his companion's expletive and glanced behind them. 'It's that fucking SS officer and his men, isn't it?' he demanded, as he spotted the lorry turning to follow them.

'You can bet your life it is. At least we've got a bit more of a lead over them now and we must be getting close to the border.' Dawson bent forward to study the map. 'Yes,' he said. 'If we're where I think we are, we've got about another four miles to go, that's all.'

Watson leant forward and patted the dashboard of the truck. 'Keep going, old girl,' he said. 'We're nearly there.'

Dawson again checked behind them. Some 700 yards distant, the German army lorry showed no signs of giving up the pursuit.

CHAPTER 33

14 SEPTEMBER 1939

The banging from the wheel with the blown tyre was getting worse, and the truck was clearly travelling much more slowly.

'Sorry, mate,' Watson said, wrestling with the steering wheel, 'this is as fast as we can go.'

'Somehow, we've got to stop that lorry, or at least slow it down,' Dawson said. 'If they catch up with us, we'll be outnumbered and out-gunned, and there's only one way that will end.'

'Any ideas?' Watson asked.

'I'm working on it.'

'What about blocking the road? Drop a tree across it or something? Maybe use the grenades?'

'That's not a bad idea, but we'd have to pick the spot carefully. In open country, they'd just drive around the obstacle. We'd need to do it in a forest or valley, somewhere like that, where they'd have no option but to shift it.'

Watson pointed ahead. 'Looks like we're heading into a sort of forest right now,' he said.

In front of them, the road curved gently to the right

and disappeared behind a clump of trees, and the land beyond was quite heavily wooded.

Dawson nodded. 'I suppose we could use a grenade or two to fell a tree.'

'You're supposed to be the bloody explosives expert, Eddie. You tell me.'

'The problem is the direction of the explosion. Trees are pretty bloody tough. It might take three or four to do the job. Even then the tree might not fall the way we want. We'd just be wasting the grenades and we've only got six left.'

'There's a steel cable in the back,' Watson said. 'We could attach it to a tree and pull it over.'

'Any tree small enough for us to pull out of the ground with this truck,' Dawson replied, 'is also easy to shift with that three-tonner. They could probably just drive straight over it – slowly, of course – and then they'd be right behind us. No, we need something else, some other way of getting them off our backs.'

When the truck drove into the forest, Dawson reckoned that the lorry was now only about 500 yards back, and gaining on them. Their slender lead was being steadily eroded and, unless they did something bloody quickly, the Germans would be on them in minutes.

The truck swept round the corner and into the shelter of the trees, the shade from the leaves and branches immediately cutting out the daylight. Dawson glanced round at the trees that edged the road. It would take more than a couple of grenades to bring one of them down. They were massive, maybe three feet in diameter.

Watson accelerated as the road straightened out in front of them, the banging and crashing from the blown

tyre now louder and more pronounced. Dawson leant out of the cab and peered back. Most of the ruptured tyre had vanished, but the shreds of the carcase that were still attached to the wheel were slamming into the mudguard as the wheel turned, and the steel wheel itself was crashing into the ground, digging furrows in the track.

'Just keep going,' he said. 'We don't have any option.'

Dawson checked the map, looking for inspiration, then sat back. The road they were on went through the forest for another couple of miles, as far as he could see, then emerged into open ground again. If they were going to slow down their pursuers, they really had to do something while they were still surrounded by the trees. Or, he suddenly thought, looking back at the map, perhaps there might be another way.

'Slow down a bit,' he instructed Watson.

'Slow down? What the hell for?'

'Look, we can't outrun that fucking lorry and we can't bring down one of these trees in time.'

'So?'

'We need that lorry to go away, right? Let's allow it get ahead of us. If we can hide and the Jerries still think we're in front of them, they'll just keep on driving. They won't know we're not ahead until they come out of this wood.'

'So we drive up some track and wait until they've gone past?'

'Exactly,' Dawson said, and pointed at the map he was holding. 'There are tracks and paths marked on this, but I can't tell how wide. We'll just have to pick one that looks big enough. So slow down a bit.'

Watson slowed down more, and they both started

looking at the undergrowth on either side of the road. They passed several narrow tracks that seemed to be more like footpaths, then a succession of wide pathways.

'Take that one,' Dawson said, pointing to one on the left-hand side of the road that led away into the wood at an oblique angle.

Watson braked, dropped down two gears and turned the steering wheel to the left. The moment the truck left the tarmac, it started bouncing, the suspension crashing and banging over the rutted surface.

The track ran fairly straight for perhaps twenty yards, then swung right around a stand of large trees, before bending back to the left. After another thirty yards or so it ended in a small clearing, occupied by a tiny wooden hut, the door hanging open and the building obviously empty. Watson braked the vehicle to a halt and switched off the engine.

Both men jumped out, grabbed their machine-pistols and ran back down the track, then cut through the forest itself until they reached a point where they could see the road. Then they ducked down into cover, though they knew there was almost no chance they could possibly be seen by anybody in the speeding lorry.

A few seconds later, they heard the sound of a diesel engine running at full power and, moments after that, the German army lorry swept past, heading west.

Both men watched it carefully as it passed them.

'Three in the cab, maybe ten or twelve in the back,' Dawson said. 'If we get involved in a shoot-out with that many Jerry soldiers, we're dead.'

'So what now? Do we head back the way we've come, or what?'

Dawson considered for a few moments. 'We still have to head west: if we head back we'll just meet the main road and the German convoy again. Let's try and change that bloody blown tyre first. There's a spare wheel bolted on the side of the truck just behind the cab.'

'We'll have to be quick. There's a chance that, as soon as they clear the forest, they'll see we aren't in front, and then they'll double back and start looking for us. We've got to hope that there's some way to get off this road before that happens.'

The two men ran back up the track to the clearing. Watson grabbed a jack and wheel-brace from the toolkit in the back of the truck while Dawson checked inside the wooden hut, which was deserted and derelict. But he wasn't looking for German woodcutters, only for wood. There were a couple of short planks inside that had been used as a pair of simple shelves. He ripped them both off the wall and went back outside with them.

'Here,' he said, handing them to Watson, who was kneeling beside the truck and starting to raise the jack under the axle.

'Thanks,' Watson said, positioning them under the jack. Without some kind of support, the jack would simply sink into the earth under the weight of the vehicle.

Dawson looked at the back and sides of the truck and shook his head. The steel was punctured by dozens of holes where rifle bullets had smashed through it. It was a miracle that they hadn't lost a tyre before, and the only reason they weren't dead was because there was so much metal behind them that none of the bullets had penetrated as far as the cab.

The moment they'd finished, Dawson glanced at his watch. The whole operation had taken them under six minutes. 'Right, let's go,' he said.

Watson started the engine and reversed the truck, then swung it round and drove back down the track to the road, their progress much smoother and quieter, even over the rough ground, now they had all six wheels and tyres again.

'So which way do we go?' Watson asked, slowing down as the truck approached the road.

'West,' Dawson decided, again studying the map. 'We've got to get across the border into Luxembourg, and this is the only road marked in this area that's going in the right direction.'

'Then let's hope we don't meet those fucking Jerries coming back this way,' Watson said, swinging the wheel left and powering the truck off the track and back up on to the tarmac.

He accelerated down the road, going up through the gears, but kept the speed moderate, just in case the German army lorry *was* heading straight for them and he had to stop or drive off the road.

Beside him, Dawson made sure a couple of the remaining stick grenades were close to hand, checked that two of the Schmeisser MP 40s were fully loaded and ready to fire, then picked up one of the Mauser K98k rifles, checked that the magazine was loaded and chambered a round. Then he held the weapon in front of him, ready to aim and fire it if he had to.

Watson steered the truck around the first bend, the tension evident in his knuckles, which were white as he clutched the wheel. But the straight stretch of road that

came into view was empty of any signs of life, and he relaxed a little.

'They must know by now that we're not in front of them,' he said.

'I don't know,' Dawson replied. 'It all depends on what the visibility's like where the road leaves this forest. If it's clear for a mile or more, they'll know because the truck will have vanished, but if there are more trees or lots of bends it's possible they could still be driving away from us, hoping to catch up.'

But as they rounded the next corner, it was obvious that the lorry wasn't still heading west, because it was right in front of them, perhaps 200 yards away and parked in the middle of the road facing them. German soldiers were fanning out on both sides of the road, obviously looking for any sign of the truck in the forest.

CHAPTER 34

14 SEPTEMBER 1939

'Oh, fuck,' Watson said, slamming on the brakes and immediately swinging over to one side of the road to do a U-turn.

'That SS bastard is fucking clever,' Dawson muttered, aiming his rifle towards the oncoming soldiers. But he didn't fire because he knew that at that range, from a moving vehicle, he'd hit nothing.

'You said that before, but you're right.' Watson swung the truck round to face the other way, the tyres bumping over the grassy verge, then pressed down on the accelerator pedal. 'He's bloody well one step ahead of us again.'

The truck started to head back the way it had come. Then a volley of shots cracked out as some of the German soldiers spotted it and opened fire with their Mausers. But within seconds Watson had driven the vehicle around the bend and they were shielded from view by the trees and were safe – at least for a couple of minutes.

'So now where the hell do we go?' Watson demanded. 'Those fucking Jerries will have mounted up by now and that lorry will be coming after us.'

Dawson was desperately studying the map, looking for a way – any way – out. They couldn't go too far east, because that would take them back to the main road. Taking one of the tracks through the forest would be a risk, because he didn't know exactly where they were, and most of them only seemed to penetrate a short distance into the woods, according to the map. The worst possible outcome would be to leave the road, get stuck up some path that ended only yards from the road and be sitting ducks when the lorry-load of German soldiers appeared.

They didn't have many options, as usual. Dawson tossed the map back on the floor and looked ahead, searching the woods on either side of the road. 'I don't like it, but we're going to have to take to the forest again, Dave. It's our only possible way out. If we keep heading this way on the road, we'll end up trapped between the main road and that lorry.'

'Which track?'

'Buggered if I know. The map's no help – it's not detailed enough for that. Just pick the first track that looks wide enough to take this truck, and preferably too narrow for that bloody lorry.'

Watson slowed down – if they were going to leave the road, he wanted to drive straight up whatever track they picked, not have to reverse and manoeuvre, because they hadn't got time to do that.

'That one looks OK,' Watson said.

Dawson saw where he was pointing and nodded.

Watson steered the truck across the road to the left-hand side. The vehicle bounced over the verge and plunged between two large trees down a track that was

a couple of feet narrower than the vehicle itself. Not that that mattered, because at the speed the truck was travelling, it simply smashed all the undergrowth and vegetation out of the way.

'Good choice,' Dawson said, looking back over the rear of the vehicle towards the road. 'The lorry can't get through that gap.'

'That won't stop the bloody Jerries following us on foot, though, will it?' Watson muttered gloomily.

'No, so keep going as long as you can. Then we'll have to bail out and start hiking.'

The trail was narrow, and getting more so the deeper they went into the forest. Soon it petered out almost completely, but Watson kept the truck moving, smashing down saplings and bushes, making his own trail. Then they found themselves heading steadily downhill, with rising ground on either side of them.

'I don't like this, Eddie. Do you want me to turn round and try and find another route?'

Dawson shook his head. 'No. Just keep going. We've covered well over a quarter of a mile since we left the road. If the Jerries are following on foot, we've got a lead over them.'

'They'll be able to follow this track easily enough,' Watson pointed out, gesturing at the churned-up ground behind them and the torn branches.

'I know, but I don't think that matters. In fact, it might even help us. Maybe we can use this vehicle to slow them down a bit.'

'How?'

'Let's find a good place first, then I'll show you.'

The ground in front of them continued to slope

269

downwards, and the land on either side still rose steadily as they headed down into a narrow and steepening valley. The truck ploughed on, bouncing and shuddering as it crashed into small trees and bushes.

'There,' Dawson said, pointing straight ahead.

In front of them, the ground levelled out slightly into a reasonably clear area, and the only way forward was through a gap between two huge rocks embedded in the rising sides of the valley, a space perhaps only four or five feet wide.

'That's ideal. Drive the truck into the gap between those rocks. We'll leave it there and walk. That'll block the track behind us, and hopefully it'll look as if we tried to drive it through and got stuck.'

'They'll be able to drag the truck out, or just climb over it,' Watson said.

'I hope they do – or rather, I hope they try to.'

Watson shrugged and drove the truck into the gap until it jammed against the sides, then switched off the engine. 'What now?' he asked. 'I suppose we might as well dump these fucking coal-scuttles.'

Dawson shook his head. 'No, we've got to hang on to them, at least for the moment. They might come in handy again. Let's grab our stuff and get the hell out of here, once I've left a little present for the Jerries.'

The two men picked up their own British-issue helmets. Then they each slung a Mauser over their shoulder and a Schmeisser around their neck, and took the grenades and all the ammunition they could carry, climbed over the front of the truck, through the gap and out the other side.

Dawson turned round, opened the bonnet of the truck

and peered inside. Then he took one of the stick grenades and removed the cap from the end of the handle, which he lobbed away into the undergrowth. Then he carefully tied the cord and ceramic ball around the oil filler cap and rested the grenade itself beside it, perching it on top of the engine. Then he gently closed the bonnet and walked away.

'If they start the engine, or even try to climb over the truck, that grenade will topple,' he said. 'Not even that German officer will have expected that, I hope. Now let's move.'

Dawson glanced at his watch, then checked his compass and pointed. 'That's west,' he said, and the two men started jogging away as quickly as they could.

The woods were quiet, birdsong the only sound they could hear, apart from their own laboured breathing as they struggled to cover as much distance as they could, as fast as possible – not easy with the ground underfoot fairly soft and leaf-strewn and laden down as they were with weapons and ammunition.

The valley continued downwards for some distance, ending in a stream that was barely more than a trickle, and then the land started to rise on the other side. They crossed the stream and continued up the slope.

'OK,' Dawson said, his breath rasping in his throat as they crested the next rise, 'let's take a breather.'

He looked back down the slope towards the point where they'd abandoned the truck. There was no sign of the place through the trees, nothing visible at all, which meant they were themselves invisible to the pursuing Germans.

'We must have come about two or three hundred

yards now, so let's move a bit more slowly and carefully. Those bastards are bound to be tracking us soon, if they aren't already.'

The land in front of them was more level, though still uneven, and they started working their way forward.

'How far have we still got to go?' Watson asked.

Dawson stopped, slung his Schmeisser behind him and fished the map out of his pocket. He unfolded it and studied it for a few seconds.

'That's the road through this forest,' he said, pointing at a minor road that was shown as passing through an area shaded light green on the map. 'I reckon we left it somewhere near here.' He pointed a grubby finger at a spot on the map, then moved it to point slightly further to the north. 'So we're probably about here.'

'Where's the border?'

Dawson unfolded the map to the next section and gestured at a wiggly black line running more or less north–south. 'That's the border,' he said, 'so we're maybe two and a half miles away from it now, more or less.'

'What's that other line?' Watson asked, indicating a dotted line in grey that ran east–west, almost through the town of Münzingen.

'Hang on a second,' Dawson looked at the map and opened it wider. 'It's nothing,' he said. 'Just the boundary between two different German districts. To the south of it is Saarland, and north of it is Rheinland-Pfalz. That's all.'

Suddenly, the silence of the forest was shattered by a single loud crack, and both men spun round to stare back the way they'd come.

Dawson looked at his watch. 'That sounded like our

stick grenade alarm clock, and it's just over eight minutes since we planted the weapon, so that's how far they are behind us. It'll take them a while to either drag what's left of the truck out of that gap or risk climbing over it, so I reckon we've got at least a quarter of an hour's start on them, maybe twenty minutes.'

'Fifteen or twenty minutes isn't a hell of a lot,' Watson said.

'No, but the further we go into the forest, the bigger the search area gets, and the more chance we have of slipping away. That SS officer has probably guessed we're trying to get into Luxembourg, but he can't know where we'll try to cross the border, because we don't know ourselves yet – depends what we find when we get there.'

'So he's *got* to follow us if he's going to stop us? Is that what you're saying?'

Dawson nodded as he replaced the map in his pocket. 'Yes. So we keep moving, keep heading west, and try to avoid leaving any traces. I haven't heard any dogs, so as long as we don't do anything stupid like drop a bit of equipment or break a branch off a tree, that kind of thing, we should be able to lose them.'

He checked his compass again and pointed through the trees in front of them. 'That way,' he said, and they set off once more, walking at a steady pace. 'Move carefully, but keep up a reasonable speed and we should reach the border in about two hours.'

'It'll be dark soon,' Watson pointed out. 'So that should help us.'

'Yeah, and hinder the bloody Jerries.'

CHAPTER 35

They'd been walking for about fifteen minutes when Dawson spotted a distant movement in the trees over to their left and raised his arm to stop Watson.

'Wait,' he whispered urgently.

'What is it?'

'I just saw something, over there.'

Both men peered in the direction Dawson had indicated.

'Like what?' Watson asked.

'I don't know, a movement.'

'Maybe it was a deer or something. Do they have deer out here?'

'No idea,' Dawson said, still staring out to the left.

Then they both saw it. About a hundred yards away, a shape like a grey-green ghost flitted through the gathering gloom, moving slowly between the trees towards them.

'That's a fucking Jerry soldier,' Watson spat, as they ducked down behind a clump of bushes. 'How the hell did they get here so quickly?'

'Buggered if I know.'

For a few seconds the two sappers just watched the distant figure.

'I can only see one man,' Watson said. 'Where are the others? There must have been a dozen men in that lorry.'

'I wonder,' Dawson muttered, his mind working out the logistics and coming up with the only possible answer. 'That Jerry didn't follow us here from the truck. That bloody SS officer's worked out what we're trying to do.'

'What? He knew where we'd be?'

'Not exactly. When he saw we'd dumped the truck to the north of that road, I bet he guessed we'd be heading towards Luxembourg. He's sent some of his troops through the forest, hoping one of them would spot us. It's the only explanation that makes sense. Fuck me, he's a cunning bastard.'

'So that leaves two questions. First, is that soldier over there by himself? And, second, do you reckon he's seen us?'

Dawson shook his head. 'I don't see anyone else. If I'm right, he's got to be alone. And he can't have seen us or he'd have fired at us by now, just to get his mates heading our way.'

'So do we take him out, or what?'

'We have to. If we move, he's going to see us. But we can't shoot him, obviously.'

Watson glanced over at Dawson, then looked back towards the approaching German soldier, then only about seventy yards away from them. 'Use a knife, you mean?'

'Yeah,' Dawson replied, drawing the Mauser bayonet from his belt scabbard. 'There's no other choice.'

Both men fell silent then, watching the soldier walking towards them. They could now see him quite clearly.

The German was carrying a Mauser rifle in his hands, his right forefinger resting on the trigger and swivelling his head from side to side as he searched the forest for his quarry.

'How are you going to do it?' Watson whispered. 'If he carries on in that direction, he's going to miss us by about thirty or forty feet. If you rush him, he'll hear you coming and shoot you down before you get half-way to him.'

'I know. Either I have to try and sneak around and get behind him, or . . .' Dawson's voice died away.

'Or what?' Watson whispered, not taking his eyes off the enemy soldier.

'Or we could try a diversion, I suppose.'

'What sort of a diversion?'

'You could surrender to him. Leave all your weapons on the ground and stand up with your hands in the air. While he's looking at you, I'll creep up behind him.'

'No fucking chance,' Watson snapped. 'I'd lay money these bastards have had orders to shoot us on sight. I'll machine-gun the fucker myself before I do that, and take the consequences.'

Dawson sighed. 'Yeah, you're right. It's too dangerous. OK, we'll use Plan B instead.'

'Which is what?'

'I don't know. I'm still working on it. Give me a minute.'

'We don't have a minute, Eddie,' Watson said urgently. 'He's only forty yards away. He'll hear us talking soon. Or step on us.'

Dawson nodded, decision made. 'OK,' he said, his voice barely above a whisper. 'Change of plan. I'll stand up, my Mauser pointed straight at him. You cover him from here. If he surrenders, we'll disarm him and knock him out. If he swings his rifle towards me, we shoot him down and then run like fuck.'

Watson nodded. 'That should work,' he said.

The two sappers held their breath as the German soldier paused suddenly about twenty yards away. He scanned all around him, then resumed his slow and cautious progress towards them.

Watson aimed his Mauser at the enemy soldier and nodded that he was ready.

Dawson waited until the German looked away from their hiding place, stood up unhurriedly, braced his legs apart and brought the rifle straight up to his shoulder. He pointed the Mauser at his target. At such point-blank range, there was scarcely any need to use the sights.

The German turned his head towards Dawson and did an almost comical double-take when he suddenly saw the British soldier in front of him. He froze, one leg bent in mid-step, and just stared. Dawson could almost see the man's thought processes reflected in the expressions on his face: first disbelief at the sudden appearance of an enemy soldier only twenty yards away; then recognition that the same soldier was armed with a rifle pointed straight at him; then the realization that his own weapon – his Mauser – was pointing in an entirely different direction; then his life-or-death calculation – could he bring his rifle round to the aim before the British soldier could fire his rifle?

At that point, Dawson very deliberately shook his

head and motioned upwards with the barrel of his Mauser.

The German nodded and removed his right hand from the trigger of his rifle. Then, moving very slowly and carefully, he raised his right hand above his head and lowered the Mauser to the ground with his left.

'OK, Dave,' Dawson said, his aim never wavering and his eyes staying locked on the German's face. 'Go and grab his weapon. Check he's not carrying grenades or a pistol. Stay clear of my line of fire, just in case he tries anything.'

Watson stood up and walked towards the soldier, holding his machine-pistol in front of him, aiming it straight at the man's stomach. When he was about six feet away, he motioned with the Schmeisser, gesturing for the German to step back a couple of paces, and only then did he bend down to pick up the discarded Mauser.

'No pistol or grenades, Eddie,' Watson called out.

'Right.' Dawson stepped forward and crossed over to where Watson and the soldier were standing in a kind of frozen tableau, staring at each other with undisguised hostility.

'You are both walking dead men,' the German said suddenly, his English stilted and heavily accented.

'Probably,' Dawson replied, 'but we're still alive at the moment. If you hadn't dropped your Mauser, you'd be dead right now and you know it.'

'You cannot hope to escape,' the German said. 'There are twenty soldiers looking for you in these woods, and others waiting outside.'

'Are they all as stupid as you?' Dawson asked. 'Because if they are, we shouldn't have any trouble

walking out of here. Thanks for the intelligence. It always helps to know the exact strength of the enemy.'

The German's eyes widened in anger and his lips compressed. 'You will not escape,' he repeated.

'Yeah, well that's up to us, isn't it? And we seem to have done pretty well so far,' Dawson said. 'But you're wrong about one thing, Fritz.'

'What?'

'We're not trying to escape. We're on a search-and-destroy mission. We're trained in sabotage and demolition and we haven't hit our main target yet, so we'll be around here for a while. We're just waiting for the explosives to be dropped for us.'

'I do not believe you.'

'Do I look like I give a fuck what you believe or don't believe?' Dawson said, then nodded to Watson. 'OK, Dave.'

Watson stepped behind the German, flipped his helmet forward off his head and cracked the steel butt-plate of his Mauser into the back of the man's skull. The soldier collapsed as if he'd been pole-axed.

'Hope you didn't kill him,' Dawson said. 'I want him to pass on the intelligence I just gave him to that SS bas-tard when he comes round.'

'So we're on a sabotage mission, are we?'

'Best I could come up with.' Dawson grinned. 'If he survives that crack on the head, it might set the Jerries running round like headless fucking chickens looking for a strategic target in this area, and for somewhere a plane could drop a parachute-load of explosives.'

'We take his weapon?'

'No, just the ammunition, and take out the bolt. Don't

want him waking up unexpectedly and firing the bloody thing. Right, let's get out of here.'

Watson picked up the German's Mauser, pulled out the bolt and threw it as far as he could into the forest, then pocketed all the rifle ammunition the man had been carrying.

Dawson checked his compass and then both men strode away into the darkening forest.

CHAPTER 36

14 SEPTEMBER 1939

'Christ. So near yet so far.'

It was now after eight, and darkness was falling. The two men were standing a few yards from the edge of the forest, hidden under a canopy of trees, and looking out across a fairly level stretch of land towards the border with Luxembourg. About 200 yards in front of them, a road ran from north to south, the occasional vehicle – all military, as far as they could tell – driving along it. But that didn't mark the border. That would have been too simple and convenient.

Beyond the road, they could see the border itself perfectly clearly. In fact, it was quite difficult to miss, because the south-east border of Luxembourg was marked by the River Moselle. The river ran south-west from Trier to a point on the border between Mesenich and Metert, and then followed the border all the way down to Schengen, which lay at the very south-east tip of Luxembourg.

'Looks like a fucking big river,' Watson said, staring at the wide expanse of water that lay in front of them.

Dawson couldn't argue with that. When he'd seen the

map Lieutenant Charnforth had pinned up back at the British camp near Dalstein, he'd barely registered the fact that there were rivers in the area – he'd been far more interested in what he was being tasked with doing and where he was supposed to be going.

'I knew there was a river on the border between Germany and Luxembourg, but I never thought it'd be anything like this,' he said.

'How the hell are we going to get across it?'

'Right now,' Dawson said, 'I don't know. What I *do* know is we won't be using a bridge, because they're going to be stuffed full of troops, at least on this side of the border. I don't know if Luxembourg's got an army, but I'll bet that, at the very least, they'll have armed police guarding their end of every bridge that links their country to Germany. So even if we slipped past the Germans, we'd probably get shot by the Luxembourgers, or whatever they're called.'

'Maybe we could find a boat?' Watson suggested doubtfully.

'Perhaps, but my guess is we'll have to swim for it. Or, to be absolutely accurate, *you'll* have to swim for it and I'll try and float across on a bit of wood or something. In fact, we'll need something like a couple of logs for buoyancy, because we'll have our weapons as well.' He paused and gestured at the thick forest that still surrounded them. 'There must be one or two logs in here somewhere.'

'So what now?' Watson asked.

'We'll have to wait for a while, but there are a couple of things we can do.' Dawson looked across the open ground that separated the edge of the forest from the

road and the riverbank, and at the German troops they could see standing there. They were positioned at intervals along the road, about 100 yards apart, most of them facing towards the forest, into German territory, which at the very least hinted at why they were there, strung out along a neutral border.

'They're looking for us,' Dawson said. 'They missed finding us in the forest, so they've mounted a patrol line right here, where we'd have to show ourselves if we were intending to cross the border.'

'It's that fucking SS officer again, I'll bet. Keeps coming back like a bad dose of the pox.'

'It's probably his work,' Dawson agreed. 'If he's ordered these troops here, then there's no point in moving up or down the riverbank. He'll have positioned soldiers all the way along it. We might as well just cross here.'

'You said there were two things we could do. What have you got in mind?'

'I'm not kidding. I can't swim. I'm frightened of water.'

'Yeah, I noticed you don't wash much,' Watson interrupted, a slight smile on his face.

Dawson grinned at him. 'Right. If I'm going to get across that bloody river, I need a raft or something that'll float. Two or three logs lashed together, something like that, something to support me and our weapons. That's the first thing.'

'And the other?'

Dawson pointed at the German soldiers. 'To get across unnoticed, we're going to have to take out one or two of those soldiers before we launch ourselves into the

water. Otherwise they'll either see or hear us. So we need to check out what they do. Do they stay in one place all the time or patrol up and down? When are they relieved? That kind of thing.'

'It'll be dark in a few minutes,' Watson pointed out.

'I don't mean now. We're here until at least tomorrow night, so we can do all that – check out the routine the Jerries are following and build a raft – in the daylight tomorrow. We'll cross tomorrow night, in the early hours of the morning, probably.'

Dawson turned round to face back into the forest. 'Let's find somewhere to hole up until tomorrow.' He shivered slightly and glanced up at the nearly cloudless sky. 'It's going to be a long, cold night,' he said. 'We've got two canteens of water and no food, unless you've got any chocolate hidden away somewhere.'

'No chance, mate.'

'Fucking gannet. So that's supper – water and water. At least we're still alive.'

The two men retreated a couple of hundred yards into the forest, moving slowly and carefully, trying to make as little noise as possible and to leave no trail. They needed somewhere where one of them could sleep while the other kept watch, and where nobody could easily sneak up on them.

'It's not perfect,' Dawson said, pointing to a tangle of undergrowth that had sprouted up around a fallen tree close to a small hillock, 'but it'll do.'

They checked all around the area, but spotted nothing suspicious. Then they crept between two bushes and sat down with their backs to the trunk of the fallen oak. There was a space on one side where a man could stretch

out – that would do as a bed – and the V-shape formed by one of the branches of the tree offered a useful vantage point over the surrounding area.

'You want to watch or sleep?' Dawson asked, replacing the cap on his water canteen.

'I don't care. If I had a coin, I'd toss you for it.'

'OK, then. You get your head down first. Let's do four-hour watches, and don't move out of here. If you need to have a slash or a crap, do it over there, in that corner.' He pointed to a spot amongst the exposed roots of the oak, then checked his watch. 'Right. I'll give you a shake just after midnight.'

CHAPTER 37

15 SEPTEMBER 1939

'God, I ache in every single muscle and joint in my body,' Dawson moaned.

It was a little after five in the morning, and Watson had just woken him from what could hardly be called a good night's sleep. The ground hadn't felt too bad when he lay down at one o'clock and Watson took over his uneventful watch, but after only a few minutes he'd felt as if he was being stabbed by stones and branches and brambles and God knows what else. He had finally drifted off, but every time he moved he woke up, albeit briefly.

Dawson felt hungover – a joke because he hadn't so much as smelt a beer in days – and absolutely exhausted. He was filthy dirty, and what had started out merely as stubble on his chin was now well on its way to becoming a full beard. It was no consolation that Watson looked – and probably felt – exactly the same.

'You know, Dave, if I wasn't so sure those fucking Jerries would shoot us on sight, I'd almost consider surrendering, just to get a bath and a hot meal.'

Watson nodded. 'You'll be taking a bath pretty soon,

if we're going to get across that river. A hot meal's going to take us a bit longer to find. Now, let's get going, mate.'

'I know. Let's see if we can find some logs. You told that officer at Catterick you were a proper engineer because you built things. You should be able to knock a raft together, no problem.'

Watson stared at him. 'I built bridges, mate, stuff like that. I used rivets and bolts and welding torches and sodding great lengths of steel. I didn't bugger about tying lumps of wood together to give a non-swimmer a fighting chance of getting across a river without drowning.'

'Well, now's your chance.' Dawson grinned. 'Come on, let's get on with it.'

The two men eased out of their overnight accommodation, again checked all around them to ensure there was no sign of any German soldiers and started searching for some fallen branches that would be suitable.

But it wasn't as easy as either of them had hoped. The forest floor was littered with leaves but very few lengths of fallen timber of any size, and most of the branches and tree trunks they did manage to find were obviously old and already fairly rotten, and rotten wood was no good to them. The majority of the branches that had fallen more recently were too small to support their weapons and ammunition, let alone a man.

'I thought this would be the easy bit,' Dawson muttered as they looked at yet another branch that appeared to be almost welded to the forest floor by an extensive growth of moulds and fungi. 'Christ, all we need are two or three decent lengths of timber.'

'Trees usually only fall over when they're dead and

have been for a while, unless there's a gale or something. This could be a wild goose chase.'

'Any ideas? Apart from a boat, obviously.'

Watson shrugged. 'If we can't find anything on the ground, we could cut the timber we need. We'll get what we want, but the problem is how much noise we make doing it.'

Dawson looked around them. They were deep in the forest, probably at least half a mile from the soldiers on the riverbank, so as long as they didn't make too much of a racket, Watson's idea might be feasible. The biggest risk was if the Germans had sent patrols into the forest itself. But right then, he hadn't got any better ideas.

'OK, Dave, let's go for it. We'll head east, away from the river, find a tree and cut what we need. One of us can stand guard while the other does the work. That way, we should be able to spot any Jerry soldiers heading our way.'

They spread out, to cover more ground, but kept each other in sight as they started looking. They needed a tree with branches big enough, but close to the ground – they weren't equipped for climbing. And they only had a couple of Mauser bayonets to do the job, so they couldn't tackle anything really substantial.

They'd been searching for about ten minutes when Watson gave a low whistle and held up his hand.

Dawson immediately stopped, checked all around him, his Schmeisser held ready to fire, but he saw nothing, then looked back at Watson.

His partner gestured, holding the fingers of his left hand open like a claw, while he moved his hand down

on to the top of his steel helmet – the military 'come to me' or 'formate on me' hand signal.

Dawson glanced round again and moved quickly but silently across to where Watson was standing. 'What is it?' he asked, his voice low.

'I might have solved our little problem,' Watson said, and pointed.

Perhaps fifty yards away, Dawson saw a long, low black shape through the trees. It looked a bit like an upturned rowing boat, but it was massive. 'What is it?' he demanded.

'We've seen a few tree stumps here and there in the forest,' Watson said, 'so we know there must have been woodcutters working here. That's the fruit of their labours. It's a pile of cut timber, ready to be loaded on to a cart and hauled away.'

Dawson looked more closely and realized Watson was right. Now he could see that it wasn't a single object, but a collection of pieces of timber. He should have expected to find something like that in a forest.

'Any sign of the woodcutters?'

'Not that I can see. You go right, and I'll go left, OK?'

'OK.'

Cautiously, the two men separated to approach the woodpile from opposite sides, just in case there were any German civilians – or even German soldiers – anywhere near it. They checked everywhere, but saw nothing. Dawson guessed the forest had been cleared of civilians, just like the farms and villages.

Almost simultaneously, they stepped into the clearing and walked over to the massive heap of wood. They could see now that it wasn't actually one pile – it was several.

Dominating the clearing was a mound of massive logs. One look was enough to tell both men they wouldn't be carrying any of them away – they were just too heavy.

'Probably telegraph poles,' Watson murmured, confirming Dawson's unspoken thoughts.

Beside that pile were half a dozen heaps of other, smaller logs, varying in length from about fifteen feet down to three or four feet, with varying diameters.

'Good news.' Dawson pointed at a number of logs about six to eight feet long. 'Two or three of those should do the trick.'

Watson nodded. 'And better than cutting fresh wood. These will have dried out a bit. They'll be lighter to carry and more buoyant.'

They walked over and looked carefully at the logs. They both doubted they'd been booby-trapped – a pile of timber in the middle of a German forest could hardly be described as a strategic target – but it was still worth checking.

'Don't see anything,' Watson said, standing up after peering beneath and behind the logs that were lying on the top of the pile.

'Neither do I. OK, let's pick out a couple and start hauling them back towards the river.'

They stood at opposite ends of the woodpile, slung their weapons over their shoulders and each grabbed one end of the six-foot log lying on the very top of the pile.

'Bugger me, that's heavy,' Dawson muttered as the two men strained to lift the piece of wood. 'Are you sure this will float?'

'Wood floats, trust me,' Watson said, staggering

slightly under the weight. 'I think we'll only need two of these.'

'Bloody good job too.'

'Let's get it on to our shoulders,' Watson suggested. 'It'll be a lot easier that way.'

Working together, the two men lifted the length of wood up. Watson was right – it did make carrying it easier. It left them each with one hand free, though using a weapon would still be impossible unless they dropped the log first.

They walked slowly, trying to make as little noise as possible, about 100 yards from the clearing where they'd found the woodpile, then lowered the log to the ground. Then they walked back, picked up a second one, and repeated the process.

Then they stopped for a breather. Dawson took out the map and checked it, then placed his compass on the ground beside it.

'If you remember,' he said, 'when we stood at the edge of the forest yesterday and looked over at the river, there was a big bend in it, and then we could see a longish straight section in both directions. According to this map, there are only two places in this area where the Moselle has a bend like that, and they're fairly close together.'

He pointed at the map. 'The first is here, near this town called Wehr. In fact, Wehr is almost on the bend, so I don't think that's where we are. The road by that bend is quite a long way from the river. The other bend is about a mile to the south of that, and that's where I reckon we are. See, the road runs right beside the river, and it's a much bigger bend. I think that fits better with what we saw.'

Watson studied the map where Dawson was pointing. 'I'd agree with that,' he said. 'So what?'

'So nothing. Just establishing where we are. According to this map, there aren't any towns or villages close to this point over in Luxembourg, so hopefully nobody will see us land.'

'We can't ask people over there for help, then?'

Dawson shook his head. 'I don't know, but if we can, we should just slip through into France without anyone even knowing we were in Luxembourg. I don't know what our status would be there, but we'd certainly be classed as armed combatants illegally entering a neutral country. I'd guess we'd be arrested at the very least, maybe even handed back to the fucking Jerries. I doubt the people of Luxembourg want to irritate Uncle Adolf. If the Germans found out that they'd harboured Allied troops, that might give them an excuse to invade, neutral territory or not.'

'No chance of a hot meal and a cold beer, then?'

'Pretty bloody unlikely. Anyway, we'd better get moving.' Dawson folded the map and put it back in his battledress pocket. 'We ought to just shift these logs a hundred yards at a time, and leave them somewhere close to the edge of the forest. How long will it take to tie them together to make a raft? And what can we use to do that?'

Watson shrugged. 'A couple of minutes, that's all. We can lash them together using our belts. We'll have to do that right by the water's edge, though. We can't carry two logs at the same time. And we'll have to get past those guards somehow.'

'Got it in one. We have to get ourselves and these lengths of timber from the forest and then into the river without being spotted. How the hell we're going to do that, I've no idea right now.'

CHAPTER 38

A couple of hours later, they'd shifted both the logs to a position just within the forest boundary, which only left them with the final 200 yards or so to cover, over almost completely open ground, and with German soldiers still patrolling the road that lay between them and their objective. Dawson still hadn't worked out how they were going to get past them, though he had the glimmerings of an idea.

'Now we watch, yes?' Watson asked.

The two men had returned to the same spot they'd occupied the previous evening, on the very edge of the forest. It provided good cover and had a reasonably unobstructed view of the road and the river beyond.

'Yeah,' Dawson agreed. 'We need to work out their routine, find out what they do and when they do it. It'll be bloody boring, but we have to know what's going on out there before we can try and get across the river. Have you got something to write with?'

Watson tapped his pockets and eventually came up with the stub of a pencil and a grubby sheet of paper. 'Will this do?'

'Perfect. Just check your watch. Mine says ten-forty-three.'

'Ten-forty-five.'

'That's close enough. Right, we can see four sentries from where we are now, so we'll name them from the left and call them Able, Baker, Charlie and Dog – straight out of the phonetic alphabet. Write those names at the top of the page. Every time one of them does anything, make a note of it, with the time. We'll soon find out their routine. When we know that, hopefully we'll find a way to get past them, preferably without killing one of them.'

'Any ideas?'

'I've got a kind of a germ of one, but it all depends on what we see today – and on the moon,' Dawson added.

'The moon? What the hell's the moon got to do with it?'

'I'll tell you later. Right. I'm going to get my head down. You've got the binoculars, paper and pencil, so just keep watch and record everything that happens. Give me a shake in a few hours and I'll take over. A mug of tea would be nice when I wake up.'

'Dream on, mate,' Watson said. 'I can offer you a swig of water and that's it. Anyway, just shut up and try to grab some sleep. It's going to be a bloody long day and a longer night tonight, is my guess.'

By the time he woke Dawson, Watson had jotted down several notes on his piece of paper and, as the afternoon gradually slipped into evening, Dawson added several more. When he woke his companion just after nine, the paper was covered in scribbles.

'How are we doing?' Watson asked, sitting up and stretching.

'About the same as usual – pretty average.' Dawson handed him a water canteen.

'You got a plan yet?'

'I might have,' Dawson admitted. 'I thought we might use German efficiency against the German sentries.'

Watson rubbed his eyes. 'You'll need to explain that to me. And slowly and carefully, because I'm still half asleep.'

Dawson grinned and glanced down at the piece of paper in his hand. 'I saw the same routine you did,' he started. 'Those sentries stay in more or less the same spot all the time. They occasionally walk up and down, but for most of their watch they just stand there, keeping an eye on the forest. They do four hours, then they're relieved by another soldier. The new men arrive in the back of a truck that drives along the road from south to north, picking up the soldiers at the end of their watch at the same time. Then the vehicle drives back down the road, heading south, so I assume that the main German camp or whatever they've got is somewhere down there.'

Watson nodded. 'I figured the same. And it looks as if each Jerry finishing his watch briefs the new man on what's been happening – which probably consists of the German equivalent of "fuck all".'

Dawson looked at the paper again. 'Right. The watch change-over that you saw was at twelve noon. I watched the same thing at four this afternoon, and again at eight this evening.'

'So the next ones will be at midnight and four in the morning, I suppose?'

'Exactly. As well as the sentries, there's a two- or three-man roving patrol, armed with machine-pistols. They walk along the road about half-way through each watch and have a chat to each of the sentries. Like the truck, they come from somewhere down to the south, walk north, and then come back down the road about half an hour later. I think they're the key.'

Watson looked interested. 'How?'

'If we try and cross from here to the river, especially carrying one of those bloody logs, one of the sentries will be certain to spot us, because we'll have to go within about fifty yards of where he'll be standing. But if we can take out one of them, we should be able to get across, because then the closest soldiers will be a hundred yards away.

'I mentioned the moon. If it was going to be a bright night, this wouldn't work, because we'd be seen even at that distance. But it's not. We've got pretty much full cloud cover, which means the visibility will be poor once night falls. And that's what we need.'

'So we hit one of the sentries? Is that what you mean?'

'Yes, but we'll have to do it quietly, and that means getting right up close to him,' Dawson said.

'But he'll see us coming, surely?'

Dawson nodded. 'Of course. The trick will be getting close without arousing his suspicion. And there is a way we can do that, I hope. It'll be too dark to see much more than the outline of a figure tonight, so we make sure that our outlines are what he'll be expecting to see. We've still got the coal-scuttle helmets, which are pretty distinctive, and in the dark he won't be able to tell the colour of our uniforms. We'll also be carrying German

weapons – the Schmeissers – so I'm hoping that the sentry will see us heading towards him and just assume we're the roving patrol.'

'Suppose the real patrol comes along?'

'That, I hope, is the clever bit. We wait until after the patrol has been up the line and gone back down to the south. We give them a few minutes to get clear, then we walk up to the sentry. With any luck, he'll think the members of the patrol have forgotten something, and he won't realize who we are until we're right beside him.'

'And then we kill him?' Watson asked flatly.

'No, not unless we have to. I know the Germans are the enemy, and in a fire-fight I'll try and kill them because I know that if I don't they'll try to kill me. Face-to-face, where we have a choice, it's different. I'd far rather just knock him out. But if we have to kill him then, yes, that's what I'll do.'

'And then what?'

'Then we drag the timbers over to the river, tie them together, strip off and put all our gear on the raft and paddle it across to the other side. When we get into Luxembourg, at least the Jerries won't still be chasing us, so we can relax a bit, then just cross the border back into France.'

It sounded easy the way Dawson said it, but neither man had the slightest doubt that what they were going to attempt wasn't 'easy' in any sense of the word. But there didn't seem to be much in the way of alternatives.

'So when do we do it?' Watson asked.

'The next watch change will be at midnight. The roving patrol should be along some time after one in the morning, and should be walking back to the German

camp about three-quarters of an hour later. Let's start moving the logs out of the forest and part-way to the river a little while before midnight, because the sentries will be less alert at the end of their watch. Then we find ourselves some cover out there' – he gestured towards the open ground between the edge of the forest and the road – 'and wait until just after the roving patrol's walked past, heading south. Then we stand up, cross over to the road and walk down it towards the sentry, as if we owned the bloody place. If you can muster the odd word or two of German when we get closer, that would be even better. That will make the sentry assume we're just a couple of German soldiers. By the time he realizes we're not, we'll be too close. It'll be too late.'

'Time to go,' Dawson murmured, just after eleven-twenty by his watch. 'Leave the weapons here – we can't afford to make any noise.'

The two men took off their various belts and straps and placed all their equipment on the ground. Then they walked over to where they'd left the two baulks of timber, picked up the first one and hoisted it on to their shoulders.

It was a dark night, the moon only fitfully visible as a dimly seen and ghostly shape through the thick veil of cloud that covered the sky.

They reached the edge of the forest and stopped for a few moments, using their ears more than their eyes, but could detect no sounds that might indicate trouble. Then they stepped forward, walking slowly and carefully over the uneven ground, balancing the heavy timber between them.

'This is far enough,' Dawson whispered.

They stopped and lowered the wood to the ground, and looked all around them. They were, Dawson thought, probably only about eighty yards from the road and the nearest sentry, quite close enough for the moment. Then they turned and walked back to the safety of the wood.

'Bloody hard work, that,' Watson muttered, as they stepped back between the trees.

'Yeah. We'll take a five-minute break, then do the other one.'

By eleven-forty, both lengths of timber were positioned ready for the final part of their journey to the river.

Dawson had decided their best option was to move out of the forest before the watch change-over. Both men had stood watches before, many times. They knew that towards the end of a very boring few hours, the attention of the sentry would be focused on the arrival of his relief, not on what he was supposed to be doing. So it made sense for them to get into their final position before the new, more alert, soldier arrived to take over.

They'd left their British helmets, and the Mausers and their ammunition in the forest – rifles would be no use to them now – and had just taken the remaining stick grenades and Schmeisser machine-pistols with them. They found a suitable hollow in the ground about sixty yards from the road and ducked down into it. It didn't offer much cover, but it would do. They were invisible from the road, in that light, unless any of the sentries or occasional vehicles they saw passing had powerful torches, and so far they'd seen no evidence of that. The sentries had small hand torches, but that was all.

They had a long wait ahead of them. First the watch change-over would take place, within the next half-hour. Then they'd have at least an hour before the roving patrol passed them going north, and another forty minutes or so before it returned. Only then, when the patrol was out of sight, would they be able to move.

CHAPTER 39

16 SEPTEMBER 1939

It was ten minutes after midnight before they saw what they'd been expecting.

'Slow-moving truck, left ten o'clock,' Dawson whispered.

'Got it.'

The two men watched in silence as the vehicle approached. In the light from its partially blacked-out headlamps they could see two of the other sentries waiting patiently to be relieved.

'It's stopped where sentry Able was positioned.'

As Dawson made this observation, the truck started moving again.

'Now Baker.'

Again the lorry braked to a stop. Dawson and Watson couldn't see anyone climb out of the vehicle or get into it, because the back of the truck was in darkness, but they had no doubt about what was happening on the road in front of them.

'And that's Charlie,' Watson murmured.

'And Dog,' Dawson added, a couple of minutes later,

as they watched the vehicle drive out of sight towards the north.

Twenty minutes later, what they assumed was the same lorry drove back, heading south along the road. The sentries, briefly illuminated by its headlights, acknowledged the vehicle's passage with raised hands or nods.

'That should be it for another hour or so,' Dawson whispered.

Ninety minutes later, they heard, rather than saw, two men walking down the road, though the cigarette one of them was smoking indicated their position reasonably clearly. The patrol stopped by each of the sentries and talked briefly with them – Dawson and Watson could just about hear the faint sounds of their conversation – and then the soldiers walked on.

'Another half hour or so, they should be on the way back. Then we can move,' Dawson said.

It was actually closer to an hour before they saw the two-man patrol walking back down the road beside the river, and this time both of them were smoking.

'Sloppy, that,' Watson muttered. 'On a clear night you can see a cigarette being smoked a quarter of a mile away. It's a dead giveaway.'

'Yeah,' Dawson replied. 'But they're not that bothered. They're well inside Germany, surrounded by other Germans. But it's good news for us.'

He glanced at the illuminated dial of his watch. 'We'll give them ten minutes,' he said. 'That should be long enough for them to get well clear of the area, but not so

long that the sentry will be too suspicious when he sees two men coming towards him.'

'Right,' Dawson said. 'Time to go.'

The two men stood up, slung their Schmeissers and settled the German helmets on their heads.

'You want a fag, for realism?' Watson asked, fishing a packet out of one of his battledress pockets.

'Yeah, but we don't light up until we feel the tarmac under our feet, OK?'

Dawson led the way, walking slowly across the open ground, and aiming to intercept the road midway between the two sentry positions that they'd named Baker and Charlie. They'd already decided that their target would be Charlie.

In a couple of minutes, Dawson saw the hard surface of the road directly in front of him, and turned right, towards Charlie, Watson following right behind him. After they'd walked a few yards, they paused, and Watson lit two cigarettes. Dawson closed both eyes tight as he did so, to preserve his night-vision, then took one of them from him.

Ahead, they could hear the sentry moving. Obviously the sight of the match had alerted him to their presence, but at the same time the fact that somebody was on the road and felt able to light a cigarette should reassure him that they were a couple of German soldiers rather than hostile troops.

They strode on towards the sentry, making no attempt to walk quietly.

Suddenly Dawson saw a dim shape ahead, perhaps ten yards in front of them.

Watson muttered a couple of German words – he only knew a handful – and Dawson grunted in reply, attempting to sound natural.

The sentry switched on his torch as they approached him, shining the beam towards them. He obviously saw the Schmeissers slung across their chests, and the German helmets, and gave no sign of having noticed the different colour and type of uniforms they were wearing.

And then they were right beside him.

Dawson knew they had to act fast and decisively, because within a matter of seconds the sentry would realize they weren't Germans. He walked straight up to the man and without a moment's hesitation smashed his fist straight into the sentry's stomach. The German soldier had no time to react. He doubled up, retching painfully, and Dawson followed up his first blow with a rabbit punch to the back of the man's neck. The German collapsed senseless to the ground.

Watson bent down and picked up the sentry's Mauser, pulled out the bolt and sent it spinning away into the darkness, rendering the weapon useless. 'Nicely done, Eddie,' he whispered, undoing the man's belt and starting to lash his arms together behind his back. 'You sure you don't want to kill him?'

'No,' Dawson said firmly. 'He's out of it now. By the time he comes round, we'll be in Luxembourg.'

'I bloody well hope so, after all this.'

Less than a minute later, Dawson and Watson were crossing back over the road, heading for the spot where they'd hidden the two lengths of wood. They'd left their weapons and other equipment near the unconscious and

incapacitated sentry and moved as quickly and sound-lessly as they could.

'Over here,' Watson said, as he spotted the timber.

'You reckon we can take both of them at the same time?' Dawson asked, looking at the pale grey shapes lying on the grass in front of them. 'That'd reduce the time we're exposed out here.'

'Let's give it a try.'

They moved one of the logs so that it was about two feet away from the other one and lying parallel to it, and then stepped between them. Together, they bent down and wrapped one hand around each of the logs.

'On three,' Dawson muttered. 'One, two, three.'

They straightened their backs, grunting with the effort, and lifted both logs up to waist level. They were heavy – they already knew that, having carried them all the way from the woodpile deep in the forest – but Dawson thought they'd be able to manage, as long as neither of them stumbled or tripped over anything.

'You OK, Dave?'

'Just about,' Watson replied. 'Ready?'

'Yeah. We'll do it on three again. One, two, three.'

The two men took a step forward simultaneously, and began walking slowly back towards the river. Fortunately, the ground they had to cross was fairly level – if it had been full of tussocks and dips they would certainly have had to make two journeys.

They'd covered maybe fifty yards before Dawson felt the strain on his arms becoming intolerable.

'Gotta take a break, Dave,' he muttered, and began slowing his steps.

'Me too. OK, start lowering now.'

The logs thudded softly on to the grass as the two men bent down and released their grip on them.

Dawson rubbed his hands together. His arms, he noticed, were quivering with the strain, but he was pleased. They'd already carried the timber about a quarter of the distance they needed to cover.

'We'll just take a couple of minutes, Dave,' he murmured, 'then we'll do it again.'

The second time, they managed to lug them a little further, perhaps seventy yards, before they stopped again.

'Nearly there,' Dawson said. 'One more lift and that should be it.'

In fact, they only managed to get the logs just to the river side of the road before they had to lower them to the ground again, but then the water was only about twenty yards away, so they were able to carry them to the riverbank one at a time. That took them less than three minutes.

'You get the stuff, Eddie. I'll start tying these together.'

'Right,' Dawson replied and walked back up the bank towards the road.

Three minutes later he was back, carrying their two Schmeissers, webbing belts and all their other gear in his arms.

Watson had already tied a belt around one end of the logs. 'Give me another couple of belts, Eddie,' he said. 'That should be all we'll need.'

Dawson helped him secure two more belts around the lengths of timber, effectively turning the two round logs into a long and narrow raft, which they hoped would be

enough to keep their gear clear of the water and fairly dry as they made the crossing, and keep Dawson afloat as well.

Silently, the two men stripped off their uniforms and bundled them up. They just kept on their underwear because it was going to be cold in the water and they would need some kind of protection. They placed the uniforms, with their boots and the Schmeissers and grenades and everything else, on the logs.

'Now let's see if this thing floats,' Dawson said.

'It had fucking better,' Watson muttered. 'OK, I'll get this side.'

The riverbank where they'd positioned the logs had a reasonably gentle slope down to the surface of the water, and their makeshift raft was pointing almost straight down the bank.

'Grab hold of both logs at the same time,' Watson instructed, 'but don't put any strain on the belts.'

'Understood.'

'Right, we'll pick this up between us and just walk forward into the river, OK?'

The two men bent down and lifted the raft cautiously, being careful to balance it and keep it level, and slowly moved forward.

'Bugger, that's cold,' Watson muttered as he stepped into the river. 'OK,' he said, as Dawson splashed in behind him. 'Now just lower it down, but keep a firm hold on it. We don't know how strong the current is, and we daren't let it get swept away.'

Moments later, the raft was floating on the surface of the Moselle. Dawson looked at it critically, partly to take his mind off the crossing, which he'd been dreading.

'These logs are floating a bit low in the water, aren't they?' he asked.

'I expected them to. This isn't properly dried and seasoned timber, so the logs are heavy. But don't worry about it – this'll float, no problem.'

'So how am I supposed to do this?' Dawson asked, his teeth already chattering – the water was very cold.

'Easy. I'll go at the front end, you stay at the back. We'll just walk forward until we're in the water up to our necks, then you just hang on to the logs. I'll swim along beside the raft, and if you can kick out a bit with your feet, that might help as well. Just don't panic. If you hold on to the logs, you can't possibly sink, OK?'

'OK.' Dawson forced out the response.

Watson moved forward. 'Right, I'm swimming now, so just let yourself go as soon as you like.'

Dawson took another step forward, then another. Suddenly his probing foot touched nothing, and for an instant he floundered, feeling himself sinking beneath the surface. He bobbed up, spluttering and shaking his head.

'No noise, Eddie. Just take it easy,' Watson hissed. 'Hold on to the logs, and keep your head above water.'

Dawson flung both his arms over the top of the log raft and clung on desperately. The fragile craft wobbled dangerously for a few moments, then stabilized again.

'Careful,' Watson warned, looking behind him.

'Sorry, mate. Fucking terrifies me, this,' Dawson gasped.

'Just hang on.'

Watson looked behind them. The current had caught the improvised craft and had already pulled it a few yards

away from the east bank of the river. But that would never be enough – they needed to get across to the other side, not just go with the flow of the current along that bank.

He kicked out strongly, almost willing the log raft forward, across the wide river. The opposite bank was dimly visible as a dark line above the even darker surface of the water. It looked a long way off. But the good news was that it didn't actually matter where they landed – within reason – though the further downstream they went, the further they'd have to walk through Luxembourg to get to the French border.

The current didn't seem too strong, and Watson's efforts did seem to be driving the craft out into the middle of the river. He glanced back at Dawson, who was still clinging on to the logs, his hands visibly shaking with the strain.

'Eddie, just relax, OK? And if you could wiggle your legs about a bit that'd help me.'

Dawson looked at him, then seemed to shake himself. 'Sorry,' he said again, and slid back off the logs, still keeping his hands on them for support. His head dipped down, but didn't go under the surface, and he started kicking out.

'Great stuff, Eddie,' Watson said.

'I'm still fucking terrified, mate, but I'm trying to think positive. If I hold on, I can't sink, right?'

'Right.'

'So I'll try and help. Where are you aiming for?'

'West, basically,' Watson replied. 'Anywhere on that far bank will do.'

'OK.' Dawson continued kicking, though he wasn't

entirely sure his efforts were actually helping propel the raft forward.

In five minutes, they'd drifted quite a way downstream, but were well over half-way across the river. Dawson was just starting to think they were going to make it, when it all went badly wrong.

CHAPTER 40

16 SEPTEMBER 1939

Dawson and Watson heard a shout, and it was from behind them, from the German side of the river. Then other voices joined in, and they could see running figures, torch-beams bouncing as the men moved around.

'What the hell's all that about?' Dawson muttered. 'Can you make out what they're saying, Dave?'

Watson listened intently for a few moments. 'I heard one of them shout something about *der Fluss*,' he said. 'That means "the river",' he added.

'Oh, shit. Don't like the sound of that.'

The two men redoubled their efforts, kicking out as hard as they could with their feet, trying to propel the raft ever faster towards the bank on the Luxembourg side of the river.

Behind them, they heard the sudden rumble as a big diesel engine sprang into life, then the sound of grating gears. Then two dim beams of light swept across the river towards them as the lorry was manoeuvred into position. Moments later, the brightness of the beams increased dramatically as the blackout covers were removed from the headlights.

'They haven't got a searchlight, so a truck's head-lamps are the next best thing,' Dawson muttered. 'One of those bastards must have seen us.'

At that moment, the beam from the headlamps swept over them, and stopped a short distance behind them. Then it started moving back towards them, to the accompaniment of a revving engine and the crunching of gears as the German driver of the truck tried to manoeuvre the vehicle into the correct position to shine on that part of the river.

And then they were illuminated, caught like moths in a flame, the headlamp beams dazzling them.

'Get behind the logs,' Watson ordered. 'Keep as low as possible. Water's the best defence there is against bullets.'

A rifle shot rang out from the east bank of the river. Splinters of wood flew off one of the logs as the bullet ploughed into the timber a mere six inches from Dawson's head.

'Oh, fuck,' he muttered, took a deep breath and ducked beneath the surface, his fear of being shot instantly overcoming his terror at being in the water. He felt the two logs above his head and slowly moved under them before bobbing up on the other side, where the timber would provide a measure of protection.

Watson had already done the same. The two men stayed as low as they could behind their floating barricade as a fusillade of shots rang out, a discordant assault on the silence of the night. Bullets ploughed into the wood beside them and splashed into the water. A couple of them even hit Dawson, but Watson was right – their passage through even three or four feet of

water slowed them right down, and they were a mere irritation.

'Keep moving,' Watson called. 'We've got a long way to go to reach that bank.'

'Yeah,' Dawson agreed, 'and when we climb up it, we'll be fucking sitting ducks.'

'We'll be a lot further away then, so we won't be anything like as visible. Let's sort it out when we get there, OK?'

Another volley of shots was fired from the opposite bank. A bullet smashed into one of the Schmeissers and knocked it off the makeshift raft and into the water, where it immediately sank before either man could reach it.

'Bugger this,' Dawson muttered and he reached up and grabbed the other machine-pistol. He pulled himself up slightly on the logs, braced the weapon as best he could, sighted roughly towards the German side of the river, towards the twin headlamps of the truck, and pulled the trigger. He fired a short burst, released the trigger, and then fired again.

He heard shouts of alarm and a cry of pain – a lucky shot must have hit one of the German soldiers – but then the MP 40 jammed. He ducked back behind the logs and worked the action of the weapon, trying to shift the jammed round from the breach. He freed it, pulled out the magazine, grabbed another one from the webbing belt on top of their clothes and snapped it into place. Then he took aim at the headlamps of the lorry and fired again, and again, heedless of the bullets whining around him and crashing into the raft. All he could hope to achieve was to make the Germans keep their heads down

– the dazzling beams of the truck's headlamps meant he couldn't see even a single target. He'd have liked to take out the vehicle's lights, but it was a challenging shot even with a rifle, firing it from a lump of wood bobbing about in the middle of the Moselle river. With a machine-pistol, it was all down to luck. And luck wasn't something they seemed to have a lot of that night.

The Schmeisser jammed again, after Dawson had fired perhaps half the magazine and, as the machine-pistol fell silent, the rate of rifle fire from the other bank increased markedly. Dawson ducked back behind the wood again and wrestled with the Schmeisser, freeing the jammed cartridge from the breach and swiftly re-loading the weapon.

Watson was still kicking out furiously, driving the raft closer and closer to the Luxembourg side of the river, ignoring the bullets flying around him. He knew the timber would stop anything the Germans could fire at them, and the bullets hitting the water were essentially harmless, their energy spent in a few feet. His only worry was if his head became exposed over the logs for long enough for one of the Germans to target it, so he kept as low as possible, lying on his back and dragging the lengths of wood – and Dawson – through the water as fast as he could.

Dawson levered himself up again, ready to fire the machine-pistol, but as he did so the raft was caught by a sudden eddy current and slipped out of the cone of the headlamp beams from the bank, into the welcoming darkness.

'Ignore the weapon,' Watson called again. 'Just keep kicking. We have to reach the bank.'

Dawson put the Schmeisser back on top of the raft, grabbed the timber with both hands and did as he was told.

On the German side of the river, they could hear angry shouts and the sound of the truck's engine revving as the driver shifted the vehicle to try to illuminate them again. But although the beam of the lights passed close by them a couple of times, the raft was now moving more quickly in the current, and it didn't pick them out. The rate of firing suddenly diminished.

Dawson and Watson were still kicking out as hard as they could, easing their raft over to the Luxembourg side of the river.

'Only about ten yards to go,' Watson gasped, his voice harsh with exertion. 'We're nearly there.'

'We've still got to get out.'

But they were getting closer to the riverbank, and a few seconds later, while the Germans were still manoeuvring the truck to try to pick them out again with its lights, Watson's feet touched the bottom of the river. He dug in his toes and forced the raft closer to the shore.

'I'm touching the bottom,' he said.

Moments later, Dawson felt both the muddy bottom of the river under his own feet and an immediate sense of relief.

The two men moved quickly towards the shore, dragging the raft behind them. Dawson grabbed his pile of clothes and tossed it on to dry land as soon as he was close enough to do so, then stepped back towards the raft and grabbed for the Schmeisser.

But as his fingers stretched out for the weapon, the headlamps swung towards them again, and another

couple of shots rang out. Dawson fumbled for the machine-pistol, but it slipped from his grasp and fell into the water.

'Forget it,' Watson snapped, already heading for cover away from the water's edge. 'Let's just get the hell out of here.'

Dawson scrambled up the bank, ducked into the undergrowth and lay flat, just as the beams of the head-lamps swept over the raft and then steadied on it. Yet again, a barrage of concentrated fire rang out, bullets ploughing into the wood of the raft and the water all around it.

Then there was a colossal explosion from right in front of them. The last thing Dawson heard before unconsciousness overcame him was Watson's sudden yell of pain.

CHAPTER 41

16 SEPTEMBER 1939

It could have been minutes, or it might have been hours. Dawson had no idea, except that it was still dark, though the moon was now visible and casting a dim light over the landscape.

He came round slowly, painfully, with no clear idea where he was or what had happened. But gradually his mind reassembled the fractured memories, and realization dawned. One of the shots fired by the Germans on the opposite bank must have hit the stick grenades, and the whole lot – the five or six they had left – must have exploded simultaneously, in a sympathetic detonation.

Dawson was, he knew, lucky to be alive. The riverbank must have acted as a shield, preventing the blast from hitting him directly. He assumed that he'd simply been knocked out, perhaps even concussed, by the explosion.

Then he remembered something else. Dave Watson. He'd been closer to the bank, he thought – though his memory was still confused – but Dawson did very clearly recall that his companion had cried out in pain. That, in

fact, had been the last thing he *did* remember. So where was his friend? And how badly was he hurt?

Dawson cautiously eased up into a crouch and peered across the river, but in the darkness he could see nothing. The truck's engine was silent and its headlights extinguished – in fact, he couldn't even see the vehicle – and there was no sign of the troops who'd been shooting at them. But just because he couldn't see them, it didn't mean that they weren't still there.

He looked round. A few feet away he could see a shape, silent and unmoving. He scrambled across and knelt beside his companion.

Watson was still unconscious – that much was immediately obvious – and his chest and left arm were soaked with blood. For a single heart-stopping instant, Dawson thought he was dead, but then he noticed the man's chest rising and falling as he breathed. How badly was he wounded?

The bundle of uniform that Dawson had flung ashore was a couple of yards away. He bent over it and rooted around until he found the trench knife, which had a sharper blade than the Mauser bayonet, the only other weapon he had left. Then he lifted the bottom of Watson's blood-soaked vest, slit it all the way up and peeled away the material to look at his friend's chest.

Even in the dark, the wound that had caused the bleeding was obvious. A chunk of shrapnel, presumably from the explosion of one of the stick grenades, had embedded itself in Watson's left shoulder, a couple of inches below the collar bone. The wound didn't look that deep, but it had bled a hell of a lot.

Dawson stretched out his hand to remove the lump

of twisted metal, then stopped. If he pulled it out, that might make the situation worse. Maybe the shrapnel was actually helping plug the wound, reducing the flow of blood. But a rip in Watson's vest showed that the shrapnel had dragged some of the material into the wound, and Dawson knew he had to get that out if he was going to avoid infection.

Before he removed the metal, he needed to make up a pad or something he could apply to the injury. They had no medical kit – most of their standard equipment had been left in the lorry back in the Warndt Forest – so he grabbed the cleanest item of clothing he could see, which was his shirt. He used the trench knife to cut it into strips, tying them together to make rudimentary bandages, and wadded up what was left into a pad that he could apply to the wound.

Before he did anything else, Dawson stepped over to the water's edge and quickly washed his hands – not the most effective way of disinfecting them, but better than nothing, he hoped – then bent over Watson's still body. He held the pad ready in his left hand, and reached out and grabbed the piece of shrapnel with his right.

The twisted lump of metal was perhaps two inches by one, and slippery with blood. He seized it between his thumb and forefinger, took as firm a grasp as he could, and pulled.

Watson moaned as the pain penetrated his unconscious mind.

Dawson ignored his friend's complaint, because he knew he had to get the metal out, and if he could do it while Watson remained unconscious, so much the better.

His fingers slipped off the steel. He wiped his hand

on his vest – that, his underpants and a pair of socks, now more holes than material, were all he was wearing – and grabbed the shrapnel again. The steel fragment was twisted and bent, and had penetrated deep into the flesh. He had to put down his makeshift pad and hold Watson's shoulder as he gently eased the metal out of the wound.

When the shrapnel finally came free, there was a sudden rush of blood from the wound. Watson screamed in agony and then woke up.

Dawson seized the wad of material and pressed it firmly against his companion's injured shoulder.

'You're OK, mate,' he said. 'You just took a lump of steel in your shoulder, but it's gone now.'

Watson groaned and tried to sit up, but Dawson put a hand on his chest to keep him lying still.

'Don't try and move,' he said. 'I've got to bandage the wound in a minute, but for now just stay still while I keep the pressure on to stop the bleeding.'

'Jesus Christ, that hurts,' Watson muttered.

'It will do,' Dawson replied. 'That was a pretty big lump of steel I pulled out of your shoulder.'

'Not that. My shoulder is just numb, but it feels like there's a man with an axe cutting his way into my skull.'

'Where?'

'The left side, just above my ear.'

Dawson leant forward and looked at the side of Watson's head. There was a huge bruise there, badly swollen.

'That's quite a crack you've got there, Dave. At least it wasn't a piece of shrapnel, otherwise you'd have bled to death by now. You were hit by something large and

solid. Maybe when the grenades blew, a chunk of wood off one of the logs shot up the bank. You've got a bruise and a graze, but the skin isn't badly cut.'

Dawson eased the makeshift pad away from the wound on Watson's shoulder and looked at it critically. He could see a piece of fabric sticking out of the cavity – a strip of Watson's torn vest – and knew he had to remove that as well.

'Just lie still, mate,' he said. 'I've got to shift some debris from your wound. I'm sorry, but it's going to hurt.'

Watson grimaced. 'OK. Just be quick.'

Dawson dried his hand, took a firm grip on the edge of the material and pulled. There was another sudden rush of blood as the sodden strip of cloth emerged. Watson moaned in pain. Dawson pushed the pad into place and held it firmly.

'It's still bleeding,' he said, 'but not too badly. Before we can move, I'll have to try to strap it up. Are you OK to sit up now?'

Watson tried to nod and grimaced as another wave of pain shot through his skull. 'Yes,' he said weakly.

'Right, I'll help you. Just hold this pad in place.'

Dawson waited until Watson had placed his right hand over the wadded-up remnants of the shirt, then stepped over his body. He seized his friend's uninjured shoulder and helped him sit up.

'You OK?' he asked anxiously, as Watson seemed about to collapse.

'Bit dizzy. Hurting.'

Dawson grabbed the cut-up lengths of his shirt and looped one of them under Watson's arm and round his

neck. The wound was in an awkward place. He knew that trying to keep any degree of pressure on it was going to be difficult, especially if they were walking – and they were going to have to get moving pretty soon. He was also worried that his companion had lost quite a lot of blood.

'You'll need to keep the pressure on that pad, Dave. I can't get it any tighter and you're still bleeding.'

'Fucking crap doctor you are,' Watson said. 'Give me a hand to get dressed.'

Dawson helped Watson pull on his shirt and trousers, then laced his boots. Only then did he get dressed himself, and take stock of their situation.

The good news was that they were undeniably out of Germany and in Luxembourg, and so they were safe from the Germans, but that was pretty much all that was good. Watson was weak and hurting, and Dawson knew he wouldn't be able to walk far, or fast. They were both famished and thirsty. They'd had no food for what felt like a week, and their water bottles had presumably either fallen off the raft to drift away downstream, or had been blown to pieces when the grenades blew up. And he had no idea how any Luxembourgers would react to meeting them, but he doubted very much if they'd be welcomed with open arms.

They needed to move – and move quickly – and find somewhere they could hide for a while, plus they needed food and water, and much better bandages or something for Watson's wound.

'Can you stand?' Dawson asked. 'And walk?'

'I can't run, if that's what you're going to ask next,' Watson said, with a flash of his old spirit.

'I wasn't expecting you to. Here, let me give you a hand.'

Dawson stepped behind his companion and helped him stand up. Watson groaned as the wound in his shoulder sent a stab of pain across his chest, and swayed slightly. Then he nodded. 'OK. I think I can manage. But for Christ's sake, just take it slow. Where are we going?'

'Bloody good question. I've still got the map in my pocket, but the compass has gone, not that we need it.' Dawson gestured to the east, where the dark waters of the Moselle were flowing silently past the bank. 'That's a bloody great river, and if we keep it on our left-hand side, we have to be heading south. So we just keep walking until we reach the border. That's my plan, anyway.'

'Weapons?' Watson asked.

Dawson shrugged his shoulders. 'One trench knife, and one Mauser bayonet. That's it. Everything else went down when the grenades blew the raft apart. I even lost the pistol. But it doesn't matter now we're here in Luxembourg. In fact, if we still had the Schmeissers I'd suggest we dumped them.'

Watson nodded. Dawson noticed he was swaying slightly. He obviously needed something to support him when they started walking.

Dawson looked around the bank. 'Hang on here just a second,' he said, and walked across to a nearby clump of trees. He took out the Mauser bayonet and selected a branch about six feet long. Half a dozen blows from the bayonet severed it from the trunk of the tree, and another dozen trimmed all the smaller branches from it.

'Here, Dave,' Dawson said, walking back to his

companion. 'Sorry this is a bit rough, but it should help you walk. Are you OK to start now?'

Watson took the trimmed branch in his right hand and hefted it, then nodded. 'Thanks,' he said. 'This should help a bit. Right, let's go.'

Dawson stayed close beside Watson as the two men started walking away from the bank of the river – if there were still any Germans over on the opposite side of the Moselle, they didn't want to be close enough to be seen once dawn broke.

Dawson glanced at his watch. 'I think it should start getting light soon,' he said. 'I'd really like to find somewhere to hide out before daybreak.'

'Somewhere in the woods, you mean?'

'Probably.' Dawson nodded. 'According to this map, there aren't any towns very close to the border, so we shouldn't have a problem staying out of sight.'

The area was quite heavily wooded, and Dawson was convinced that once they moved away from the riverbank they'd be safe from German snipers.

He and Watson moved slowly into the shelter of the trees. The sky to the east was lightening, and their visibility was slowly improving, even under the canopy of leaves above their heads. Watson was obviously hurting badly, and could only walk quite slowly, so Dawson knew they'd have to stop pretty soon.

They'd covered perhaps 500 yards from the spot where they'd crawled ashore before he found anything suitable, and even then it wasn't ideal. He'd have preferred to put a bit more distance between themselves and the place they'd landed, just in case the Luxembourg police or anyone had spotted them.

But Watson couldn't walk much further, so it would have to do. Two large trees surrounded by heavy undergrowth were backed up against a sharp rise in the ground, and formed a natural vantage point. It offered a place where they could hide and lick their wounds, and allow Watson time to recover.

'Let's get in there, Dave,' Dawson said. 'That's as good a spot as anywhere I've seen.'

He led the way through the bushes, Watson following close behind him. Between the two trees was a more or less level area, and Dawson helped his friend sit down on it, then eased him backwards until he was leaning against one of the trees.

'Let's take a look at your shoulder, Dave.'

Dawson undid the buttons on Watson's shirt and pulled it open. The pad he'd tried to tie around the wound was sodden with blood, and when he eased it away from the skin, he could see that the injury was still bleeding, although the flow seemed a bit less than before. But one thing was perfectly obvious – Watson needed medical attention, and quickly, or at the very least the wound would have to be strapped up.

'Right, Dave,' Dawson said, forcing himself to sound a lot more cheerful than he felt. 'You stay here. I'm going to go off and try and find some food and drink for us and I'll try and grab some bandages or a medical kit or something for your shoulder, OK?'

Watson just nodded. He looked absolutely exhausted, grey with fatigue and loss of blood.

Dawson checked he had both the trench knife and the Mauser bayonet – there was no point in leaving one of the weapons with Watson, as he was plainly far too

exhausted to use one – and stepped back out of the clump of undergrowth into the forest.

He glanced around but saw nothing and nobody. Then he looked back, mentally fixing the appearance of the spot in his mind, before he turned and walked away. Behind him, the sun was just starting to rise, so he kept it at his back, to ensure he was heading west. He needed to keep away from the border, and ideally wanted to find some kind of outlying farmhouse. He didn't want to break in and steal stuff, but because of his situation – and more importantly due to Watson's fragile condition – he didn't see that he had much option. If he couldn't find food and drink and a medical kit, he guessed his friend might be dead by evening. There was no way Dawson was going to let that happen.

The forest started to thin out slightly as he walked further west. He scanned the ground ahead, looking for any signs of habitation, but it wasn't a house, as he'd hoped, that he saw first. It was a track, deeply rutted with the marks of what looked like a horse-drawn cart – he couldn't see any tread patterns that might indicate the tyres of a motor vehicle – and the centre bore the unmistakable signs of horses' hooves.

He arrived at the track at an oblique angle – it looked as if it ran more or less north-east to south-west – and for a few seconds Dawson just stood there, looking along it in both directions, trying to decide which way to go. South-west would take him deeper into Luxembourg itself, north-east towards the River Moselle and the border, and there was no way he could tell which way the farmhouse, or whatever the track served, was located.

The track might lead to a group of fields near the river, or perhaps some kind of habitation.

Eventually Dawson cut a mark on a tree to ensure he'd know exactly where he'd joined the track, then flipped a mental coin and turned left, away from the border. Even if the track didn't lead to a farmhouse, by going deeper into Luxembourg he should – sooner or later – find a farmhouse or cottage.

He trudged along the track, keeping close to the left-hand side so that he would be able to dive off into the forest if he encountered anyone, though at that early hour he was hopeful that everyone in the area would still be in bed.

After about 300 yards, another track ran off to the right. Dawson kept on the original route because the other track looked a lot narrower. In another 100 yards, it looked as if his decision was justified.

Directly in front of him, around a slight bend, the track ended in a muddy yard, a small house on one side and what looked like a hay barn on the other. Beside the barn was a large shed or equipment store, and sticking out of that was the front end of a wooden cart. In a field to the left of the barn a heavy horse – it looked to Dawson's amateur eyes like a shire horse or something similar – was standing, contentedly munching a break-fast of grass.

Neither the hay barn nor the equipment store was likely to hold stocks of food or drink, but beside the house itself was a small brick building that looked like a wash-house or perhaps a storeroom. That, to Dawson, looked a lot more hopeful. There was no sign of activity in the house, so with any luck he could get into the

building, find what he was looking for and get out again unnoticed.

He checked around him once more, then started walking towards the house, keeping among the trees and out of sight as much as he could. He reached a position behind the equipment shed which shielded him completely from the house and strode quickly across to the building. Dawson peered round the corner, towards the house. Still no movement. There was a stretch of open ground in front of him, between the shed and the small outhouse, and no way to go around it, so he simply ran.

He reached the wall of the outhouse and for a few seconds just stood there, catching his breath. The lack of food had left him feeling weak and feeble. He was surprised how much that brief exertion had taken it out of him.

When his breathing returned to normal, he risked a glance around the end of the building, over towards the house. There was still nobody in sight and no sign of any movement within the property, so he slipped around the end of the wall to the outhouse door.

There was no lock, just a simple handle, and the door was actually standing slightly ajar. As Dawson pushed it open, the hinges creaked alarmingly. He stepped inside, but left the door open – he didn't want to make the same noise when he left.

In the gloom, Dawson looked round, and was immediately disappointed. It had perhaps been a long-shot, hoping that the family might have stored food there, but the building was obviously nothing more than a wash-house, for both clothes and bodies, by the looks of it.

On the left-hand wall was a large square ceramic sink,

and above it a single tap – a slightly more sophisticated arrangement than the outside pump he'd seen at the farm in Germany where he and Watson had taken temporary refuge, what felt like weeks earlier.

The tap meant water and he badly needed a drink. Dawson turned the tap, waited for the water to flow so he could at least check the colour, then stuck his mouth under the spout and drank greedily. He came up for air, then drank again.

As he straightened up, water running down his unshaven chin, he was aware suddenly he was no longer alone.

Standing in the doorway of the wash-house, framed against the rising sun directly behind her, stood a young woman of perhaps twenty. It looked as if she was still wearing her night-clothes and had just pulled on a simple housecoat over them.

Dawson noticed two things about her immediately. The first was that, despite being almost in silhouette, she was obviously very pretty, with slightly tousled long blonde hair framing her face.

The second was the fact that she was holding a double-barrelled twelve-bore shotgun, both hammers pulled back into the firing position, which she was pointing directly at his stomach. It looked to Dawson as if she knew exactly how to use it.

CHAPTER 42

16 SEPTEMBER 1939

Dawson was effectively unarmed – the Mauser bayonet was in its scabbard on his belt and the trench knife was tucked into his right boot, but against a shotgun both blades were useless – so he did the only thing he could. He straightened up very slowly and raised both hands high.

The girl nodded in approval and barked a sentence at him.

Dawson understood not a word of it, so he shook his head slowly. 'I do not understand,' he replied, enunciating each syllable of each word very carefully. 'I am an English soldier. Do you speak English?'

The girl lowered the weapon very slightly, so that it was pointing at his groin rather than his stomach – though to Dawson, this didn't seem like much of an improvement – and stared at him for a moment. Then she said something else, again in a language Dawson didn't know, though it sounded guttural, like German.

He shrugged – not easy with his arms above his head – and tried on a smile for size.

The girl didn't return his smile, just gestured with the

muzzle of the shotgun towards Dawson's bayonet. 'Take that out,' she ordered, her English fairly fluent. 'Put it on the floor and kick it towards me.'

Dawson did exactly as he was told.

The girl nodded. 'Now, that looks like a knife in your right boot. Do the same with that.'

Again Dawson complied, because there was nothing else he could do.

The girl stepped back a couple of paces and for a few seconds glanced down at the two weapons lying on the floor near her feet. Then she kicked them both over to the side of the wash-house, out of his reach.

'I know weapons,' the girl said. 'I have shot rifles and shotguns since I was child. That is a Mauser bayonet and Wehrmacht trench knife. If you really are an English soldier, why do you carry German weapons?'

'It's a long story,' Dawson said.

'Why don't you tell me? I like stories. I have all day to listen.'

'But I haven't.'

'You are in no position to argue. How do I know you're not a German spy?'

'Because I don't speak German?' Dawson suggested.

The girl stared at him for a few moments, then again spoke in what sounded like German.

'*Ich hasse die Engländer. Ich werde dich erscheissen.*'

Then she raised her weapon to her shoulder and aimed it carefully at Dawson's head.

And, again, there was nothing he could do except shrug his shoulders.

Then the girl lowered the shotgun. 'I think you *are* English,' she said, almost reluctantly. 'I just told you –

in German – that I hate the English and that I am going to shoot you. If you *are* German, I think, when you look down these barrels, you would have admitted it. There is another reason too,' she added, but didn't elaborate.

Dawson heaved a sigh of relief. 'Do you hate the English?' he asked.

'No. You can put your arms down now,' she said. 'Who are you?'

'My name's Eddie Dawson and I am a British soldier. Your English is very good.'

'I am Celine. I had an Englishman as my teacher at school. My parents paid for extra lessons for me. If you are English, you should know Luxembourg is neutral, so what are you doing here in this country, on my land?'

Quickly, Dawson explained how they'd been cut off behind the German lines and apparently abandoned by the French.

'Of course,' Celine muttered, when he told her about Capitaine de St Véran.

'You don't like the French?' Dawson asked.

'They talk good fighting and then they always run away,' she said. 'So what happened then?'

Dawson finished his tale by explaining that his fellow soldier had been wounded when the stick grenades blew up on the river and was hiding out in the woods nearby.

'I don't think he's very badly injured,' Dawson told her, 'but he must have lost a lot of blood so he's very weak. I need bandages and pads to keep the bleeding under control. And we haven't had much to eat or drink ever since we escaped from the Warndt Forest.'

Celine nodded. 'Where is he – exactly?' she asked.

'I can't really tell you,' Dawson said, 'because I don't know this area, but I can find my way back to him.'

Despite her apparent friendliness, Dawson was very conscious the girl was still holding the shotgun, and might simply be trying to identify Watson's position so she could send the police or troops after him.

'I understand,' Celine said and then, as if reading Dawson's mind, she lowered the hammers on the weapon and leant it against the wall beside the door.

'Actually,' she said, 'Germans I hate. Arrogant bastards. Right, you stay for a few minutes. I will get food and water and medical supplies, and then we go and find your friend.'

Without another word, Celine left the wash-house and walked across the yard to the house. The moment she opened the house door, Dawson walked across and retrieved the Mauser bayonet, then picked up the shotgun. It was obviously old but perfectly serviceable. He opened the weapon and extracted the two shells – both were filled with buckshot. At the range Celine had been standing, they'd have blown him apart if she'd fired. Dawson nodded, slid them back into the breach and replaced the weapon by the door.

About five minutes later Celine walked back across to the wash-house, a large woven fabric basket in her hand. She was now dressed in a checked blouse and blue farmer's overalls tucked into heavy boots, but somehow managed to make even this unpromising outfit look as if it was the latest fashion.

Now she was no longer standing in silhouette, Dawson could fully appreciate her natural beauty for the first time – full red lips, brilliant blue eyes, golden hair

and a figure he knew he was going to dream about for months to come. If he survived, of course.

'Ready?' she asked, and Dawson nodded. 'You carry the gun,' she said. 'You are a better shot than I, I am sure.'

'With two loads of buckshot, you don't need to be that good a shot.'

Celine grinned at him, and Dawson's heart performed a strange manoeuvre in his chest.

'You checked. I thought you would,' she said. 'Now, which way?'

Dawson pointed towards the track that led into the forest. 'I came down there,' he said, 'and I marked one of the trees so I'd be able to find my way back again.'

Ten minutes after leaving the farmhouse, Dawson stopped at the side of the track and looked at the trees that lined it. 'It's somewhere near here,' he said, scanning the trunks. Then he spotted it – a vertical line he'd cut into the bark of one tree at about chest-height.

'That's it,' Dawson said. 'Now we start heading east. I had the rising sun behind me all the way as I walked over to this track.'

Once they were in the forest, Dawson moved quickly, eager to get back to their hiding place and do what they could for Dave Watson.

'He's over there,' he said at last, pointing at the two trees and patch of undergrowth he remembered.

With Celine beside him, Dawson strode across to the spot and slid through the gap in the bushes.

It was much gloomier in the shelter of the undergrowth. For a moment Dawson couldn't even see Watson. When he did, for a few seconds he thought his

friend was dead. Watson lay unmoving, flat on his back in the hollow between the two trees, his right hand pressing a bulge under the left-hand side of his shirt, a shirt now liberally soaked in blood.

'Dave?' Dawson called out. He stepped quickly across to where the man lay and bent over him.

Watson's eyes flickered open. 'You've been a long time, mate,' he said, his voice strained and weak. Then his eyes widened in surprise as he caught sight of Celine standing behind Dawson. 'Is she why you've been a long time?' he asked, a smile forming despite the pain he had to be suffering. 'You jammy sod.'

Dawson shook his head. 'We've brought you some food and something to drink. Can you sit up?'

'If there's beer and chips in that woman's bag, I can even stand up.'

Celine smiled slightly and shook her head. 'Chips I have not, but I bring you a bottle of beer.'

'If that isn't a bad joke, I may have to marry you,' Watson muttered.

With Dawson's help, he levered himself into a sitting position and leant back against the trunk of one of the trees.

'Are you still hurting?' Dawson asked.

'What the hell do you think?' Watson snapped.

'Yes, that *is* a stupid question, Eddie,' Celine said, then stepped over to the wounded man. She took a bottle of clear liquid out of her bag and offered it to him.

'What's that?'

'Water. I have beer, but for now take a few sips of this. Now, Dave – I may call you Dave? – let me look at your shoulder.'

She gently undid the buttons on his shirt, eased the material away from the wound on his shoulder and then lifted off the makeshift pad Watson had been holding there.

He cried out in pain as the pad came free – some of the blood had congealed and the very act of removing the material caused it to grab and tug at the wound itself.

Celine peered at it closely. 'It is a nasty wound. Very ragged edges,' she said. 'I need to clean it.'

'Are you a doctor?' Watson asked hopefully, taking another drink.

'No, but I treat animals on our farm, so I know about wounds.'

'Wonderful,' Watson muttered. 'Bloody man takes hours to find anyone, and then comes back here with a vet.'

'A vet with beer in her bag,' Celine pointed out. 'If I was real doctor, I would say no alcohol. So shut up and let me fix you.'

Behind Celine, Dawson smiled slightly when he caught Watson's eye.

She took another bottle of water and a pad of some kind of white wadded material from the bag. 'This will hurt, I'm sorry, but I must see if there is anything in the wound – any pieces of shrapnel. Then I will bandage you. I'm sorry, but that is the way it must be.'

'Go ahead, doc,' Watson muttered. 'I'll just sit here and think of the beer I'll enjoy when you've finished.'

Celine was quick and thorough, and as gentle as she could be, but Watson still shouted with the pain a couple of times. When she'd finished, he lay back, white and sweating. She also checked his head injury, where the

swelling was by now beginning to subside, though it was still very tender to the touch.

'There is nothing in the shoulder wound,' she said to Dawson, 'and no sign of infection. Now I will bandage it up and, with luck, it will heal over a few days.'

It took her only a couple of minutes, and at the end of it she rummaged around in her bag again, took out a bottle of beer, opened it and handed it to Watson. 'I promised,' she said. 'Enjoy and have some of this too.'

She pulled out a loaf of bread, and a packet of dried sausage and thick, juicy slices of ham, passed him a selection and then offered Dawson a similar feast.

The two men ate hungrily – they were both famished – while Celine sat watching them with a slight smile on her face. When they'd finished, she produced two more bottles of beer for them.

'This is just like the pale ale we get at home, Eddie,' Watson murmured, holding up the bottle to inspect the contents more closely.

'It is local beer,' Celine said. 'And now we must decide what to do.'

'Now we're here in Luxembourg,' Dawson replied, 'we hoped we could just walk south until we reach the French border. After all, now we're safe from the Germans.'

Celine nodded. 'Yes, you are, but not completely. You are not safe yet. When I saw you in our wash-house, I guessed who you are before you even spoke to me. Very early this morning, the police came outside the house, looking for two British criminals who came from Germany across the Moselle, and who killed many civilians as they got away.'

Dawson shook his head. 'We're not criminals, and we didn't see a single civilian the whole time we were in Germany.'

'But we did kill a few people, Eddie,' Watson commented.

'Yes, but no civilians,' Dawson insisted.

'I understand,' Celine said. 'It is not difficult to understand. I heard an explosion over to the east after midnight – it woke me – and a few hours after that the police came. The Germans must have guessed you came into Luxembourg and asked the police here to arrest you and give you over to them. Germany is powerful neighbour, so the police must appear to help. But they only visited the outlying farms, not the forest, which is obvious to do if they were serious to track you down.'

'So if we *are* caught,' Dawson asked, 'what will happen to us?'

'If police catch you, they will give you to the Germans. There is nothing else they can do. But I think they are not searching hard to find you.'

'So we have to keep out of sight?' Watson asked. He looked and sounded a hell of a lot better now he'd had something to eat and drink.

'Exactly. Now, we are only six kilometres from France, but you cannot walk that far – not until you are stronger. So the best thing is for you and me, Eddie, to go back to farm. We have a cart there, and a horse to pull it. We can bring it to the track. If Dave can walk then to the cart, I can take you both south. I can take you to somewhere a kilometre from France.'

Dawson nodded his thanks but asked the obvious question. 'Why, Celine? Why are you doing this? Don't

get me wrong – without your help, Dave here would be in a pretty bad way, and I'd probably be living on a diet of roots and berries, so we're really grateful. But you could have just given us food and drink and then walked away and left us to our own devices.'

Celine shrugged. 'For the same reason I look after sick animals, I think. You are both hurt, hungry and thirsty. I cannot turn away from you. Also,' she added, 'to help you two get away will make the Germans very angry!'

'Well, we really appreciate it. Do you want to go back to the farm now?'

'Yes, we must.' Celine walked across and handed Watson another bottle of water. 'We will be back before an hour. Just stay here and do not move your arm too much. It will bleed again.'

'Whatever you say, doc.' Watson sounded almost chirpy. The food and drink he'd had had definitely revived his spirits.

Dawson led the way through the undergrowth and out of their hiding place, the old shotgun held ready in his hands, but the woods appeared to be deserted.

In a few minutes they were walking back down the track that led towards the farmhouse.

'Is it your farm, then?' Dawson asked.

Celine shook her head. 'No, not yet, anyway. My mother and father have it. I have it when they pass away. In fact, the land we own is not big, only a farmhouse and outbuildings and two fields near house. We rent the rest.'

'Is it reasonably profitable?'

'No, not really. It gives us a living, but no more.'

Dawson stopped suddenly and grabbed Celine by the arm. 'Hear that?' he said urgently.

'What?'

'That sounded like a truck engine, a diesel engine, and I think it was heading this way.'

'Could be anything,' Celine murmured.

'I know, but it could be the police or somebody out in the woods looking for us. Let's get off this track, just in case.'

Silently, they stepped aside, melting into the scrubby undergrowth and into the shelter of the trees.

'I heard it for a few seconds, but I hear nothing now,' Celine said. 'You?'

'No.' Dawson shook his head. 'I think it's stopped. But maybe we should stay off that track, just in case.'

Moving through the wood slowed them down, but it still seemed to both of them to be a safer option than walking along in the open, just in case Dawson's guess was correct, and the noise had been caused by a lorry delivering a group of the local police to start a search of the woods for the two fugitives.

They were nearly at the clearing where the farmhouse was located when they both heard another sound, quite unmistakable and infinitely more sinister than a truck's diesel engine.

CHAPTER 43

16 SEPTEMBER 1939

'That was a shot,' Dawson said, stating the blindingly obvious, 'and it sounded pretty close to us.'

Celine nodded. 'I think a rifle or a pistol,' she said, 'but not a shotgun. And that is strange. Most farmers here have shotguns, but few rifles in this area, and I know no one who has pistol.'

'Let's get moving, find out what's going on.'

They walked faster now, covering the remaining 100 yards or so to the clearing as quickly as they could, but still keeping within the shelter of the trees.

When they reached the final bend in the track that led to the farmhouse, they came to a stop about ten feet from the edge of the forest and stared at the scene in front of them. Parked outside the property was an army truck, and the grey-green uniforms of the soldiers milling around it left them in no doubt of their nationality.

'Those are Germans,' Celine hissed, the intensity of her anger and hatred unmistakable. 'What are they doing here in Luxembourg? How did they get into the country?'

The front door of the farmhouse was open, and, even

from the distance they were standing, Dawson and Celine could see that the lock had been blown apart, presumably by the bullet they'd heard being fired a few moments earlier. And then, in a matter of seconds, what had clearly been a bad situation turned infinitely worse.

The front door of the farmhouse suddenly crashed back on its hinges, and two German soldiers stepped out, dragging a struggling woman behind them.

Beside Dawson, Celine tensed. 'Oh, God. My mother,' she moaned.

Moments later, another two soldiers emerged from the house, this time hauling out a middle-aged man. Dawson really didn't need Celine's whispered confirmation to know that this unfortunate civilian was her father.

The Germans slammed the man and woman against the wall of the house and held them there, as if waiting for someone.

'I must to do something,' Celine hissed. 'Give me the shotgun.'

Dawson shifted the weapon to his other hand, away from her. He absolutely understood her fear and emotion, but he also realized the odds they were facing. He just hoped the Germans would have to be cautious in their actions, simply because of where they were. He assumed they'd managed to talk their way into Luxembourg on the pretext of being in hot pursuit of the 'British criminals', but he didn't expect them to be violent towards any of the people they were questioning.

'No, Celine,' he said. 'Right now, there's nothing we can do. If we run out there now brandishing that shotgun, they'd cut us down before we'd covered ten

yards. And I don't think the Germans will hurt your parents, because they shouldn't even be here in Luxembourg.'

'But what they want? Why are they here? They still hunt you?'

For a moment, Dawson didn't reply, because he'd just spotted the man he'd hoped he'd never see again. The high-peaked cap with the *Totenkopf* emblem made him stand out from the other men, and the SS runes on his lapel only confirmed the identification.

'Oh, shit,' he muttered.

'What is it?' Celine asked.

'That man over there, the one wearing the officer's uniform. He's SS – in fact, they're probably all SS – and it's him and his squad of men who've been chasing us ever since we busted out of the barn back in Kesslingen. He nearly caught us a couple of times. He's really sharp.'

The German soldiers moved aside as the SS officer stepped forward, their deference towards him quite obvious. He crossed to where the four soldiers had pinioned the man and woman against the wall of the farmhouse, stopped directly in front of Celine's father, just a foot or two away, stared at him for a few seconds and then barked something, some question, but the wind whipped his words away, and Celine couldn't hear what he was saying.

The old man shook his head. The SS officer stepped even closer and prodded him in the chest and shouted something else at him.

'What do they want?' Celine asked again.

'Us, at a guess,' Dawson said shortly. 'Watson and me. We didn't kill any civilians – in fact, we didn't even see

any – but we had quite a few encounters with German soldiers and each time we came off best. Until now, that is,' he added. 'I don't think that SS bastard is ever going to give up chasing us.'

Celine seemed to relax slightly. 'Well, my parents cannot tell them anything about you. They know nothing. They did not wake up when the police arrived last night and they were still sleep when I saw you go into the wash-house this morning.'

'So with any luck, they should just give up and move off in a few minutes,' Dawson suggested, never taking his eyes off the SS officer.

And that looked as if it was going to happen. The officer stepped across to Celine's mother and presumably asked her the same question or questions, with exactly the same result – she just shook her head.

The officer moved away and barked orders at the soldiers, some of whom started heading back towards the lorry they'd obviously arrived in.

But then there was another shout, and a soldier pushed his way hurriedly through a group of his comrades towards the officer.

'What happens now?' Celine asked.

'I don't know,' Dawson replied, apprehension colouring his voice.

The soldier stopped beside the SS officer and handed him something, some small object, and pointed back across the yard towards the wash-house.

A sudden jolt of fear coursed through Dawson's veins, and he reached down to his right boot.

'Oh, fuck,' he muttered. 'I think they've found my trench knife.'

'What?'

'My trench knife. When you found me in the wash-house, you made me kick the bayonet and the knife over towards you, so you could have a look at them. And then you kicked them away from you. I remember I grabbed the bayonet – I've got it in my belt right now – but the trench knife must have slid under something in the wash-house, because I don't remember picking it up again.'

'You idiot! You stupid, stupid idiot! Why did you not take it with you?'

'I'm sorry,' Dawson muttered. 'I'm really sorry, but there's nothing I can do about that now.'

'So now they know you are there,' Celine said flatly. 'How else would a Wehrmacht knife be in wash-house of a Luxembourg farm?'

'Yes,' Dawson said, 'but your parents will still know nothing about that.'

'Well, I hope the Germans believe them,' Celine muttered, her voice low and angry, 'because if anything happens to them it is your fault.'

Silently, they watched the drama unfold in front of them.

The SS officer nodded to the soldier, turned away and walked back towards the two captives, still pressed up against the wall of the farmhouse, their arms held firmly by the soldiers beside them. Now Dawson could see that he was holding a knife of some sort and, as the officer reached Celine's father, he pulled the blade from its scabbard and waved the weapon in front of the old man's face.

'That must be the trench knife,' Dawson muttered. 'What are we going to do?'

Dawson was figuring the odds, looking for angles and weaknesses in the German position. The facts were overwhelming – they were looking at twelve or thirteen soldiers, most with Mauser carbines slung over their shoulders, though a couple were armed with Schmeisser MP 40 machine-pistols. Between them, he and Celine had an elderly shotgun, two cartridges loaded with buckshot, and a bayonet. He'd have thought twice about tackling even a single enemy soldier with that armoury – against the number in front of them, any attack would be suicide.

Dawson fully understood the reality of their situation, and so, he knew, did Celine. He also knew they had to do something – he could not just sit there in hiding and watch her parents be killed by the German soldiers. Not when part of the reason for their predicament was his fault. They had to do something soon – the questioning by the SS officer was already getting visibly more aggressive.

'I could get across there, behind the barn,' Dawson whispered, pointing towards the hay barn. 'That would bring the soldiers within range of the shotgun.'

'Yes? And after you fire both barrels? What then?'

'Run back here.'

'You will never make it,' Celine snapped. 'You would be dead before you get half-way here.' She looked around, then stepped back. 'Wait here,' she said.

'But what—' Dawson started to say, but she'd already gone, running lithely through the trees, deeper into the forest and away from the farm.

He had no idea where she'd gone, or what her intentions were, but he was certain she'd be back. She

wouldn't abandon her mother and father without trying to do everything in her power to save them. Maybe she'd gone for help, to try to find the Luxembourg police or somebody. He just didn't know.

But whatever Celine's intentions, Dawson hoped she'd be quick, because the situation at the farm was deteriorating – fast.

The SS officer was still shouting at Celine's father, waving the trench knife in front of his face, clearly running short of patience. He stepped sideways to stand next to Celine's mother, and repeated his questioning, with the same result. It was only a matter of time, Dawson knew, before the officer escalated the interrogation, neutral Luxembourg or not.

And even as he watched, the SS officer stepped back from the old man and gave orders to one of the soldiers standing nearby. The soldier put down his Schmeisser, undid his equipment belt and placed that on the ground near his machine-pistol. Then he removed his tunic to reveal a very grubby undershirt.

The SS officer said something else to him and he nodded agreement. He stepped forward to the middle-aged man and said something to him. But before the captive could reply, the German soldier smashed his fist into his stomach.

Despite the restraining arms of the soldiers standing on either side of him, the old man bent forward, retching and gasping for breath. A few feet away, Celine's mother howled in anguish, a high, keening wail that echoed around the clearing. Another soldier stepped forward quickly and slapped her across the face. The wailing ceased abruptly.

The first soldier reached down with his left hand, grabbed a handful of the old man's hair and wrenched his head up. Then he crashed his right fist into the man's face and stepped back.

Even from fifty yards away, Dawson could see the blood streaming from his mouth and nose as he slumped forward again, still fighting for breath. At a command from the SS officer, the two soldiers holding the man released him and he collapsed to the ground. The soldier stepped back and aimed a powerful kick at the old man's stomach, a blow so violent that it lifted his body an inch or two off the ground.

Then the soldier moved sideways to stand in front of Celine's mother, and Dawson knew exactly what was going to happen next. And he knew that, no matter what the consequences, he had to try to stop it.

The attention of all the German soldiers was concentrated on the events unfolding outside the farmhouse and none of them, as far as he could tell, was looking in his direction. That was absolutely the only edge he had.

He checked the shotgun once again, but left the hammers forward – he couldn't risk tripping and the weapon discharging accidentally.

He looked again at the soldiers, then moved to his left, still in the shelter of the trees, until the hay barn was more or less directly between him and the enemy troops, to provide him with the maximum possible cover. Then he took a deep breath, gripped the shotgun firmly, and ran.

CHAPTER 44

16 SEPTEMBER 1939

Dawson reached the wooden side of the barn and stood with his back pressed against it for a few seconds. Then he pulled back the hammer on the left-hand chamber of the weapon. Most shotguns, he seemed to recall, had different degrees of choke on each barrel, and he had a hazy recollection that the left-hand barrel usually had a tighter choke – and hence a slightly longer range – than the right. Not that it was going to make much difference. Once he fired the first shot, he knew that the German soldiers would be all over him.

He peered around the corner of the hay barn. The soldier who'd beaten Celine's father was now standing in front of her mother, clearly about to repeat the same treatment on her.

As the soldier swung back his arm to drive his fist into her stomach, Dawson brought the shotgun up to his shoulder, aimed the barrels at the main group of German troops and pulled the trigger. The old shotgun kicked like a demented donkey, slamming the steel butt-plate back into his shoulder, and the boom of the shot echoed off the few buildings in the clearing.

The closest soldiers were about twenty-five yards away, and Dawson knew that was approaching the extreme range of the weapon. But buckshot is heavier than birdshot and carries further. Three of the soldiers fell to the ground immediately, though Dawson knew that, at worst, they'd only have suffered painful flesh wounds from the heavy pellets – that's if they'd managed to penetrate their thick clothing. They'd probably dropped out of shock more than anything else.

The sound of the shot was followed by an instant of silence, then yells as the soldiers shouted in alarm and orders were given. Some of the Germans started running for cover, but others swung round, with their weapons in their hands, and started looking for a target. The first rounds from a Schmeisser machine-pistol cut through the air and slammed into the wooden walls of the barn.

Then, as Dawson watched from his vantage point, trying to decide the optimum moment when he should fire the second barrel, and disarm himself at the same time, a single shot rang out. But that shot came from behind him.

He spun round, but could see nothing – there were no German troops anywhere in sight. He looked back, just as the half-dressed soldier who had been beating up Celine's father tumbled backwards and fell twitching to the ground, his dirty undershirt suddenly a sodden mass of red.

Dawson looked back at the forest, but still saw nothing. He brought the shotgun back up to the aim, pulled the trigger and fired the second barrel towards the German soldiers, then dropped the useless weapon and

ran back towards the tree-line, dodging from side to side as shots from the German soldiers rang out behind him.

He ducked behind a tree as soon as he reached the edge of the forest and looked around him.

Another shot sounded close beside him, somewhere over to his left, and he turned to see Celine crouched beside a bush, a Winchester hunting rifle in her hands. As he ran towards her, she cranked down the loading lever to chamber another round, the spent brass cartridge case spinning out of the breech as she brought the weapon back up to the aim.

'I told you to stay right here,' she said.

'I had to do something,' Dawson replied. He spotted another rifle lying on the ground beside her – a bolt-action heavy-calibre weapon that didn't look unlike the Lee-Enfield he was used to – and grabbed it.

Celine fired again, and another German soldier tumbled backwards. 'Did you kill any of them?' she demanded.

'I doubt it, not using a shotgun at that range.'

'Shame.'

Dawson snapped off a shot but missed the man he'd been aiming at. The SS officer – who would have been his prime target if he'd been visible – had vanished from sight, but the German soldiers had clearly recovered from the shock of the sudden and unexpected attack and were already regrouping. He could see them dodging into cover and advancing towards the edge of the forest. Bullets whistled around him, cutting through the undergrowth and thudding into the trunks of the trees that surrounded them.

'We've got to get out of here,' Dawson said, working

the bolt and firing another round, more to try to discourage the enemy soldiers than with any real hope of hitting them.

'I cannot leaving my mother and father with these animals.'

'You have to or we'll both be dead inside five minutes. We'll get away from here, go deep into the forest. The Germans will follow us. Then we can circle back.'

Celine fired another shot, then nodded. 'You are right,' she muttered. 'I know you are right, but—'

A burst of fire from a machine-pistol shredded the bush right beside her.

Dawson couldn't wait any longer. 'Come on,' he snapped, grabbed her arm and pulled her to her feet.

'Wait!' she snapped, and thrust a couple of boxes of ammunition at him. 'Take these.'

Then she turned and ran, dodging between the trees, her slight figure lithe and graceful even in flight.

Dawson followed, pausing only to fire off another couple of shots as he started to run. He caught up with her after about fifty yards, when she ducked behind the trunk of a tree and fired another round back at their pursuers.

He did the same, then shouldered his rifle. 'We need to move,' he said. 'We need speed, not firepower. That's the only way we're going to survive this.'

Celine nodded somewhat reluctantly, then turned and ran, Dawson right beside her.

'Where'd you get the rifles?' he asked.

'The next farm,' Celine replied shortly. 'It is only two hundred metres from ours. The farmer is away, but I know where his keys are.'

'Where are we going? We've got to avoid where Dave's hiding.'

'I know. Don't worry – we go in the opposite direction.'

After that, Dawson saved his breath for running.

Behind them, the sound of shots was diminishing slightly, presumably because the German troops had lost sight of them among the trees.

Dawson stopped, listened for a moment for the sounds of the shots, then fired two rounds in quick succession towards where he hoped the Germans were.

'No more,' Celine said, 'unless we see them. We must double back very soon.'

A couple of minutes later, they reached a gully, at the bottom of which was a small stream, meandering towards the Moselle, Dawson guessed.

'Which way are we going?' he asked.

'Right.' Celine pointed.

Dawson scrambled down to the base of the gully, leaving heavy prints all the way down the side, waded through the stream and then stamped his foot hard into the muddy bank on the opposite side. Then he opened one of the boxes of ammunition Celine had given him, stuffed the rounds into his pockets and tossed the empty box up on to the opposite bank.

'That might convince them we've gone that way,' he said.

Together, they waded up the stream, heading west, Dawson assumed, away from the River Moselle, further into Luxembourg. Up to then, they had not bothered about the noise they made, but now they tried to move as quietly as possible. They crept upstream, keeping as

low as they could, looking and listening for any noise of pursuit. They could hear shouted orders coming from somewhere to their right, to the north of the watercourse, but no further shots, so presumably the German soldiers had – at least for the moment – lost sight of them.

Ducking under low branches and around bushes and shrubs that sprouted from the riverbank, they moved more quickly as the sounds of pursuit diminished behind them.

'Do you think we have lost them?' Celine whispered.

'For the moment, yes. Let's start working our way back towards the farmhouse.'

About fifty yards further on, the high banks on both sides of the stream flattened out, and they were able to step out of the water and on to dry land again. Celine led the way up a grassy slope and back through the forest.

They could still hear the German soldiers – or, to be exact, they could hear the sound of shouted orders – somewhere to the east of them. Dawson guessed they were probably at least a couple of hundred yards away, which was far enough, under the circumstances. But still they both kept a sharp lookout, because it was always possible that the SS officer had ordered his soldiers to carry out a wide sweep through the forest on either side of the main group of searchers.

'How far now?' Dawson whispered, as they crossed through a small open glade and then stepped back under the sheltering canopy of the trees.

'A hundred metres. I think we—'

Celine broke off, and they both ducked down, as a single shot sounded from somewhere almost directly in front of them.

It was just the sound of a shot. No bullet came anywhere near them, and after a couple of seconds they stood up again.

'What was that?' Celine asked.

Dawson already had a really bad feeling in the pit of his stomach. 'Jesus, I hope I'm wrong,' he said. 'Get us to the farmhouse as quickly as you can.'

But even as they started jogging through the forest, they heard another shot, again from somewhere right in front of them, and that pretty much confirmed what Dawson had feared.

Celine glanced at him and shook her head. 'Oh, no,' she moaned, tears springing to her eyes.

'I don't know,' Dawson replied.

Celine abandoned all caution and ran ahead of him, her rifle in hand as she sprinted through the forest.

Dawson could hardly keep up with her, encumbered as he was with his heavy uniform and boots.

A few seconds later, he burst out of the edge of the forest, to see the farmhouse directly in front of him. They were approaching it from the opposite direction, so the barn and the other outbuildings were on the far side. Ahead of him, he could see Celine running around the side of the building, towards the main door of the farmhouse.

For an instant, there was almost complete silence. The only sounds Dawson could hear were the pounding of his boots on the earth and his laboured breathing. Then a howl of anguish rent the air. The noise was chilling, almost feral in its intensity, and for a fleeting instant he doubted if it came from a human throat.

Then he rounded the corner of the building and

skidded to a halt, his rifle held ready to fire. But the yard was deserted, or at least no German troops were present.

Celine was slumped on the ground, her arms cradling the lifeless body of her mother, the result of one of the shots they'd heard now all too obvious. There was a small round hole in the centre of the woman's forehead, the skin around it discoloured by the residue from the shot, and a massive hole at the back of her skull.

Celine looked down again at the tragic ruin of her mother's face, then threw back her head and howled, a high-pitched wail of agony that told its own story of grief and rage and frustration.

Dawson stepped behind her and looked down at the body of her father, despatched in the same callous manner by a single shot through the head. The weapon used had almost certainly been a pistol, and that in itself identified the likely perpetrator. Most German soldiers carried rifles or machine-pistols and it was usually only the officers who would be armed with a handgun.

'That SS bastard did this,' Dawson muttered to himself, then turned back to Celine.

She was now standing, looking down at the bodies of her parents, the grief-stricken expression on her face now replaced by one of cold fury.

'Celine, I'm so sorry,' Dawson began, but it was as if she didn't hear him.

'Where are they?' she snapped. 'Where are the fucking Germans?'

Dawson pointed towards the forest that surrounded them. 'Following our trail through the woods, I suppose.'

Beside one of the two dead German soldiers was a discarded Schmeisser machine-pistol. She walked across

to the body, snatched up the weapon and strode over to where the German army lorry was parked. Before Dawson could stop her, she'd pulled back the bolt and emptied the entire magazine into the side of the vehicle, shredding the tyres and probably wrecking the engine.

'Now they'll know exactly where we are,' Dawson said.

'Good,' Celine snapped. 'Let them come, all of them.'

Dawson grabbed her arm. 'No, Celine. That's suicide, and you know it. We've got to move, get away from here.'

For a few moments, Dawson thought she would hit him, then her fixed expression softened and she nodded. 'Yes, I know,' she murmured. 'Now we go.'

Gently, Dawson took the machine-pistol from her and tossed away the empty magazine. He ran back to the body of the soldier, grabbed four full magazines from his equipment belt and a couple of stick grenades, pulled a trench knife from his boot and then turned and ran back to Celine.

'We go and get your friend,' she said, 'and then go across into France. I know he is weak, but he will have to walk.'

As they started to run, Dawson glanced at Celine. 'This isn't your fight, you know,' he said. 'You can just stay here in Luxembourg. That'll be a lot safer for you than France.'

'Safe in neutral Luxembourg, like for my parents? Do not make me laugh.' Celine shook her head. 'No, you are wrong, Eddie. There is nothing for me here now. When that German bastard killed my mother and father, he made this my fight. I cannot forgive or forget. If it is

last thing I do ever, I will find that SS officer and make him pay.'

'Not if I get to him first, you won't,' Dawson said, and for a moment the shadow of a smile flitted across Celine's face.

The moment they reached the edge of the clearing, they ran into the forest and then turned to follow the track, but kept within the shadow of the trees.

'Can we do this?' Dawson asked. 'There are still about a dozen Jerry soldiers out there, after our blood. Can we slip past them and get over the border?'

'I know this forest. Those German bastards do not,' Celine said, as they reached the tree Dawson had marked earlier. 'So we have a good try. If they catch us, we make sure we take as many of them with us as we can.'

He couldn't fault her spirit, but it sounded as if she was happy to embark on a suicide trip. Going down in a blaze of glory wasn't Dawson's idea of the best way to end the first week of his personal war. He still had a score to settle with Capitaine de St Véran, for one thing. He'd have to keep his eye on her and make sure she didn't compromise their position.

They strode through a heavily wooded area, still alert for any sign of enemy soldiers. The forest seemed deserted.

They stopped when they reached the two trees that marked Watson's refuge, checking that everything looked normal – Dawson hoped that they'd managed to steer the pursuit well away from that location, but the SS officer had shown a remarkable ability to predict where they'd go and what they'd do, so he wasn't convinced.

But that area of the forest, too, seemed quiet and peaceful.

'You stay here,' Dawson told Celine. 'I'll go and check on Dave.'

Dawson slung the bolt-action rifle over his shoulder, checked the Schmeisser was fully loaded and strode forward. He slid through the undergrowth and into the shadowy bower formed by the trees and bushes, and looked round, the machine-pistol held ready to fire.

But Watson was nowhere in sight. The area between the two trees, where he and Celine had left him when they went off to fetch the horse and cart, was empty. But there was no sign of violence, no bloodstains on the ground. All that was visible were the empty beer bottles left over from their meal that morning.

'Dave?' he called softly. 'It's me, Eddie. You here somewhere?'

To his relief, there was an answering grunt from the undergrowth at the far end, and a few moments later Watson's head popped into view.

Dawson stepped forward and helped his friend stand up.

'I heard shooting,' Watson explained, 'so I dived down there to keep out of sight, just in case it was the bloody Jerries or somebody looking for us. What's happened?'

'Nothing good, mate,' Dawson replied. 'Celine's parents have been killed, and somehow that fucking SS officer has found a way into Luxembourg with his squad of soldiers and they're still after us.'

As he led the way out of their hiding place, Dawson explained what they'd seen and what had happened at the farmhouse.

'The horse and cart isn't an option no more, Dave,'

Dawson finished, 'so it's back to Shanks's Pony. Can you walk?'

'If that fucking German's behind me, no problem.'

And Watson did look a hell of a lot better. Obviously the food and drink he'd had, and the fact that he'd been able to rest for a few hours, had given him a new lease of life.

'Christ, Celine,' Watson said, as he and Dawson rejoined her, 'I'm really sorry about what happened to your parents.'

Celine shrugged, but Dawson could tell she was still close to tears; only her anger held back the flood.

'We must go,' she said brusquely and turned away, leading the two men south, and deeper into the forest.

CHAPTER 45

For about half an hour they neither saw nor heard any sign of the German troops. They appeared to have the forest to themselves, but Dawson knew that was an illusion. The enemy soldiers were still out there somewhere, still looking for them. It was only a matter of time before they'd make contact with them again.

And when that happened, Dawson knew they'd be in real trouble, outnumbered about three or four to one by better-armed and well-equipped troops. They'd been lucky so far, having taken the enemy soldiers by surprise at the farmhouse, but they'd now completely lost that element. The next time they made contact, they all knew the Germans would be ready for them.

Watson was walking fairly slowly, but he was walking and hardly slowed them at all because they were proceeding as cautiously and quietly as possible. He'd insisted on taking the loaded Schmeisser from Dawson, just in case they did run into any enemy soldiers, because that left Dawson's hands free to use the rifle. And, as Watson pointed out, it didn't take a lot of strength to aim a Schmeisser machine-pistol and pull the trigger.

But their easy progress came to an abrupt halt.

Dawson was slightly ahead of Celine and Watson, leading the way, when he suddenly froze into immobility as he approached a group of trees growing tightly together. He lifted his left arm to stop his two companions advancing any further, and all three sank silently to the floor of the forest, keeping well out of sight.

Moments later, from somewhere in front of them, they all quite clearly heard a voice muttering something in German. Then there was a faint metallic clatter, perhaps as a weapon of some sort was loaded or a magazine checked, and the sound of heavy footsteps treading the ground.

Dawson moved cautiously backwards and pressed his mouth close to Celine's ear. 'At least one man, maybe forty yards ahead,' he whispered. 'He's just behind those trees in front of us and moving left, towards that clump of bushes. Did you hear what he said?'

'I think it was just a curse. He stumbled or tripped, that was all,' Celine said, equally quietly.

'They're probably setting up a line of sentries all the way from the farmhouse to the Moselle, because they know we'll have to move through that area if we're going to get across the French border.'

'So now what do we do?' Watson asked.

'We go through that line. We've got no option.'

'How?'

'I'm still working on that.'

For a few seconds, Dawson just stood there, considering the options – the very limited options – that they had. 'OK,' he said. 'We can do this quietly or noisily. Noisy and we toss a stick grenade at that sentry, or blast

him with the rifles, if we can see him. If we do that, the rest of the Jerries will know exactly where we are, and we'll have to run like hell and hope we get so far ahead they can't catch us.'

'Fine for you two,' Watson whispered, 'but not me.'

Dawson nodded. 'I know that, mate. There's no way we're leaving you behind. So we have to be sneaky.' He turned to Celine. 'How's this? The Germans are looking for two British soldiers, right? Not a woman. Suppose you leave your weapons here with us and just walk forward, picking flowers or something?'

'Do I look like woman who walks through wood picking flowers?' Celine hissed.

'No, but they won't know that. Then, while the Jerry soldier is looking at you, I'll sneak up behind him and take him out.'

'That is it? That is your plan?'

Dawson shrugged. 'I don't have any better ideas right now.'

Celine snorted – but quietly, because the German soldier was still fairly close by – and tossed her head. 'If a girl wants a man's attention, she does not pick flowers. Here, take this.' She handed Dawson her rifle, slipped the straps of her overalls off her shoulders, unbuttoned her checked blouse and tied it around her waist. Underneath it, she had on only a thin undergarment, made of a flimsy material that left little to the imagination.

Dawson's familiarity with the female figure and the garments used to clothe it was limited at best – his only sexual experiences had been essentially adolescent and frustratingly unsatisfactory fumblings outside dance

halls and the like – and what Celine was wearing looked to him like a sort of vest. Whatever it was, the effect was electrifying.

She thrust out her chest and the fabric tightened over her breasts. She looked at Dawson, a half-smile on her lips.

'That gets *my* attention,' Dawson said, his natural bravado reasserting itself, but barely able to take his eyes off her. Beside him Watson nodded enthusiastic agreement.

'Now I go and get his attention.'

'And I'll work my way round behind him,' Dawson said.

Celine shook her head. 'Do not bother. I fight off Luxembourg farm boys for ten years. I can deal with one German soldier. Give me the bayonet – or you have left that somewhere with the knife?'

Dawson shook his head. 'I'm so sorry about what happened, Celine.' He pulled the bayonet from its scabbard and handed it to her, handle first. 'Are you sure about this?'

'Yes. Do not worry.'

Dawson looked doubtful, then nodded agreement. 'OK, but I'll be watching and I'll be close by, just in case.'

Celine tucked the bayonet into the back of her overalls, where it would be invisible to anyone. Then she strode boldly forward, humming a tune that Dawson didn't recognize. She angled over to where they thought the German soldier might have been heading, and did actually stop a couple of times to pick a flower from the forest floor. Then she vanished from sight.

'I don't like this, Eddie,' Watson muttered, as he tried to see where Celine had gone.

'Nor do I, but we need to stay out of sight – if that fucking Jerry soldier catches sight of either of us, the game'll be up and no mistake. We just have to hope she knows what she's doing. She's our ticket out of this country, because she knows these forests and we don't.'

At that moment, they heard an exclamation in German, then Celine's soft voice speaking the same language, somewhere beyond the undergrowth over to their left. Seconds later, there was a grunt of pain, followed by a squeal that was clearly female.

'You wait here,' Dawson said, took the Schmeisser from Watson and ran over to the clump of bushes. He stepped behind them, the weapon held ready to fire, and glanced to his left.

Celine was crouched on the ground beside a grey-clad figure, her left hand pressed against the side of her head, blood streaming from her temple.

Dawson ran over to her. His eyes flicked first to the German sentry, but a single glance was enough to tell the tale. The Mauser bayonet was sticking obscenely out of his chest, and, though the man's eyes were flickering and his hands and legs twitching, they were just his body's reflex actions – to all intents and purposes, he was already dead.

Dawson crouched down beside Celine and gently lifted her hand away from her forehead, then sighed in relief. There was a cut on her temple which was bleeding profusely, but which was obviously fairly shallow.

'What happened?' Dawson asked

'My fault,' Celine insisted. 'I came too close to him

and his helmet hit my head when he fell.' She stood up, gave the German soldier's body a final dismissive kick, then stepped away from it. She pulled on her blouse and buttoned it, then took a handkerchief from the pocket of her overalls, wadded it into a pad and pressed it against the cut. 'We must go,' she said.

Dawson looked at the dead man's Mauser but decided to leave it there – the hunting rifles they had were every bit as good as that weapon – then followed Celine.

Watson appeared from behind the trees, and the three of them set off again, heading south into the woods, every step they took bringing them nearer to the French border and – hopefully – to safety.

But they'd hardly gone seventy yards when there was a shout from behind them, and suddenly the woods rang to the sound of shots, a couple of rounds from a Mauser ripping through the foliage above them.

'Oh, fuck,' Dawson said.

'They don't shoot at us,' Celine pointed out. 'Those bullets went high into the trees.'

'I know. My guess is another of the German soldiers has just found the body. The fastest way to alert his comrades is to fire his rifle. They'll be right behind us any minute now. We've got to get moving.'

The woods behind them echoed with shouts and yells in German as orders were passed and acknowledged, the sound of imminent pursuit unmistakable. The three of them started running, knowing their only possible escape was to put some distance between themselves and the enemy soldiers, because they couldn't win a fire-fight, not against that many troops.

But Watson was already making heavy weather of it,

stumbling along, his breath coming in short and painful gasps and his bandaged shoulder wound had started to bleed again. Looking at him, Dawson realized his friend couldn't go much further, not at the pace he and Celine were setting. Somehow, they had to slow down, and that meant slowing down the pursuit.

Dawson glanced back, looking for the first sight of any of the enemy soldiers. He caught a flash of grey moving between the trees, maybe sixty yards away, hauled the hunting rifle up to his shoulder and snapped off a barely aimed shot. The bullet ploughed harmlessly into the trunk of a tree.

'How many are there?' Watson gasped, pointing the Schmeisser back the way they'd come and looking for a target.

'We saw about a dozen back at the farmhouse, but Celine took care of a couple there, so I'd guess there are about eight or nine left now – plus that SS officer.'

'Enough, then?'

'More than enough,' Dawson agreed, the rifle aimed towards the position where he'd seen the German soldier take cover. 'They outnumber us roughly three to one.'

Watson glanced at Celine, who was also aiming her rifle in the same direction as Dawson, then back at his fellow sapper. 'Leave me here, Eddie,' he said. 'Give me a couple of magazines for the Schmeisser and the two stick grenades. I've got a good arm, and I could buy you two the time you'll need to get away. You'd be faster without me.'

Dawson didn't even look at him. 'Not a chance, mate. We're in this together, win or lose.'

Then he glanced back at Celine, and at the darkening forest ahead of them. 'But a stay-behind isn't such a bad idea,' he said musingly. 'Celine, you help Dave to that big tree over there' – he pointed at a massive old oak with spreading branches – 'while I cover you.'

Celine nodded. She and Watson made their way as quickly as they could to the oak tree.

Moments later, Dawson joined them. He checked the ammunition he had left for the rifle. 'Ten rounds,' he muttered. 'What about you, Celine?'

'Three rounds in the weapon and maybe twenty in my pocket.'

It was an easy decision. 'OK,' Dawson said, 'let's change rifles.'

'We do not have to. They both have the same calibre,' Celine replied, taking a handful of gleaming brass cartridges and handing them over.

'Thanks.' Dawson slid them into his pocket. 'Now you two go – I'll catch up with you.'

For a second or two Watson stood there, irresolute. 'Planning a suicidal last stand, are you?' he demanded.

'Hell, no,' Dawson's reply was sharp. 'I'm going to keep the Jerries at bay for as long as I can, then I'll run like hell to catch you up. Now go, before I change my mind and leave you here instead.'

Watson nodded and turned away, Celine beside him. When Dawson glanced round a few seconds later, they'd both vanished from sight among the trees to the south. Immediately, he swung back to face the direction where he guessed the German troops were massing. There was no sign of any activity there, but he knew that was where the danger lay. He checked his rifle again, then took one

of the stick grenades from his belt. He unscrewed the end cap and laid the weapon on the ground in front of him, ready for immediate use.

The oak offered plenty of protection for him against a straight frontal assault, and he was fairly sure the German troops didn't even know he was there – or not yet, anyway. But as soon as the shooting started, they'd try to out-flank him and hit him from two sides simultaneously, and he knew he'd have to get away from the tree before that happened, or he'd be dead.

There was a shallow depression beside the oak which offered a good view through the trees to the north and would keep him out of sight of the advancing troops. Dawson slid down into it, rested the rifle on the grassy soil in front of him, and just waited.

He didn't have long to wait.

CHAPTER 46

16 SEPTEMBER 1939

The first two German soldiers appeared in front of him, Mauser rifles in their hands, perhaps fifty yards away. Behind them, Dawson could see other shadowy figures moving, taking advantage of the cover provided by the trees, but still making fairly quick progress towards him.

He shifted the barrel of the rifle slightly, but ignored the leading two enemy troops. Instead, he picked a soldier some distance back in the forest, waited until the man was silhouetted between two trees and then squeezed the trigger. The rifle jumped against his shoulder. The soldier fell backwards, killed or at least badly wounded.

Then, while the German soldiers dived for whatever cover they could find, Dawson eased back behind the tree and picked up one of the stick grenades. In easy, fluid movements, he pulled down the priming cord and threw the weapon over-arm as far as he could towards the two leading troops.

But even before the crack of the grenade's detonation, Dawson was up and running, running for his life,

through the forest to the south, looking for another spot he could use for an ambush.

Shots echoed from behind him, but none came close. He guessed that the German soldiers were still stunned by the blast of the grenade and either couldn't see him or couldn't aim accurately enough to hit him.

A couple of hundred yards further on, Dawson skidded to a halt at the edge of a small clearing and looked back, but saw no sign of pursuit. He glanced at his watch and checked the position of the sun, to ensure that he was still heading in the right direction, then ran on, trying to put as much distance as he could between himself and the Germans, because he knew they wouldn't give up the chase. He guessed they were regrouping before they followed him.

And then another thought struck him. Unless the SS officer had positioned a second line of soldiers further south, and Dawson didn't think there were enough troops to let him do that, he, Watson and Celine were now through the line. There should be no enemy forces in front of them so, as long as they kept moving, and kept moving faster than their pursuers, who should now be more cautious, they had a chance of making it to the border.

Dawson grinned to himself. There were a lot of 'shoulds' in that scenario, but for almost the first time since he and Celine had run away from the farmhouse, he thought they had a real chance of making it.

Twenty minutes later, he caught up with the other two. Watson was still walking, largely unaided, and Celine was checking behind them constantly, looking out for any danger.

'Thank God, Eddie,' Watson muttered, as Dawson fell into step beside them.

'Just keep going, mate, and we'll be OK. How far to the border now, Celine?'

'Not that far,' she replied. 'Maybe two or three kilometres.'

'That's less than two miles,' Dawson mused. 'About an hour, then. Right, I've not seen any Jerries since the shoot-out. I'll stop somewhere in a few minutes while you two get a bit ahead of me, just in case they're catching us up.'

A dense clump of bushes provided the most suitable location Dawson could find, and again he settled down, acting as a sniper, to watch for any pursuit. But again the forest seemed quiet. He could neither hear nor see any sign of enemy troops. After about ten minutes, Dawson stood up cautiously and moved on.

'I think we've lost them,' he said, fifteen minutes later, when he caught up with Celine and Watson once again.

'Are you sure?' Celine sounded doubtful, at best. 'You think they just gave up, after everything?'

'Maybe,' Dawson said. 'They know we're somewhere in this forest, but they don't know where. So, at the moment, we have the advantage, not them. They know we're armed, because I've just ambushed them. If they try to move quickly, they know they could run into another hail of bullets or get a grenade thrown at them, so they have to take it slowly. I think we've simply outdistanced them.'

'God, I hope you're right, Eddie.' Watson sounded desperate. The pace he and Celine had been walking had obviously taken it out of him.

'There is maybe another reason,' Celine suggested, and both men turned to look at her.

'They could be trying to get ahead of us again, you mean?' Dawson said.

'It is possible. I destroyed their truck, but they may move quickly through the forest, but to the west, to cut us off before we get to the border. That maybe is why you have seen no soldiers.'

'Right,' said Dawson decisively. 'We can't be more than about half a mile from the border. We'll keep going, but a bit slower. Keep your eyes and ears open.'

They covered the next 500 yards or so in complete silence, listening for any sounds that seemed out of place.

Then Celine stopped suddenly and stared over to her right.

'What is it?' Dawson hissed.

'A soldier. I am sure I saw a soldier over there.'

'How far away?'

'Maybe a hundred metres. I just saw him through the trees.'

For a moment, Dawson stared in the direction Celine was pointing, then made a decision.

'We'll do the same routine,' he said, unslinging the rifle from his shoulder. 'There's enough cover here for me to hide. You two go on and I'll watch your backs. Take it slowly and quietly, OK?'

Celine nodded and led Watson away, taking advantage of the undergrowth and foliage to avoid being seen, and continued walking steadily towards the border.

Dawson ducked into cover beside a tree, a position that offered him a good view of the wooded area that

lay to the west of his position, checked his rifle and prepared the last stick grenade for throwing.

But before he saw any of the soldiers, one of the
Germans obviously spotted Celine and Watson. A shout
in German was followed by a single rifle shot from the
west, and then two more. Dawson still had no target in
sight.

He had no idea if either Celine or Watson had been
hit, or even killed, but he knew he had to draw the fire
somehow.

He sighted roughly where he thought the shots were
coming from – difficult in a forest, where the sound tends
to bounce off tree trunks – and squeezed the trigger.

Almost instantly, a volley of shots peppered the undergrowth around him, the bullets being fired from at least
two positions. It looked as if the Germans had positioned
themselves in a north–south line, and the three of them
had walked right into the trap.

Dawson snapped off another couple of rounds, but
he still had no visible targets. There was really only one
course of action left to him. He wriggled backwards out
of his hiding place, pulled the cord on the stick grenade,
threw it as hard and as far as he could over to the west,
then turned and ran, dodging left and right as he did so.

The crack of the grenade exploding was loud in his
ears, and was followed almost immediately by volleys of
shots. Dawson knew he was presenting a difficult target,
running and weaving through the trees, altering his path
every couple of seconds, but even so, some of the bullets came very close to him, smashing into the trunks of
the trees as he ran past them.

Then he felt a massive blow on the right side of his

chest, a blow that knocked him sideways. Dawson tumbled to the ground, rolling over and over on the forest floor and then lay still, lying flat on his back, his eyes open and staring at the green canopy of leaves high above him.

CHAPTER 47

For an instant, Dawson assumed he was dying. The pain in his side was excruciating – it felt as if every rib was broken. He reached around his chest with his left hand, feeling for the blood and the entry wound he was sure were there. But there was nothing to feel, only his tattered battledress jacket.

Then he glanced over at the rifle. The stock was shattered, and the weapon useless. Obviously the bullet fired by the German soldier had smashed into it. That had driven the wood into his side, and the impact probably had cracked a rib or two. But Dawson knew he was lucky to be alive. A couple of inches higher or lower and he'd have been killed.

He peered cautiously over to the west, where the shot had come from, but could see nobody. He couldn't stay where he was – sooner or later one of the enemy soldiers would run over to him – and he now had virtually no weapons at all. Dawson climbed to his knees, then straightened up cautiously, his breathing shallow as he attempted to come to terms with the pain in his side.

So he ran, because that was the only option left to him. He didn't run fast, because he couldn't, but he weaved and ducked and dived as much as possible. Shots followed him, but none hit him.

And then another weapon fired, from somewhere in front of him, and, for an instant, Dawson assumed the worst, that enemy soldiers had somehow worked their way around to cut him off and that he was caught in the cross-fire. Then he realized the shot hadn't been fired at him, but at the Germans. A few seconds later Dawson hobbled past Celine, who was leaning against a tree and aiming her rifle at their enemy.

'Go,' she said, and fired another round. 'Dave is back there.'

The two sappers – both staggering and reeling, but for different reasons – dodged through the forest, desperately searching for sanctuary as the bullets howled around them.

In front of them, the trees grew thicker, and the two men plunged between them, into deeper cover. Almost immediately the sound of shooting seemed to diminish. Dawson knew they were now invisible to the German troops.

They walked on as quickly as they could, then Dawson grabbed Watson's arm and dragged him to a halt beside a tree.

'Look there, mate,' he said, pointing ahead and to the right. 'Tank traps.'

In the clearing that lay in front of them, rows of vertical steel girders protruded from the ground, like some bizarre farmer's crop.

'That must be the Maginot Line, Dave, the first layer

of defence. There'll be minefields and all the rest somewhere in front of us. We'll have to go carefully, stay in the trees.'

Seconds later, Celine ran up to them and skidded to a halt.

Dawson pointed at the tank traps and opened his mouth to say something, but Celine beat him to it.

'That is the beginning of the Maginot Line,' she said. 'I know where we are now. Follow me.'

She led the way through the wood, keeping close to the larger trees. On one side another open area appeared, and she pointed towards it.

'That is a minefield,' she said, and glanced at Dawson, who looked at her quizzically. 'I saw the French digging the holes two years ago,' she explained, 'until they saw me and chased me away.'

She weaved her way through the trees, the two sappers right behind her. Intermittent shots still rang out from behind them, but none of the bullets came close to them.

Then they came to another open area on their right, coils of barbed wire strung across it. On the far side, a low object loomed up, a curved slab of concrete topped with a circular turret from which the muzzle of a heavy machine-gun protruded, and suddenly Dawson realized that they were in France.

'That's a Maginot Line fort,' he said, his voice exultant. 'We've bloody made it!'

'Not yet,' Celine snapped. 'Stay behind me.'

They followed her around the edge of the clearing, keeping to the trees and heavy undergrowth.

Out of the corner of his eye, Dawson noticed

movement at the fort and glanced over towards it. What he saw stopped him in his tracks.

'Celine,' he called urgently. 'Stop.'

He pointed at the fort, and they could all see that the turret had traversed to follow them, the barrel of a heavy machine-gun pointing directly at where they were standing.

Dawson lowered his rifle to the ground, and motioned to the other two to do the same. Then all three of them raised their hands to show that they were unarmed.

'Be a bastard if we were shot now,' Watson muttered.

They continued walking around the edge of the clearing heading towards the fort, the machine-gun still traversing to follow them.

Then another burst of fire echoed from somewhere behind them and the weapon lifted and pointed back into the forest. It spat a stream of heavy-calibre bullets into the trees, the thunderous roar of the machine-gun drowning out the sound of sporadic rifle fire.

Moments later, the rifle fire ceased altogether. Not even crack German troops fancied their chances against such armament and such a fortification.

Two minutes later, safe in the trees on the French side of the fort, Dawson looked at his fellow sapper and grinned. 'Bloody safe at last,' he said. 'I never thought we'd do it.'

'I did. I had faith in you – and in Celine, of course,' Watson replied, turning to look at the girl. 'Thank God you found her.'

'Yes. We'd never have done this without you.'

Celine nodded, but didn't speak, just stepped towards them and kissed each man gently on the lips. She moved

back just as an officer and half a dozen soldiers appeared from behind her, their rifles aimed straight at the two British soldiers.

Two hours later, Watson and Dawson sat side-by-side on a wooden bench in a French army camp, the remains of a decent meal on the table in front of them, Celine sitting opposite them. She'd explained to the French officer what had happened and, once their identities had been established from their paybooks, the two men had been allowed to wash and shave, and then the three of them sat down to eat.

'What will you do now, Celine?' Dawson asked. 'Go back to the farm?'

She shook her head. 'There is nothing for me there now. I think the Germans will invade Luxembourg though we are neutral. I will stay here in France. Maybe I can help the war effort. And you two? Back to the army, I think?'

'Yes,' Dawson said. 'We'll have to explain what happened to us – we've probably been listed as "missing in action" by now, so we'll have to sort that out. And I've got a bit of unfinished business to attend to back there.'

As evening was falling, a British army lorry rattled to a stop in the French camp.

Dawson looked at it, then back at Celine. 'You'll be OK?' he asked.

'I take care of myself, Eddie,' she replied.

Dawson grinned. 'I've noticed that,' he said. 'Maybe we'll meet again. Perhaps when all this is over.'

'Perhaps. You never know.'

Celine kissed him again, a lingering embrace that Dawson wished would last for ever, then stepped back.

'You had better go now,' she said quietly.

The two sappers climbed on board the lorry and lowered their aching bodies on to the hard wooden bench seats in the back. They stared behind them as the truck pulled away, Dawson with his eyes fixed on Celine's face until the vehicle swung round a corner and she was lost to sight.

A couple of hours after that, having been checked by the medics, who cleaned and rebandaged Watson's injured shoulder and told Dawson just to take it easy for a few days, they were standing in front of Lieutenant Charnforth in the British army camp just outside Dalstein. Dawson had explained exactly what had happened to them since they'd left the camp to work on the minefield in the Warndt Forest.

'A good start to your war, you could say,' Charnforth remarked. 'You might be interested to learn that – assuming your account of what happened is accurate – the two of you accounted for a higher number of German soldiers killed than the entire French advance into Saarland. And that says something about both you two – and about the French.

'Now, the Intelligence people will probably want to debrief you over what you saw while you were behind enemy lines, so you're both to make yourselves available for that. The sergeant will tell you when the Intelligence officers are expected. In the meantime, you, Dawson, will be on light duties for a week to give you a chance to recover. Watson, you're excused all duties for two

weeks, or until the medics give you a clean bill of health. And well done, both of you. It's good to have you back.'

'It's good to be back, sir.'

CHAPTER 48

16 SEPTEMBER 1939

Later that evening, Dawson – still dressed in the rags he'd been wearing when he crossed the Maginot Line and carrying a small kitbag in his hand – left the British army camp by climbing over a fence into the adjoining field and wandered down the road to where the French troops were billeted.

He found a sunny spot not far from the road, tucked the kitbag out of sight, sat down and took out a packet of cigarettes and a box of matches. He lit a cigarette and sat there smoking, looking around him with what looked like casual disinterest. In fact, he was taking careful note of the camp routine and looking out for just one man.

The sun had sunk below the western horizon when he saw a small group of officers walking along the road that led to Dalstein, laughing and chatting. Dawson assumed they'd visited the local bar and were on their way back to their billets.

As the group reached the camp, they split up and went their separate ways. As they did so, Dawson ground out his cigarette under his boot and started walking down the road. About fifty yards in front of him, a slim, dapper

officer strode along, whistling a tune. Dawson increased his pace to catch up.

At the sound of his footsteps, the French officer glanced behind him, then stared in astonishment.

'You!' he gasped. 'But I thought—'

'You thought what, Capitaine de St Véran? You thought the mine you carefully placed in the cleared zone must have killed us? Unluckily for you, my friend Dave Watson – he's still alive too, by the way – and I are very thorough, and we found it. Or did you think we might have been killed by the German soldiers that you knew were advancing towards the forest?'

'I didn't place a mine and I don't know about the Germans.' St Véran began a blustering denial, but his eyes told a different story. 'How dare you address me in such an offensive manner?'

'I'm not here to argue with you, Capitaine,' Dawson said. 'I know the truth and you know that I do. I'm not interested in your feeble excuses.'

'Then what are you here for?' St Véran demanded.

'For this,' Dawson snapped. 'To kill you.'

He bent down and in a single fluid movement he drew the Wehrmacht trench knife – the one he'd taken from the dead soldier outside Celine's farmhouse – and drove the blade deep into the French officer's stomach.

St Véran gasped in agony, eyes popping from his head and his mouth open in a soundless scream as Dawson worked the blade higher and higher.

'This isn't for me and it isn't for Dave Watson. This is for Tommy Blake and the other British lads that you abandoned along with us in the Warndt Forest, the men

who won't be coming back out because the Germans slaughtered them. That was your fault, you treacherous fucking Frog.'

As he said the last word, Dawson rammed upwards with all of his strength. The tip of the trench knife ripped St Véran's heart apart, and he slumped down dead.

Dawson dragged his body to the side of the road and tossed the corpse into the ditch that ran alongside it.

'Good riddance, you bastard,' he muttered, and walked away.

The front of his uniform was soaked in blood from the appalling injury he'd inflicted on the French officer, but that wouldn't be a problem. Dawson walked back to where he'd left the kitbag and opened it up. He pulled out a new clean battledress, stripped off the old clothes and dressed in the new uniform. He carefully folded the old battledress so that the bloodstains were on the inside, tucked it into the kitbag and walked slowly back to the British army camp. He re-entered it using the same route as before.

There were a couple of fires burning there, soldiers sitting round them smoking and drinking tea. Dawson walked over to the biggest one.

'You look smart, Eddie,' one of the men said. 'New uniform?'

'You bet. The old one was just rags, really. Mind if I get rid of it here?'

'Help yourself.'

Dawson nodded his thanks, opened up the kitbag, pulled out his old battledress and tossed it on to the flames. He sat down next to the fire, accepted a mug of tea and watched as his old uniform – and all the

386

evidence of his encounter with the French officer – was burnt away to ashes.

'Thanks, lads,' he said and stood up and walked back to the tent he was sharing with Dave Watson.

'It's done?' Watson asked, propping himself up on one elbow.

'It's done,' Dawson nodded. 'I used the trench knife I took off one of the Jerry soldiers at Celine's farmhouse and I left it there. When someone finds the body, they'll most probably start looking for a renegade German soldier.'

'Well, they certainly won't come looking for you. You've been here with me all evening. Nobody saw you leave or come back, I hope?'

Dawson shook his head. 'No. I climbed the fence at the bottom of the field.'

'So that's it, is it?'

'For St Véran it is, Dave, but I'm not quite finished yet. That's one score settled, but I've still got that bastard of an SS officer to take care of.'

'You might never see him again.'

'Don't worry, Dave. I don't know how, but somehow, somewhere, I'm going to find him. I made Celine a promise and I'm bloody well going to keep it. I don't like unfinished business.'

AUTHOR'S NOTE

I've tried to base this story as far as possible on the real events that occurred during the first few days following the start of the Second World War and described as accurately as I could the tools and techniques used by the soldiers involved in that conflict.

The Saar Offensive

It's not generally known, but French forces entered German territory in the Saarland region within about a week of the declaration of war. The ostensible reason for this invasion, which covered a very wide front but was extremely shallow, and which met no German resistance, was to assist the Polish forces by trying to divert Hitler's attention away from that country.

It didn't work. The idea was that this probing advance would be followed by an all-out assault by about forty divisions, including one armoured division, three mechanized divisions, seventy-eight artillery regiments and forty tank battalions. But on 12 September 1939 the Anglo-French Supreme War Council met for the first time at Abbeville in France and decided – for whatever

reason – that all offensive actions would stop immediately.

Maurice Gamelin, the head of the French army, ordered his troops to advance no closer than one kilometre from the German positions along the Siegfried Line, but didn't tell his Polish counterpart. Instead, Gamelin informed Marshal Edward Rydz-Śmigły that half of his divisions had contacted the enemy, and that the French advance had forced the withdrawal of at least six divisions of Wehrmacht troops from Poland, all of which was blatantly untrue.

The next day General Louis Faury, the commander of the French Military Mission to Poland, told the Polish chief of staff that the planned major offensive had been postponed from 17 September to 20 September. Simultaneously, orders were issued for the French divisions to retreat to their barracks along the Maginot Line. The major offensive never took place.

The 'Bouncing Betty'

The 'Bouncing Betty', or S-mine, was manufactured from 1935 onwards and became a vital component of the Third Reich's defensive strategy. Until production ended with Germany's defeat in 1945, nearly two million S-mines had been made. They were responsible for inflicting heavy casualties and slowing, and in some cases even repelling, advances into German-held territory throughout the war. The design was lethal, successful and later very much imitated by the arms manufacturers

ACKNOWLEDGEMENTS

I'd like to acknowledge the unswerving encouragement of my agent, Luigi Bonomi, who has always fought my corner with tenacity and enthusiasm. Profound thanks are also due to my editor at Macmillan, Jeremy Trevathan, who has, from the start, been whole-hearted in his support of this book, and for his incisive and inspired editing. On a more practical note, I must offer my thanks to Ronald Fairfax, author of *Corky's War* (Mutiny Press, ISBN 978-0-9559705-0-4), for his invaluable assistance in the vital field of research. As always, any errors of fact are mine and mine alone.

To Sara, as always